Elizabeth Moon joined the US Marine Corps in 1968, reaching the rank of 1st Lieutenant during active duty. She has also earned degrees in history and biology, run for public office and been a columnist on her local newspaper. She lives near Austin, Texas, with her husband and their son.

By Elizabeth Moon

The Serrano Legacy
Hunting Party
Sporting Chance
Winning Colours
Once a Hero
Rules of Engagement
Change of Command

The Deed of Paksenarrion
Sheepfarmer's Daughter
Divided Allegiance
Oath of Gold

with Anne McCaffrey
Sassinak (The Planet Pirates Volume 1)
Generation Warriors (The Planet Pirates Volume 3)

CHANGE OF COMMAND

Book Six of
The Serrano Legacy

ELIZABETH MOON

orbit

An *Orbit* Book

First published in Great Britain by Orbit 2000

Typeset in Melior by M Rules
Printed and bound in Great Britain by
Mackays of Chatham PLC, Chatham, Kent

Orbit
A Division of
Little, Brown and Company (UK)
Brettenham House
Lancaster Place
London WC2E 7EN

ACKNOWLEDGEMENTS

As always, quite a few people helped with technical bits. Certain parts of this book could not have been written without the help of the fencing group . . . I leave it to them to figure out who contributed which bit of necessary information or advice. David Watson helped choreograph some of the fights and advised on metallurgy, and Kathleen Jones did yeoman work in the structural engineering of a very complicated plot. Susan and Andrew both provided useful information on points of high finance I would never have thought of (stock parking?); Allen helped with naval procedure. Other assistance came from a panel at the Baltimore WorldCon, but unfortunately a computer crash six weeks later robbed me of all the names, email addresses, and even snail-mail addresses (I had put them in the computer, of course . . . and since it was the mail function that crashed . . .). But they have my gratitude though I can't thank them properly unless we run into each other at another convention. Their input changed one section greatly; remaining mistakes are all mine, including having put their addresses in a computer about to lose its memory so that I couldn't thank them properly.

CHAPTER ONE

CASTLE ROCK

Newscast: 'Today the Speaker of the Table of Ministers and the Grand Council of the Familias Regnant was assassinated while en route from the shuttleport to the Palace. His close friend and legal advisor, Kevil Mahoney, was seriously injured and is now undergoing emergency treatment in a secure medical facility. Three security personnel also died. Speaker Thornbuckle's youngest daughter, travelling in a separate conveyance, was not injured, but is now in protective custody. . . .'

BREITIS MEDICAL PAVILION

Kevil was aware of disturbing dreams, and tried to fight his way to consciousness. He felt stiff, as if he'd been in the same position too long, and somewhere in the distance someone hurt quite badly. Red and pink swirls slid past his vision; when he blinked, nothing happened but the addition of ugly green smears to the swirls. He thought he heard something, but – like the vague shapes that teased his eyes – the sounds were curiously unhelpful, blunt and unformed.

He struggled harder, and finally made out a voice, speaking some arcane language he didn't know. What was a subcue something-or-other? What was an ivy line? His fogged mind tried to show him a picture of ivy leaves lined up in a row.

'– need complete rejuv, if he lives that long –' came suddenly, with silvery clarity.

Ice, then fire, washed through him; he never knew if it was something they did, or his body's response to what he heard. His eyes opened to see a pale blur; he struggled to get his mouth open, then realized it was open, wedged with some instrument.

'Lie still,' someone said. 'Close your eyes.'

He was in no mood to take orders. He gagged on the thing in his mouth, and someone slid it out.

'What happened?' he croaked, in a voice he didn't recognize but felt in his painful throat.

Memory returned in that moment, even as he asked. Even as the people he could not yet see hesitated, he knew what had happened.

He and Bunny in the ground car. Bunny's face, taut and lined for so many months, finally relaxing. They had been chatting about the continuing problems resulting from the Morrelines' pharmaceutical plant on Patchcock, the rising price of rejuvenations and the political implications –

And then the white flare of some weapon, and Bunny's face disappearing into a mess of red and pink and gray –

He must be dead. No one could survive that. And he, Kevil Mahoney, was alive – at least for now – because his friend's head had taken the brunt of whatever attack.

The New Texas Godfearing Militia had sworn vengeance on them. Evidently it had been no idle threat.

He needed to know what had happened. Who was in charge now? What was Fleet doing? But he felt a dark chilly fog rising over him, and slipped into that darkness unsure if it was death or a drug.

Hobart Conselline permitted none of the emotions churning inside him to show in his face or demeanor. His secretary's expression of cautious solemnity proved he'd been successful; the silly man couldn't tell how his employer was taking the news. Good.

'It's been confirmed by three separate agencies, milord,' his secretary said.

'Terrible!' Hobart said, and shook his head. 'I suppose it was those terrorists, in retaliation for the executions –'

'That's the speculation at this time, milord.'

'How many were killed or injured?'

'Lord Thornbuckle and three security personnel killed; Ser Mahoney is alive but in critical condition. He is not expected to live.'

'A terrible, terrible situation.' Hobart shook his head again. Terrible for some, certainly. Bunny Thornbuckle's relatives and friends were no doubt reeling in shock and confusion. So would the whole Council be, if someone didn't take hold and give the guidance that had been so sorely needed for the past several years. If Kevil Mahoney had been uninjured, they might have turned to him, but without either Bunny or Kevil, the Families would mill about like panicky sheep, baaing uselessly at the wolf-pack around them. He knew exactly what far-sighted, strong, decisive leader should take charge.

'Send our condolences to Miranda,' he told his secretary. 'Inform my wife's secretary that I'm sure my wife will want to call on her.' Poor, beautiful, clever Miranda, so unlucky in her choice of men and her children.

Poor Brun, for that matter. Like everyone who had met

the child, he had enjoyed her scatterbrained, madcap beauty. She had needed a good husband to settle her down, but Bunny had insisted on letting her run wild, with disastrous results. Another instance of Bunny's lamentable lack of decisive, firm leadership. Nothing like that had happened to the Conselline daughters, nor ever would. Bunny's older children had turned out well enough, though young Buttons was no second Bunny. He had all his father's stuffiness and none of his father's brilliance. All the better; the last thing the Consellines needed was another Bunny Thornbuckle in that Chair.

'You have messages from several of the Families,' the secretary said.

'No doubt,' Hobart said. Those he had been talking to, in preparation for the Grand Council meeting this year, would want to know his plans now. For an instant, the internal vision of those plans blinded him to the room around him. With Bunny and Kevil Mahoney out of the picture – with Bunny's supporters in disarray, shocked and grieving – a man who knew what he wanted and moved quickly and decisively might go farther than he had believed possible.

He glanced over the messages as his secretary left the room. As he'd expected: shock, concern, fear, shock . . . with every passing moment, he felt more certain that he, and he alone, would have to act in this crisis. How fortunate that he had not left Castle Rock with the others. 'Make a list of all the Chairholders who are still onplanet,' he said. His secretary nodded. 'And set up a conference call for the Conselline Sept, all Chairholding members.'

'Sir, I have the list – I keep a current file on all the Chairholders –'

'Excellent.' He looked over it carefully while his secretary was arranging the complicated linkage of ansible and ordinary communications lines for the conference call, and realized that the opportunity would never be greater.

The Barraclough Sept, which included the lesser Aranlake and Padualenare septs, had not rallied to Bunny's side when Brun returned. The Aranlakes, with the exception of Lady Cecelia de Marktos, had supported an Aranlake candidate, Hubert Roscoe Millander, for Family head, and they'd lost. They were home sulking. The Padualenares favored Bunny's brother Harlis, who supported their claim to seniority over the Aranlakes, and their ambitions in the colonial worlds. This left only a few of the Barracloughs themselves onplanet, those closest to Bunny and therefore more likely devastated by his death.

Hobart glanced around the room, his gaze roaming from one proof of his eminence to another. Would *his* family be devastated if he were assassinated? Delphine would be; she could cry and cry until her pretty face was all swollen and splotched with ugly color. The girls would cry, but only for awhile, he was sure. They would look for another patron, another source of favor and another dispenser of luxuries. Fickle, that's what women were, unless you trained them well, as he had trained Delphine. The boys, though – if he had brought them up well, they would be planning already how to avenge him, and how to gain more power.

But he would not be assassinated. He would be more careful than Bunny, more alert to covert threats, less – not less *brave*, but less foolhardy. Brun had no doubt got her foolhardy genes from him, not from prudent Miranda.

His excitement mounted as he went on through the list. If he had had Bunny killed – and the thought had crossed his mind more than once, in the year when it seemed that nothing else would get that great fool out of an office he was unfit to fill – he could not have chosen a

better time. Best of all, he hadn't done it himself; he'd had
nothing to do with it. Fate had finally come over to his
side. He had proven himself capable of succeeding against
the worst Fate could do, and now Fate – womanlike – had
chosen him for that very energy and persistence and will to
triumph.

He closed his eyes a moment, allowing himself the
luxury of imagining the moment when he took over as
Speaker – when the faces which had ignored or turned
away turned to him – *had* to turn to him – and he could
finally show his true abilities. *I will make the Familias
great, and everyone will know who saved it from destruc-
tion.*

R.S.S *GYRFALCON*

'I didn't know they would take it out of *my* pay,' Ensign
Barin Serrano said. His voice almost squeaked, but he
couldn't help it. His entire paycheck, gone . . . *nothing* in
his credit cube, and he'd already ordered the traditional
engagement and wedding gifts.

'Well, who did you think would pay for it? Those
people have already used up the Sector discretionary
fund, and most of the recreational reserve. And they're
not even charging you for all of them, just the ones your
pay will cover.'

'Ten dependents . . .' Barin murmured. That would
eat up all his pay after he was promoted, too. He supposed he should count himself lucky that Fleet
regulations prohibited official indebtedness. 'And I'm not
even married. How could they do this to me?'

'Look at it this way, sir – it'll keep you out of trouble.'

'No . . . not really. I've just sent in my order for the
wedding . . .'

'Well, sir –'

'Attention all hands . . . attention all hands . . .' A
pause, during which Barin tried to think how to get himself out of his present financial fix. Then the captain's
voice: 'It is my sad duty to announce that the Speaker of
the Table of Ministers has been assassinated. Stand
by . . .'

Barin stared at the chief, who stared back. The Speaker
assassinated? Where? How?

And what would happen to Brun, and all those
women?

R.S.S. *SHRIKE*

'Lieutenant Suiza, there's a flash priority message, Cobalt
encryption.'

'Ummm . . .' Esmay Suiza's mind had drifted, as it did
often these days, to Barin. 'Right – well – keep a link to
the ansible and I'll get the captain.' The last priority message had been medical, directing them to relieve senior
NCOs with rejuv of duty, but they had none aboard.
Maybe this one would be useful. What she wanted was a
message from Barin, preferably with a friendly reaction
from his family. Being on two different ships really ham-
pered communication; she hoped they could meet in
person for a few days. Captain Solis knew she was due
leave; he had already said she could take the time off. But
she'd heard nothing. . . .

Captain Solis, never talkative this early in first shift,
became even more silent after the encrypted message had
gone to his console. Esmay glanced over. 'Sir?'

'I . . . said nothing, Lieutenant.' He met her eyes.
'Lord Thornbuckle is dead. Assassinated. Presumably –'
His gaze dropped to the readout of the decryption
device. 'Presumably it's the New Texas Militia, in retaliation for our execution of their Rangers.' A pause, during

which Esmay did her best not to ask the question that hammered at her mind. He answered it anyway. 'Lieutenant, you can count on all leaves being cancelled. I'm sorry. There are some things more urgent than a wedding.'

'It won't hurt to do the paperwork,' Esmay said, without thinking. Solis gave her a long look, but finally nodded.

'Good idea. Then if you get the chance . . . but in the meantime, I want a threat assessment . . . get started on that while I make the announcement to the crew.'

ALTIPLANO

Newscast: 'General Casimir Suiza announced today that the Landbride Suiza is planning to marry an outlander, Barin Serrano, also an officer in the Regular Space Service. Opposition to any such outlander marriage is expected from the Landsman's Guild; questions have already been asked about the succession, in view of the fact that Landbride Suiza continues to reside offworld and serve in the Regular Space Service. In other news, the Speaker of the Table of Ministers has been assassinated on Castle Rock . . .'

GUERNESE REPUBLIC GENERAL NEWS SERVICE

Newscast: '. . . of more concern is the threat of renewed violence from the New Texas Militia branches which were not destroyed by the Familias Regnant in their extravagant attempt to rescue the Speaker's daughter. Questions have been raised in Parliament about the involvement of Guernesi intelligence personnel in that attempt, and whether such cooperation with the Familias Regnant compromised Guernesi interests . . .'

Memorandum to the Chair of the Benignity:
Whatever the Familias Regnant hoped to gain by attacking the Texan Militia, and despite the successful extrication of the Speaker's daughter, they will find they have poked a hornet's nest. Although it is tempting to take advantage of this, I believe that any contact with the Militia would endanger our longstanding policy, and would risk alienating the Holy Father.

Our intelligence reports indicate continuing and widening splits between the ruling elements, however, which might well be exploited without entangling us with the New Texans. Project Dance has provided the most accurate assessments so far of the behaviors of major Familias septs. Project Retainer is showing a profit, and the latest data indicate that some 15–23% of the R.S.S. senior NCO corps will be severely affected within another 180 days, with peak incidence at 250–300 days. Three independent sources confirm early failure beginning over 300 days ago. It is somewhat surprising that the Familias have not cut back manufacture and distribution of the drugs . . .

Memorandum to the Admiral of the Fleet:
At the request of the Table of Ministers and the Grand Council, all ships not on high-alert status will maintain one minute of silence at 1200 hours on the day of Lord Thornbuckle's funeral, and no other recognition shall be given; specifically there shall be no salute of arms.

'One minute of silence in respect for the Speaker of the Grand Council.'

Silence dragged on. Longer than a minute, it felt like.
Esmay wondered how Brun was holding up. She had not
had time to recover from her captivity, and already she
had lost her father. Esmay murmured prayers she had
not thought of in years.

Memorandum to the Chief of Personnel, from the
Chief, Medical Services:
Urgent you refer all enlisted personnel who
received rejuvenation treatment within the past ten
years to medical immediately. Make no exceptions.
If necessary, refer in order of rejuvenation.

Admiral Vida Serrano, now securely in command of
Sector Seven, read the memorandum in silence, very
aware of the tension in Master Chief Valdos' shoulders.
She herself had forwarded the concerns of Barin and
Captain Escovar about mental deterioration in senior
enlisted personnel, under the tightest security. She had
followed the subsequent medical investigation, but the
details eluded her. Rejuvenation neurobiology was not
her field. She needed to be briefed on it, and so far –
despite several increasingly firm requests to Fleet
Headquarters – no such briefing had taken place.

How could she reassure Valdos, and others under her
command, without the information she needed?

What would happen if she couldn't?

'Get me the heads of personnel and medical,' she said.
'We have a situation I don't fully understand, and I want
to be sure we handle this with both discretion and fair-
ness.'

'Sir.' A pause. 'If the admiral permits –'

'Go ahead.'

'Is it true they're looking for ways to bump out senior
NCOs, an excuse not to offer any more rejuvenations?'

Just the kind of ideas she did not want floating around. But was it true?

'In my opinion, Chief – and it's only my opinion, but I do have some data – this may have to do with medical problems from a bad batch of rejuv drugs.'

'Problems.'

'Yes. I am not going to blacken anyone's name, because I don't know all the facts. I'm not a medical officer. I do know that investigation of something else revealed a source of contaminated rejuv drugs, and there was concern that they might have made it into our supply chain. Meanwhile, several senior NCOs began showing neurological symptoms within a few months to a year of each other – widely separated in their duty stations, and not all in the same branch.'

'Could they – have given us bad drugs, to justify later refusal to rejuv?'

'On purpose?' He nodded. 'Absolutely not. If that's what happened, I suspect it is a simple mistake – or, if not, an enemy wished to deprive us of our most valuable senior NCOs in order to make a strike easier.'

'I hope you're right, sir.' He went out, shaking his head.

She hoped she was right, too . . . and that he believed her. If the NCOs started worrying about whether they had been given bad drugs intentionally, the close-knit community of Fleet could unravel with fatal speed.

Internal Memorandum, MorCon Pharmaceuticals:
. . . despite the best efforts of our advertising departments to restore confidence in our product, the market share is still severely depressed compared to the 68% dominance of the market we enjoyed before the Patchcock scandal. Our competitors have taken full advantage of revelations

about the inferior quality of our product, and our legal staff tells us that litigation is still increasing. This has severely affected profits, which used to make up over 20% of the total for the Conselline Sept. Non-political means of recovery have been ineffective; we need legislative relief from laws that are crippling our attempt to deal fairly and honestly with the consequences of the errors made by others. We feel it is imperative that some means be found to regain market share. Lady Venezia Morreline continues to oppose this, and we have been unable to convince her that we cannot be held responsible for the acts of sabotage by a foreign agent. . . .

REGULAR SPACE SERVICE MILITARY PRISON, STACK ISLANDS, COPPER MOUNTAIN

On a cold, windy day in local autumn, the prisoners of Stack Islands Military Prison were drawn up in ranks to witness another change of command ceremony from behind barriers of both steel and invisible force shields. In front of it, in the small enclosed parade ground, all but a few of the guards were also in formation, uneasily aware of the prisoners' gazes fixed on their backs. No matter that a force shield lay between them; nothing protected them from the malevolence.

Up in front, Iosep Tolin relinquished his command to Pilar Bacarion with relief. He had not enjoyed any moment of his stay in that exile from his former sphere of power, and he had agreed to take early retirement to get quit of it. Pilar, though – he would be very glad to put the width of the Big Ocean, and later some deepspace, between himself and one of the few women who had ever been close to Admiral Lepescu.

On her part, Commander Pilar Bacarion felt an almost physical surge of pleasure in the tension on Tolin's face. He not only disliked her, he was afraid of her. He should be. They all should be, and they *would* be, in time. She smiled at Tolin, letting him see that she recognized his fear, and saw the glisten of sweat on his forehead, even in the cold. Then she released him from her gaze, and turned it instead on her subordinates.

They did not flinch. She had not thought they would. Their gaze challenged her – the first female commander this prison had ever had. Was she tough enough, their gaze asked. Could she do the job? Others – whose identities she already knew – had no doubts about her toughness. They were well aware that Lepescu had been her mentor, that she had supported his agenda. Carefully disguised in her duffle were slivers of the ears she had taken; when it had become imprudent to keep these proofs of her status, she had sliced them thin herself and found hiding places for them.

She had Hunted, in the oldest Hunt of all; she had killed. She had survived the Hunt on Sirialis, having left to take command of a ship before the game ended with Lepescu dead and Heris Serrano once more in favor with Fleet brass. But no one knew it. They were all dead, and the prisoners she'd hunted had never seen her face. Her luck was strong, and her skills – she would match her skills against Serrano directly some day; she knew she would win.

She looked past the guards, past the force screen, to the prisoners in their drab ranks. In there she also had potential allies. In time.

Tolin left at last, in the whining aircar. She wished him a nasty storm on the way to the mainland, but it didn't really matter. Let him live – and let him realize someday just what he'd seen, in their brief exchange.

The ceremony over, Pilar summoned her staff. They were unwise enough to look surprised; she allowed herself a tight smile on the way to her office, thinking how soon they would learn what she was like.

On the mainland, at Main Base, autumn had not yet moderated a brutally hot summer. It had been a dry year, and now fine reddish dust turned the sky dirty brown as the wind lifted it high into the atmosphere.

In this kind of weather, everyone who could get off-base privileges spent hours in Q-town's bars, drinking whatever was coldest. Even combat veterans accepted the crowd in their favorite watering hole. It was too hot, and too miserable, to complain.

Margiu Pardalt, newly graduated from the Academy, and the only Xavierine in her class, had a habit of coming tops in her classes. She had to; she had to do something to make up for her sister Masiu, killed by raiders years ago. Masiu had been the family genius: brilliant, brave, everything a family could hope for. Margiu was second-best, and knew it – a poor replacement for the fallen hero – so it was up to her to make her mark, to be Masiu's memorial. Her place in the Academy had been a gift from the Familias in memory of Masiu. Her place in the universe was to be her gift in return.

She had earned an evening's liberty by coming first in her class yet again at Copper Mountain, and she thought it fitting that her free hours came at a time when no rational person could enjoy them. She'd have stayed in her quarters, but her training CO had told her to get off the base – and orders were orders.

Another gust of wind howled down Q-town's main street and filled her nose with hot stinging dust. She sneezed, and her eyes watered. It reminded her too much of the Benignity's scorch of Xavier, when she and her family had wrapped torn sheets around their heads for weeks to filter the dust and ash.

Ahead, on the right, she spotted a doorway just opening as someone came out, and a gush of cooler air brushed her side. She turned into it.

It was only moderately crowded – less crowded than the two bars she'd glanced into and left – and smelled of food as much as drink. Margiu made her way to one of the open booths, and slid in, then looked around. The tables and seats looked a little strange, until she realized they were meant to look like ship parts. No, they *were* ship parts. Her quick glance took in the long dark bar – obviously hull material. The models – obviously military vessels. The battle honors hung on the walls, the photographs.

It was a shrine, then. Margiu felt obscurely comforted and lowered her head to pray for the dead and the survivors alike. Her family were Synorhines; she had learned the right forms for valediction and commemoration from early childhood.

'Do you need help?' someone asked. Margiu looked up to find herself face to face with a man in a float-chair.

'No, sir – I was honoring the dead,' she said.

His brows rose, crinkling the skin around the scars on his bald scalp. 'You knew about this place?'

'No, sir . . . but it's obvious.'

'Hmm. May I have the honor of your name?'

'Ensign Pardalt,' she said. 'From Xavier.'

'Ah. Xavier.' He looked her over carefully. 'And you were at the Academy when –'

'No, sir. I was home . . . on Xavier, I mean.' She knew already that to Fleet personnel, Fleet was home, and the planet of origin was just that – the planet of origin.

'And you survived the Benignity – your family as well?'

'Most of them.'

'You're welcome here anytime, Ensign. You've earned it.'

But she hadn't earned anything. Not yet. The way she saw it, everything she had, Masiu had earned. Still, she was not going to contradict someone like this, a combat veteran.

'Thank you,' she said instead. And then, carefully, hoping she'd read the signals right, 'May I offer you a drink?'

She saw a reaction, but she wasn't sure what. 'As it is your first time in my establishment, I hope you will honor me by accepting one.'

She dipped her head. 'I would be honored.' Then, as he waited, she realized he wanted her to name it. She wasn't used to that, but she glanced at the menu display and chose a dark ale spiced with ginger.

When the mug arrived, heavily frosted, it came with a bowl of raw vegetable sticks on shaved ice.

'If you like spiced ales, I thought you might like these,' the man said. Margiu nibbled one; it had a refreshing bite. He sipped his own drink, watching her over the rim. She found it disconcerting.

'We had Lieutenant Suiza in here when she was on a course,' he said finally.

That name she knew, of course. Suiza had been added to her family's prayers, and she had heard a lot about Suiza in the Academy and after. 'I've never met her,' Margiu said. 'But we owe her a lot.'

'You remind me of her,' the man said. 'She's quiet too.'

'She's a real hero,' Margiu said. 'I'm just a very green ensign.'

'You might surprise yourself,' the man said.

She did fantasize about that, sometimes, but she knew it was ridiculous. She could be serious, careful, diligent, prudent – and none of those were heroic virtues, as she understood heroism.

ZENEBRA; *EVENING SPORTS WITH ANGH DIOR,* CHAUNCY NETWORK

'Lady Cecelia de Marktos, who returned to competition several years ago on one of the D'Amerosia string, has qualified for the Senior Horse Trials at Wherrin this season on a horse bred at her own stables, Seniority. With the veteran rider/owner up, Seniority won the Challenge Event for rising novices, then the Stavenge. The pair are expected to threaten the reigning champion, Liam Ardahi, and the experienced champion Plantagenet, competing under the colors of Orregiemos Combine . . .'

Viewers saw Lady Cecelia's pleasant, bony, somewhat horselike face, beneath rumpled red-gold curls . . . then a shot of her exercising Seniority over fences, the horse's gleaming red coat only a shade darker than her hair, then a shot of them over the last fence of the Stavenge. The video shifted to Liam Ardahi guiding Plantagenet over the Wherrin Trials' B Course big drop-bridge combination the year before, freezing on the instant before landing, while the commentator recited their previous record.

Cecelia grimaced at the display. Like any expert rider, she could find flaws in everything she did, and would have much preferred to have the vid show her over the seventeenth fence – where she and Seniority had made neat work of a difficult combination – than that last fence, where Seniority had jumped flat, and her own hand position showed why. She'd lost concentration for a crucial few seconds.

Why had she been thinking about Pedar Orregiemos and the Rejuvenants, and not Fence Thirty?

WHERRIN EQUESTRIAN PARK

Two days later, Cecelia brought Seniority in from the gallops in exactly the shape she wanted – pulse and respiration had recovered beautifully, and he could have gone another mile without strain. But any more fitness now, and he would peak before the Senior Trials. No, a long hack this afternoon, then tomorrow –

'Cece! Have you heard?' Colum was waiting for her at the entrance to the gallops, as he usually did, but he spoke first.

'What?' She loosened the strap of her helmet, and pushed back under it the one lock of red hair that always managed to get loose and tickle her forehead.

'Lord Thornbuckle's been killed – it's on all the newsvids –'

She felt a heaviness in her chest as if she'd been kicked. 'Bunny?' A swift montage of pictures ran through her mind – Bunny at the head of the table, Bunny on horseback on Opening Day of the hunt season, Bunny taking over from Kemtre at the Grand Council, Bunny and Kevil, heads together, discussing something . . . 'It can't be –' He was younger than she by twenty-odd years; he was healthy as a horse –

'They say it might be those terrorists.'

Reality came back as Seniority reached down to rub his face on his leg, and yanked the reins; Cecelia blinked, looked around, saw the subdued flurry of activity near the barns. The first acid bite of sadness seeped through the shock. If it was true, this was going to hurt a lot. Colum seemed to understand that she could say nothing; he flung a cooler over the horse's back, and put a hand to the rein. Cecelia sat there, as he led Seniority on into the aisle between the barns, where the look on the grooms' faces told her that the newsvids were playing this straight.

'You heard?' That was Roz, her head groom.

'Yes.' She slid down, ran the stirrups up, automatically coordinating with the groom as they untacked the chestnut horse and began the after-workout rubdown.

'You knew him, didn't you?'

Already past tense. Cecelia shivered. 'Yes. For a long time.'

'It's terrible. It said on the news there wasn't even enough left for a neuroscan. No chance –'

She didn't want to hear this; she didn't want to think about this. Her rejuvenated body felt alien suddenly, the reverse of the way she had felt when her young mind lived in her old one . . . now she felt trapped in a body that could not feel what she felt emotionally.

'Do you think they'll cancel the Trials?'

Cecelia looked over at Roz, who flushed in unbecoming splotches. 'I doubt it,' she said. 'They didn't stop the Trials when Kemtre abdicated.'

But even as she said it, she felt uneasy. Whether the Trials went on or not, should *she* ride? What was the right thing to do? She paused in her strokes down Seniority's muscled haunch to calculate travel times. She could not possibly make it to Castle Rock for any memorial service, even if she gave up the competition. That being so, what good would it do Bunny for her to withdraw?

What good would it do someone else?

She stood watching as Roz and Gerry began sponging the horse down, wondering why that had come to mind . . . why, at some level, she did not believe that awful milita group had killed Bunny. But who else? And how was she going to find out?

'Cece –' Dale, her trainer, had Max in tow. 'I know, it's awful, but you've got to ride this guy.'

She wanted to say she couldn't, but she knew she

could. And whatever happened to humans, horses needed their unbroken routine. She let a groom give her a leg up onto Max, and headed back to the gallops.

As always, just being on a horse in motion cleared her mind. Max was no Seniority, but he was maturing into a very nice ride over shorter distances, and he would bring a good price when the time came.

If the time came, with Bunny dead. Who knew what that meant politically? She didn't, though she had paid more attention than she used to. Bunny had been a good executive, except perhaps for his frenzy when Brun was taken – a frenzy no one could blame. Things had gone well – her investments had prospered, and if hers prospered then surely the economy was doing well. Except for the volatility in rejuvenation pharmaceuticals, which had pretty much smoothed out this past year. The Consellines had lost face – and market share – but they certainly weren't ruined.

And what about Miranda, and Brun? Would they move back to Sirialis? Would they – she hated the thought that forced itself to the top of her mind – would they still have foxhunting?

That wasn't the important thing, of course – the important thing was finding out who had killed Bunny and dealing with him. Or her.

Max took advantage of his rider's wandering mind and shied at a rustle in the hedge beside the field. Cecelia caught him before he could bolt, and sent him on firmly. Best think about the horse; that was something she could control. For the rest of the two-hour hack, she managed to keep her sorrow and her worries at bay.

They returned when she handed Max over to the grooms. Roz looked almost as grim as she felt – she had worked two seasons on Sirialis, Cecelia remembered, and had a scrapbook on the Thornbuckle family. 'It'll never be the same,' she muttered to Cecelia. 'Young Buttons is a fine man, but he's not his father.'

'No . . . but Kevil will help him.'

'He was hurt too, you know. Really bad – he might die.'

'Kevil Mahoney?'

'That's what the newsvid said. If you can trust them. Damn those terrorists anyway; I don't know why they have to make more trouble in the world, as if there's not enough.'

'Lady Cecelia –' That was Dale, more formal than usual. 'You have a caller.'

The last thing she wanted. She turned away, leaving Roz and the new girl working on Max, and stripped off her gloves, tucking them in her belt.

He was lounging in the stable office, flipping through the stable feed records.

'Get out of that,' Cecelia said, but without much heat. She herself had sneaked a look at the hay receipts for other owners, wondering if they had a better source. Everyone snooped in stable offices.

'You're looking splendid,' Pedar Orregiemos said. 'Still – terrible news, terrible news.'

'Yes, it is.' Cecelia sat down heavily in one of the battered leather chairs. 'I'm still not really grasping it.'

'I came over because I knew you'd been close to both of them,' Pedar said.

Cecelia looked up sharply. 'Both of them?'

'Bunny and Kevil, I mean. At least, that's what the word was, the past few years. People were even twitting young George about it.'

'About me and *Kevil*?'

He shrugged. 'And why not?'

'Kevil and I are friends,' Cecelia said, almost spitting the words out. 'Friends, not lovers.' Well, only twice, after which they'd both agreed it wasn't working nearly as well as they'd hoped. 'Yes, I spent a lot of time with him after my rejuvenation, because I needed his legal advice to untangle my affairs. But that's all.' She was aware of the heat in her face, mixed anger and shame.

'Well, a friend, then. But still . . . I was sure you'd be upset, so I came over to check on you.'

Disgusting little climber. Yes, he was rich, and yes, his family was Seated, but he was, compared to her, a minor twig on the very large and ancient Conselline elm . . . her branch of the Aranlake Sept made up a much greater percentage of the even larger and older Barraclough oak.

Cecelia pushed that back down. She wasn't the sort of person who worshipped a family tree; people didn't get to choose their parentage. Pedar's mannerisms, more pronounced in old age and despite several rejuvenations, had been there from the day she first met him, at someone's birthday party. He wanted to be a protector . . . bad luck for him that she didn't need protecting.

'I'm fine, Pedar. I'll be fine – I'll grieve, and then I'll get over it.'

'Why don't you let me take you to dinner?'

As so often, the kind impulse that was exactly wrong. 'Not tonight, please. I just want to go back and cry a little. Another time, perhaps.'

'I'll hold you to it,' Pedar said, and bowed politely. Go away, Cecelia thought, as loudly as she could while holding a polite smile that made her face ache. He bowed again and left.

She and Bunny had laughed about Pedar, from time to time – trusting each other not to share that fact. His stiff little bows; his exaggerated courtesies; his passion for antique clothing and sports even more useless than fox-hunting and eventing.

She would never have Bunny to laugh with again. She would never see that long, foolish face come alight with intelligence, with his quick wit. She would never warm herself at the glow of the love between Bunny and Miranda . . . a love she had watched grow and deepen over the many decades she'd known them both.

Tears ran down her face, and when Dale came back to the office, she was curled into the big chair, and didn't hear him step in, then quietly close the door behind him when he left again.

CHAPTER TWO

CASTLE ROCK, THE OLD PALACE

The day of Bunny's funeral dawned clear and cold. Miranda woke before dawn, and watched the light seep into the eastern sky. She lay still beneath the covers, feeling the weight of them; reluctant to leave that warm nest and face what would be a long and difficult day. Their room – her room – was not cold, but she had not felt warm since that first horrible moment when they'd told her Bunny was dead.

A faint click, then music so soft she could barely hear it – the music she had chosen herself. She reached over and punched up the volume – no sense in that slow crescendo if she was already awake – and threw off the covers in one angry gesture.

Bunny was dead. Nothing would change that, not the music, not the dawn, not whatever mood she was in. Beneath her feet, the carpet was still soft and thick. Around her shoulders, the fleecy jacket warmed her.

Bunny was dead. She was alive, and beautiful (she heard people whispering, and after all it was true) and very, very wealthy.

Faintly, through the closed door, she heard a lusty cry.

Wealthy, and the grandmother of bastards whose fathers were, if not dead, criminals and no doubt partners of those who had killed Bunny.

Miranda had not told Bunny how she felt about those babies. Grandmothers were supposed to have a natural love for grandchildren, but she could not see those boys as anything but vandalism perpetrated on her daughter.

Bunny had seen it differently. Bunny had assumed she would love them, if Brun couldn't; Bunny had assumed she would organize their care.

Bunny was dead.

She stood, unable to move for a long moment. It wasn't supposed to be like this. People their age were supposed to be adult, mature, stable . . . they were resigned to loss, said the books she'd read.

She wasn't resigned. She wanted to shake her fist and scream at the sky; she wanted to fall off a cliff and drown. The secret was that the rich had hearts too . . . she had loved Bunny the way girls in romance storycubes loved their heroes, and forty years of marriage had not changed that.

And he was dead.

And she was alive, with children and grandchildren and bastard grandchildren who were not at fault for their fathers' sins, and a daughter still healing from what had been done to her, and all Bunny's hopes and dreams for the peace of the world crashing down around them, shattered.

When her maid knocked, Miranda smiled and calmly accepted a cup of tea, which she drank with perfect composure while her maid ran her bath.

Brun Meager had wakened even earlier, when the twins cried, as they often did, in the middle of the night. They should be sleeping through the night, the nursemaids said, but they hadn't done so more than one night in four since they were taken from Our Texas. And Brun had discovered, to her annoyance, that when they woke, she also woke, even if someone else was doing the feeding and cleaning.

She used the time to exercise, the exercises she never skipped these days. By the time her maid knocked, she had already worked herself into a sweat, and showered herself back to normal. In the mirrors of the bath, her face stared back at her, strange after nearly two standard years without a mirror . . . an older face, a harder face, but – in spite of everything – a face of memorable beauty.

Something would have to be done about that . . . but not today. Today she would walk with her mother, her brothers, her older sister, in the funeral procession; today she would hold her head high in the face of the universe. They had forced her to bear their children. They could not force her to hide.

PALACE SECURITY, CASTLE ROCK

Colonel Bai-Darlin had not slept all night. Organizing a state funeral had always been – would always be – a nightmare of protocol and endless complicated detail, but ordinarily a state funeral was not mixed with a top-level security concern. Even when a head of state was assassinated, that usually ended the threat. Only 23.87 percent of political assassinations in the past five hundred years had been followed by subsequent assassinations.

But this was different. The other branches of the New Texas Godfearing Militia had specifically threatened Lord Thornbuckle and his family, with additional threats to Hazel Takeris, the Rangers' wives and female dependents, and several members of the Regular Space Service, including Admiral Vida Serrano. Fleet, Colonel Bai-Darlin thought, could protect its own. His responsibility was the safety of the civilians, specifically those who would be present, vulnerable, in the funeral procession.

His predecessor, Colonel Harris, was even now trying to explain why they had not taken sufficient precautions, why Lord Thornbuckle had died, and no one – not one single Militia member or sympathizer – had been captured.

He would have to assume they'd try again. He would have to assume that everything Harris had done was wrong – that Harris had missed something vital.

Unless it wasn't the New Texas Godfearing Militia after all. Bai-Darlin's head lifted, as if scenting game. What if it were someone else, someone trying to use the hotheaded NewTex as a cover?

In that case, the funeral would probably go off without a hitch. Which, at the moment, was all he cared about.

Brun eyed her mother as they came out onto the porch, into the cold sunlight. Security, dark-uniformed and obviously armed, hovered around them. Five cars, all identical polished burgundy with black and gold trim, awaited them.

'Five?' Brun said.

'Security,' her mother said. 'Four of them are drags.'

'Ah.' Four would lay false trails, though since everyone knew where the funeral would be held, she didn't see how that would help.

She could at least notice who was here, and who had not been able to – or wanted to – come. No Lady Cecelia . . . well, it was the Wherrin Trials, after all, and she might not even have heard yet. Her sister Berenice, though, and her brother Abelard. No Raffa or Ronnie –

absurd how she had missed them. Raffa's Aunt Marta
Saenz, such a support to her father while she was missing – her mother's report of that had been just a touch
acidic – had gone back to her own world as soon as Brun
returned. No George – but of course the odious George
had his own critically wounded father to watch over. Of
their own sept, her father's younger brother Harlis, and
his son Kell, who didn't look to have improved from her
last memory of him. A whole raft of Consellines, most of
whom she didn't know well enough to put names to, and
Venezia Morreline.

In ordinary times – not that the death of her father
would ever have been ordinary – Kevil Mahoney would
have given the eulogy. Instead it was her Uncle Harlis,
and the eulogy slid into a subtle critique of her father's
policies. A fine man, a man with strong family loyal-
ties . . . to his children, a man of great abilities who had
perhaps not quite lived up to them . . .

'Ballocks!' That low mutter was a great-great-uncle in
the Barraclough main line. He took the floor next, praising Bunny the way Brun had expected him to be praised.
That was the father she remembered: generous, loyal,
intelligent, capable.

Others followed. Political friends, describing how Lord
Thornbuckle's tactful but firm handling of the government had held it together when Kemtre abdicated.
Political enemies, praising with delicate cuts at her
father's occasional mistakes, and being so tactful in ignoring the obvious one that Brun found herself the target of
one covert glance after another.

If it hadn't been for her – if it hadn't been for her idiot
rashness – her father would still be alive, and in power,
and these sly critics would be silent. She glanced down at
her mother's hands, and saw the knuckles whitening the
skin, though Miranda's face betrayed nothing. Guilt,

sorrow, shame . . . and a deep, deep anger. It was her fault – in part – but it was not *all* her fault. Their maneuvering, their use of her misfortune and her father's death – that was *their* responsibility.

She had been determined to go away, to change herself into someone else, and break the connection with the rash young Brun who fell into captivity; but watching her father's enemies – enemies she had not known he had – at her father's funeral, that resolve weakened.

Prima Bowie sat embroidering a collar with a row of tiny green leaves, and kept a sharp eye on her household. It was hard to realize that only a short time ago she had been Prima Bowie in truth, Mitch's first wife and mother of nine children, with a real household to manage, a household with a garden and weaving shed, with courtyards for the children, and servants and tutors. Now she was Prima Bowie on her new Familias identity card, because that's what Hazel had told them, and even Hazel didn't know that wasn't a name but a title. She had been called Ruth Ann in childhood, long before she was any man's prima, but no one had called her that since her father died. And Mitch's last name wasn't Bowie – that was his title. He was really a Pardue. So her name ought to be Ruth Ann Pardue.

Should she tell someone? It would not be fitting to be called Prima Serrano, when that young woman became his first wife. She knew that, even as she hated the thought of being second or third behind such a young thing – and, what was worse, a heathen abomination who was actually in the military.

'Prima?' She looked up, to see Simplicity in the doorway. 'Hazel's here, Mama . . . Prima . . .'

Simplicity had never learned not to call her *Mama*. Prima wished again that Mitch had not made such a fuss about it, but he had, and she'd had to send the child to the servants' hall even before she was out of the virgins' bower. It occurred to Prima that now she could reverse that decision.

'It's all right to call me Mama here, Simplicity,' she said softly. The girl's expression relaxed.

'Mama! But the Ranger —'

'Isn't here. You may say Mama.'

Simplicity ran over, just like the small child she was inside, and hugged Prima clumsily. 'Love you, Mama.'

'I love you, Simplicity,' Prima said, greatly daring. She patted the girl on the shoulder. 'There now. Go to the kitchen and bring us some lemonade.'

'Yes, Mama.' Simplicity had always been biddable and sweet; Prima could not help wishing Mitch had appreciated that sweetness more.

Hazel tapped at the doorframe. 'Prima?'

'Yes.' Prima pushed the needle through her work, and laid it aside. 'Come in, have a seat. What is the news?'

Hazel looked at her. 'You could turn on a vid.'

'Full of nonsense,' Prima said. 'All that arguing, and bad language, too.' She didn't mention the other things she had found there by accident. Men and women with no clothes on, doing things she had never imagined they could do.

'Lord Thornbuckle's funeral was today,' Hazel said.

Prima knew that. Everyone knew that. Even with the vid turned off, there was no way to avoid knowing that the Speaker of the Table of Ministers, whose daughter had started all the troubles, had died and was being — not buried, because they didn't do that here, but . . . but whatever they called it, today.

It was all his fault, really. Prima wanted to believe that, wanted to believe that if that one arrogant blond man had not been so bad a father that his daughter had fallen into cåptivity, then she would still be Prima Bowie, first wife of a Ranger, safe and happy in the household she had known – had helped make – since her wedding.

That was a comfortable thought. All his fault, and Mitch the innocent dupe of heathens. Herself an innocent victim. The children . . . Prima sighed. Try as she might, she could not convince herself – quite – that it was all Lord Thornbuckle's fault. Or even his daughter's, though she loathed the tall yellow-haired woman.

'Prima –' Hazel was leaning forward. 'I'm sorry, but – I really need to talk to you about your plans.'

'My plans?' Prima stiffened, her fingers pausing for a moment in their busy work. 'What do you mean?'

'Everyone wants to know what you are going to do – about the children's schooling, about supporting yourself –'

'Supporting myself!' Prima fastened on that; she was not about to discuss sending the children out to one of the heathen schools. 'But the Serranos promised protection –'

'Protection, yes. But there are hundreds of you, all told – they can't afford to support all of you, not like this –'

Like this, in a warren of indoor rooms in a tall building, with windows that looked out on more tall buildings. Prima would have given anything for a bit of ground to walk on, sky to look at.

'And there are laws about the children, about schooling.'

That she could answer. 'I am not sending my children to some heathen school to be taught vileness –'

'There are religious schools,' Hazel said. 'I brought you a cube –'

A cube. Which she could access only with a cube reader. A machine. Machines, the parsons had always said, would make women lazy.

'I need to change my name,' she said abruptly. Hazel looked surprised. 'I'm not Mitch's Prima anymore,' she said. 'Ruth Ann was my birth name, and I should be Ruth Ann again.'

'Ruth Ann,' Hazel said softly, tasting it in her mouth. 'It's a pretty name.'

'It sounds strange to me; no one's called me that since my parents, years ago.'

'Didn't they keep calling you —?'

'No, it wouldn't have been fitting. I was Prima Pardue from the day I married Mitch, and Prima Bowie from the day he became Ranger.' She fidgeted a bit, wishing she didn't have to ask what she wanted to know. 'Hazel . . . I never see anyone like Simplicity, even on the vid, when I do watch it. Surely your people have children that turn out . . . not quite . . . right?'

'Not many,' Hazel said. She flushed; Prima knew something forbidden was in her mind. 'I know you don't like to hear it, but — people do tests and medical treatment even before babies are born, to be sure nothing is wrong with them. Then, if something happens during pregnancy or birth, they fix it.'

'Fix it.' Like a door? But people weren't doors and shutters and shoes and . . . 'How can you fix a mind?' she asked, greatly daring.

'I don't know.' Hazel's flush faded. 'I'm still young; I haven't finished my schooling, and I never studied any medicine.'

'Could they fix . . . Simplicity . . . now?'

'I don't think so,' Hazel said. 'I can ask. But I think they have to be younger.' She cocked her head. 'But Prima — Ruth, I mean — there's no need to "fix" Simplicity. She's a sweet, loving person the way she is.'

'Your people don't value sweetness,' Prima said. 'They value intelligence.'

Hazel paused, looking thoughtful. 'There are many places in the Familias where that's true, but there are also many places that will value Simplicity for her gentleness, her kindness. I think you misjudge us. If you want to find a place –'

'No. I don't want to send her away! That's what Mitch said!' That's what Mitch had done. It still hurt her, that Simplicity had had to endure months in that nursery away from the home she loved.

'I didn't mean send her away. I meant go with her to a place where she'd be welcome.'

'I can't go anywhere without my – without Ensign Serrano's permission.'

'You could tell him what you want.'

'Hazel – you know I can't do that. He's my – well, not husband, the way he should be, but he's our protector. It is for him to decide what to do with us.'

'That's not how it works, here,' Hazel said. Prima had heard that before, but it was hard to believe. Ensign Serrano was her protector, on the guarantee of his grandmother; he had the right to decide where they would live, and how. 'He'd probably be delighted if you found a place where you and the others could be happy.'

'I don't know how to do that,' Prima said. 'I don't know where to start.'

'You could ask Professor Meyerson.'

'Waltraude?' This had not occurred to Prima; she knew that Meyerson claimed expertise in Texan history – though a very strange version of it, from Prima's viewpoint – but what could she know about other worlds?

'She's a professor – finding things out is what she does best.'

'Could you explain it?' Prima asked. She was much more comfortable with Hazel, even Hazel in men's pants, than with Waltraude in a dress. Waltraude looked at them all as if they were carrots and beets and potatoes on the kitchen table – as if she were considering how they would fit in a stew.

'If she comes back in time. Prima – one thing I came to tell you – I'm leaving later today. I should be on my way to the ship now – clearing customs is going to take longer than usual. I'm going back to my family.'

'Oh.' She had known, in a way, that Hazel would leave, as the former captive women had left. Those women – she still worried about them, but they had all insisted on going, some to restorative surgery, others with voice synthesizers, back to their families if they had any, or a life of independence that Prima could not imagine wanting. 'I'll miss you, Hazel,' Prima said, feeling the hot tears rise.

'You were good to me,' Hazel said, and came to hug her. Prima could feel the girl's young breasts now . . . Hazel was breeding age, but she would not breed. She would do – might already have done – terrible things to herself so that she would have no babies until much later. She might already be an Abomination.

Yet Hazel was a good girl – honest, kind, gentle. She had been so desperately worried about the two little girls, in the beginning; she had been so sweet to all the children. If she'd been Prima's daughter, Prima would have been proud of her. But now she'd go off to some school, or fly on a ship, or – Prima could not even imagine all the possibilities, and knew she couldn't. How could a child like this know what she wanted, what was right?

'God's blessing on you,' Prima said, greatly daring in offering a blessing to a heathen. She wanted to tell Hazel not to use any abominable technology, but she knew that was futile. The girl was the product of that technology; her family used it, she would use it too. She prayed silently that God would keep Hazel safe.

SECTOR SEVEN HEADQUARTERS

'We now know what happened, Admiral.' The chief medical officer touched the display controls, and blurred blots of color sharpened into focus. 'The Surgeon General's office sent this out by ansible; the research labs finally figured it out. In a normal rejuvenation, on the left, the metabolites of the rejuv drugs are each involved in scavenging specific degradation products.'

'In plain language?' Vida Serrano asked. She knew, and knew they knew, what was meant, but she was determined to make them say it in language that anyone could understand. She had already been briefed, very secretly, by Marta Katerina Saenz.

'The rejuv drugs break down in the body into other chemicals, and those chemicals – metabolites – bind to and remove the chemical compounds characteristic of aging.'

'Very well.'

'In a normal rejuvenation, that leaves only healthy, undegraded tissues as a matrix for replication, the second part of the rejuvenation process.'

'So the first part throws out the old, as it were, and then the second part builds up the new?'

'Yes, Admiral. But on the right – if you'll look right here – you can see that these tissues, which stain green, are not being removed. No green on the left, and green –'

'On the right. Yes. And I presume that means that age-deteriorated tissues are left in the matrix when the rejuv proceeds.'

'Exactly. Which replicate into age-deteriorated tissues, so that after some years – it depends on the amount of deterioration in the original as well as the exact kind of faulty drug – the deterioration affects brain function like any other senile dementia.'

'So – how do you fix it?'

'Unfortunately, we don't know. It appears that if no actual functional degradation has occurred, then a rejuvenation with good drugs produces a fresh start. But when we tried that on one of the first patients, it didn't work. The body rejuvenated to a young age, but the mental function stayed the same. We have been observing him for months now, and while the deterioration has not progressed, it has also not improved.'

'What about other treatments? Surely you had something for this kind of problem before rejuv?'

'No, not really. Admiral – I know that nobody likes to hear this, but medical miracles are rarely miracles.'

Marta had told her the same thing, but she'd hoped for better news.

'How early can you detect the problem?' If they couldn't reverse it, perhaps catching it early would work.

'Within a year of a bad rejuv, which is plenty of time to correct it. But the tests take weeks – maybe we can speed it up later, but not yet – and we have a lot of people to test.'

What were they going to do with those whose rejuvs had failed, who had already been damaged . . . Vida shuddered. Rejuvenate them to youthful bodies and senility of mind? Who would take care of them? For how long? Or . . . let them die? Neither horn of the dilemma seemed tenable, and for once she was glad that it wasn't her decision. Let the Grand Admiral and the Surgeon General figure it out; the mathematics of equity in this escaped her.

ZENEBRA, TWO DAYS BEFORE THE SENIOR TRIALS

For dinner, Pedar had chosen Raymond's, that year's fashionable restaurant. She steered him away from discussing the Trials – he wanted her to dissect all the other competitors for his amusement.

'It's not right,' she insisted. 'They're my friends as well as my fellow competitors; it's not honorable to pick them apart like that.' She touched the table controls and brought up the chessboard. 'Let's play.'

'Don't be naive, Cecelia,' Pedar said. Had he rejuved yet again? She couldn't tell. He still dressed more like an actor in some deep-historical play. Her interest in history didn't extend to clothing styles, so she wasn't sure what period. 'There's no place in real life for honor. In sports, perhaps –' He picked up a black knight and a white, and made them bow to each other. 'But even you know that what really matters is winning.' He clashed the pieces together.

'If you break the rules,' Cecelia said, trying to be reasonable, 'they eliminate you.'

Pedar tilted his hand. 'Then you might say that Bunny broke the rules.'

She could not believe what she was hearing. 'You –'

'Cecelia – the rules are on a different level, when you're talking about realities . . . surely you know that.' His tone indulged her, the knowledgeable adult to the ignorant adolescent. 'Men like Bunny make the rules . . . until someone else displaces them.' He pushed the white king along the board, knocking the other pieces askew, until it rested on the edge of the board. 'Yet there are always rules beyond rules . . . the rules that keep a man in his place – or move him away.' His finger touched the game piece; it teetered a moment on the edge of the table, then fell.

Her body tensed, as if she had seen an unexpected ditch looming beyond a jump she thought she knew. His expression shifted, reflecting hers; she hated that he had noticed. But he kept smiling, waiting her answer. She couldn't think what to answer. She had to say something, though; she could feel his smile beginning to stiffen in place, like overbeaten egg whites.

'I see,' she said, buying time. She didn't understand about Bunny yet, what rules he had broken that brought this man and his faction to the desperate action they had taken. She didn't understand why he had hinted so broadly, or what he expected her to do about it. But she did see that none of it was accidental, not Bunny's death, or this dinner meeting, or anything else Pedar did. Perhaps as far back as the Trials several years ago, her first ride in years. He had tried then to talk to her about the politics of the Rejuvenants, and she had dismissed it as mere fashion. 'I do wonder,' she said after a long pause, 'what, if anything, the New Texas Godfearing Militia has to do with Rejuvenants.'

He relaxed just that fraction which told her she had chosen the safer alternative at that conversational fence.

'People need something to blame for their disappointments,' he said. 'As some opportunities are foreclosed, others must be seen to open. Or unrest might become general.'

Cecelia puzzled at this. Again, he waited for her, that indulgent smile which told her he expected her to be slow to understand. She hated that patience; if this was what she would become, as a Rejuvenant, she might just as well run her horse over a cliff and be done with it. Opportunities foreclosed – that had to be because Rejuvenants could live well-nigh forever, and who was going to give up power and privilege while still young and capable? Mentally, she transferred the problem to horse breeding, where it made more sense to her. If the old horses didn't die off, and you kept breeding at the same rate . . . well, of course.

'I wonder if rejuv drugs would work on horses,' she said, before she could get a lock on her tongue.

Pedar burst out laughing, and the bald man at the next table looked up. 'Cecelia, my dear! Only you would think of rejuvenating a horse!'

She could feel the heat in her face. Yet – if he laughed at her like that, he was not afraid of her wits. She allowed her voice to carry a little sting. 'I see what you mean, Pedar. Those who cannot afford rejuvenation, or who are simply impatient, see ahead of them a lifetime of blocked opportunities – blocked by the Rejuvenants. But the universe is large – if they are discontented and ambitious enough, there are colony worlds –'

'Theft is always more profitable, until the thief is caught,' Pedar murmured.

'That's –' She was about to say ridiculous, when a tension in Pedar's face silenced her.

She had too much to think about, and she did not really want to think about any of it. Of what use were her wealth, and her skills, and her rejuvenated body, if she couldn't do what she liked without having to worry about the rest of the universe? What she had wanted – what she hoped to gain – was a long life full of her own particular pleasures . . . which began, though they did not end, in that stable block on Rotterdam. Which centered on horses and the people who had identified themselves as horse people since long before humans left Old Earth.

She reminded herself that she had time for both, now. No longer need she fear the advancing years, the aging of joints and bones that would make her slower, clumsier. She could afford to spend a few months now dealing with whatever complication Pedar meant, without losing it.

But she didn't want to.

And Pedar knew that. As she dipped the asymmetrical spoon always used with Biaristi cold soups, as she refreshed her mouth afterwards with a sip of Eran ale, and went on to the crunchy-coated strips of spiced rock grouse, she was aware that Pedar, in sounding her out, was expecting exactly the retreat she most wanted to make. He had turned the conversation back to the Trials, to her chances, and his. She answered automatically, but watched as from a distance the subtle signals of his expressions.

What a toad the man was, after all. He would dangle some conspiracy in front of her for his own amusement, sure that she could not concentrate on anything but horses for long enough to learn anything dangerous, or do anything . . .

'I think you're quite right to ride anyway,' Pedar said. 'After all, it's too late to attend any ceremony.'

'The horse is ready,' Cecelia said, fighting back an urge to change her mind and not ride after all. 'And so am I. You're staying too.'

'For the same reasons,' Pedar said. 'I'm ready; my horse is ready, and my competition . . . is here.'

And because it gave him a strong apparent alibi. While someone had plotted Bunny's assassination, Pedar had been very publicly visible a very long way away, supervising his horse in training for the Senior Trials. Cecelia knew it would have been possible to have it done — anyone knew that — but finding and proving the links would be more difficult. And dangerous.

She was, she discovered on the day, more ready than she knew for this particular event. While nothing could make the Senior Trials effortless, she was hardly aware of the effort she exerted. Seniority reacted well to her detached calmness, and put in faultless cross-country and stadium rounds . . . which, in the end, were enough to win, when the dressage leader (also faultless in cross-country) had a rail down the next day. Liam Ardahi had to withdraw during the cross-country, when Plantagenet refused the water repeatedly. Cecelia wondered if that were entirely an accident; Plantagenet had always been bold into water. But if Pedar wanted her distracted by a major win . . . he was ruthlessly competitive, but he had won a much larger competition – as he saw it.

She smiled for the press on her victory gallop, and remembered to thank all her staff, enclosing a personal note with the bonus credit each received. At the reception that evening, she wore her amber necklace carved in the likeness of Epona. Like that enigmatic goddess, she smiled and accepted congratulations, finally pleading a sore elbow in order to leave before midnight.

An hour later, wearing a groom's overall, she was hacking down the dark road to the spaceport on Max, whose alert ears and brisk movement revealed that the horse, at least, thought this was a fine idea. If anyone asked, her groundcar was parked in the stable lot, and everyone knew that she was likely to have gone to the stables to end the night's celebration there. Colum had had Max saddled for her – an extra hack would do that one no harm – but had been out of sight when she led the horse out.

Five kilometers away, where a service road met the tracks of A Course, Phase C, Dale waited with the truck and trailer, in which a horse stamped its impatience; Roz had driven her own battered little groundcar. Cecelia swung off Max, helped load him in the trailer beside Dulcy – Max could be difficult to load in an empty trailer – then struggled with the car's cranky driver-side door. Roz slammed it from outside, and climbed into the truck; Cece drove off alone to the regional airport.

The advantage of piloting her own ship was that her flight plan and her actual destination need have nothing to do with each other. She had discussed with her staff the training schedule for Seniority and Max for the rest of the season, and told them she was going to visit EquiSite's lab before returning to Rotterdam, to check on a new gene-sculpting technique only recently applied to horses.

Then she filed a flight plan for Rotterdam, knowing that her staff would not comment.

Her new planet-to-jump craft allowed her to bypass Zenebra's crowded station. She expected Pedar to check on her flight plan, and her jump vector. Fine. Let him check. The exit vector for Rotterdam actually led to the first intermediate jump point, and from there she could route to Castle Rock easily. She spared a moment to thank Heris for suggesting that she get a license and learn to pilot her own craft.

Though she did miss the luxury of *Sweet Delight*, and the deference accorded a full-size yacht. What she really wanted was another long, hot bath and a massage. She had managed to cram in a small wet-bath facility and the necessary recycling gear by eliminating any possibility of inviting someone else along. So a shower and no massage, and she would expect to wake up stiff in the morning. Even a rejuvenated body couldn't do the Senior Trials without strain.

Still, it was worth it. *Pounce* had more speed than her old yacht, as well as the ability to land onplanet. She was past the orbital station now, following the beacons out to the system's jump point.

CHAPTER THREE

Two uneventful transits after leaving Zenebra, Cecelia was in Castle Rock's nearspace, confirming that Miranda was still onplanet and still in residence in the Old Palace. When she called, the staff person who answered reported that Miranda would indeed be willing to see her. Cecelia made her shuttle reservation while waiting for the station tug to bump her gently into the docking harness. The paperwork necessary to clear the Rockhouse Major Dockmaster and Customs seemed to take forever (had Heris really coped with this much, or was it worse because of the assassination?) but she made her shuttle with a few minutes to spare. She saw no one she knew on Rockhouse Major, and no one familiar on the down shuttle. That suited her; she was in no mood to talk to any of her acquaintances.

But when she came out of the shuttleport entryway, looking for a hirecar, she saw one of the long black official cars, with the Familias seal on the doors, and the driver clearly recognized her.

'Lady Cecelia?'

'Yes?'

'Lady Miranda sent us for you. Your luggage?'

'In the dump,' Cecelia said, handing over the ID strip. The driver nodded to his second, who took the strip and went off toward the dumps. Belatedly, Cecelia wondered if she should make sure of their identity and authorization – Heris, she thought, would be scolding her if Heris were here. But the driver was now holding out a flat packet.

'Lady Miranda wanted you to have this first,' he said.

Cecelia opened it. A note from Miranda, and a flatpic of the driver and assistant. 'You may not be worried,' the note said, 'but we have learned we must all take precautions. I look forward to seeing you.'

In minutes, the assistant was back with Cecelia's few pieces of luggage, all marked with the striped tape that meant they'd passed Customs. Cecelia got into the car and wondered, as it shot forward into traffic, if they were taking the same route Bunny had followed the day he was killed. She didn't ask.

At the Palace, everything seemed normal at first. The same uniforms at the gate, at the doors. The same quietly efficient staff who guided her first to her guest room overlooking a small garden, and then, when she had showered and changed, to Miranda's suite. It was hard to remember, in this quiet gracious place, that Bunny was dead, and all their peace in peril. She found herself expecting to see him coming down the corridor, his pleasantly foolish face lighting with a smile.

Until she came face to face with Miranda, and saw the devastation of that legendary beauty. Cecelia wondered how the same exquisite curves of bone, the same flawless skin, could now express a wasteland. After the rituals of greeting, when the staff had placed a tea set on the low table and withdrawn, Cecelia could wait no longer. No need, when the porcelain surface had already shattered.

'Miranda, what have they told you about it – about who did it?'

'Nothing.' Miranda poured a cup of tea and handed it to Cecelia; the cup did not rattle on the saucer. 'I know the news media say it was the New Texas Militia, in retaliation for the executions. I know that the former head of security is on administrative leave. But they have very gently let me know that investigations are in progress, and I will be informed when it is time. Do have a pastry; you always liked these curly ones, didn't you?'

Cecelia ignored the offered pastry. 'Miranda . . . I don't think it was the NewTex Militia.'

'Why?' Miranda's face had no more expression than a cameo.

'I think it was someone . . . inside.'

'Family?' Her voice was cool. Why wasn't she upset? Why wasn't she frightened? Had she been through too much?

Cecelia waited a moment, then went on. 'Pedar said . . . that Bunny broke rules.'

Miranda's mouth twitched; it might have been grimace or grin. 'He did. He was so . . . so quiet, so . . . compliant, it always seemed. But from the first time he brought me a tart he'd filched from the cook, when we were children, and showed me where we could hide from our governesses . . . he broke rules.'

'More important than that,' Cecelia said.

'I know.' Miranda stared past Cecelia's left ear, as if she saw something a long way away, but was too tired to pay much attention.

'Miranda!' Even before Miranda turned her eyes back, Cecelia had bitten back the rest of it, all that she wanted to say. You can't give up now. You have to keep going. You have a family –

'I have a family,' Miranda said, in that cool level voice. 'I have responsibilities. Children. Grandchildren. You don't want me to forget that.'

'Yes . . .' Cecelia had lowered her voice, and strove to sit quietly.

'I do not care.' Miranda turned that cameo face full on Cecelia. 'I do not care about the children – not even Brun, whom I most desperately want to care about. I do not care about the grandchildren, those bastard brats forced on my daughter –' Her breath caught in a ragged gasp, giving the lie to that *do not care.* Cecelia said nothing; there was nothing she could say. 'I do not care,' Miranda went on, 'about anything but Branthcombe. Bunny. Whom, in this day and age, and in spite of rejuvenations and genetic selection and everything else we invented to spare us the pain of living . . . I loved. All my life, from the time he brought me that cherry tart, and we ate it in alternate bites, sitting on the back stairs . . . I loved him. It was a miracle to me that he loved me. That he survived the hunting season we still make our young people go through, that he remembered me after my years in seclusion at Cypress Hill, that he married me. And fathered my children, and no matter what stayed loyal and decent and –' Her voice broke at last, in a gasp that ended in sobs.

'My dear . . .' Cecelia reached out, uncertain. Miranda had been, for so long, another exquisite porcelain figurine in Cecelia's mental collection of beautiful women – like her sister, like all the women of that type – and she had never touched any of them for more than the rituals of class affection – the fingertips, the cheeks. But Miranda didn't recoil, and leaned into her as if Cecelia were her mother or her aunt.

The sobs went on a long time, and Cecelia had a cramp in the small of her back from twisting to accommodate Miranda's position, by the time Miranda quieted.

'Damnation,' she said then. 'I thought I was over it.'

'I don't think you can get over it,' Cecelia said.

'No. Not really. But over it enough to function. You're right, I have to do that much. But I really do not know how.'

'Your advisors –'

'Are vultures.' Miranda gave Cecelia a sideways glance and pulled back a little; Cecelia took that hint and stood, stretching. 'You, never having married, may not realize just how complicated the situation is. Your estate is all yours, and you have the disposal of it –'

'When my ham-fisted relatives don't interfere,' Cecelia said. She had tried, and failed, to put out of her mind her sister's interference in her will. The legal repercussions had dragged on for several years.

'True. But what I have is Bunny's legacy in several separate realms, some of which I stayed out of. The political –'

'Surely no one expects you to take over as Speaker –'

'No.' Miranda's voice was sour. 'Everyone is sure that the political realm is the one I know least about. More's the pity – since I actually do understand it, and could take over, if they'd only let me.'

Cecelia managed not to gape, by a small margin. Miranda politically minded? Then she thought of Lorenza, who certainly had been, and repressed a shiver. She sat down again and poured herself a cup of tea.

'Lorenza,' Miranda said, in another uncanny echo of Cecelia's thoughts. 'Now there was another case of backstage expertise. She and I used to play the most delicate games of power . . . it would bore you, Cecelia, unless you could think of it in equestrian terms, but . . . if you could imagine yourself on a very, very advanced horse, which despised you but had, for some reason, agreed to obey exactly your commands.'

'I had one like that,' Cecelia said, hoping to divert Miranda onto a more congenial topic. Miranda's hiss of annoyance stopped her.

'We are not talking horses. Did you ever fence?'

Fence. Possible meanings ran through Cecelia's mind, the most recent out of her *Spacepilots' Glossary of Navigational Terms*; she couldn't imagine Miranda as a jump-point explorer probing into unknown routes.

'Ancient sport,' Miranda said. 'Derived from an ancient method of warfare. Swordfighting, also called fencing.'

'No,' Cecelia said, feeling grumpy. She had just spent a half hour comforting a woman in collapse, and now she was being questioned like a schoolgirl about a sport she had always considered supremely silly. For one thing, it had nothing to do with fences that horses could jump over. 'I don't . . . er . . . fence.'

'You should,' Miranda said. She stood, and moved restlessly around the room, touching the surfaces as if she felt her way, rather than saw them with her eyes. Curtain, curtain, bureau, chair . . . 'It's an excellent discipline, and apt for use aboard spaceships, for instance.'

'Swords?' Cecelia could not quite keep the astonishment out of her voice. Was Miranda losing her mind? Tears, then politics, then swords?

'They do less damage to bulkheads,' Miranda said. 'If your only purpose is to kill people, why destroy the ship?'

She must be crazy. It must be, Cecelia thought, an effect of whatever had kept her so lovely for so long. Could she have been given bad rejuv drugs?

'Cecelia, I am not crazy. Well . . . not very crazy. Distracted with grief, and frustration, and anger, but not

in the way we usually mean. Fencing – if you knew anything about it – is the ideal metaphor for what Lorenza
and I did, just as Bunny and her brother Piercy – but no.
You don't know the terms.'

Cecelia felt her temper gathering like a boil behind her
eyes. She squeezed them hard shut, and spoke with them
closed. 'Miranda. I know you're grieving; it was good for
you to cry. But please quit treating me like a silly
horsecrazy schoolgirl –'

'But you are,' Miranda said, in that same flat cool
voice. 'You always have been; you refused to grow up –
just like Brun, that way. It was ridiculous of Bunny to
send Brun to you, of all people –'

'You – blame me? For Brun?'

'Not really . . . I mean, intellectually I know we chose
her genetic type, we chose to increase the risk-taking and
the responsiveness. But there you were, such a model for
such a girl – every hunting season, egging her on over
bigger fences, as if horses were all that mattered. And
what did it get her, to take someone like you for a model?
That . . . that degradation!'

Astonishment had blown out anger for the moment.
'She isn't like me,' Cecelia said, feeling her way.

'She's not horse-crazy, no. But that – that stubborn
insouciance, that willingness to shed responsibility –'

Cecelia felt the anger gathering again just beyond her
vision. 'I didn't know you considered me irresponsible,'
she managed to say quietly.

Miranda's hand tilted quickly, a diminishing gesture.
'Not in everything, of course. But no sense of family, no
loyalty to the Familias –' Her head swung away; the bell
of golden hair swung wide a moment, then stilled into
new perfection. 'And she pulled that harebrained stunt to
rescue you – she could have been killed then –'

'I didn't ask her to,' Cecelia said. Something tapped at

the alarms in her brain, a tiny hammering. 'I couldn't. She just –'

'Loved you,' Miranda said. Under mint-green silk, her shoulders rose and fell; Cecelia could not hear the sigh but knew it had been given.

'She loved her family,' Cecelia said. 'And you didn't need rescuing.'

'No.' Miranda turned back, face composed as usual. 'No, I never did.' For a long moment, she stood motionless, silent. Cecelia found it hard to breathe. Miranda shrugged again. 'Kata Saenz said we provided the wrong models for Brun; she told Bunny that, in the planning for Brun's rescue. I was glad of it at the time; I knew we'd done something wrong, though our other children turned out well. And the shock of being told it was partly his fault got Bunny out of his fury with the Suiza girl, and in the end she saved Brun's life. I just can't understand her, though she's my child.'

'How about the rest of the family? Buttons and Sarah . . .?'

'Are wonderfully helpful, as far as they can be. Buttons, of course, expected to take over as his father's heir. But Bunny's younger brother Harlis – you remember him?'

Cecelia nodded. Harlis had all the arrogance, all the faux-aristocratic foppery, and a third less sense, than Bunny had had. Bunny could always go in an instant from the foolish foxhunting lord of the manor to the sensible, practical, and very capable politician. Harlis was Harlis – all surface and no substance.

'Harlis is challenging the Family structure, and I'm not sure Buttons can stop him. I did tell Bunny three years ago that he ought to clarify the situation just in case, and he and Kevil were looking into it, but then Bubbles – Brun – disappeared.'

'And of course Bunny wasn't thinking of it then.'

'No, nor of anything else. Harlis managed to convince some of the distant relatives that Bunny's mind had gone, and that any of Bunny's children were likely to carry the trait. And some of them accepted that, and have thrown in their influence with Harlis. He's acquired an astonishing amount of stock in several of the corporations; even old Trema left him her shares –'

'Will you be all right?'

'Probably, but I'm going to lose a lot. And I wanted it for Brun – for her and the twins. She needs a safe place; Sirialis would have been perfect –'

'Harlis isn't taking Sirialis . . .!' Cecelia's first thought was that Harlis had never liked foxhunting and might end the annual hunting season; she slapped that thought down, ashamed of herself. Maybe she was as selfish and narrow-minded as Miranda thought.

'He's trying.' Miranda dropped her voice, mimicking Harlis's. '"Oh, you'll always be welcome, Miranda, of course. You'll always have a place. But it was family property, not Bunny's alone." As if I would go there to lurk in the apartment he so generously offered, while he strides about pretending to be lord of the manor!'

Cecelia forebore to say that he would be the lord, and no pretense, if he had his way. 'And what are you doing about it – I assume you have some plan.'

'Yes. But I haven't decided . . . it would mean tearing up much that Bunny built . . . family relationships, friendships, alliances. I can call on my family –' Of the founding Families, Miranda's had been known first for information management, and later for the development and manufacture of a variety of devices that were to the ordinary computer as a top event horse was to a child's pony.

'But it's – it was Bunny's, and it's rightfully yours –'

Inheritance had been the one immutable aspect of law, concentration of assets within a Family, the foundation of Family power. Angry as Cecelia had been with her sister for questioning her will, she knew that if she had left her assets within the family, even to a distant relative, the will would not have been challenged.

'Cece – you don't understand how threadbare the fabric has become, since you exposed Kemtre and Lorenza. I suppose it had begun before, but that's when it became obvious.' Miranda paused, frowning a bit in thought. 'Bunny and I, and Kevil, were holding an alliance of Families by the skin of our teeth. All those years of social connections, business connections, and Kevil's legal skills and intuition. I swear he knew more about the ragged skeletons in Family closets than anyone had ever guessed. Bunny would talk them around, and I would smile and be gracious and work through the wives and mistresses. We were holding it together, just, but the crises kept knocking it out of balance. Kemtre's abdication, that Patchcock mess – the scare about bad rejuvenation drugs, and the Morreline/Conselline Family collapse, and then Brun's abduction . . .' Her voice trailed away.

'And I went back to Rotterdam to play with horses,' Cecelia said.

'Yes. I understand it, in a way. Venezia Morreline had her pottery, and you had horses, and Kata Saenz had her research. Most people do have their private interests, and that, after all, is what a good political system is supposed to do – leave you free to do what you are best at, whatever it is. People want to do the work they love, marry and have children, have some fun. But if too many people do that, Cecelia, it leaves gaps for people who want power for its own sake, and who may use it in ways that later degrade your life.'

Like Bunny using Fleet resources as if they were personal, to rescue Brun. She didn't say that; she knew that Miranda knew what people thought. 'How is Kevil?' she asked instead.

'Alive.' From her tone, Cecelia couldn't tell if Miranda were pleased about that or not. Then she sighed. 'I can't wish Kevil dead, only Bunny alive as well. Kevil was badly hurt – days in the regen tank, and then the head injury – he's still not himself. He may never be, the doctors say. And without Bunny – or me, if I could only find a way – he doesn't have the backing to do what he did for us before.'

'I should visit him,' Cecelia said.

'Yes, you should. You should tell him what you told me, with all the names you know. He might know something useful, something that would give us leverage.'

'And Brun?'

'Brun . . . has a crazy notion of changing her identity. Going to the Guernesi and getting a rejuv and biosculpt that will make her a new person from the bones out. I think she got the idea from the prince's clones.'

'She doesn't want the children,' Cecelia said, not asking.

'Would you?' Miranda shivered, then sighed. 'No, she doesn't want them. I don't want them myself, really. Bunny did. Bunny had some crazy idea that they could grow up to prove their existence wasn't a disaster, but it is.'

'That's a lot of burden on them.'

'Yes. Unfair, too. I know that. But nothing can make them other than they are: bastards, Brun's ruin, the ruin of all our hopes for the Familias. They are the lit fuse, poor little brats.'

'What are they like?'

'Babies. Toddlers, really, at this point. Neither looks

like anyone in our family, and they aren't identical. One has the brightest red hair I ever saw, and the other's is brown. Brun says one of the men was a redhead. . . .'

Cecelia noticed that Miranda had not used names; before she could ask, Miranda went on.

'The gene scan showed up some interesting anomalies – according to one geneticist, who's also looked at the women and other children, these people were seriously inbred, with a lot of undesirable recessives concentrated. They had noticed that children born of captured women were less likely to be disabled, but considered that as proof of their God's blessing on capturing women. Of course, we had the boys treated at once, although it was too late for a complete washout.'

'What do you call them?' Cecelia finally got a word in.

Miranda blushed. 'We don't actually . . . have names. Brun never did, and she refuses to talk about it. Their nurses call them Red and Brownie. I know –' She held up a hand. 'Those are names for dogs or ponies, not boys. Nicknames, at best. I just don't – Bunny and I had been talking about it when he was killed.' She moved her cup restlessly. 'Would you like to see them?'

'Of course.' Cecelia stood.

Down the hall, past several doors and now she could hear the crowing of a happy child, the chuckle of another. Miranda paused just before the open door. Cecelia looked in. Two young women in colorful smocks, a floor strewn with toys, and two sturdy toddlers. One, the redhead, was bouncing up and down, clapping his hands. The other, sitting in a scatter of blocks, looked quickly toward the door, grinning.

They were normal children, not monsters. Happy children, not monsters. Children who were more than 'lit fuses' – who were potentially normal, if only they didn't grow up burdened with a past they had not made.

'You have to send them away,' Cecelia said, surprising herself. 'There are people who want children and don't have them; there are places where these boys will be treasured as they should be.'

'Bunny said –'

'Bunny's dead. They're alive. They can have a good future – and the universe is big enough that they need not be anyone's pawns in some power game.'

'And you know who –?' A tone suspended between sarcasm and hope.

'No, but I can find out. Will you let me do that? Find them homes where they'll have a chance?'

Miranda sagged. 'I . . . don't know.'

'Miranda. You have other grandchildren, and will have more. Children you can love naturally. Children whose political importance, if any, comes with a family commitment. You haven't even given these boys *names* – you know yourself that's wrong. Give them up; give them a chance.'

'Brun wants to . . .' Miranda said. 'She said . . . she doesn't want to hate them, but she can't live with them around. But neither of us can face the thought of an orphanage.'

'She's right,' Cecelia said. 'You said we were alike – we may be, that much. If I had borne them, in her circumstances, I'd have to give them up. It's a big universe; they need never know.'

She left Miranda in the doorway and went on into the room, nodding to the nurses, and sitting on the floor. Red, his hair an orange flame, put a fat thumb in his mouth, but Brownie grinned at her. Cecelia pulled out the ring of keys from the stable and jingled it. His grin widened, and he came to her, grabbing for the keys. Though he looked little like Brun, his boldness and the sparkle in his blue eyes suggested Brun's attitudes.

Cecelia did not think of herself as a religious person, but she found herself praying to something, somewhere, to give these boys a better life than their beginning.

'Lady Cecelia!' That was Brun; Cecelia turned.

'You look well,' she said. Brun looked well physically – her tall body trim and fit, her tumbled gold curls in a riot around her head. But the clear gaze was shadowed, darkening when she looked at the boys.

'I'm fine,' Brun said. 'Considering everything.'

'I agree with you and your mother,' Cecelia said. 'These boys need a proper home, not to mention names.'

Brun's face stiffened, then she grinned. 'Still tactful, I see.'

'As ever,' Cecelia agreed. 'My dear, I'm almost ninety, and rejuvenation did nothing to soften my personality. Why don't we do it today?'

'Today?' Both Miranda and Brun looked shocked; so did the nurses.

'They're starting to talk; they understand even more. Every day you wait makes it harder on them.'

'I . . . want to be sure they have good homes . . . that they lack for nothing . . .' Brun said.

'A good home is a loving home,' Cecelia said, with all the confidence of the childless. 'And right now they're lacking the most basic needs of all – a name, a parent –'

'But what will you do with them?'

'Take them to a safe and loving home. Brun, you've known me all your life. Have I ever lied to you?' Brun shook her head, tears rising in her eyes. Miranda started to speak, but Cecelia waved her down. 'I have told you the truth, even when it wasn't what you wanted to hear. I tell you the truth now – if you let me have these boys I will see to it that they find a good home. I will do it myself. . . .'

'But your schedule –'

'Is my own. Miranda, you were twitting me with my

self-indulgence. This is what self-indulgence is good for. I can help you, right now, because I have no other obligations in the way.' She softened her voice. 'Please let me.'

Brun looked down, then nodded. Cecelia could see the gleam of tears in her eyes.

Miranda stared at Cecelia a long moment, then said, 'All right. And I still have money for them – a start in a new life –'

'Good.' Cecelia tried to think what next. She had said *today* without really thinking what that would mean, but now the two nursemaids were watching her, waiting for orders. She had no idea how long it took to pack up two children, or where to take them, but she knew she must not hesitate. She spoke to the nursemaids.

'Are you full-time employees, and would you be able to travel for a month or so?'

'Yes, ma'am,' said one of them. 'We're from Sirialis, originally, but we thought we'd be staying for years . . .'

'Then will you please start packing – or have someone help you pack – the boys' things? I need to talk to Miranda and make some arrangements –' She would need a bigger ship – a momentary pang, when she thought of how easy it would have been with *Sweet Delight*, and Heris Serrano, to take the twins and their nursemaids anywhere. Reservations on a commercial liner? No, too much chance of publicity. She'd have to lease a ship and crew. No, to start with she'd need another room – set of rooms – in her hotel. She'd made reservations for one. Or perhaps another hotel. Ideas whirled through her head like leaves before a wind. 'Miranda, let's go to your suite – we have business.'

'Yes, Cecelia.' Miranda nodded at the nursemaids, already beginning to gather toys. 'I'll send a maid in to do the packing; just be sure the boys are clean and dressed. And I'll take care of your salaries and references.'

Then she led the way to her suite. Brun came along with them, her face once more stiff with misery.

'Do you have any notion where you're going with them?' Miranda asked, when they were again in her sitting room.

'Yes.' The thought had come as she walked down the passage. 'I know the perfect planet, and probably the perfect couple. Do you want to know?'

'Not . . . now. Later, maybe.' Brun sat hunched, her eyes on the carpet.

'Fine, then. Miranda, I'll need the use of your comset –'

'I'll just call Poisson –'

'No. I'll make the reservations myself.' Only as far as the first hotel, she told herself. From there, she would arrange transportation. And she wanted no records in the Palace computers, where reporters might already have a tap.

'I have resources –'

'You said you were feuding with Bunny's brother –'

'In my own right. At least let me help.'

'Of course.' Cecelia turned politely to Brun as Miranda opened a line to her bank. 'Brun – have you heard from that girl – Hazel, wasn't it? – lately?'

Brun looked up. 'I worry about her. She seems to be doing fine, for someone who's been through so much, but she never has admitted how bad it was. She keeps wanting to get me to meet with that Ranger's wife – Prima Bowie.'

'Why?'

'I don't know.' Brun shifted restlessly. 'Hazel liked her, I think. Says she was kind. Hazel feels sorry for her, being a stranger in our society. But she chose it; she wasn't abducted.'

'Are they all still together, all those women?' asked Cecelia.

'As far as I know. I don't . . . really care.'

Miranda broke in. 'I've deposited a lump sum in your account, Cecelia; I can send more later if –'

'Don't worry about it,' Cecelia said. 'Tell me – do the maids take the boys out to play? In a park or anything?'

'Not off the grounds. The news media are bad enough as it is.'

'Then – how about Palace employees with children? Are there any?'

'I'm sure there are, but I don't know who. . . .'

'Perhaps the maids will. We don't want publicity when we take the children out.'

The little crocodile of children from Briary Meadows Primary School being herded through the public rooms as part of their field trip acquired a short tail. They didn't pay much attention; they were tired of glass-fronted cases full of trophies, letters, gifts to this or that famous person by another famous person, the rooms of interesting furniture which they could not touch, the silken ropes on which they were not supposed to swing, the constant admonitions to pay attention, be quiet, quit straggling or crowding.

The children had been promised a stop at Ziffra's, the famous ice-cream parlor, if they were good, and only a steady murmur of commands kept them from trampling one another on the way out the door. The nursemaids, now wearing the green smocks of adult helpers in the school, complete with dangling nametags, brought up the rear, each with a toddler on her hip.

Outside, the remaining media scavengers waited for any sign of Brun or her children, but ignored the confusion of piping voices and busy adults. They had seen bright green buses with the school name arrive, and crowds of obvious schoolchildren arrive, teachers hustling them into neat lines and adult volunteers scampering to catch the inevitable escapees. At least one such field trip arrived every day; the Palace had always been a favorite tourist site, and busloads of children, retirees, and convention attendees showed up so often that no one in the press corps paid them any mind.

Now, as the chattering youngsters piled into the buses, and the harried adults counted, compared notes, and shut the doors, they ignored the confusion, keeping an eye out instead for the return of Lady Cecelia, whose limousine waited at the other end of the car park.

A half hour later, Cecelia left, smiling into the holo lens and accepting congratulations on her win in the Senior Trials. She fielded a couple of questions about her breeding program, expressed sympathy for Bunny's family, and stepped into the waiting limousine, which took her to the medical center where Kevil Mahoney was still listed in critical condition.

And later that afternoon, the two school volunteers whose green smocks and nametags had been borrowed for a time walked out the service entrance with other Palace staff who lived offsite. No one paid attention to them, either.

Miranda listened to the silence and felt something shift inside her mind. She had not really been able to hear the twins, but knowing they were not there, that she could not hear them even if she walked down the hall, tipped her toward some distant horizon. She glanced at the clock. Was it still so early? Surely Cecelia had not been able to get them offplanet yet. She could check . . . she stopped, her hand outstretched to the comunit.

No. As if it were a robotic arm she were operating, she concentrated on her hand, and brought it back to her lap.

They were gone. They were gone forever.

Lightness filled her, as if she were a transparent husk

of herself. She might blow away . . . but of course that was nonsense. She was tired, very tired, and –

'Mother?'

Weight and darkness returned so suddenly she could hardly breathe. 'Yes, Brun?'

'You do think they'll be all right.'

'Of course.' Miranda took a deep breath. 'Cecelia is reliable, in her own way, and she will make sure of it.'

'Good.' Brun came into the room tentatively, as if she were unsure of her welcome. 'I feel . . . strange.'

Of course she felt strange. No one could survive what she had survived, and not feel strange, the moment life gave time to stop and notice.

'Sit down,' Miranda said. 'Have some tea.' Cecelia had not even finished hers. Brun sat as gingerly as she had come in. They nibbled pastries in silence for awhile, then Brun set down her plate.

'What's going to happen with the family holdings?'

Not the question Miranda had expected, but one she was glad to deal with at the moment. 'It's going to be very difficult,' Miranda said. 'When your father mobilized the Fleet to go after you, he antagonized a lot of people, his own family included.'

'Too much for one person,' Brun murmured.

'It wasn't their daughter,' Miranda said. 'And it wasn't your decision; it was his. But Harlis gained ground with the rest of the family then – he'd already been working on it, claiming that Bunny was spending too much time and energy on Council business, and neglecting the family interests. He said Buttons was too young and inexperienced; he started demanding silly, time-wasting reports, and nitpicking everything. Buttons has had a lot to learn in only a few years, but he's doing very well. It's just that Harlis promises he could do better. And now – well, he's determined to get Sirialis.'

'That's stupid,' Brun said, with some of her old arrogance. 'That's not profit; the place has never made a profit –'

'That's partly Harlis's point. He claims it could, if it were managed properly. Which does not, of course, include foxhunting . . . or only as a commercial enterprise. He's strong on commercial enterprises. I don't know if you've kept track of the branches he manages –'

'No,' Brun said.

'You can look it up later, then. He thinks Sirialis would pay as a mature colony prospect –'

'Bring in colonists!?'

'Yes. In his view, the planet is full of wasted space that ought to be put to profitable use. Buttons pointed out the agricultural areas, but he insists that this is not enough, and he's claiming that Bunny's title was only a life one. Kevil had been working on this, before the attack, but – but now he can't help either.'

Brun scowled. 'I wonder if dear Uncle Harlis had anything to do with the assassination.'

'No, dear. It was not Harlis.' That came out with more emphasis than she intended, and Brun looked at her with dawning comprehension.

'Mother – you *know* something? You know who did it?'

'I know it wasn't Harlis.' Damn, she'd have to figure out something, or Brun would go charging off, straight into danger again.

'You don't believe it was the NewTex –?'

'No. Although that's still the official line, I do not.'

'Then who?'

'Brun, I am not having this conversation with you. Not now, at least. We need to talk about your father's family, and their probable actions, and some of the other economic matters. These things must be dealt with now. Your father's murderers . . . can wait.'

'The trail –'

'Will never be too cold. Brun, please. For once in your life listen to me – we must be careful.'

Brun had blanched at that; the muscles along her jaw bunched. 'I want to go to the Guernesi Republic.'

'No. I need you here.'

'For what, an exhibition?'

'No, for an ally. If we are to defend our position, we must all help. Your sisters are already busy – up to their eyeballs in their family responsibilities, but trying to line up support. Buttons and Sarah are both working flat out. I need help, someone whose loyalty is undoubted – I need you.'

'Oh . . .' Brun looked past her, into some distance Miranda could not imagine.

'You were willing enough to help Cecelia,' she said, and hated the sharpness in her voice.

'You really need me?' Brun asked.

Miranda gave her a sharp look. 'Of course – no, let me say that more precisely. Yes, I need you. No one else can do what you can; no one else in the family has the training and experience.'

'You're serious . . . but you've never needed me. I'm just the troublemaker . . .' Still, an uncertain note had come into her voice.

'No. You're the one who can survive trouble. Brun, please – help me.'

Brun's face twisted. 'I don't know if I can . . .'

'You can if you will,' Miranda said firmly. 'I want to find who murdered your father, and who is trying to dismantle the Familias Regnant, and for what purpose. I am not sure they are the same person or organization, but they might well be.'

Brun watched her perfect, serene, immaculate mother with amazement. For her whole life, she had seen her mother as the icon everyone thought her. Her father was the active one, the doer and maker and shaper of events. Her mother smoothed his way by smiling and standing by.

Now she saw the real person behind the label of 'mother' and 'Bunny Thornbuckle's wife' . . . a woman as intelligent, tough and knowledgeable as her father had ever been. As dangerous, perhaps, as Lorenza had been. From the gleam in Miranda's eye, her mother had just noticed that recognition, and was enjoying the surprise.

'I made no mistake, picking Brun *Meager* for my nom de guerre,' Brun said, testing her hypothesis.

Her mother smiled. 'Quite so. I'm glad you recognize it. Now – are you with me?'

'Yes. If I can . . .'

'You can. Not all at once, but – let me go on here. I warned your father, after that disgraceful affair on Patchcock, to beware of his relatives doing what that Morreline woman did. Granted, her brothers deserved it, but others could do the same with less reason. He was sure he had it taken care of, in part because old Viktor Barraclough had always been his friend and mentor. But about the time of the Xavier invasion, he and Kevil found irregularities . . . purchases of company shares they couldn't put a name to, changes in some of the boards of directors which didn't make sense. The military crisis had to come first, of course; and after that, with proof of traitors in Fleet, they were far more concerned with that, and with Grand Council business. But what it's come down to is that Harlis has enough shares, and enough votes in various boards, that he can make a plausible case that much of your father's estate was actually not his personally. I think he'd fiddled the files, but I haven't had time to work on it. And I can't do it here.'

'Could you do it at Appledale?'

'Not really . . . I need to go to Sirialis; that's where we stored the backup data. Your father thought I was paranoid, sometimes, but I insisted that we take a complete readoff every half-year, and just archive it. I think that's why Harlis is so determined to get Sirialis; he suspects that the data are there somewhere.'

'Then you should go to Sirialis,' Brun said. 'He can't keep you away, can he?'

'Not yet. But I couldn't leave you alone here –'

Brun interrupted. 'You wanted my help; let me give it. Nothing's likely to happen at the next Grand Council meeting anyway; they're probably still in shock, and they'll waffle for days.'

'I'm not so sure; that Conselline fellow got himself elected interim Speaker –'

'Whatever happens can't matter as much as stopping Harlis. Go on. I'll attend the Council meeting, and let you know what happens. Promise.' Brun reached over and patted her mother's arm. 'We aren't going to let Harlis take everything, and we aren't going to let some idiot Conselline ruin the Familias. If that's what's happening.'

Her mother gave her an appraising look. 'Sometimes, Brun, you are remarkably like your father.'

'Sorry . . .'

'No. Don't be. All right – first we'll clear out of this –' With a wave of her arm, she indicated the entire Palace. 'Then I'll go to Sirialis.'

Cecelia stopped on the way to the hospital to contact her hotel, and reassure the front staff that the two young women and two children were the individuals she had authorized to register in her name. Another two bedrooms? No problem. Cecelia grinned to herself; she had been so wise to invest in a hotel here on Castle Rock, rather than depending on the hospitality of friends.

When she got to the hospital, she was told that she had just missed George. She went upstairs, and stood in the corridor outside Special Care, looking at the motionless form in the bed.

He looked wretched, she thought; she wondered if she had looked as bad. He wasn't conscious, they told her; they were still struggling to control the pressure on his brain, and he was deeply sedated except for weekly checks of neurological function. Cecelia blinked back tears, remembering herself in that drug-induced coma . . . wondering if Kevil were more conscious than they realized . . . and silently promised him she would return and get him out of there, no matter what. She found it hard to leave, but she had something even more urgent to do.

At the Laurels, she stopped at the concierge's desk to ask for assistance in leasing a yacht. The Laurels expected such requests; it took only a moment for the concierge to connect Cecelia to the booking agent for Allsystems Leasing.

Her inspiration had been her nephew Ronnie. Ronnie and Raffaele, as newlyweds, had taken off for the frontier – to Excet-24, a world newly opened to colonization. Cecelia hoped it would have a more euphonious name before it qualified for full membership in the Familias. At last report, Ronnie and Raffa had no children yet, but were 'hoping.' Cecelia wasn't sure who was hoping – the young people or their parents – but she remembered Raffa's problem-solving abilities, and was sure that Raffa could find the boys a good home if she didn't want them herself.

But this meant a long trip – six weeks at least. She discussed the route with the leasing agent, and ordered the Premium Platinum package of consumables. She didn't mind doing Bunny's family this service, but why should she suffer for it? She wanted fresh food again.

On Miranda's advice, Cecelia hired three more nurse-maids. One wanted to emigrate, and was glad to accept a colony share in lieu of salary. She brought along her own children, a two- and a four-year-old. Five people to care for four children might be overdoing it, Cecelia thought, but she herself didn't intend to wash a single diaper or wipe a single drippy nose.

By midnight, Cecelia had arranged everything. The yacht would not be ready immediately, of course; even with the assurance of large sums of money, it took time to prepare a large spaceship for a luxury voyage. But Cecelia had arranged for one of the nursemaids from Miranda's to take the boys to a park with the newly hired maid and her children, leaving the suite clear for at least some hours of the days. No one had seen pictures of them for months; no one, Cecelia was sure, would notice two more young women with children in a park full of young women with children. She had discussed with the nursemaids what clothes would be needed for the voyage and for six months afterward; she didn't know how easy it would be to find children's clothes on a colony world. She set up credit lines so that purchases by the nursemaids would not be traceable to her or to Miranda.

Then she fell into bed with a glow of conscious virtue. When the twins woke, bawling, at two in the morning, she pulled a pillow over her head and went back to sleep. That part of it was someone else's problem.

By the time they boosted from Rockhouse Major, Cecelia felt sure that no one had suspected anything. As far as anyone outside the Palace knew, the twins were still there. The news media had shown no more than normal interest in her doings, and seemed to accept her offhand comment that she had leased the big yacht because she was tired of doing all the work in her little one, and wanted someone else along to cook and clean.

The two boys thoroughly enjoyed the company of other children; Cecelia pored over their medical records in her stateroom, and came to the same conclusion as the doctors and psychologists. Normal children, who could expect to have normal lives. The real question was . . . should she tell Raffaele and Ronnie who they really were? In her own mind, the boys should not know – that they were adopted, yes, but not that their fathers had raped their mother and kept her captive. Of course they must have access to their medical records someday; advances in therapy might make it possible to finish cleaning up their genome.

She saw moral and emotional shoals in either direction.

CHAPTER FOUR

Excet Colony 24 looked, from space, like a paradise, sapphire seas and emerald forests, tawny drylands and olive savannas, all spatched and streaked with white water-vapor clouds. It had been seeded two hundred years before with the usual package of invader species, and closely monitored thereafter. Originally, colonization had been planned for a century later, when the introduced ecosystem would be more stable, but oxygen levels had never fallen dangerously low; the original system here had already been oxy-carbon.

The colony spaceport, in contrast, was a dirty little dump, in Cecelia's view. Her chartered yacht had its own shuttle, whose wide viewscreen gave a clear view of the mess. Discarded cargo containers lay scattered near either end of the runway. The single runway. The spaceport buildings were ugly piles, too much like the Patchcock port. The white plumes of cement factories, the lime kilns where limestone and shale were converted to cement for construction, lay gently on a background of rich green forest in the near distance.

Customs consisted of a harried young woman with a nearly impenetrable accent, whose only concern was whether the new arrivals had colony shares.

'I don't *need* a colony share,' Cecelia said. 'I'm not staying; I'm just here to visit —'

The young woman glared, took Cecelia's IDs, and inserted them in a machine. After a moment, she turned to give Cecelia a long look.

'Yer not stain.'

'I'm not staying, no. I'm here to visit my nephew and his wife. Ronald Vandormer.'

'Aow! Rownnie! Whyntcha sai so?'

'I tried,' Cecelia said.

'He's at th' office, about naow,' the woman said. 'Ya kin gover.' She pointed out the 'office,' a two-story cube of concrete.

Like most colonies, this one had been given a head start by its investors: the spaceport town had a small grid of paved streets and a larger grid of gravelled ones. The first hundred or so buildings had been put up of substantial materials — in this case concrete blocks. Beyond that were rickety constructions that Cecelia could only call shacks — crudely built of raw timber. Cecelia noticed, as she walked along, the number of people who were carrying things by hand . . . the absence of hand trucks, let alone vehicles.

The two-story building had a low wall enclosing a courtyard to one side, where a group of men were working on some piece of machinery she didn't understand. She started to speak up and ask them about Ronnie, when one of the faces in the group suddenly looked familiar. Ronnie? She blinked in the brilliant sunlight, and it still was . . . in face. The glossy young aristocrat, who had always been just one hair from a dandy — and that only because his friend George had been born with creases and a shine, as they said – stood there in tan workshirt and pants, with smears of mud or grease on both. She couldn't even tell what color his boots had been. But it was Ronnie – as handsome as ever, or more so.

Before she could call out, he turned and went inside; the men went back to doing something with machinery and wood. She followed him inside, to a rough-walled room with a concrete floor, and found him jotting something down on a deskcomp.

'Ronnie –'

He looked up, then his eyes widened. 'Aunt Cecelia!'

'I sent word,' Cecelia said.

'We never got it.' He shrugged. 'It's probably in the batch somewhere but everyone's been too busy . . .' He looked out the window at the bustle in the courtyard.

'It looks like a lot of work,' Cecelia said, eyeing him. This was not a change she had ever expected to see in Ronnie. And why hadn't he said anything about Bunny's death? Or asked about Brun?

'It is. It's not something I thought I'd ever be doing, to tell you the truth.'

'Who's your colony governor?'

'Er . . . I am, now that Misktov ran off.'

'Ran off?'

'Yes . . . it's easy enough. He stowed away on an outbound flight with most of our negotiable resources.'

'But – but that's criminal.'

'So it is,' Ronnie said. 'But I didn't see any police force around to stop him, and we don't have ansible access down here. No money, no communications.'

'Oh.' Perhaps he didn't know about Bunny's assassination. Cecelia took another look around the room. Not an office, exactly – she saw furniture she recognized from Raffa's mother's summer cottage. A dining room table covered with data cubes and books. A sofa piled with more books and sheets of plastic and paper that looked like construction drawings. Over everything, a layer of gritty gray dust and ash.

'But we're doing well, considering,' Ronnie said, before she could organize her thoughts. 'It's just . . . there's a lot I didn't know. Don't know yet. You know, Aunt Cecelia, no matter how many cubes you study, there's always something . . .'

'For instance?'

'Well . . . the cement plants are working all right, and we've got plenty of sand and gravel, so we're fine for unreinforced construction. But my cubes said unreinforced concrete is dangerous . . .'

'What does your colony engineering team say?'

'Engineering team? We haven't one. I know, the prospectus says we do, but we don't. Aunt Cece, ninety percent of our population are low-level workers . . . which makes sense . . . but these people are low-level workers in a high-level system. They're used to a more advanced infrastructure. They know how to do their work in a world where everything's already set up, not how to work from scratch. The farmers know how to grow crops in big fields, but they don't know how to level them. The plumbers know how to connect pipes in standard modular buildings, but they don't know how to set up a plumbing system from scratch. That's what the engineering team is supposed to do, make the connection between standard designs and standard practices, and the conditions we have locally. But we don't have one.'

'If it's that bad, why don't you leave?'

Ronnie looked stubborn. 'We don't want to leave, Aunt Cecelia; we want to make it work. We sank all our money in it – even the wedding presents –'

'Even your reserves?'

He flushed. 'Not at first, but when Misktov ran off we

had to do something. We could've bought ourselves out and run home like silly children, but . . . the colony needed help. So we blew the last on enough to keep the rest alive while we worked it out.'

This was a very different Ronnie from the spoiled boy she'd known. Not a hint of petulance or whine anywhere in his voice or manner – he'd been dumped into trouble, and he was going to handle it.

'How's Raffa?' she asked.

'She's fine . . . tired, though.' Ronnie grinned, but his eyes were worried. 'She's trying to get a school started, but it's hard – the parents say they're too busy, they need the children at home.'

'Don't these colony groups include trained teachers?'

'On paper, yes.' Ronnie grimaced. 'There's a lot I didn't know, in the old days. I thought every standard colony dropped with prefab housing, the five-year-contract engineering team, the education and medical backups that are on the contract.'

'And they don't?'

'No – at least, right before Misktov ran off, while we still had the credit for it, I made some inquiries and found that many colonies are shorted. But they're stuck on some planet, mostly uneducated people who haven't a clue who to contact in the Colonial Office . . . no one ever knows. Even me – I sent messages out, but never got any back. We haven't heard from our families in over a year, though we've scraped up enough to piggyback messages to them three times.'

'Um. Well, Ronnie, I may have added to your burdens, but –'

'Cecelia!' Raffa came through the door like a burst of spring breeze. 'I'm so glad to see you! The only thing about this is that I miss my friends sometimes!'

The girl – no, young woman – looked healthy enough,

and genuinely glad to see her. Cecelia braced herself for what she must do.

'Raffaele, Ronnie . . . have you heard about Bunny?'

'Bunny? No – what's wrong?'

'He was assassinated several months ago, supposedly by allies of the men executed after Brun's capture –'

'Wait – Brun was captured? By whom? Is she all right?'

How long had they been out of contact? Cecelia could hardly believe they didn't know. She gave them a quick review of what had happened, ending with, 'So you see, when I started thinking of a good home for the babies, I thought of you – I was sure you could find a home for them.'

'Brun's babies?'

Now she'd done it. 'Yes.'

'Of *course* I want them,' Raffa said, almost fiercely. Then with a glance at Ronnie, 'We do, don't we, Ron?'

'Of course,' Ronnie said, but he sounded tired again. 'I don't exactly know how, but we'll manage.'

'I've brought along nursemaids, including one with two children of her own who wants to stay. And some money Miranda sent, for their education later.'

'If it's enough to hire a teacher,' Raffa said, 'we can start that school . . .'

Cecelia had no idea if it was enough, but she would pry the necessary out of Raffa and Ronnie's parents if she had to. She would also, she thought, find out why incoming messages, including hers, weren't getting through.

'Where are the babies?' Raffa said, looking around.

'Still in the shuttle,' Cecelia said. 'I doubt I'd ever have gotten them past that . . . that person in the terminal.'

'Oh, Ganner . . . she was Misktov's girlfriend, and he left her here, marooned her. She thought she was going to be the governor's lady, and lord it over everyone, but here she is. She hates everybody.'

'Except handsome men,' Raffa said, with a touch of asperity. 'Lady Cecelia, you should see how she fawns on Ronnie. I know he's not susceptible, but it's a little disgusting sometimes.'

'It's handy when I want something,' Ronnie said. 'Come on, let's get those babies out of the shuttle. If I have babies crawling all over me, I'll bet Ganner finds me less attractive.'

By the time she left again, Cecelia knew that more was wrong with Excet-24 than one scoundrelly governor and a missing engineering team. She'd never paid much attention to colony worlds – why choose to live uncomfortably if you didn't have to? – or colonial policy, but surely it hadn't been intended to work like this. The nursemaids had been understandably wide-eyed at the conditions on the planet, and Cecelia had had some difficulty persuading them to stay until she returned.

'I'll find out why messages aren't getting through,' she promised Ronnie. 'And find you some of the experts you need. You've done wonderfully –' She didn't really believe that, but the young couple had tried, and weren't whining, and that counted for a lot in her private gradebook. 'It'll be a few months, you understand –'

'That's what they all say,' Ronnie said, but with no sting in it.

All the way to Sirialis, Miranda had planned what to do. If she tried to call on her family's expertise, Harlis might find out, and would certainly do his best to stop her. She had to assume he'd figure it out; she had to assume she had only a limited lead before he found some way of separating her from the data she needed to explore.

Bunny had teased her, at first, when she insisted on having her own archives, separate from the family, in

machines not physically connected to anything but a
solar power supply. Paranoia, he'd said, ran in the
Meager family line. She pressed her lips together tightly,
remembering that laugh, and her scornful reply . . . she
had been so young, so sure of herself.

And so right. Not for nothing had her family been in
information technology for centuries. She had insisted;
Bunny had given in; her personal and very complete
archives lay not at the big house – though she kept a
blind copy there, as a decoy – but in a remote hunting
lodge. Every hunting season – and in between, if they
were in residence – she added another set of records,
stripping the current logs.

It would have been easier if she could have had Kevil's
help, but she could do it herself, given enough time. That
was the trick, finding enough time.

The staff at Sirialis met her with the sympathy and
respect she'd expected. Harlis might have local spies and
supporters, but they wouldn't show themselves yet. She
spent the first few days as anyone would expect, taking
sympathy calls and answering what questions she could
about the future of their world.

The big house felt empty, even with all the servants in
it . . . knowing Bunny would never come down those
stairs, never wander out of that library, never sit at the
head of the long table. She missed him almost as much in
the stables and kennels; although she had ridden to
hounds every season, foxhunting had never been her
favorite sport; she had done it because Bunny enjoyed it
so, and enjoyed her company.

That first evening, alone in the big room she had once
shared, her mind wandered back to Cecelia's visit. Where
had she taken the twins? She had seemed to know exactly
where she was going . . . well, that was Cecelia, and
always had been, though it usually involved a horse.

But before the twins, what was it she'd said? About Bunny's killers, about some plot — Miranda struggled to remember, past the confusion of the last weeks, the urgency of her concern about the estate, and the travel-induced headache. Finally she shrugged, and gave up for the night.

The name didn't come to her until she was at the hunting lodge far north of the main house, where the snow still lay deep on the shadowed sides of the mountains. She'd made copies of all the critical data — astonishing herself with the number of cubes it took to hold it all — and then packed it neatly into her carryall for the flight back. It was too late that day — she didn't want to risk a night flight, as tired as she was — so she'd heated up one of the frozen lumps of soup, and settled in by the fire-place with a mug of soup and another of cocoa. She felt — not smug, exactly, but pleased with herself. She had the backups, which she could work on at the main house, and her surveillance link showed no ships in the system. That meant Harlis could not possibly get there in time to discover her hiding place.

Her mind wandered off to the twins again, and from there to Cecelia, and then — as if a cube were playing — her memory handed her the first part of their conversation. Not the NewTex Militia — well, she'd been doubtful of that herself, though they were certainly capable of killing and maiming. But . . . Pedar Orregiemos?

Cecelia hadn't mentioned it, and perhaps didn't know it, but Pedar had once wanted to marry her. She hadn't loved him; he was older than Bunny, and fussy pomposity had never attracted her — but he'd been convinced she married Bunny just for his money. He'd even said so, one afternoon in the rose garden. She hadn't quite smacked his face, but she'd been tempted.

Pedar? Could it be? She couldn't imagine him doing it himself, except perhaps with a smallsword — he had been quite a fencer in his day, and probably kept it up. And Cecelia might have misunderstood. What could be the reason? What could Pedar gain from killing Bunny, or having him killed?

She did not realize, until the handle snapped off the cocoa mug, just how agitated she was. Luckily the cocoa had cooled; she wiped up the mess, put the broken bits in the trash she'd take back to the main house, and tried to quiet the racing of her heart.

Pedar was, after all, a Rejuvenant — not merely someone who had had rejuvenations, as she and Bunny had had, but someone who felt threatened by those who hadn't. She remembered six — no, seven, at least — eight years ago, an argument about Rejuvenants and Ageists at one of Kemtre's parties, when Pedar had insisted very loudly that it would end in bloodshed. *They will kill us out of envy, or we will kill them in self-defense,* he'd said, and then some other men had hustled him away and sobered him up.

Would he have had Bunny killed for that? Was he one of a group who would have done it? And who else?

She tried to turn off these thoughts — she needed rest; she had a long flight the next morning, and a lot of work to do after it — but she lay long awake, tossing, her stomach roiled with anger.

The next day, back in the main house, she walked past the glass cases of antique weapons as she had done so often before, and paused. Bunny had fenced only because it was an expected social skill, keeping her company in the salle as she kept him company in the hunting field. But he had had a strange passion for old weapons, both blades and firearms.

It was a mixed collection, though displayed with all

the organization possible: long blades in this case, short blades in that one, short-barrelled firearms here, long-barrelled ones there, glass-topped floor cabinets with helmets and breastplates and mailed gloves.

Miranda stopped in front of the wall-hung case of swords. The broadest blades below – the single broadsword, the two sabers, one straight and one curved slightly. Two schlagers, a rapier, five epees, four foils – the latter displayed in pairs, angled and opposing, their tips crossed.

On a whim, Miranda opened the case and took down the broadsword, turning its blade to the light to see the dappled pattern of refolded and beaten steel layers. When she rapped it with her knuckles, it rang a little, and its edge was still sharp enough to cut.

She wished she knew its history. Bunny had suspected it of being an ancient reproduction from the early space era, not a genuine prespace relic. But when they'd done a forensic scan on it, there'd been human blood in the runes incising the blade. Only a trace, and the scans weren't able to date it closer than a couple of hundred years, but . . . she'd always wondered.

The sabers were easier to date. One of them had been a presentation sword made for one of Bunny's ancestors as a fiftieth wedding anniversary present, with a dated inscription. It had never been used for anything but ceremony – carried upright in processions, or laid along the top of the coffin at funerals. The other had been an officer's saber – also ceremonial, she assumed, inherited over the blanket from a family she'd never heard of, some two hundred years before.

The schlagers at least were old – one was certainly 20th Century old reckoning – but while she had drilled with such blades, they hadn't ever warmed her interest. The rapier, so seemingly similar, did. This one, with a graceful swept hilt, balanced easily when she lifted it out, and swung it around.

She put it back almost guiltily. What was she thinking? Nothing, she told herself. Nothing at all. She closed the case and locked it. These were priceless antiques, not toys; if she wanted to practice, the salle held modern weapons and equipment far better suited for her sport.

And she had no time. She headed back to the big square office that had been Bunny's estate office, and was now her workplace as she tried to figure out just what Harlis had done.

ALTIPLANO

Luci Suiza had expected the furor over her cousin Esmay's engagement to an outlander to dispel interest in her own plans, but somehow the discussion at the dinner table spilled over onto her. She had a mouthful of corn soup when Papa Stefan opened with a volley of complaints about the quarterly accounts.

'– And that ridiculous expense for equipment we don't need, to develop a foreign market we've done very well without for centuries. We're not that sort of people, is what I say. Luci! You can't tell me this was all Esmaya's idea!'

Luci swallowed quickly, burning her throat on the soup, but managed not to choke. 'No, Papa Stefan. But we were talking about the future of her herd, and I had researched –'

'Researched!' Papa Stefan in full huff would interrupt even generals; unmarried girls didn't have a chance. 'You don't know what research is. You were seduced by all those outlander magazines you read. If my mother were still alive –'

Luci found that she had inherited the gene for

interruption, surprising herself. 'She's not. Esmay's the Landbride, and she approves. The outlanders need our stocks' genetic input, and we need theirs.'

'You interrupted me!' Papa Stefan did not quite roar, but he looked as if he might.

'You interrupted me first,' Luci said. She heard the shocked mutters of her parents, but ignored them in the excitement of attack. 'And the genetic equipment was my idea, and is my responsibility, and I did check with the Landbride, who approved the expenses, which she thoroughly understood.'

'Not like a Landbride at all,' Papa Stefan growled. 'A Landbride should conserve resources, not waste them on crackpot schemes –'

'Like the Barley River irrigation project?' That was Sanni, who could never resist a dig about Papa Stefan's one big mistake. As a young man, he'd been convinced that irrigation of dry coastal land with water from the Barley would be practical and profitable. His mother, then only newly Landbride, had allowed him enough money to unbalance the estancia budget for a decade.

'It's not the same thing at all,' Papa Stefan said.

'It's not,' Luci said. 'My idea is on schedule and on budget, and in fact it's costing us less than the Landbride approved, because I got support from other breeders.'

'Which is another thing,' Papa Stefan said, ignoring the part about on budget and on schedule. 'You went outside the family to bring in outsiders –'

'Our allies for generations,' Luci said. 'After all, I'm marrying Phil –' It had slipped out, not at the moment she'd planned.

'Philip? Philip who?'

'Philip Vicarios,' Sanni said quietly; her quick glance admonished Luci. Papa Stefan stared a moment, then turned to look at Casimir and Berthold.

'She's marrying a Vicarios?'

Luci had not really doubted what Esmay told her, but now a chill sank through her as she saw, in their faces, additional confirmation.

Berthold shrugged. 'She has Esmay's approval, I understand.'

'And you, Casi?'

Casimir nodded. 'The family is our ally. Paul is my friend –'

'Does she *know* –?'

'Children, you may be excused,' Sanni interrupted. The younger cousins, eyes already wide, scrambled away from the table with only the briefest duck of the head to the elders. Luci's younger brother gave her a look that meant she would be ambushed later and expected to Tell All. When the door closed behind them all, Luci spoke into the silence.

'I know. Esmaya told me. She said it didn't matter, that she held no grudge against the family, and if Philip was kind –'

'Kind! Marriage is not about kindness!' Papa Stefan had turned an ugly red.

'It is,' Sanni said. 'Not that you would know –'

'Quiet!' Casimir rarely interrupted at these family fights, but this time he did, with all the power of command built over years of active service. 'Too much is at stake here to rehash old battles or waste energy and patience yelling at each other. As the Landbride's Trustee, I know that she did in fact approve Luci's desire to marry Philip Vicarios. She did in fact approve Luci's expenditure of equipment to allow us to export gene-stock, and her reasons were sound enough to convince me, and the other Trustees, that this was a good idea. This is not, after all, the real issue. The real issue is, the Landbride wants to marry an outlander, and continue to

live offplanet, and the other landholders would like to
use this as an excuse to reduce our influence in the Guild.
I see no chance of changing Esmay's mind – for all the
reasons we know about – so I suggest we turn our attention to minimizing the damage to the Suiza Family, and
quit inflicting more on ourselves.'

Luci had not expected her uncle Casimir to be so sensible. To her surprise, Papa Stefan went back to his meal,
stabbing the sliced cattlelope as if it were an enemy, but
silent. Sanni sipped the rest of her soup in thoughtful
silence; Berthold helped himself to a pile of potatoes in
red sauce, and began eating steadily. Casimir looked at
Luci.

'Have you any more bombshells to drop, Luci?'

'No, Uncle.'

'Did Esmaya mention anything to you about passing on
the Landbride duties?'

Luci felt herself going hot. 'She did . . . in a way . . .
but –'

'She spoke of you.' It was not a question. Casimir
tented his hands and looked over them at her. 'Did you
agree?'

'I told her it was too soon,' Luci said. 'I'm only –'

'The age that two Landbrides were invested, in the old
days. A year older, in fact, than Silvia.' Luci had never
heard of Silvia, though she had, like all the children,
memorized a hundred years of Landbrides Suiza. 'It may
be that having her designate you Landbride-to-be would
help – that plus your marriage to a Vicarios would prove
that the Suizas were not involved in interstellar politics.'

CHAPTER FIVE

Hobart glared at Oskar Morreline, former head of the Morreline branch of his sept. 'You were outmaneuvered by Venezia,' he said. 'That fuzzbrained sister of yours cost us market share and dropped profits twenty-eight percent –'

'It's not my fault,' Oskar said. 'If –'

'Oh, yes, it is,' Hobart interrupted smoothly. 'Your daughter Ottala – what is it with the women in your family, anyway? – goes haring off to Patchcock and gets herself killed. That's what started it – a daughter you didn't control any better than Bunny controlled Brun –'

Oskar had flushed an ugly color; Hobart enjoyed that as he always enjoyed exercising power. 'No, Oskar. I can't trust you to do it right, whatever it is. I cannot give you a Ministry. In a few years, I expect the public climate will change, and then, perhaps, we can find something for you.'

'You expect my vote but you aren't giving me anything?'

'I expect your vote because you know where your

advantage lies. Even if they had it to give, you would get nothing out of that clique Bunny ran. And they do not have it to give, not anymore.'

Oskar glared, but subsided, as Hobart had known he would. Oskar was a blusterer, but if that didn't work he had no second weapon. Hobart always had a second weapon – and a third and a fourth, he thought to himself. He changed his tone, and went on; if Oskar could get it through his head what the problem really was, he might be useful.

'Whoever controls the rejuvenation process controls everything – as long as the public doesn't rebel against rejuvs. We must take steps against the Ageist conspiracies; the shortlifes, if they realize the danger they're in, outnumber us at this point and could be dangerous.'

'But Venezia says –'

'Venezia is a fool. Yes, something had gone wrong there, something serious. A Benignity spy, if I understand the little that's been declassified. But it's not as bad as all that. Women are so excitable, not to mention sentimental, and Venezia in particular –'

Oskar nodded eagerly; Hobart smiled to himself. How the Morreline brothers hated having Venezia in charge! 'All she ever did was play with pottery –' Oskar said.

'Quite so. How could she know anything about the real world? She could not be expected to realize how many lives would be disrupted – prematurely ended, with the shortage of rejuvenation drugs – because of her finicky insistence on exact procedures.'

'But Hobart – how do we get it back? How do we get her out of there?'

Exactly the opening he'd hoped for. 'By doing precisely what I tell you,' Hobart said. 'I need your support at all the Grand Council sessions; I will let you know what I need you to say, and how to vote. With more sympathetic, more cooperative Ministers, we should be able to ease dear Venezia back into her supportive role.'

'She won't like it,' Oskar said, puffing out his plump cheeks.

'I don't care whether she does or not,' Hobart said. 'I am not going to let one woman stand in the way of progress for the Conselline Sept.' He looked forward to that moment, probably more than Oskar did. Venezia had been a constant nuisance at sept board meetings, poking her nose into all sorts of inconvenient corners. He'd had to roust her out of his own offices more than once, where she chatted up the clerical staff and wheedled who knows what out of them. She seemed to think she had a moral mission to clean up the whole sept.

'Our responsibility to the whole Familias . . .' she would say, while Hobart ground his teeth. They had no responsibility to the whole Familias; they had a responsibility to Family shareholders. Period. He wasn't going to urge her to go on making faulty drugs. Bad for business, and people would be watching carefully. Beyond that, though, it wasn't their business to be saints, if that's what she had in mind.

'If Kemtre had not been a weak man, none of these disasters would have happened. He drugged his son into stupidity, and then created those damned clones.'

'I don't see that cloning is such a bad thing.'

'No, nor do I, except that we have a rapidly growing population anyway. We don't need clones; we need sensible strong men who know how to handle the hysterics. No offense.' He eyed Oskar, but Oskar didn't mind if Hobart called his sister hysterical. 'Now, Oskar, I want you to have a word with the Broderick Institute, and tell them to do their homework a little better –'

'The Broderick Institute? What have they done?'

Sometimes he wondered if Oskar had a brain. Venezia,

for all her impracticality, had wit enough. 'Oskar, the Broderick Institute is where Dr. Margulis works.' Oskar still looked blank. 'The same Dr. Margulis whose report on the so-called bad drugs coming out of Patchcock started a near panic in the market –'

'Oh – *that* Dr. Margulis. But I thought –'

'He's come up with more – the man is a closet Ageist, I'm sure, just looking for any excuse to scare people away from rejuvenation. Broderick has given him free rein for the past fifteen years, and look what that so-called independent research has led to. It's cost you, and me, and the whole Familias. He needs to be controlled; at the very least, someone needs to do *impartial* research showing how beneficial rejuv is. And since the Conselline Sept provides over two-thirds of the money to support the Broderick Institute, they need to be reminded of the importance of truly even-handed science.'

'Won't they complain about academic freedom?'

'They're not a university; they're a privately funded research facility. If you're tactful, they'll get the point without blowing up. That's your job.'

Oskar left, finally, and Hobart puffed air out explosively. *Idiots.* He was surrounded by idiots and incompetents, and they all wanted something from him. He glanced at his desk and told his secretary to send in Pedar Orregiemos. Another idiot. Minor family, major nuisance, but also a born bootlicker, and those could be useful.

Pedar came in looking smug about something. Hobart had no time for Pedar's self-congratulation. Besides, he would be even smugger, with more reason, very shortly.

'We have a problem coming up,' he said. Pedar's expression shifted quickly from smugness to concern. 'As you know, I was elected temporary Speaker at the emergency Council meeting immediately after Lord Thornbuckle's assassination.' Pedar nodded. 'The next meeting will be crucial. If we are not to lapse back into the ineffective vacillation of the previous administration, if we're to meet the challenges that threaten us, we need to take action quickly. Will you help me?'

'Of course,' Pedar said. 'What can I do?'

'In the long run, you can be my Minister of Foreign Affairs.' Hobart paused, and enjoyed the sight of Pedar completely silenced, for once. He had not expected that high an honor . . . good, then he would be the more willing to earn it. 'But not immediately: first there are changes in the bylaws which need to be approved. I'll give you the texts; I want your analysis of the probable response.'

'Of course; right away.'

'I'm calling the next meeting almost immediately; it would be unethical not to have a general meeting as quickly as possible.' Pedar nodded like a child's toy. Did he even grasp the importance of that? Did he realize how critical the timing was, how this haste would work to Conselline advantage? For an instant, Hobart thought of explaining it to him, sharing some of his data on Family movements, his basis for knowing who could attend, and thus how the votes would go. No. Better not let even Pedar know how much he knew.

Hobart went on. 'After that meeting, I'll be making some ministerial changes; Foreign Affairs will be high on that list, but I can't give you an exact date. What you must understand is where the real threat is.' Hobart leaned closer. 'It's not war, no matter what anyone says. We're large, strong, healthy, with a vigorous military — well, mostly vigorous. Anton Lepescu was more than a little crazy, but that doesn't mean all his ideas were bad. He had the right idea about the military and war, for instance. If he'd been assigned to the rescue mission, do you suppose we'd have had any problem with leftover terrorists?'

Pedar shook his head; Hobart allowed himself a smile.

'Of course not,' he went on. 'He'd have made sure there weren't any. None of this idiocy of bringing back hundreds of women and children – born troublemakers, every one of them. And to whom do we owe that diplomatic and political problem? Bunny Thornbuckle's friends, the Serranos. Who, as we all know, have no direct loyalty to any of the Chairholding Families.'

'Well, but, Hobart, none of the Fleet families do now –'

'Not directly, not now, but they *did* in the past. That's my point. I've read history; I know what's supposed to have happened. But how do we know that the Serranos weren't involved in the massacre of their patron Family? What proof do we have?'

Pedar looked surprised, then thoughtful. 'I hadn't ever considered that. But they're powerful . . .'

'Yes. Thoroughly entrenched. And I'm sure there are decent, loyal soldiers among them. But overall, their influence is questionable. We need a Fleet we can count on to crush any opponent, protect our shipping, protect the new worlds we need to open for our colonists.'

After Pedar left, Hobart stared out the window, musing. His brother Guilliam had always been the pet of the family. Everyone loved Guilliam; Hobart had suspected his parents of having that easy charm built into Guilliam's genes, while he – he had been given the steel-hard core Guilliam lacked. He had been designed as the unloved workhorse, who was to stand back, walk behind, and do all the difficult tasks that were too much for Guilliam.

People still talked about Guilliam. Too bad about poor Guilliam, they said. Hobart knew what they really meant – too bad that they had to deal with him instead of his softer brother. Guilliam took no part in Family business – hadn't since their parents died, when an escalation in his addiction to starplex-tree resin resulted in permanent brain damage which even rejuv could not repair.

Guilliam would not be at the next Council meeting, any more than he'd been at the others. And on Hobart's side . . . he ran through the list again, ticking names off his mental list. The minor Families – Derringer, Hochlit, Tassi-Lioti, all that crowd – were yammering now for leadership, and would probably follow anyone strong enough. Harlis Thornbuckle, Bunny's own brother, wanted control of Bunny's estate bad enough to deal . . . though he probably wasn't trustworthy in the long run. If Kevil Mahoney had been capable, he might have talked some of the waverers into the other camp, but he was still in the medical center, and the opposition was no more than a confusion of Barracloughs, more intent on fighting over leadership within their sept than on threats from without. Since Mahoney wasn't on his side, just as well not to have him active at all. In the future, he expected to talk Mahoney over; the man needed a power base. It was purely an accident that he had been Bunny's friend; he could just as easily be Hobart's friend.

With any luck, no one from Bunny's family would attend this Grand Council meeting anyway. They would expect this one to be unimportant, with a weak Speaker elected to finish out Bunny's term. This was his window of opportunity. He could take hold of the weak, flaccid, rudderless ship of state – catch the winds of time, and take them all to a better future than anyone else saw.

And he would be taken seriously this time. Not as a substitute for Guilliam, but as the leader he knew himself to be. Young and vigorous, even without rejuv – and when it came time to rejuv, he would know exactly what source to use.

His scheduler chimed; Hobart silenced it with a snap of the fingers. He toyed with the idea of skipping his exercises for once, but habit had already brought him to his feet. Iagin, the Swordmaster who supervised his own fencing coach, was there for his twice-annual analysis of Hobart's progress.

The pine-and-sandalwood-scented changing room shifted his mood, as it was meant to, and focussed his attention on his body. Hobart stripped off his business clothes and dropped them into the hamper. His exercise clothes hung on racks . . . today, for his fencing lesson, he chose a skinsuit and the leather armor. His coach didn't approve of leather, but he was in no mood to pamper his coach.

He glanced at himself in the mirror with satisfaction. Barrel chest, flat belly, well-muscled legs, erect posture, firm mouth. Not a slack, flabby fiber in him, mind or body. A man fit to lead.

In the exercise room itself, he warmed up with the standard sets, then stretched. As he was twisting himself into a pretzel, trying not to look at himself – he hated these stretches, which were at best undignified – the door opened and the Swordmaster came in. His own coach would not have dared; Hobart had made it clear that he needed no supervision in warm-up. But the Swordmasters were an old, proud breed, and he put up with their arrogance for the sake of their skill. Bunny had never taken up fencing, and had resolutely refused to have a Swordmaster at his estate even when most Families did. Well, and who had just died?

'Lord Conselline,' the Swordmaster said. 'Your form needs improvement.'

'Instruct me,' Hobart said, proud of conquering a flash of anger.

The Swordmaster bent and twisted his own body into the stretch, and held it. 'You are not keeping the knee straight,' he said, from under his arm. 'And you are bending the spine too much in the thoracic span, and not enough in the lumbar.' He unwound, not red in the face or breathless. 'Try again.'

Hobart twisted and tangled himself into the required knot. He knew what it was for, but he disliked it and knew he had been skimping on it for months. The Swordmaster's hands steadied him, and then pushed and pulled . . . Hobart felt a *pop* in his spine, and the sudden ease of a cramp he had not realized he had.

'Like that,' the Swordmaster said. 'You really should let Orris spot you in this for several months.'

'I'll consider it,' Hobart said, untwisting carefully.

'Good. If you are ready . . .' The Swordmaster nodded toward the salle.

'Is it true,' Hobart asked, as they passed through the archway, 'that all Swordmasters must have killed with the blade?'

'It is a tradition,' the Swordmaster said.

Hobart wanted to know what it felt like but could think of no polite way to ask. And which blade? The Swordmasters taught the use of all blades, had mastered all styles.

Orris held out practice masks, transparent reinforced ceram with touch-signalling circuitry embedded, and the warm-up blades. Hobart glanced at Orris, wondering what he'd told Master Iagin; he suspect Orris of reporting on more than his fencing skill. He did, after all, have to take the occasional call during a lesson, and Orris might have overheard scraps of conversation. But nothing important, he thought. Nothing that would interest a Swordmaster anyway.

Masked and gloved, with blade in hand, he faced

Master Iagin on the strip. The salute – old-fashioned, formal, an utter waste of time, and yet it set the emotional tone for what followed. The initial touches . . . boring, when all Hobart wanted was to get this session out of the way so he could return to his plotting.

Master Iagin's tip smacked into his faceshield, which flared red. For an instant he could not speak for anger, and then he grunted. 'Touch.'

'Your mind wandered, Lord Conselline,' Master Iagin said. Behind the arc of gleaming protection, his expression was unreadable – quiet, a little stern, but neither anger nor apprehension.

'My apologies,' Hobart said. This was, after all, one of the reasons he had stayed with fencing, the need to concentrate utterly on what he was doing. But Orris usually gave him a few minutes to settle in. The man had never struck him so early in a session. Still . . . the Swordmaster was who he was, and probably thought fencing was the most important thing in the universe. In his, it may have been. Hobart collected these scattered thoughts, locked them away, and focussed on Master Iagin's blade.

Just in time, for it flicked toward him again, and his parry was only just enough. He missed the riposte, but by the next parry was able to riposte . . . only to meet Master Iagin's parry and a riposte so powerful it blew through his own and punched him lightly in the chest.

'Touch,' he said, this time more cheerfully. He was not expected to defeat a Swordmaster, only to show that he had been working.

He had indeed, and his next attack actually achieved a touch. His spirits soared. He had never made a touch on the Swordmaster from seven before. All that work with weights must have done it. Twenty touches – sixteen to the Swordmaster and four to him – then a break to stretch out again before taking up the heavier blades.

'Your right forearm is definitely stronger, Lord Conselline,' the Swordmaster said.

'Orris has me doing weight work.'

'Good. But I notice that your left arm is still substantially weaker – there should be no more than five percent difference in strength, unless someone has suffered an injury. Have you?'

Hobart scowled. 'It's stronger than last year.'

'Indeed it is. But the imbalance affects more than your offhand fencing, milord. It also affects the set of your spine and your gait. You need to balance them, just as you balance work and play.'

Hobart's scowl deepened; he could feel the tension in his neck. 'I have no time for play, Swordmaster. Surely you have heard of the terrible crisis that faces us? Lord Thornbuckle was killed by terrorists –'

'Yes, of course,' Master Iagin said. 'But that makes my point. You must be balanced to withstand such blows. It is the failure of balance in your society which makes it vulnerable – the undisciplined who stagger and fall when the blow falls.'

'I do not intend to stagger and fall,' Hobart said. He caught a glimpse of himself in the mirrors that lined the salle – flushed and truculent. Dangerous.

'Nor will you, milord, I'm sure. Your work here – the discipline needed to achieve the level you've achieved – sustains you, along with your native talents. But as each movement balances contraction of one muscle group with extension of another, so the steadfast must balance strain and relaxation.'

'I find relaxation in this,' Hobart said with a wave to include the entire exercise suite.

'That is good,' Master Iagin said. 'You have a warrior's heart, which finds ease in growing stronger.'

Praise, of a sort. He would take it. A warrior's heart

he knew he had, and he could feel himself growing stronger.

When the lesson ended, Hobart invited Master Iagin to dinner at the family table, but the Swordmaster declined. 'With your permission, milord, I will walk in your gardens; I must take ship tomorrow, and I am not often able to stretch my legs in such beauty.'

'Of course.' He still did not understand Master Iagin's fascination with the garden, but he anticipated that request. Discreet surveillance had revealed that the man did not tumble a maid behind the hedges or use any sort of communications device to contact a confederate. He always did what he asked permission to do – strolled along the pebbled garden paths, stopping now and then to sniff a flower. He pretended to fence with the topiary knight, and if one of the gardener's cats appeared, he would pick it up and stroke it. At the far end of the garden, he always paused to watch the black-finned fish in the lily pond. Not what Hobart had expected of a Swordmaster, but they were known to have strange habits. Most of them, for some reason or other, liked gardens.

At dinner, Delphine asked if the Swordmaster were still there. Hobart gave her a look that shut her up instantly, but then he answered her. 'He's here, but he's leaving tomorrow. Why?'

'I just wanted to meet him . . .'

'You have no reason to meet him; you do not take fencing seriously.' Delphine could strike a pretty pose with foil in hand, and in fencing whites, and in the garden in front of the rose hedge, looked quite exciting that way. But her footwork was execrable, and she had never shown any determination in learning better. He would not have been too pleased if she had, but her failure to oppose him even on this was another proof of her weakness. Luckily, he had been able to choose other gene lines for his sons.

Delphine picked at her shellfish and changed the subject. 'I called Miranda today, but her private secretary wouldn't put me through. I was able to make an appointment for tomorrow, when she's taking condolence calls.'

'That's good,' Hobart said. A quick flash of anger that a secretary prevented his wife – *his* wife, Lady Conselline – from contacting Miranda Thornbuckle flared and died. It wasn't important, after all. Miranda would find out soon enough that what power she had had through Bunny was gone, water into sand.

'Hobart – are *you* in danger?'

'Me?!' He smiled at her, surprised and pleased by her solicitude. 'No, my dear. Bunny made enemies I have not made.' He had others, but none that would dare have him killed. 'And besides, I am more careful. We have excellent security. Do not worry about me, or about yourself and the children.'

'It's all so terrible,' Delphine said, putting down her fork. 'Pirates capturing Brun, and then the terrorists –'

'It won't happen again,' Hobart said firmly. 'I'll see to that.'

Her eyes widened, the periwinkle-blue eyes that he loved. 'But Hobart – how? You aren't –'

If she said he wasn't important, he would kill her right there; he felt himself stiffening, and saw in her face the reaction to his expression. Her mouth snapped shut; tears filled her eyes and she looked down at her plate.

'I know it's hard for you to believe,' he said quietly, through his teeth. 'But I am not a nonentity –'

'Oh, Hobart, I didn't say – I didn't mean –'

'And I can and will keep you safe. And others. It's my duty, and I have never shirked my duty.'

'Of course not,' she said. Up came her napkin, to dab at the tears.

'We have had laxity in high places,' Hobart said firmly,

feeling the phrases in his mouth. 'With all due respect for Lord Thornbuckle – and I have known Bunny all my life – he simply did not have the . . . the moral fiber to do what was necessary. I will not make that mistake. When I am First Speaker – and I shall be, Delphine, in a matter of days – things will be handled very differently. None of his weak deference to the entrenched bureaucracy which is always afraid to make changes lest it mean the loss of influence. I will make the decisions, and I will save the realm.' He looked up, to find her staring at him, eyes still wide. He pointed his knife at her. 'And you, my dear, will say nothing of this to anyone. I have no doubt that the Grand Council will be glad to elect someone who has a clear vision of what should be done, but I don't want them confused by your version of events first, is that clear?'

'Yes, Hobart.'

'You will say nothing to Miranda tomorrow.'

'No, Hobart.'

'And you will quit messing about with that crab, and eat properly.'

'Yes, Hobart.'

That was better. If she would just confine herself to doing what he told her, and not argue, she would be an exemplary wife. He could imagine her in the Palace, greeting those he invited to the necessary social events. Delphine was good at social events. Decorative, tactful, soft-voiced. Like Miranda, Bunny's widow, in that respect. But his wife. His tool.

R.S.S. *GYRFALCON*

Barin Serrano checked his appearance in the mirror yet again. Like all his class who had not actually disgraced themselves, he had his promotion to jig, and in an hour the ensigns were to appear for the promotion ceremony in the captain's office. His parents, in accordance with tradition, had sent him their old insignia – a pair from each – and a credit chip for his contribution to the celebration in the junior officers' mess. That was handy, given that his pay was now zeroed out. They'd said nothing about that, in their accompanying note. He wondered if it had been written before they found out. He wondered if they simply couldn't think of anything to say.

Luckily, these lower-level promotions didn't require dress uniforms, and he had a natural knack for looking trim. His mind strayed, as it often did, to Esmay Suiza, whose fluffy brown hair sometimes appalled her as much as it delighted him. She would never understand, he was sure, how those stray wisps made him feel.

He hadn't heard from Esmay in weeks, but they'd both been shipbound. They'd expected it. He hadn't expected to be quite so susceptible to everything that reminded him of her, but he assumed that would pass.

'C'mon, Barin!' came a call from the hatch of the ensigns' bay. With a last glance (no, hairs had not suddenly sprouted from his ears) he turned and followed the rest to the ceremony.

The ceremony itself was brief, but the aftermath wasn't. Each newly promoted jig had, by tradition, donated a dozen drink chits into the pool, and the first twelve enlisted personnel who recognized the new rank each got one. Barin, one of the last in alphabetical order on this ship, found that he was being ambushed at every crossing until his last chit was gone.

Four hours later, the first of the new ensign assignees came aboard, a ship-to-ship transfer from the *Cape Hay* which had ferried them from Sector HQ. Two were already partway through their progress from newly commissioned to jig, but three were this year's graduates, so

wet they squeaked. Barin, still most junior in ship duty of
the jigs, found himself assigned to escort them to the
junior wardroom. He'd known the more senior ones at the
Academy; Cordas Stettin was, in fact, a kind of cousin
through his mother's family, and Indi Khas had been in
his cadet unit. They looked incredibly young; he couldn't
believe he had ever been that green. He kept almost looking behind himself when one of them called him *sir*.

The *Gyrfalcon* was on what would have been a routine
patrol, if it weren't for the persistent fear that the New
Texas colonies were up to something. Normally, Sector
Seven was quiet; the transit points into it from Benignity
space made invasion from their main enemy unlikely.
Now, however, they were expecting trouble. Within the
ship itself, all routines were performed under the restrictions of Level 2 alert. A few days of this, Barin thought,
and people would start slacking off: not quite dogging
down the blast barriers, not remembering to close off the
shower-room drains after use, forgetting one or more of
the niggling little details that might – if they came under
surprise attack – save lives, or waste them.

Junior officers and senior NCOs were the only defense
against this natural relaxation of precautions, and they
had lost eight senior NCOs to the medical restrictions on
rejuv recipients. Barin took his turn at inspection with a
keen understanding of its importance. He had, after all,
lost an uncle to someone's failure to dog a blast barrier,
and had grown up with the story.

But *Cape Hay* had brought new orders, and Captain
Escovar called Barin in to discuss them.

'You remember that professor who's been staying with
your wives – er, dependents?'

'Yes, sir.'

'Well, we're going to stop by to pick her up, and take

her with us to Sector One HQ, where we're to meet a diplomat of some sort from the Lone Star Confederation and transport her back to Castle Rock. And it might be a good idea for you to try to convince those women to do something other than sit there eating up Fleet resources. They may not listen, but they've been telling Professor Meyerson they can't do anything without your permission. Oh, and you have mail.'

Barin read the message cube as soon as he had a free moment, which was hours later. His parents had recorded it, but the full weight of the Serrano dynasty lay behind it.

He was young to marry anyway, and with Fleet having already assigned him responsibility for the maximum number of dependents, how could he even think of marrying? Of course they were sure that Lieutenant Suiza would understand, and if she truly cared for him, she would see to it that she made things easier, not harder, for him. There need be no unseemly haste, assuming –

Barin argued with the message cube in resentful silence. How could he think of marrying? How could he not? Unseemly haste? They had known each other for years now, they had been through a Bloodhorde attack, the machinations of envious troublemakers, a very tricky hostage extrication, and he was not – NOT – going to be told he was too young, too inexperienced, too anything else to get married. He was a jig, not some wet-ears ensign fresh out of the Academy.

He loved her. She loved him. It was so simple, if only other people would leave them alone. Perhaps she could get leave and they could meet somewhere . . . privately . . . he toyed briefly with the idea of running away and getting married secretly, in spite of his family. That wouldn't be fair to Esmay though. The Landbride Suiza would expect – would require – more than a hasty ceremony before some local magistrate. Still, with the ship detached for diplomatic duty, maybe – just maybe – they could manage to meet.

CHAPTER SIX

R.S.S. *SHRIKE*

'Mail drop, Lieutenant.' Chief Conway handed Esmay the hardcopy list. Esmay managed not to sigh. All these new security procedures ate time, since every piece of incoming mail at every mail drop required her to check and initial it. Luckily, they could pick up mail only when reasonably near Fleet relays. Still, she could not believe that all these security measures were necessary on a small ship like this. She ran her eye down the list, noting that the chief had flagged three names, a pivot-major and two sergeants minor. They had received more than a sig beyond the mean number of contacts, and from multiple sources.

'No packages,' Esmay murmured, checking the columns.

'No, sir, not for them. There's one for you, though. And Pivot-major Gunderson is getting married at the end of this tour. The return addresses match his next-of-kin address, his future in-laws' address, and the medical center on Rockhouse Major.'

'Medical center?' Then it came to her. 'Oh – of course.'

Gunderson was neuroenhanced, and — 'Is his betrothed also a NEM?'

'No . . . civilian softsider. Gunderson's trying to get a control implant approved.'

That made sense — he wouldn't want to tear his spouse apart by accident. 'Still . . . a civilian marriage?'

'Security's been all over it,' the chief said, correctly interpreting her scowl of concern. 'The family's not Fleet, but they've been subcontractors for two generations.'

Esmay let her gaze drift to the next name.

'Farley's parents have sicced the whole family on her to get her to leave Fleet and work for their shipping consortium. She says she's been hassled for years, and just trashes the notes.'

A message cube from Barin. Esmay put it aside for later viewing. It bore the sticker that meant it had passed censors at Sector HQ. He must have told his family by now — his grandmother already knew; this was probably about their response to his telling them about Esmay. She still hadn't heard back from her own family, though with the long transit times the new security regs imposed, that wasn't too surprising. She hoped they'd reply promptly. She and Barin would have only a short window of opportunity for their wedding, and while they wanted it to be small and informal, she still wanted it to feel like a wedding, which meant family present.

Her other mail was all official business, addressed to her position on *Shrike* . . . all but the package, much battered after its passage through one checkpoint after another, with Brun Meager's name in the sender ID square.

A package from Brun? Esmay hadn't heard from her since she left for Castle Rock with her babies. She noticed the rumpled sealtape, where security had tried to open it, as required by the new rules. She laid her hand on the ID plate, wondering momentarily how Brun had acquired her handprint, and the sealtape flicked free. Esmay unfolded the wrapping, aware of security watching her.

The last of the paper folded back to reveal . . . a strip of embroidery so exquisite that Esmay could not repress a gasp of pleasure. As wide as her hand, a long strip – she unfolded it carefully – that was nearly as tall as she was. And every centimeter covered with white-on-white embroidery and lace. She hardly dared touch it with bare hands; she felt she should be wearing white gloves to protect it. She laid it gently across her lap and went back to the box.

Under the folded strip was a square of some sheer white fabric, more like a net, encrusted with tiny seed pearls. And under *that*, several pages of drawings, sketches of a gown – a wedding gown, Esmay realized, with long sleeves and a high collar. It was more severe than she would have expected Brun to choose; it had almost the suggestion of a uniform about the shoulders.

The data cube in the same package explained. 'Barin's acquisitions need a way to support themselves, Hazel told me, and you need a wedding gown. Handwork of this quality is rare; if they're working for a good designer, they'll be paid well for it. So I took the liberty of talking to some designers. I assume you don't want to pay a year's salary on it. For the Fleet hero who rescued me, and an introduction to the craftswomen doing work of this quality, Goran Hiel is willing to design your gown. He's not considered as good as Marice Limited, but I liked the slight military flair.'

It was not the first time Brun had tried to plan their life for them. This was . . . the fourth, Esmay thought, trying not to resent it. Brun had grown up expecting things to go her way; money and beauty and luck had failed her only once. No wonder she wanted to go back to running the

world – or at least her friends' lives. She was only revert-
ing to normal; she didn't mean to flaunt her power.
Probably.

Esmay looked at the drawings and embroidery again.
For a moment, Esmay imagined herself in that gown,
made of such gorgeous stuff. She would look . . . no, she
must not think about that, not now. It was far too grand a
gown for her, for a plain lieutenant in Fleet who wanted
a quiet family wedding.

But for the Landbride Suiza?

It was not too grand for the Landbride Suiza, but she
was not marrying Barin as Landbride . . . she paused in
folding the strip of embroidery to replace it in the box.
Was she not, indeed?

A cascade of difficulties unfolded in her mind, beginning with her position as Landbride Suiza. What if
someone thought her marrying Barin had anything to do
with that? With the historical position of Suiza of
Altiplano and the Regular Space Service, or Altiplano's
ambiguous position within the Familias Regnant?

What if her family thought that? What if – she did not
like even thinking about this, about the land link that
was supposed to have been formed with the Landbride
ceremony – what if the land itself, Land Suiza, thought
her marriage to Barin Serrano meant something beyond
love?

And she hadn't yet made formal application for a
status change. Quickly, without stopping to think about
any of it, she called up the relevent forms.

OFFICER APPLICATION FOR LIFE PARTNER CEREMONY: *Procedures
and Requirements.*

Although she had known about the official forms in an
intellectual way, having them actually loaded onto her
deskcomp felt very . . . serious. First came a long, depress-
ing series of warnings, restrictions, and discouraging

statistics: she had to initial each paragraph as having been read. Formal life partnerships (also known as marriages, the text informed her prosily) failed even among individuals of longstanding Fleet background. The report cited all the possible reasons, including some Esmay hadn't thought of (Were there really people who were confused about their gender as adults? And how many people converted to a religion requiring celibacy after marrying someone?).

She read on, doggedly initialling one paragraph after another, until she came to the section warning officers against entanglements with persons of planetary importance. And right there, in a list that included governor-general of this, and assistant general secretary of that, and commander of the other, she found 'Altiplano: Sector Commanders, immediate families of, and Landbride/Landgroom.'

Landgroom? There wasn't any such title on Altiplano. The whole point of the Landbride was . . . her mind caught up with the warning and she glanced back at the heading. 'Officers are specifically warned to avoid political entanglements, including liaisons either casual and permanent with the following classes of persons.'

She could hardly avoid a liaison with herself, but – what would this mean to Barin? She was a commissioned officer of the Regular Space Service. Surely they couldn't hold her Landbride status against her . . . not her . . .

But if they did . . . she hadn't been a Landbride when she and Barin met and fell in love. She had been just another ensign . . . *just another ensign who had survived a mutiny and saved a planet* . . . but basically, a Fleet officer. She hadn't done anything wrong in falling for Barin, or he for her. What difference did it make that she was also the Landbride Suiza?

Come to think of it, had she ever *officially* informed

Fleet that she was the Landbride? Lady Katerina Saenz knew, but she had been concentrating so on helping get Brun free – that was far more important – and she wasn't at all sure she'd turned in the form. Esmay called up her personnel stats. Planet of origin, family of origin, religion, local awards and decorations . . . the Starmount, she had put that in. But she hadn't mentioned Landbride.

Feeling guilty already, she hunted through the Personnel Procedures database for the right form, and didn't find one. Well . . . not that many officers became Landbride. In fact, she was the only one. But this meant discussing the lapse with Captain Solis; he would not want to be surprised by it later.

'Captain, could I speak to you?'

'Certainly.' He looked up from his work, much less menacing than she had once thought him.

'It's about these forms for a change of status,' Esmay began. 'The warnings to personnel –'

His brows rose. 'I don't imagine you're in any trouble – you and the young man are both Fleet officers. Unless you still think you're robbing cradles.'

'No, sir. But the section on planetary entanglements –'

'I know your father's a prominent person, but you're a Fleet officer –'

'And a Landbride.'

'Landbride? What is that?'

'A proscribed position, it says here.' Esmay handed over the printout she'd made. 'I don't know if it applies – I am a Fleet officer, and when we met I wasn't Landbride Suiza –'

'Umph. Landbride must be something extraordinary. What does a Landbride do, Lieutenant?'

That was not something she could explain, when she didn't half understand it herself. 'It's – the Landbride represents the family's bond to the land – to the soil itself – in the family holdings. She's a symbol of the family's commitment to the land. It's . . . sort of religious.'

'I didn't even know you were a Landbride,' he said.

'It happened during my leave home, after my great-grandmother died,' Esmay said. 'When I came back, we were so busy with the rescue mission, I guess I forgot to put it in . . . I didn't think about its being important.'

'Yes . . . we were all somewhat preoccupied right then. But you need to report it now. Personnel will definitely want to know, and they may have some concerns about your duties. How much time you'll need to be away from Fleet, and so on.'

'I won't,' Esmay said. 'That's what my father said –'

'But religion . . .' He looked thoughtful. 'Religious positions usually require some actual commitment of time and effort, Lieutenant. If you aren't there –'

Esmay thought suddenly of the spring and fall Eveners, when her great-grandmother had ridden out to do something – she didn't know what – in the fields. No one had mentioned that to her, but –

'It all happened so fast,' she said. 'And then I came back . . .' She hated the sudden pleading tone in her voice; and stopped short.

'You need to get it straightened out, whatever it is, before you marry young Serrano,' he said. 'Not just because of regulations, but because you both need to know what you're getting into. And I see here you're in double jeopardy, with your father being a sector commander.'

'Yes, sir,' Esmay said. 'But they knew that when I went into the prep school.'

'But you weren't then about to marry one of the oldest families in Fleet,' he said. His tone held no rancor, but the very matter-of-factness of it set a barrier of steel between her and what she hoped for.

Esmay nodded, and withdrew. Master Chief Cattaro, after rummaging in the Admin database for the correct form, gnawed the corner of her lip. 'There's a procedure, Lieutenant . . . there's always a procedure. Let me just check . . .' Another dive into the database. 'Ah. What I think will work is a 7653, an *Application for Exception, Unspecified*, and a 78B-4, an *Incident Report, Personnel Infraction, Unspecified*, and then you'll need a 9245 . . . no, actually, two of them. One to accompany each of the others.' Chief Cattaro grinned, looking happier with each additional form. 'And it might be just as well to file your 8813 – your application for permission for permanent bond – linked to the code tag for your pre-commissioning records, because that will have your prep-school classifi- cations, and of course you'll need . . .'

'Chief, I'm not going to have time to do all that at once.'

'Best get started then,' Cattaro said. She had the quiet twinkle of the senior NCO who has just been able to dump a load of work on a junior officer. 'I'll just pipe it to your desk, shall I? Or would you rather work in here?'

She could always fill in the blanks while working on something else.

'My desk, please, Chief.'

'Yes, sir.'

Filling out the forms to Chief Cattaro's satisfaction kept her busy the rest of that shift and part of the next, along with her other work. For reasons known only to the forms designers in Personnel, none of the forms asked for the information in the same order, or even the same format, which made it impossible to simply port data from one to the other. Family name first here, but last there. Middle name or names as initials in this form, but spelled out in that one. Planet of origin by a code from a table, or spelled out, or by a code from another table, which didn't agree with the first.

They really did not want Landbrides to marry into Fleet, Esmay decided.

Barin's message cube – when she finally had time to put it in the reader – was less informative than she'd hoped. He loved her – she couldn't hear that too often – and he was still waiting to hear from his parents. He was afraid they'd be upset by the administrative decision to make him responsible for the support of the women brought back from Our Texas. It was going to be hard to convince Personnel to approve the paperwork for a status change, when clearly he couldn't afford any more dependents.

Esmay wondered if someone in Admin had gone bonkers. Why were they demanding that Barin pay support for these women? He had included the data he thought she'd need – evidently he hadn't yet found the sections of the application which forbade her to exist, or him to marry her. He promised to write again, but pointed out that with his entire salary going to the support of the NewTex women, he would be limited to ship-to-ship transfers within the Fleet postal system.

Esmay added his information to her paperwork, and then completed what she could of her application, along with the belated NOTICE OF RELATIONSHIP papers. It was all so silly. They'd known she was a sector commander's daughter when they accepted her into Fleet, and Altiplano had no desire to influence the Familias Grand Council anyway. It had never even tried to get a Seat in Council. Why was it on the proscribed list? And if they were going to put Landbrides on, why hadn't they done the elementary research to find out that there was no such thing as a Landgroom? Cursing the anonymous 'they' in silence, Esmay finished the forms, stamped and thumb-sealed them, and took them back to the captain's office for his clerk to make the required copies and ready them for transit.

She went back to the rest of the message cube later. The former Rangers' wives, now settled uneasily in an apartment block on Rockhouse Major, were constantly asking Barin for assurances he could not provide.

'Grandmother knows why I did it – and agrees that it was justifiable under the circumstances – but she warned me that Fleet would not be pleased, no matter what kind of report she turned in. Headquarters feels I overstepped my authority, and created a huge financial obligation for them, not to mention a publicity nightmare. They've insisted that I contribute to their maintenance, though my whole salary won't pay the grocery bills alone. Everyone – from the women to the admirals – seems to think it's my place to come up with a solution. And I'm stumped. Those women don't seem to be capable of anything but sitting around complaining, and now the civil authorities are jumping on *me* because they won't send their children to school.'

Esmay thought of the women she'd seen in the shuttle during the evacuation: the long-sleeved, long-skirted dresses, the headscarves, the work-worn hands. If they were as religious as the Old Believers on Altiplano, they'd be very uncomfortable on a space station, or even one of the more – her mind struggled for awhile, looking for a different word, but finally settled on the first – *advanced* planets.

She hadn't thought much about the women and children removed – or rescued – on that mission since leaving the task force. She'd assumed the women who had been prisoners had received medical treatment, and that 'someone' had done 'something' about the others.

Apparently not. Though it was hardly fair to land all the responsibility on Barin, if he was going to be held accountable, then clearly she herself had to do something. What a nuisance it was, being stuck on a different ship! They couldn't just talk it over, share ideas, come up with solutions.

She prepared queries for Barin and the Fleet library-search service, and at the next downjump sent them off.

The idea woke her out of a sound sleep some nights later, and she lay there wide-eyed, amazed at herself. The women needed a place to live and raise their children, preferably on a planet. They needed a way to earn a living. Brun had suggested the latter, with her comments about their skill in handwork. And now Esmay had herself thought of a solution to the former problem. Altiplano. As the Landbride Suiza, she could settle them on Suiza lands. In their own village, if necessary, where they could follow their own customs. Their handwork could be exported, along with the genestock, to fill out their income beyond what they could produce from the land; she would be willing to give them a start of livestock from her own personal holdings. Their children could grow up as Altiplanans; in a few generations, they'd be assimilated completely.

The more she thought about it, the better it seemed. The women might even find husbands on Altiplano, if they wanted them. Since their beliefs fit somewhere on the great branching tree of religions that had grown out of Old Earth Christianity, surely they would find the tone of Altiplano's Old Believers congenial. She tried not to think of those passages in her child's history book about the religious disputes. Her great-grandmother had insisted that they were all the result of insufficient humility and excessive arrogance. And anyway, religious

freedom was now part of the Altiplanan legal code,
though Altiplano lacked the diversity of culture of Fleet
or the more cosmopolitan planets.

Since she couldn't go back to sleep, she turned on her
desk unit and recorded a cube for Barin with the gist of
her idea, then one for Luci, telling her cousin all about
the wedding plans, and Barin's problems, and asking
about vacancies on Suiza lands. In her mind's eye, she
saw them settled somewhere in the south, in a tidy little
village of stone houses, with kitchen gardens. Something
very like what Barin had described as the households
they'd come from.

By the time she'd populated their pastures with Cateri
goats and cattelopes, and imagined them all cheerful and
productive, with laughing children playing in the lanes,
she was sleepy again. She went back to bed sure that all
problems had solutions and this one had just been solved.

Next morning she was not quite as sure – she thought
she remembered that they were free-birthers, or at least
their men were – but she put the cubes in the outgoing
mail collection anyway, and went on with her work.

ALTIPLANO, ESTANCIA SUIZA

Luci Suiza came through the front hall on her way in
from the polo fields – she needed a shower before the
Vicarios family showed up for dinner, and had let
Esmay's half-brother ride her pony cool. That was one
reason, and the other was that she'd seen the little red
mail van driving up to the house. Philip had been sending her a note every day; when she was lucky she got to
them before anyone else. She picked up his note, and a
message cube from Esmay, and took them up to her room.

She read the note before she showered, stripping off
her sweaty clothes and tingling all over from the phrases

he'd used, as well as the cooler air wafting in through the window. Tonight – tonight the parents would have their final meeting, and after that, they would be betrothed.

After her shower, wrapped in a fluffy white robe, Luci fed Esmay's cube into the reader in her room, and brushed her hair as the message came up. Esmay was fine; she hadn't heard back from Barin about his family yet; Brun had sent her gorgeous samples of embroidery and sketches for a gown; Fleet had a lot of silly rules about who could marry whom, so she was having to fill out lots of forms . . . Luci paused, pinned up her hair, and glanced at the clock. She still had time. She made a long arm, pulled her cosmetics closer to the cube reader, and tried to do her makeup and watch the message at the same time.

Fleet didn't approve of officers marrying Landbrides. *So resign*, Luci thought to herself, and sure enough the next bit was a long, rambling apology and then the admission that Esmay thought she should resign. Was Luci interested?

Luci was interested; Luci heaved a sigh at her absent cousin, and applied lip color. No matter what anyone said, there was no way to play polo and end up with soft moist lips, without using cosmetics. The message continued; Luci kept an eye on the clock. She liked her cousin; she admired her intensely, but Phil would be here in twenty-five minutes.

Esmay's wonderful idea of settling the women from Our Texas and their children on Suiza lands took her by surprise; the eyeliner she'd been applying so carefully swiped up and away, a dark streak across her face before she caught herself. What?! *Nineteen* women, and their children – dozens of children – all to be settled on Suiza lands? Free-birthers, from a planet with a barbarous religious cult . . . she could just imagine what the priests would say about *that*! Esmay babbled on about their handwork skills, their experience on low-tech planets. *We are not low-tech*, Luci thought angrily. *Idiot. Fool.*

Then she caught sight of her face in the mirror, and the clock, and the anger roared in her like a brushfire. Esmay had no right! Esmay was not a proper Landbride – no one who really understood, who really cared, could have considered that for an instant . . .

Luci dashed into the bathroom, nearly trampling two of the younger children.

'Luci, what happened to your –'

'Be quiet!' she snarled at them, and scrubbed the makeup off her face, leaving streaks on the facecloth. Stupid Esmay. Ridiculous Esmay. It was a good thing she'd left, and a good thing she wanted to resign as Landbride, and Luci would pluck her hair herself if she had a chance.

When she got back to her room and looked out the window to see if the Vicarios vehicle was coming yet, the alternating blue and gold of shadow and late sun streaking the grass of the polo fields stabbed her heart. It was so beautiful, so beautiful it hurt. How could Esmay not want this? How could she care so little, that she would think of violating the land for a bunch of outlanders?

She rested her forearms on the windowsill and drank in the cool air scented with early roses and apple blossom. Somewhere in the distance, horses whinnied; the grooms would be mixing evening feeds. This was what she wanted, what she had always wanted – well, this and Philip to share it with. Land to cherish and nourish and protect, beauty to nurture, the ancient cycles of the land.

Light reflected from something moving on the road, then flashed straight in her eyes when the vehicle turned into their drive. The Vicarios, no doubt, unless it was her father returning late from the city. No time now for cosmetics, though she touched her chapped lips with color again. The blue-and-white overtunic and white skirt of the courted maiden. After tonight, she would wear the blue skirt of the bride-to-be.

Esmay, you fool! was her last thought as she closed her door and ran down the upper passage to the stairs.

The Vicarios family had gone back to their city house by midnight. At this third of the formal meetings (alternating from one family's home to the other's), the parents had been pleasantly relaxed. The exchange of gifts, the ritual speeches, the contrived – but still effective 'unexpected' visit of the priest who put her hand in Philip's, and tied a silk scarf around the pair of them – all had gone without a hitch. Luci and Philip had a few minutes alone in the rose garden as their elders watched from the lighted door-way; he kissed her respectfully on the brow, and murmured her name.

Philip went with his parents when they left, of course. From now on, no more stolen moments, let alone hours, in which to discover each other . . . from now on, they were formally betrothed, and that betrothal had its own rules. Maddening, perhaps intentionally so. Luci filched another stuffed date from the tray a sleepy maidservant was carrying back to the kitchen, and followed her father into the library. Her uncle and grandfather, already relaxed in chairs by the fireplace, looked up as she came in.

'Luci, you should be in bed.'

'Papa, I'm not sleepy.' He raised his eyebrows at her, but she didn't move. 'Papa, I had a message cube from Esmay today.'

Her uncle Casimir sighed. 'Esmay . . . now there's another problem. Berthold, did you get anywhere in the Landsmen's Guild?'

'Nowhere. Oh, Vicarios won't oppose us, but that's because of Luci, and his support is half-hearted. It would be different if she hadn't left so young, I think. They don't really remember her, and even though they awarded her the Starmount, and consider her a hero, they do not want a Landbride – any Landbride but especially our Landbride – connected to an outlander family. Cosca told me frankly that even if she moved here, and also her husband, he would oppose it. *Nothing good ever came from the stars*, he insisted.'

'And the votes?'

'Enough for a challenge, Casi, I'm sure of it. No, the only way out of this is for Esmaya to come and talk to them herself.'

'Or resign.'

'Or resign, but – will she?'

Luci spoke up. 'She mentioned that in her cube.'

'What – resigning? Why?'

'Her precious Fleet seems to think about us the way the Landsmen's Guild thinks about them. She says they have some kind of regulation forbidding officers to marry Landbrides.'

Her father snorted. 'Do they have one forbidding officers to *be* Landbrides? How ridiculous!'

'Are you serious?' Casimir asked. 'They have something specific about Landbrides? How would they know?'

'I don't know,' Luci said. 'That's just what she said. And she said why didn't we take in all those women brought back from Our Texas – she was sure they'd fit in.'

A stunned silence, satisfying by its depth and length.

'She *what*?' Casimir said finally. 'Aren't those women –'

'Free-birthers and religious cultists,' Luci said, with satisfaction. 'Exactly.'

'But – but the priests will object,' Berthold said.

'Not as badly as the Landsmen's Guild, if they hear of it. Dear God, I thought she had more sense than that!'

'She is in love,' Luci pointed out, willing now to be magnanimous. 'Apparently Fleet is taking Barin's salary to pay for their upkeep – at least some of it – and Esmay's trying to help him out. Nineteen of them, after all, and all those children.'

'At our expense.' Casimir shook his head. 'Well, that settles it. She'll have to resign, as soon as I can get word to her. The Trustees will certainly not approve this, if I were willing to let it be known.' He gave Luci a hard look. 'You didn't tell Philip, I hope.'

'Of course not.' Luci glared at her uncle. Esmay might not have any sense, but *she* knew what the family honor required.

'I hope she does name you Landbride, Luci,' Casimir said. 'You'll be a good one.'

Luci had a sudden spasm of doubt. Was she being fair to Esmay, who after all had had so many bad things happen to her? But underneath the doubt, the same exultation she had felt when Esmay gave her the brown mare . . . *mine, it's mine, I can take care of it, nobody can hurt it. . . .*

'I wonder if we could place an ansible call,' Casimir said.

'Surely it's not that urgent,' Berthold said.

'What if she just packs them up and ships them to us? Better safe than sorry.'

'She won't,' Luci said. 'I'm sure she won't.' She didn't know how she knew, but she knew – probably by now Esmay had figured out for herself why it was a bad idea, and the next mail would bring apologies.

'I hope not,' her father said. He yawned. 'Oh, do go to bed, Luci! I'm exhausted.'

Luci gave him a kiss and went up to bed, sure she

would not sleep for the warring emotions inside her. She undressed quickly, hung her clothes up, and slipped naked between the sheets, taking great lungfuls of the fragrant night air. She hoped Esmay felt this way about her Barin . . . if her poor cousin couldn't be Landbride, she at least deserved a great love.

R.S.S. *SHRIKE*

Esmay came onto the bridge to find Captain Solis scowling. Now what had she done or left undone?

'I was afraid I'd lose you,' the captain said.

'Lose me?'

'New orders. They're sending me a new exec, and you over to line ships again. I knew they would eventually. Even though we can always use someone with your talents in SAR, they consider it a waste.'

He handed over the message cube. 'It's all in there; we'll be dropping you off at Topaz.'

'Topaz –' A civilian station.

'In transit between ships is a good time to use a few days' leave, Lieutenant. Assuming you have a use for it.'

Barin. Her heart hammered. Now if she could only figure out how . . .

'*Navarino* is in Sector Six. *Gyrfalcon*, I hear, is going to be detached from picket duty and sent back to Castle Rock, and thence to Sector One –' Solis did not crack a smile, but she did. She knew the regulations: all she had to do was show up at the right time. The route she chose from Topaz to Sector Six HQ was her own choice. There was at least a chance that she could meet Barin at some intermediate station. If she could get word to him. If she could get leave.

CHAPTER SEVEN

BENIGNITY OF THE COMPASSIONATE HAND
NUOVO VENITZA, SANTA LUZIA

Hostite Fieddi, Swordmaster and troupe leader, bowed to the Chairman's box, then to either end of the Grande, where the notable guests of state and industry were seated, and finally, that cold chill down the spine which this required movement always brought, turned his back on the most dangerous man in his universe to salute the mortal representative of that Holy One who was even more dangerous, having dominion over all universes.

Protocol, he thought sourly, was invented by the devil, for the ensnaring of innocent hearts. Not that his was innocent; he had been debriefed by his superior in the Order, and had still to face confession. In between . . .

Trumpets blared, the old curled rams' horn trumpets, and from the corner of his eye, Hostite saw the doors open in each corner, dark mouths. In each, a gleaming figure poised in one of the Attitudes. A low drumroll . . . the first figure in each doorway stalked forward; and behind it a second.

Eight now, each demonstrating one of the Attitudes, a

Full Square. The drums shifted to a subtle beat, step and step; the figures moved forward, in toward the open space where Hostite waited. Four were female, four were male. Four belonged to the Sun: pure gold, copper-red, rich bronze, and brass. Four belonged to the Moon: silver, steel, lead, platinum. And he, the dance's Shadow, gleamed obsidian in the light.

Sabre dancing had its roots in ancient days, long before the first men left Earth. More than one sword-bearing culture had its sword and knife dances, and more than one had used them as training. More than one had also the spectacle, where the rich and powerful watched as their servants danced and bled for their amusement. There had always been, for some, the heady linkage of lust and danger.

But not until the Benignity had the old threads wound into such a line of life and death as this. Hostite smiled behind his mask. Here was the imperial circus, and here were the holy warriors, and here were the dancers . . . and here he ruled.

The gleaming figures had formed the circle, with him in the center . . . the Spanish circle, he knew from his studies with its elaborate figures. He turned slowly, enjoying as much as the Chairman, he was sure, those fine-tuned bodies beneath the gleaming paint. Unlike his mask, theirs were transparent – invisible, to all but those who knew exactly where to look. Instead, their faces – biosculpted to be as beautiful as their bodies – gazed back at him with impassivity.

Tonight's music, chosen by the Chairman, was Imetzina's 'Quadrille for Evening by the Sea.' The Chairman beckoned; the opening phrase began. Hostite signalled Four and Seven, brass and lead. So much was tradition, and the Dance began with what might seem dullness.

Gracefully, yet with a severity imposed by the weapons, Four and Seven stepped out of the circumference, into the circle. In practice, they danced naked but for wrist, elbow, and knee guards, but here – in formal performance, with Someone certainly watching from behind the curtain – Four wore the small, metallic-scaled breast medallions, the pleated metallic-scaled skirt that hung from her hips and swirled when she moved. Seven wore the loincloth that was hardly more than a codpiece strapped in place.

The blades were all steel, but coated to match the dancers' colors. Hostite's blade alone was not steel, but true obsidian, brittle but sharper than any other.

The traditional quadrille required each dancer to face each, first in the pairs, and then by fours. Hostite worried a little about Four – this was her first performance in the Grande, and though she had seemed completely solid in rehearsal, he knew that the excitement of a first performance could cause a fatal misstep. But Caris, who usually danced the Four, had hyperextended her knee while instructing a junior class: some careless student – not a student any longer – had left a lump of wax on the floor.

Pelinn should have had another half-year in the second company, Hostite thought, but she was very talented and very dedicated, the best of the understudies. He hoped she would not be marked badly tonight.

The music brought the dancers together, blade against blade, and whirled them apart. Four moved perfectly in time to the beat, and as the figures followed one another, including the difficult change of hand during pirouette, Hostite relaxed a little. Even though brass and lead danced the false art, a much less dangerous design than the true, they could mark each other permanently if they erred.

Eight and Two followed Four and Seven: platinum

and copper, the maximum contrast of color, and the minimum of gender – both were women. Genetic twins, differentiated only by makeup and costume. Hostite smiled indulgently to himself. They were at the height of their powers now, and after all the years of training together, they always produced a spectacular show. Whirling, leaping, throwing kicks as well as rapid thrusts and sweeping strokes, it seemed they must slice one another to bits – but they never did.

Bronze and steel next, Three and Six, this time both males. Not twins, nor matched in height or style. Steel Six had four centimeters on Bronze Three, with a corresponding reach – but Three, born of a family of acrobats, matched him easily in the dance. Their corded muscles stood out; their weapons rang ever more loudly – and always on the beat.

Hostite signalled for the pairs next: One and Five would dance alone at the end, but for now joined Four and Seven. Gold and brass, lead and silver ... the false art and the true danced both with and against each other. For many patrons, this was the best part of any dance, with its interlocking symbolism, but for the Master it was always a problem. In the finale, One and Five must be capable of the most difficult movements, which meant they must not suffer injury now – and yet they must demonstrate the True, and its superiority to the False. Hostite worried again about Four; she must be shown to be inferior, without injuring Five, or being too badly hurt.

Again he was reassured by her steady, even rhythm under the spectacular moves required. She had the true dramatic temperament; when pressed by the true art, she grimaced, leaned back, seemed on the point of imbalance – but never quite fell. The few thin lines of red on her skin were only enhancements, not serious injuries that would take time from her training or performance.

The dance continued, with the other pairs replacing those: Two and Eight opposing Six and Three. Here, where Hostite expected no problems, Six missed his footing in a turn – perhaps the floor was sweat-slick there, or perhaps he lost concentration. Whatever the reason, his left foot slid sideways as his weight came on it, and Two – they were in the second figure by then – opened his leg across the knee from the lateral thigh to the posterior calf, exposing bone at the joint, just before the gush of brilliant blood that proved an artery had been severed. A gasp, almost a moan, came from the watching seat. Hostite ignored that, and gestured to his dancers. Three and Eight moved aside, without missing a beat; Two backed away and knelt, weapon outstretched. Hostite looked at the Chair's box. Which would it be?

A hand outstretched: the music stopped, mid-phrase. The dancers stopped, held their poses. Silence, then, but for Six's harsh breathing. He lay where he had fallen, in a widening pool of blood, struggling not to make a sound. Hostite knew already it was a crippling blow. He might live, and walk, but he would never dance again, even if the joint held.

'Steel,' the Chairman said. 'Our thanks for your service. It is ended.'

Before anyone else could move, Hostite moved, his obsidian blade slicing through the air and Six's throat. He bowed to the Chair's box.

'Continue,' the Chair said. Hostite returned to his place; the music resumed mid-phrase where it had paused. Two still knelt, having no partner. Three and Eight moved with the music, dancing, avoiding both Two and the dangerous bright blood. It honored the honorable dead, to dance before them, around them.

At the end of that figure, the Chair gestured again, and again the dance paused. Now Hostite closed the dead

'I suppose.' Goonar was much less interested in who might be a Benignity agent than in how such information could be turned for profit. 'So . . . either they're going to find out it was a bad batch, and the price of any remaining Morreline/Conselline stock will drop through the floor, and the whole combine will be bankrupt, or they'll find the basic process is flawed and all rejuv-related products will go down?'

'You lot!' Kaim glared at him. 'Is profit all you care about? Doesn't it mean anything to you that if all the master chiefs go bonkers, we can't possibly stand against a Benignity or NewTex invasion?'

'New Texans are amateurs,' Goonar said absently. 'That silly drunk –'

'Isn't the whole story. Just as you said, any organization has traitors, and any organization also has fools that get drunk.'

'Still,' Basil said, with a silky tone that alerted Goonar. 'Still, I do not see that finding your traitors – assuming you have them – is our responsibility. We do, on the other hand, have a responsibility to the family which, by paying taxes, pays your salary too, Kaim, so I wouldn't be so smug about your moral purity.'

Goonar spread both arms. 'Stop it, both of you. None of us wants to see the Familias fall to invasion, and none of us wants to see the Terakian family go broke. We're one blood.' Which might, in a few minutes, be mingled on the porch floor, if the other two didn't quit posturing.

'Daddy!' Basil's daughter burst through the door from the dining room, leading her mother by a good ten feet. 'Found you!' Basil scooped her up, and the child flashed a wide grin at the other men. 'Lunch time!' she announced.

'Sounds good to me,' Goonar said, pushing himself up. 'Come here, little one, and let your father get up.' The child bounced from her father's lap to Goonar and he lifted her slight weight to his shoulder, where she crowed in delight. 'Don't forget to –'

'Duck,' she said, leaning over his head. Inside, her mother shook her head.

'Sorry, Goonar. Lydia's Jon had put something down the toilet in the children's bathroom, and we were coping with the overflow. Jessie got away from us.'

'Good timing,' Goonar said in an undertone. Berish was almost as pretty as little Jessie, and he envied Basil at times like this, remembering those first years of marriage, when the children were sweet lumps of brown sugar and a wife was an inexhaustible cavern of enchantments. He'd thought of remarrying, but the pain of losing Sela and the children still stabbed; he could not risk that again. He swung Jessie down, and followed the others to the great dining table.

After lunch, the rain stopped for a while, and Goonar chivvied the men into a walk along the shore, past the orange squares of fish pens. Here, with the distractions of uneven footing and a breeze freshening into a blustery wind, Basil and Kaim were less inclined to quarrel. Kaim opened his mind, like the net of a fisherman, spilling a mixed lot of information which Goonar knew he and Basil would pick over at leisure. By dinnertime, when the wind had blown the clouds south for a time, Kaim was clearly enjoying the once-hated planet.

Goonar himself wanted nothing more than to be back aboard one of the Terakian family's ships, preferably one with the new decryption algorithms, that could intercept transmissions via the financial ansibles. He tried to settle calmly to the after-dinner word games, but he couldn't concentrate. After the third time that Kaim crossed his entry with a 10-point bonus, he gave up.

'I'm fuzzed,' he said. 'I'm going up to bed.'

'To bed?' Basil asked. 'It's not that late.'

'No, but I'm that tired.' Goonar yawned, and climbed the stairs to his tower room. Basil undoubtedly knew what he was going to do, and could be counted on to keep Kaim out of the way. The problem was that no security system could really keep his communications clean, not down here. He opened a line to the family headquarters on Caskadar, requested a data dump of the past two days of market reports, and told the duty operator he'd be in the next day to put something in the batch for the ansible.

'By midday, local, Ser,' the operator said. 'It goes off at 1300, and we have to have all the data encrypted.'

'I'll be there by 1000,' Goonar promised.

When Basil came up, hours later, Goonar was still picking through the data dump.

'I thought you were fuzzed,' Basil said.

'I am.' This time the yawn was genuine. 'But I'm also worried. There's something going on with the Consellines – look at this –'

'Not now. In the morning. I had to ply Kaim with more brandy to keep him downstairs, and if I don't sleep now I'll be very sorry in the morning.'

'You'll be sorry longer if you don't look at this. I'm serious, Bas. Something's going on, and it's big. Look at the fluctuations in the rejuv index.'

'It's been volatile ever since the Patchcock mess,' Basil said. 'Took it six months to recover at all, and every little rumor shakes it like a windchime.'

'So quit talking and look,' Goonar said. He tapped the chart.

'Oh.' Basil pushed his lips out and back in. 'What about the raw –'

'Over the top,' Goonar said, shuffling through the pile to find what he wanted. 'There – I can't be sure without getting a hook in one of the big lines, but I'd bet that's from the Conselline plants; they're the only single source big enough to draw those resources this fast.'

'And they'd lost market share, and . . . damn, cuz, I wish we could access the employment figures.' Basil shook his head as if to clear it. 'So – we tell –'

'The Fathers,' Goonar said. 'And we don't tell Kaim. I'm preparing an ansible load for tomorrow.'

'Today. What time does it have to be in? You want help?'

'Just keep Kaim out of my way.'

Goonar's line of command ran through Basil's father, not his own – typical of the Terakian family's organization. So he was surprised when the next message came from his father.

'Goonar – tell Basil to keep Kaim onplanet another 48 hours without fail. Then get yourself on the next shuttle up.'

'As God wills,' Goonar said, with both piety and practicality: the family code for 'What's going on?'

'In his grace,' said his father and signed off.

So he had put his finger on the lion's eyelid. Well, now to convince Basil to trap Kaim and let him run off.

The shuttle ride to the orbital station seemed to take forever, though he knew it was the standard flight time. When he arrived, he went directly to the Terakian Shipping offices, where staff were bustling around as if a ship were arriving.

'Who's coming?'

'We just got word by ansible. *Flavor* is on her way through fast-transit, with something urgent. If you want a lift, I'm sure they'll have room for you.'

Favored-of-God, nicknamed *Flavor*, was the Terakian's

fast courier . . . and the family's most advanced recon vessel, loaded with the best scan equipment money or influence or trickery could obtain. 'There she is –' one of the techs said, pointing to the display board. A bright splash on the screen meant something had come through the jump point at max vee, and the color shift meant she was making a dangerously fast approach.

So whatever it was, the Fathers were willing to let everyone know they had some urgent chore in hand. Usually Terakian ships moved in the same stately arcs as any other commercial carrier, never showing all their capacity unless they ran into trouble.

'What's his ETA?' Goonar asked.

'At this rate? Under twenty hours.'

Twenty hours . . . so why had his father told him to leave downside immediately?

So he would be gone before word of *Flavor*'s arrival got to the surface? So perhaps Kaim wouldn't connect the two? So there would be no transmissions to the surface which Kaim might intercept?

Goonar sighed. While the station had a perfectly comfortable lodging house for transients, and he had more than enough credit to use it, he knew – without even asking – that his father expected him to stay in the office. In the off-duty bunkroom for low-level staff, with its hard narrow beds.

'I'm going over to Spotted Lamb for lunch,' Goonar said. 'If anyone wants me.'

He was almost through with dessert – honeyed figs stuffed with chopped bitsai nuts – when the call came. A tightbeamed packet for him from *Flavor*.

Adhem, the office manager, gave him a look, which Goonar had no trouble intepreting. He wasn't that senior in the family; he was just another of the young men moving up through the ranks . . . so why was he suddenly

in the office at just the right time for the appearance of
Flavor on a fast run, and why was he getting this packet,
instead of someone more senior? He was moving up, not
down or sideways, because he knew better than to give
Adhem any information at all.

Flavor's commander met him at the hatch and threw her
arms around him. Laisa, Basil's sister, had the same dangerous energy as her brother. As Goonar's chain of
command went through his uncle, so Laisa's went
through Goonar's father.

'You're coming with us,' she murmured in his ear.

'That's nice,' Goonar said, detaching himself. 'Basil
says to give you his love.'

'We're fuel-and-go,' Laisa said. Goonar nodded, and
went through the hatch ahead of her.

In the next few hours, he briefed her on what he
thought he had learned from Kaim and the more accessible data channels.

'Here's what you don't know,' Laisa said, when he was
through. 'There was a distant family member captured
with the *Elias Madero* – a young girl, Hazel Takeris. Some
seventy years ago, a Terakian boy fell in love with a
Chapapas girl –'

'A Greek!'

'Yes, from Delphi Duetti. Of course both families dis-
approved, so they changed their names – called
themselves Takeris. Had lots of children, in defiance of
everyone, including six boys, who continued the habit of
defying parents by becoming perfectly ordinary merchant
crewmen who married late and had few children. This
girl is his great-granddaughter – her father was a son of
the second son, and his wife died young, leaving him
with one daughter. He was killed by the NewTex that
boarded *Elias Madero*, and the girl captured.'

Goonar listened, trying to find some connection with the news he'd brought from Kaim. Laisa went on.

'At the time we heard about the ambush, we didn't know that. The original connection's name was off our books. Then Aunt Herdion saw a news report and thought the newsie had misspelled Terakian. You know what she's like – she got on the com, all ready to chew bones. They gave her all the information they had, just to get her off their backs. Shortly after the rescue, when the newsies reported Hazel's survival, she barged into the remaining Takeris family discussion of Hazel's future, and insisted on having a say. In fact, she was all set to adopt the girl herself. They're not too happy with her, but they're also not rich, so her offer to pay for Hazel's education sweetened the deal.'

'Yes, but what does this have to do with rejuvenation drugs and rejuv psychosis?'

'Not much – but you need to know that, to understand some recent decisions by the Family Council, which will affect everything from the contracts we take to the way we select crew. The Family Council hadn't paid much attention to your report from Zenebra about the NewTex saboteurs there, but now they consider that the NewTex forms a possible serious threat to Terakian Shipping specifically, because of the way we have been casual about picking up replacement crew. And because you and Basil caught that agent on Zenebra. There's also concern about spies in shipping agents' staffs. They're convinced that the raiders knew about the *Elias Madero*'s deviation from its filed flight plan.'

Goonar snorted. 'I'd say half the merchanters who work in that area know about that shortcut.'

'No more. At least, not Terakian ships. We're restricted from anything but green-lined routes –'

'That'll put paid to our fast-courier service –'

'Yes, but we won't be subject to piracy. At least not that kind of piracy.'

'So — what about this rejuvenation stuff? I still think we need to suck some data off the financial ansibles —'

'We have. I'm not sure what it all means, though.' Laisa handed him several cubes. 'That one's from Benedictus, and this one's Caskadar three weeks ago. We'll suck it again on the way out.'

'Where are we going?'

'Where God and the Fathers will. I haven't been told yet.'

Goonar settled down to data analysis. While the price of rejuv drugs had bounced up and down with every rumor of contamination or scarcity, the price of the raw materials had been growing . . . slowly at first . . . since the Patchcock mess. Somebody was buying the stuff, in quantity. Rejuv drugs used some of the same raw materials as many other pharmaceuticals, but some were unique to that process. He highlighted them – the prices rose steadily. So . . . somebody was buying, and presumably using the raw materials to make the finished drugs, for which they had – or expected to have – a market.

He kept digging, paused to eat, slept awhile, and woke to Laisa's call. 'We have the new squirt.'

He rubbed his eyes and groaned. 'And a destination, O beauteous one?'

'Marfalk.'

Marfalk. An obscure world; he'd heard the name but knew nothing about it. 'How long?'

'Eight days, about.'

'I'm going back to sleep.'

But he didn't sleep; the new data he hadn't seen kept him awake. Finally he rolled out of the bunk, muttering curses in four languages, and punched it in.

'You didn't tell me you intercepted a memo,' he said to Laisa over the shipcom.

'You were sleepy,' she said.

'Not now.' It had been encrypted, but *Flavor*'s systems were designed to handle all the standard commercial encryption schemata. Under the first level of encryption was another – as usual, simpler. The decryption machine made short work of that, too. Then, finally, the code. Goonar looked at it, and let his mind freewheel. Whose code was it? Something about it looked familiar . . . then it came to him. Conselline senior family branch. His breath came short. 'Laisa . . . do we have a code chip for Conselline senior branch?'

'Not on board. Is that what you think you've got?'

'Looks like it. We can start running it past the other chips, but I'm betting on that one.' He tipped his head one way, then the other. The Conselline memo looked almost readable as it was, but he knew that was deceptive. Nothing was ever that simple. Then the pattern popped out at him, as if someone had outlined words in red ink.

CHAPTER EIGHT

CASTLE ROCK

Brun called the Mahoney residence and, for a wonder, George answered.

'George – it's Brun.'

'Oh . . . if you want my father, he's still not –'

'No, I know that. I was after you.'

'Brun, I'm sorry I didn't come to see you after your father – I mean, I've been so busy with Dad in the hospital –'

'I know, George. I'm not upset; I just need to talk to you.'

'Um . . . I should tell you, I've been going out with your cousin.' George, of all people, sounded embarrassed. And what did this have to do with his father's injuries, her father's assassination, or the political situation? Still, she knew what to do with that opening.

'Seriously?'

'Looks that way. We're both in law school.'

'Which cousin?' Brun had a sudden cold worry that this was the leak through which Harlis had gained information.

'Not Harlis's – Jessamine's.'

Her mother's sister's child. The one she had dismissed so blithely back on Sirialis, the first year the girl came for hunting. 'Sydney?'

George laughed. 'No, that's her older sister. This is Veronica. What did you want, Brun?'

'Information, of course. Where is everyone in our crowd and what's going on. Since I got back . . . things have happened too fast, and you're the only one here I can ask without getting a lecture.'

'Ronnie and Raffa are off pioneering – you knew that, didn't you?'

'Yes, though I still think they're crazy. Do you know where?'

'Some dismal colony world; I can look it up if you want. I send mail via the Development Office – rather, I did at first, but they don't answer. What with law school –'

'Never mind, George. I hope your father's better soon.'

'It's – he's not like himself at all, Brun. I remember when you were getting Lady Cecelia out . . . I never realized what it's like when someone you know doesn't even seem to recognize you. And he can't talk; he just makes these noises –'

She didn't want to think about that. She couldn't, and stay reasonable.

'George, I'm so sorry. If it's all right, I'll call again – we should stay in touch.'

'All right.' He sounded tired, worried, miserable. Brun felt guilty for a moment, but then turned her mind to the more pressing problem of finding out what was going on in politics. She still didn't expect anything much to happen in the Grand Council meeting, but it was always better to be prepared. She checked the directory her mother had left with her, frowning as one name after another came up absent. Apparently a lot of people thought nothing much was going to happen, and had not bothered to stay on Castle Rock and find out.

Brun slipped her card into the slot, unlocking her chair's displays and communications, and settled into her chair. Aside from the formal presentation, when she became old enough to have a Seat, she had not been to any meetings, and none of her dreams in the years since had involved taking part in a routine Council meeting.

At the far end of their Family table, her uncle Harlis glowered at her, then leaned over to speak to her cousin Kell. Well, she already knew she could expect no help from him. She smiled, trying for the serenity that had always been her mother's trademark.

The Ministers straggled in, no longer in the formal robes she remembered – when had they quit wearing them? Had her father put an end to it?

Hobart Conselline stood at the Speaker's podium. Brun blinked, surprised. The Conselline family had lost ground in the wake of the Patchcock scandal, because the Morrelines were in their sept. Even though no one could prove that the Consellines had known about it, other Families had taken advantage of the opportunity to take market share from the largest and wealthiest of the septs. When had they regained their influence? And what did it mean? She skimmed the minutes of the emergency meeting after her father's death.

As she adjusted the viewer to bring each face into focus, she noticed something odd. To the Speaker's right, the Ministers' faces expressed suppressed glee mingled with impatience and even anger. To his left, the faces seemed lifeless, sodden with despair.

What was going on? She looked around for anyone she

knew, who might give her a clue, but she had been away
too long. The seating arrangements had rotated again; no
one was where she expected. She called up the seating
chart. No one – wait – Sarah's older sister Linnet had a
chair one row over and four up. She entered the callcode,
and her own name. The screen lit, and letters appeared.
Good to have you back, Brun.

Thanks she entered, then glanced at Linnet, who
smiled and nodded. *Any idea what's going on today?*

Yes, but I won't put it onscreen. We'll talk at the break.

That was clear as mud. Brun glanced over; Linnet
nodded again, this time without smiling. Well . . . she
would have to figure it out for herself. She referred again
to the desk's databank. The unhappy Ministers first . . .
her father's appointees, she realized by the dates. The
longest in office. Foreign Affairs, Cabby DeLancre. Minor
family, but a good solid man she knew her father
respected. Defense, Irion Solinari. Another minor
family – her father had long promoted the view that
minor families should take their turn in major roles. The
Clerk-Minister, Emilie Sante-Foin, who supervised the
clerical staff.

The gleeful ones were all new. Her father had
appointed one, at the Council meeting just before his
death: Elory Sa-Consell, Legislative Affairs. A Conselline,
but one Kevil had recommended – she'd found that in her
father's papers. The others had been appointed at the
emergency session held immediately after her father's
death. A new Minister of Internal Security, to replace
Pauli de Marktos, who had obviously just failed in his
duty, and whose offer to resign had been accepted so
swiftly. Bristar Anston Conselline. A new Legal Advisor,
replacing Kevil Mahoney: Sera Vesell. Born a Conselline,
Brun noted with a quick flick of the data to the bio section. Judicial Affairs: instead of Clari Whitlow, who had

held the post since before Kemtre's abdication, Norum Radsin, whom even Brun had heard of as a troublemaker in the legal profession. Colonial Affairs: Davor Vraimont.

So . . . it looked like a Conselline coup. In that case, why was her uncle looking so complacent? Did he not see it, or had he known already?

The excitement started before the meeting. Kemtre Altmann, the former king, came forward to stand in front of the Table. He had evidently rejuved again since she'd seen him last; he looked smooth and healthy, with only a decorative streak of white in his hair, though there was still the faint suggestion of a drooping eagle to his posture. Shocked murmurs followed him, and finally died away.

'I yield the floor to our beloved former king,' Harlis Conselline said in a voice that practically dripped butter.

'Thank you,' Kemtre said. 'I just want to ask you all to put the realm – the Familias – first, as you think about the issues before us. There's been a lot of dissension, a lot of anger, a lot of conflict among us –'

There had? Brun had heard nothing of it from her father in their brief time together, but perhaps he had concealed it from her.

'We need to think about the good of the whole Familias Regnant,' Kemtre was saying. 'In the face of all the threats to our stability, we must not fall prey to internal bickering. The welfare of all is more important than any petty personal grievances.'

From somewhere behind, Brun heard an angry exclamation. Across the chamber, a man stood up and yelled, 'Don't you start, Viktor!'

Brun scrabbled at the databank controls trying to figure out who these people were, even as Kemtre bowed and made his way back up the aisle to a sprinkling of applause, clearly stronger in some areas than others.

Viktor – that had to be Viktor Barraclough, a distant relative, the eldest of the elder branch of the Sept, though not the elected head of the Family – and the other man – she looked again at the seating chart. Alfred Sebastian Morreline-Contin.

Political instincts she had not known she possessed told her the whole thing was a setup . . . Hobart Conselline had pulled a coup, and Kemtre appealed for unity because he knew there was none. And her uncle Harlis was not surprised or dismayed, as he should have been when a rival Family grabbed so much power, which meant that he had known ahead of time. He had been bought, with what coin she thought she knew.

Contested inheritances were heard in the Court of Wills, and the Minister of Judicial Affairs had the right to appoint justices to that court. Hobart's new Minister had promised Harlis a deal.

Rage blurred her vision a moment, as Hobart stood up and began speaking . . . something about this sad occasion and the need for clear direction. Hobart's voice had an unpleasant tone – monotonous and yet insistent – which made it hard to listen to the sense of what he was saying. Brun's mind drifted to the odd division of expressions on the Ministers' faces. She had never missed Kevil more. He would have known why Emilie Sante-Foin glowered and Davor Vraimont smirked. With a few low-voiced phrases, he could have made clear the relationship between Vraimont Industrial Arts and the opportunities implicit in being the Colonial Affairs Minister.

Buttons came down the long aisle to the table; Harlis glared, and Buttons nodded. Then he smiled at Brun, with the weary amity of someone who is too exhausted to fight.

'I'm sorry business kept me away –' he murmured.

'It's not your fault,' Brun said. 'Someone had to keep things going. I'm glad you did.'

He looked surprised at that. What had he thought she'd say? Scold him for not rushing to her side?

'Have you seen the agenda?'

'No – it wasn't posted. Mother said it was, but I couldn't find it.'

'What are you whispering about?' Harlis said in a harsh voice. 'It's almost time for the meeting.' He looked as confident as Buttons had looked worried, and his gaze passed over Brun with none of the affection he had once lavished on her younger self. She doubted she could flirt him into her camp now. His son Kell leered at her, the sneer on his face making clear what he was thinking about.

'My brother and I were exchanging greetings,' Brun said. 'Do you have a problem with that?'

Buttons laid a hand on her wrist; she ignored it.

'Well, he should have come earlier,' Harlis said.

'You never came at all,' Brun said, deliberately misinterpreting the temporal cue.

'I was at the funeral!' Harlis said, more loudly; other heads turned to look at him, and Hobart Conselline paused in his speech, glaring.

'I wasn't talking about the funeral,' Brun said, her voice deliberately lower. 'Before. When I first got home.'

'Wasn't any need,' Harlis muttered, flushing.

Brun merely looked at him, until the gavel banged on the podium and the bell rang, signalling the end of the introductory speech.

'The first order of business,' Hobart said, 'is to vote on the proposed changes in the Corporate Bylaws.'

'I object!' That was Viktor Barraclough again. 'The proposals have not been submitted to the entire Council in sufficient advance –'

'You're out of order,' Hobart said. Brun could hear the gloat in his voice. 'Besides, these changes are familiar to everyone; I presented them last session —'

'And they were voted down,' Viktor said.

'You're out of order,' Hobart said again. 'If you inter-rupt again, I'll have you thrown out. Now sit down. If you have anything worthwhile to say, you may say it during the discussion period.'

Brun felt her muscles tightening and took a deep breath. She had never seen anything like this in the Grand Council. From the shocked looks around her, no one else had, either.

'The full text is available at 34-888-16,' Hobart went on. 'The annotations are at 35-888-29. Please try to follow along as I go over them.'

As if they were little children and Hobart Conselline their teacher. Brun called up the two files, and read quickly, with growing dismay. Proposal to limit the fran-chise to those presently Seated — offspring to be Seated as space allowed and in strict order of seniority. Proposal to take 'suitable measures' to meet the threat of Ageists . . . what threat? Proposal to create a special commission to investigate Ageist influence in the Regular Space Service, and another to investigate the inappropriate use of Space Service resources for private purposes. With a chill, Brun realized that this was aimed at her rescue. Proposal to restrict access of news media . . . to restrict public access to records of Grand Council meetings : . . to reduce the quorum for voting on Corporate Bylaws.

Every proposal had been presented before — the links told her when, and by whom — and had been voted down before. But that had been with time for discussion, with men like her father and Kevil Mahoney to explain why the proposals were not in the best interests of the Familias as a whole. She could remember, now she was sitting here, that on the occasion of her taking her Seat, Hobart Conselline had stood up to propose limiting the franchise. On that occasion, he'd said the influence of the Grand Council was being diluted by mere fertility — that the unSeated populace had lost respect for the Grand Council because all it took to get a Seat was being born to the right parents.

She sent a private message to Buttons: *Was he always like this?*

Ever since I've had a Seat, Buttons replied.

Brun tuned back in to what Hobart was saying.

'While no one would wish such a vicious attack on anyone, it is perhaps fortunate for Lord Thornbuckle that he cannot stand before us to justify his actions.'

Brun stiffened and glanced at Buttons. His expression did not change, but his stylus pushed his pad so hard that a red light came up on the margin.

'I am truly sorry,' Hobart went on, 'if this distresses his daughter, who has chosen this time to take her place among us —' The tone implied that her doing so was in the worst taste. 'But private feelings must defer to public weal, in this case.' He looked up at her Seat with an expression that made her want to wipe her face with a clean cloth. She expected the chamber to erupt in her defense — but no one moved or spoke. Hobart gave her a stiff little smile and nod, and went on.

'Since Lord Thornbuckle is dead, and cannot reply, some might consider it unnecessary to detail the charges that might have been brought against him. But I believe in full and fair disclosure. The changes I propose to the bylaws are not trivial, and you need to know why I would suggest something so drastic. The fact is, the Familias Regnant is sick, on its deathbed, and if we don't act quickly, the patient could die. Will die, I believe, without our intervention.'

Buttons muttered something Brun couldn't quite hear. She glanced at him; for an instant, with his mouth compressed, he looked exactly like his father in a rage.

A light flashed on the panel: someone asking for the floor. Hobart shook his head and went on. 'There's no time for discussion, we need to get this done, get it out of the way, so we can move forward.'

'There's always been time for discussion –' someone yelled loudly, from a few rows over. Brun queried her panel. Minor branch of the Dakkers Sept, coded turquoise in the Family database.

'That's the trouble, all we do is talk!' yelled someone else. Conselline, minor branch, Hobart's third younger brother.

A gabble of voices rose, and lights flashed on the panel. Hobart banged the gavel repeatedly and finally the turmoil died down. Brun, looking around, saw angry, flushed faces everywhere, all glaring tight-lipped at one another.

How had Hobart Conselline become Speaker? Brun raced through the database, trying to figure out the story behind the story. It had been the emergency Grand Council meeting, held in the hours after the assassination. Emergency meetings did not require the same quorum of Seats . . . so response was limited to those attending in person, or immediately available on an ansible link. Only 23.2 percent of the Grand Council had been polled. Naturally, Lord Thornbuckle's family had not been present or available, nor had most of their friends. Hobart Conselline had received a majority of votes cast, but it amounted to only 15.8 percent of the whole. Yet he was acting as if he had a large majority of the entire Council.

'Look behind the obvious,' one of Brun's instructors had taught her. 'Who benefits?' The Consellines, clearly, but how? They were already filthy rich – as rich or richer than the Barraclough Sept – so why this grab for power? What more did they want?

'We're going to vote now,' Hobart was saying. 'Right now, and get it behind us, so we can move on to important external issues.'

The warning chimes of Vote in Progress rang through the chamber, and Brun's screen lit with the proposals. Had Hobart really read through all of them? She struggled through the convoluted legalese, trying to figure out what they really meant. Kevil Mahoney had always said that legal language had more subtext than any fiction ever written, but she had not actually studied law. Some didn't look that bad; the reasoning as given had a plausible ring to it. She chewed on her lip, struggling to find the hidden meanings.

Safer to vote against all of them, just in case. She hoped that was safer. She entered her votes, and sat back to watch the others. Kell, tip of his tongue just showing, was marking his votes slowly, one by one. Harlis had finished. And Hobart Conselline . . . Hobart was watching *her*, she realized.

Time dragged on, as they waited for others to complete their votes. Most seemed to have had their minds made up ahead of time, but a few earnest souls were bent over their desks, clearly checking every word of every proposition, and comparing it to other texts.

The outcome of the voting was less a surprise than it might have been . . . the bylaws changes passed, and the next vote confirmed Hobart Conselline as Speaker for a normal term. The speeches had been confusing; on both sides of what was clearly becoming a deep division, speakers seemed choked with outrage, incoherent. Brun kept quiet, watching carefully and making notes. Buttons, she saw, did the same.

After the meeting ended, they went back to Appledale

in the same car, by mutual consent talking only of things they could see from its windows. After supper, they settled to business, and finally Brun's big brother treated her as an equal.

'I have to say I was impressed with your performance today.'

'I didn't do anything.'

'You didn't pout, flounce, flirt, or storm. You sat there being attentive, intelligent, and menacing.'

'Menacing?'

'Didn't you see our new Speaker watching you during the voting?'

'Yes. Made me itchy.'

'As well it should. The man's odd, Brun. Well – Mother's gone to Sirialis, I hear. Are you staying here?'

'For now, yes. I'd planned to be the person on site to deal with the Grand Council, unless you want to take it over.'

'Are you sure? Because if you can keep an eye on the Council, then I can concentrate on what our dear uncle was up to with the various family companies. It's hard without Kevil –'

'I'm sorry,' Brun said.

He looked at her a long moment, and she knew that he knew what she meant – sorry for everything, for becoming the issue by which the Family lost ground, as well as the reason for their father's assassination.

'Don't be sorry for being yourself,' Buttons said finally. 'And don't be sorry for coming back – it'd be worse if you hadn't.'

'I don't see how,' Brun said.

'I can think of a dozen ways,' Buttons said. 'And so can you, if you take the trouble. But that's not what matters right now. We've got attacks on all fronts – where'd you put the babies, by the way? I don't want them used as hostages against us.'

'Cecelia de Marktos took them somewhere. She's trustworthy –'

'Well, unless she puts them in a barn and tries to turn
them into racehorses,' Buttons said, with the first genuine
grin she'd seen on his face. 'Grooms, I wouldn't mind, but
you never know with her.'

Brun laughed aloud. 'You're right – but I don't think
she has them with her.'

'Good. As long as they aren't going to cause us trouble –'

'Not for another ten or twelve years . . . I don't want to
think about them as teenage boys. . . .'

'If we have a Familias Regnant in ten years, we can
worry about it then.' Brun glanced at him; his face had
gone somber, and he looked far older than his age.

'Buttons – do you agree with Hobart about that?'

'That the Familias is in danger, yes. That it's in danger
because of lax leadership in the past, no. It's his policies
that endanger it most. This business of restricting the
franchise – one way we've had of relieving strain between
Families is that the small know they can enlarge by
having more Seatholders. That's let them take in outsiders as clients. Dad said the movement of power from
one sept to another was a major factor in keeping the
Familias stable. That's why they instituted the kingship,
originally.'

'Why can't Hobart see it?' Brun asked.

'I don't know. Back when I was a boy of maybe ten –
and you were still in the nursery – I overheard some of
the adults talking about how the new rejuv methods
might change things politically. But of course, I was too
young to follow it. I remember Dad and Uncle Harlis
arguing, though. When I asked questions in school,
nobody seemed to understand them, and later, when I
was in the Royals, everyone talked as if the repeating

rejuvenations were just a way to stay young for a normal lifespan, not an actual extension. It was – oh, the year that Lepescu came to Sirialis, I think it was, that Charlie Windetsson got drunk at a mess dinner and pointed out that if our parents never grew old, we had no reason to grow up. There was no future for us. Everyone laughed, and drank, and – I remember a sort of cold chill. I left the party early, called Sarah, and that's when we decided to marry.'

'I didn't know that.'

'Well . . . you were being wild at the time. Most of our set were, and I suddenly saw it myself. Our parents had been more grown up – working in family business in some way – by the time they finished their education. Sometimes even before. But their parents barely lived past their Centuries, and retired from Family work in their eighties. The first rejuv upset that a little, but the new one . . . I came home, and talked to Dad about it. He promised that he and Mother would resign their duties while I was still young – he transferred stock to me right after that Hunt Ball, and encouraged me to be active in Council as well as business.'

'And I thought you'd gone all stuffy . . .'

'So I had. But I didn't want to go from childhood to childhood – rich enough to rejuv and be twenty or thirty all my life, with nothing to do. That's no way to live –'

'But Uncle Harlis,' Brun said. She wanted information, not a lecture on lifestyle. 'What about him?'

'He saw multiple rejuvs as a way of maintaining Family power. He wanted rejuv restricted to the Seated Families at first. So did some others, but the proposal didn't pass. Then he tried an age restriction: no one under eighty should be eligible. That didn't pass either, of course. The Ageists, who had used the biological problems with the earlier procedure to make repeated rejuvs illegal, expected his support with the new procedure, but he didn't go along.'

'So . . . you're saying the population grew?'

'Not just that. The birth rate in our set actually dropped, because people could wait to have children until they were fifty or sixty or older. It's the shape of the population that really changed, and the power structure. Age always did confer an advantage of experience, and now it could do so without losing any advantge of physical strength and energy. Younger people needed to find new opportunities because the old weren't dying – or even retiring. And of course people wanted rejuv, and especially when they found out how useful it was in some kinds of illness and injury. Everyone rich enough wanted it. And the Consellines wanted the profit.'

'Ummm . . . which meant expanding, somehow . . . like Dad's proposal to open new colonies?'

'As a temporary measure. Some others wanted to annex adjacent territories, but Dad opposed spatial expansion, on the grounds that we couldn't serve all we had. And why alienate neighbors when we had planets within the Familias outline which could be settled? But he wanted more support for colonies, too – he had been pushing the Colonial Office to make allowances for the less stable ecosystems of the worlds now being opened. That translates into concessions for the companies – and families – purchasing settlement licenses.'

Brun shook her head. 'I don't know enough to follow this.'

'Well, you can learn. Basically, the longer a world is allowed to stabilize after the terraforming treatments, the more easily it can be colonized. Until recently, this required such long-term investment that very few Families would attempt it. When the Familias Regnant came together, the Council agreed to a joint investment at one world a year. We only know how much better the old-treated planets are because of the Lost Worlds.'

'Paradise, Babylon, Oasis,' Brun said, to prove she was listening.

'Yes. All treated in the second wave of outreach, and all lost to the records for centuries in the Cluster Wars. So they had between seven and eight hundred years of stabilization after treatment. Nothing like the mature ecosystem of a planet in its natural state, but for human purposes vastly superior to most of the worlds we used . . . only now are others approaching the quality. The scouts who found Paradise found mature forests with 300-year-old timber . . . grasslands with deep soil, not a shallow dark layer . . . estuaries rich in shellfish rather than a few colonies that had still to be nurtured. A stable climate, reasonably predictable. Nobody had known what difference another five centuries could make. If we could let all terraformed planets have that long, colonists would have a much easier time. Not easy – it's never easy – but easier.'

'But temporary, you said. Was he thinking of enforcing a limit on reproduction, or on rejuv?'

'I'm not sure. He talked about both, from time to time. But the Familias is so complicated . . . you know, we have planets populated mostly by free-birthers, and others with mostly zero-growthers, and probably eight dozen religions, not even counting the fringes. Any policy one group approves will offend someone else. And meanwhile, the percentage of the population that had been rejuved was going up every year. Every survey taken showed that Rejuvenants wanted and expected to rejuv again.'

'I wonder how the Guernesi have handled it,' Brun said. 'They've had the process as long as we have, and they aren't falling apart.'

'I don't know . . . it's a good question. Do they have our diversity of beliefs?'

'And I don't know that one.' Brun shook her head. 'This is seriously complicated stuff, Buttons.'

'It's a seriously complicated universe, and we're right in the middle of a whirlpool if we don't figure it out.' He gave her a long, steady look. 'You're a grownup now, and you've volunteered for the job of being Council watchdog for our family. This is what it takes.'

'Being a dizzy blonde was such *fun*,' Brun said, but her heart wasn't in it.

JESSAMYN ESSENCE, ESSENTIAL TRANSPORT LTD.

In the working passengers' mess, the men had played the newsvid cube of the assassination and aftermath three times already without more than a few muttered cuss-words. Then one of them, the oldest, shut off the player.

'So we're too late and somebody got 'im first, so what do we do?' His glance challenged them.

'Git the rest of 'em. If he's dead maybe they won't be watchin' so close. I could take that yellow-haired slut.'

'I keep thinkin' about the chillen, Dan . . . by rights, they should be our'n.'

'Ben's right,' another said. 'Somebody stomps the rat-tler's head, no matter how it thrashes around it's not gonna attack nobody. We don't need to be goin' around killin' people like criminals. But gettin' our chillen back, that's a good thing to do.'

'But how're we gonna find 'em? Sposin' they've already been sent to new homes?'

Dan held up his hand. 'We don't know that yet. First thing is, we'll look for 'em in a group. Prob'ly we'll hear, if we keep our ears open. Every port we come to. Now mind – nobody gets drunk, like that idiot on Zenebra –'

They all knew about that; a whole shipload had been captured. 'No fights, no arguments. We have a mission – a new mission – and that's the rules. Got it?'

'Yessir.'

The next day, the *Jessy* came into Goldwyn Station, and the working passengers debarked after checking off their assignments with the captain. For once, the captain thought, working passengers had actually worked – without complaint – and he added the optional minimal pay chit to their goodbye handshake. Whatever anyone said about fanatics, he always liked to hire the pious brotherhoods, because he could count on them to work hard and keep their fingers off the cargo.

The Goldwyn spacers services section, or S-3, offered a variety of cheap lodging, food, and drink. This was an all-civilian station, rarely visited by R.S.S. ships, and the diversity of Familias spacefaring cultures showed up in decor and cuisine both. The men followed their noses to something with a familiar smoky-meat odor, and settled at one long table. On one wall, a newsvid showed scenes from some business meeting, but they didn't recognize any of the faces or references. Then a face they did recognize, a blonde woman with short curly hair.

'– Any comments on the outcome of the meeting, Sera Meager-Thornbuckle?' The announcer's accent was hard to follow.

'No . . . you realize our family is still in mourning . . .' The blonde woman's accent was, if possible, worse.

'Yes, Sera, but what do you think of a Conselline as Speaker?'

'Excuse me –' She turned away, and the camera followed showing her getting into a long dark-maroon car.

'Damn,' one of the men said. 'It's *her*!'

'You men are all the same.' That was a waitress in red

checks and blue denim, slapping menus down in front of them. 'Just because she's young and rich and pretty —'

'We'll have chili,' Dan said. 'All of us — a bowl of chili each and some crackers.' His glance silenced the others, who looked ready to say things they must not say.

'An' some beer?' the waitress asked.

'No . . . not yet, anyway.' Not until they'd found out what they wanted, where the women and children were. If they could find them and bring them home — even some of them — they'd be honored among men, maybe even more than if they'd managed to kill the Speaker themselves. That would stop the Rangers of Texas True from saying they were nothing but a bunch of wifeless drifters causing trouble.

'Look —' Ben touched Dan's arm and nodded at the newsvid. There it was again, the picture that had infuriated them all — women and children in the traditional clothes walking down a corridor from a ship's hatch, guarded by battle-armored troops of the Familias Fleet.

Dan had trouble following the accent of the newsvid announcer, but he did understand Baskar Station. Was that where the women were in the picture, or where they were now? He didn't know, but they could always go and find out. Somewhere there'd be a bar, and men talking, and someone would know, if he asked the right questions.

CHAPTER NINE

CASTLE ROCK, OLD PALACE

Hobart Conselline ran his hand over the wide gleaming surface of the desk – *his* desk now, as it had been Bunny Thornbuckle's, and before that Kemtre Altmann's – and felt a glow of satisfaction. His Delphine now had the suite Miranda had occupied, and to him had come every perquisite he had once envied, from the skilled silent staff to the deference of those who had been his peers, and were now his subordinates.

He had worried, when he saw Brun and Buttons both at the Thornbuckle tables, but neither of them had offered to speak. And however they had voted, the count had gone his way. Their own uncle supported him – for a specific reason, but that didn't matter. He would have appointed new ministers for legal affairs and internal affairs anyway; he would have appointed new judges. There were certain legal actions in progress within his own sept which made that prudent. If Harlis benefitted, and assumed it was all for his own benefit, well – that was a cheap profit, and he had never scorned a cheap profit in his life.

He leaned back in the chair and gave himself up to reverie for a few minutes. He was relatively young, and with the aid of repeated rejuvenations he would remain young . . . and powerful. They had seen what happened with a succession of Speakers, generations back, and then what happened when they made leadership hereditary, with the Altmanns. Prosperity had followed prosperity, an upward trend with only minor adjustments. But no one had yet seen what he would show them: the stability and wealth that would come with one leader who would never fade into senility. Year after year, decade after decade, he would be there to serve and protect . . . to guide and lead. . . .

His desk chimed at him, and he sat up, scowling. That was the future, but now he had to deal with the problems his predecessors had left him.

'Milord, Colonel Bai-Darlin, head of the Special Security Unit, would like a meeting.'

'Send him in.' He would show them how hard a real leader worked. He would be tireless for the good of the realm, as he had always been tireless for the good of his Family, and his sept. And realistically speaking, given the importance of his sept in the economy of the realm, what was good for the Consellines could not help but be good for the rest – at least most of them.

Bai-Darlin came in with a crisp salute and heel-click that convinced Hobart the man was efficient. But was he smart? Was he tireless?

'Milord, I thought you might like to be brought up to date on the investigation into the death of Lord Thornbuckle –'

'It was those NewTex terrorists,' Hobart said. 'I can't imagine why you haven't caught them yet.'

'Milord, the preliminary investigations have found no trace of anyone from any of the worlds on which they operate being on Castle Rock since the Rangers were brought to this system for trial.'

'Then the investigators are incompetent! What does it take, a bright red stripe painted on someone's head? They threatened to kill the Speaker, and the Speaker was shot. What more do you want?'

Bai-Darlin looked at him in a way that made Hobart feel uncomfortable. 'Evidence, for a start.'

'You have evidence; Lord Thornbuckle's dead body. The damage done to Ser Mahoney, to the vehicle.'

'Yes, milord, but none of that points to the New Texas Godfearing Militia. We have no indication, on travel manifests, on hotel registers, that they were here.'

'If they weren't here, they must have hired someone.'

'According to our best sources, they do not hire criminals to work for them, and what we know about the types of weapons used does not fit with them either. They like direct confrontation; they would be far more likely to walk up to an intended victim on the street.'

'Excuses,' Hobart said firmly. 'Although, if it wasn't the Militia, I can think of another disruptive element it might be.'

'Yes, milord? Anything you could suggest –'

'Ageists,' Hobart said. 'Lord Thornbuckle was a Rejuvenant, and so was his wife, a multiple.' Bai-Darlin's gaze shifted to Hobart's ear. Hobart shook his head. 'These are jewelry, Colonel. I support rejuvenation, of course; any sensible man does. And a man in my position must wear his colors, so to speak. I will rejuvenate when I need to, in another ten years or so; I'm quite a bit younger than Lord Thornbuckle was. In the meantime, these rings –' he touched his ear – 'these rings reassure the older rejuvenants that I am serious when I support their interests.'

'I see, sir. And you think it possible that Ageists

assassinated Lord Thornbuckle because he was rejuvenated? Does this mean that you think they will attack you?'

'I don't think it was Ageists – I think it was the
NewTex Militia, as I told you. But if I'm wrong about
that, I'd look at the Ageists next.'

Bai-Darlin did not look convinced. 'I was hoping,
milord, that you might share some insights into possible
elements among the Seated Families . . . perhaps Lord
Thornbuckle had aroused a particular animosity there?
He seemed a popular Speaker, but there's always someone . . .'

Hobart waved his hand. 'Minor resentments perhaps.
Certainly there were those who felt he misused Familias
resources in going after his daughter the way he did. A
number of us thought so, and expressed ourselves at the
time. But I'm not aware – and I wouldn't be, necessarily,
since I've little to do with the internal workings of
Barraclough Sept – of anything serious enough to cause
someone to kill him.'

'Very good, sir. Thank you, milord, for your time.'

'Catch those killers, Colonel, and I'll see you get a
medal.' Instead of the eager grin Hobart expected, Bai-
Darlin gave him a dark, brooding look before turning
away. Strange fellow. Perhaps not as efficient as he had
seemed.

Several days later, Hobart found himself glaring at the
same desk he had coveted so much. That was the natural
result of having to deal with obstructive fools, he told
himself. A man had a right to have Ministers he could
work with. Why should any of Bunny Thornbuckle's
appointees expect to stay in office, if they were going to
cause him trouble? They should have learned from
his first dismissals and replacements, but they still
obstructed him. They would have to go, root and branch;

he was not going to deal with any more of this insubordination.

Hobart considered his options. Who should be replaced first? Defense had been making noises lately about rejuvenation in the enlisted ranks, something about aged NCOs going crazy or something. Their idiot medical branch had put a hold on all rejuvenations, and seemed to be determined to investigate thoroughly. He'd pointed out to Irion Solinari that it would be expensive and inefficient to hold a prolonged investigation into something like that, and that it would be better to cut their losses and simply discharge the affected personnel as medically unfit. But Solinari argued – Solinari did nothing *but* argue, Hobart thought, remembering that Solinari had also argued with Bunny, who had appointed him. Just a difficult personality, and not one suited to a responsible position like Minister of Defense.

If Solinari went – if he had his own choice in as Defense, then . . . he could also ease out the more difficult of the admirals. Perhaps *their* rejuvenations would fail? Those had all been done with the original Guernesi drugs, so if they failed it would take the burden of public opinion off the Patchcock connection. They didn't actually have to fail, if only Fleet could be persuaded to take them off active duty out of concern about the rejuvenations. Right now the medical branch and senior officers were being completely unreasonable, and Solinari was backing them up – or stirring them up, he wasn't sure which. Solinari definitely had to go.

He opened his private pad and began drafting a letter to Solinari, explaining his reasoning. He didn't want to be harsh, but the man had to realize that he just was not qualified. And even if he had been, his negative attitude, his contentious nature, made him unfit. More in sorrow than anger, Hobart told himself, was the tone he wanted

to take. Not that Solinari had any friends worth worrying
about. A bunch of backbiting, acid-tongued nonentities in
the minor families, that was all. They'd soon find out
what they were dealing with.

Admiral Vida Serrano rarely concerned herself with civilian matters, unless they seemed likely to precipitate a
war. The change from one head of state to another should
have been – usually was – a matter of ceremony and
speeches, which affected the Regular Space Service no
more than the change from one Grand Admiral to
another.

Certainly Lord Thornbuckle's assassination had been
shocking, but she expected that it wouldn't make much
difference in the long run. Someone else would be
elected, a few Ministers might change, and the inertia of
the very large organization would keep everything going
very much as usual. What could be frustrating when she
wanted to make a change reassured her when she wanted
stability. Her business, as she saw it, was to make sure her
command was ready to deal with any exterior threat,
which might see the momentary confusion as an opportunity to cause trouble.

To that end, she had put herself on the list for updates
on the rejuvenation problem, and had come to the same
conclusion as the first blue-ribbon panel charged with
investigating it. A bad batch of rejuvenation drugs, pur-
chased because they were slightly less expensive, and
almost certainly manufactured at the Patchcock plant she
had seen. The solution was also clear: repeat rejuvenations with clean drugs for those who had not yet suffered
significant damage, and supportive care for those who
had, for whom another rejuvenation would mean prolon-
gation of senile misery. She had cosigned the report,
when it was forwarded upstairs, and had also cosigned a

letter suggesting that the manufacturer bear the expense of the repeat rejuvenations and the supportive care.

And nothing had been done. The update list had disappeared; she'd asked Headquarters, and been told it was 'discontinued pending investigation of security problems.' She'd heard rumors that one of the big independent research labs was itself under investigation for possible falsification of evidence and misuse of public funds. Headquarters had suddenly cut off funding for repeat rejuvenations, without explaining why. Surely they understood how important it was – Fleet needed those people back at work, not to mention the individuals' own need to be saved from senility and death. Vida approved as many rejuvenations as she could out of her discretionary fund, but she didn't have the money for all of them. She thought of contacting Marta Katerina Saenz, whose pharmaceuticals she trusted. But Headquarters had put a gag order on rejuvenation; she wasn't even supposed to discuss it internally. Going outside would be grounds for court-martial, if she were found out.

She wished she knew where all this nonsense was coming from. Was it someone in Fleet? Someone in the government? The Grand Council meeting the day after the funeral had elected Hobart Merethal Conselline as the new head of government, and he had appointed some new people to various defense-related committees. But Irion Solinari was still Minister of Defense, and he'd always been solid. She toyed with the idea of contacting him directly, but admirals who got involved with Ministers went up like a rocket and down like the stick, in her experience. It was almost as bad for a career as marrying into a Seated Family.

Most of these new appointees were only names to Vida Serrano. The Con.sellines and Morrelines had been involved in the Patchcock mess – everyone knew that much – but she had searched the databases a long time to find Hobart Merethal Conselline, and then the only information she could get was a short official biography on the occasion of his taking his Seat in Council. Nothing in it indicated why the other Families would choose him, unless it were a general desire to repudiate Thornbuckle and all his friends.

She had reached this point in what had become an all-too-familiar reverie when her clerk called.

'Admiral – there's a courier here from Headquarters with a hand-carry.'

Hand-carries were an outdated pain, in Vida's opinion, but some of the mossybacks at Headquarters believed in them. Especially the Chief of Personnel. Maybe it was the information she'd requested on the progress of other sectors in returning their rejuvenated senior NCOs to active duty.

'Send 'em in,' she said.

To her surprise, Heris Serrano's acquaintance, Commander Livadhi . . . Arash? Aram? . . . came in with the case under his arm. Not commander, she realized, as the obviously new star on his collar twinkled. Admiral minor.

'Congratulations,' she said. 'I hadn't heard about your promotion.' She hadn't heard that a promotion board was even meeting. She should have heard. Another tiny alarm rang in her head.

'Admiral, I'm sorry to be the bearer of bad news, but thank you anyway.' He looked shamefaced, almost as if he wanted to dig a guilty toe in her carpet.

'Excuse me?' He might be an admiral minor, but she was an admiral major, and she made the words a challenge.

'I don't know if you heard that we have a new Minister of Defense –'

'No! Solinari's out?' A major alarm, now.

'Yes. Out and gone – nobody had a chance to talk to him; the word is he left Castle Rock and went home, and he's not giving interviews to anyone.'

'I see.' What had they done to Solinari, who had never shrunk from interviews, who had spoken his mind in spite of everyone? What could send a Solinari back to – what was that world he'd come from? – and put a lock on his tongue? She felt cold, considering.

'The short of it is that the new Speaker didn't like what Solinari told him about the rejuvenation problem, and he's appointed someone who will do what he's told without question. The new Speaker does not believe that the problem with NCO rejuvenations is entirely the fault of the pharmaceuticals –'

'Of course it is,' Vida said. 'The data clearly show –'

'Data can be manipulated,' Livadhi said. 'The Speaker seems convinced that the data *were* manipulated, perhaps by special interest groups influencing scientists in the research facilities.'

'He *wants* the data manipulated,' Vida said, anger rising in her like a storm.

'That's not for me to say,' Livadhi said. He paused, and Vida stared at him, taking in the warning she'd just been given.

'And what else, then?'

'Given the possibility, yet to be investigated, that the failure of the NCO rejuvenations was not entirely due to problems with the drugs, but to some idiosyncratic response . . . right now, they're talking about the level of inbreeding in Fleet families, I understand, though you didn't hear that from me.'

'As if *their* families weren't inbred!'

'We are not Registered Embryos . . . so they said.' He waited, while she seethed quietly, then went on. 'Given that possibility, they say, then there is concern about the stability of rejuvenations of senior officer personnel as well. It has been decided that all rejuvenations of Fleet personnel must be investigated thoroughly, beginning with those of flag rank.'

'They can't be serious!' Vida Serrano stiffened in her chair.

'Yes, sir, they are. They've extended the medical hold to all personnel – officers included, and specifically including flag officers – whose rejuvenations are more than ten years old. They're to be relieved of active duty until medical evaluations are complete.'

'But –'

'Admiral, I know it's unprecedented.' To his credit, Livadhi looked almost as unhappy as she felt. If he felt any triumph, he was concealing it well. 'This whole mess is unprecedented. It is leave with pay – at least, full pay for those below commander, half-pay for those above.'

'Which is nearly every officer involved.' Vida scowled. 'Besides, they *know* my rejuv is stable. I was one of the first – it's been over twenty-five years –'

'Yes, sir, but –'

'And who do they think is going to take over, all of a sudden? The losers they didn't want to waste rejuv on? Or even promote? No – don't answer that. I didn't say it; you didn't hear it. Blast!' This was how Livadhi had been promoted, and she was sure that other commanders were even at this moment pinning on the stars they had not expected to receive for another half decade or so. She wondered briefly if Heris had become the newest Admiral Serrano.

Vida swung her chair away from her desk, staring through the bulkhead into decades of memory. All lay clear to her inward sight, vista after vista, crisp images, faces, names, relationships. They were wrong – they had to be wrong. Nothing blurred her mind. She swung back. 'Fine, then. I'll take myself off duty, hike down to Medical, they can take a look and put me back on.'

'No, sir. Please – would the admiral look at the orders?'

'Which you didn't draft, I presume. All right.' She looked at them, read them carefully, every word of every old-fashioned paper sheet.

Worse than bad. Mandatory immediate release from active duty. Immediate replacement by officers speci- fied – in her case, Admiral minor Livadhi. Immediate surrender of all communications devices, encryption/ decryption devices, data access devices . . .

'I'm not – I'm sorry, Admiral, I think it's unreasonable and ridiculous to make flag officers leave their quarters and their duty stations so fast –'

'Makes sense if someone really wants us gone, though,' Vida said. She was past the first flash of anger now, and her brain had moved into combat-speed computation. 'Rush us out, make sure we can't contact our friends still on active duty except by monitored channels, make sure we have no access to files –'

'I have a room in the Transient Officers' Bay,' Livadhi said. 'I see no reason to enforce this to the letter –'

Vida looked up and caught sympathy on his face. Heris had said he had his good points. 'Don't you? Then you're more a fool than I ever thought, young man. When the wind changes, so must the sails. If you don't enforce your orders, you won't last long. I'll be out of here by the deadline.'

'Yes, but – I'm not even sure what I'm supposed to do –' That was almost plaintive. Vida gave him a wide Serrano grin, full teeth, and he paled, the freckles stand- ing out.

'You'll do your job, son, the same way I did mine – and learn it the same way too. Scary to get what you always wanted, isn't it? Now if you'll excuse me, I need to clear my desk.' She punched for her clerk. 'Sandy — come on in; we have a situation.'

Within the hour, she had started the process that would transfer command of Sector Seven to Admiral minor Livadhi. No big change-of-command ceremony, because there was no time for it if they were to make the deadline. She called in her staff, advised them of the orders, and had them start briefing Livadhi, who had just come from Sector Five, about the peculiarities of Sector Seven. While they did so, she began peeling out her personal files from the official ones stored under her codes. She would definitely take with her the files on rejuvenation, for instance — should she offer Livadhi copies? No. If he were found to have them, he might get in trouble. What about the scant information she'd collected on the new powers in the Grand Council? Maybe. Lists of family members on active duty, people from whom she might legitimately — well, almost legitimately — seek information . . . all the Admirals Serrano had been rejuved, so all would be affected. From Davor, now a third-year at the Academy, to Gossin — her nose wrinkled at the thought of trying to work with Gossin, who was one of the rare light-skinned Serranos (though that was only the most obvious of her problems) — the list included nineteen — no, seventeen, because Heris's parents had just retired. Barin's mother was still on active duty, but his father had retired to take over as the Serrano family's agent.

Her com chimed. She punched it live. 'Vida? It's Gadar Livadhi. Have you heard this ridiculous order taking rejuved admirals off duty?'

'Just saw the orders, Gadar,' she said. 'One of yours brought them to me, in fact. Nice shiny new star young Arash has.'

'Well . . . what are we going to do about it?'

'I don't know about you, but I'm going to take myself off active duty. Were you one of the experimentals too?'

'Yes, and there's not a thing wrong with my brain but the smoke coming off it from this nonsense.'

'Gadar – this is no time –'

'– To start trouble. I know. But at a time like this, with Thornbuckle gone, we need experienced leaders.'

'If we've done our job, our juniors can take over.' She knew she didn't believe that, and Gadar's snort told her he didn't believe it either.

'You're an optimist. By the way, what do you hear from Copper Mountain?'

'Nothing,' Vida said. 'Should I?'

'Well . . . you know my brother Arkad's in the judicial division . . .'

'Yes . . .'

'He's been investigating the records of prisoners sent to Copper Mountain's secure facilities – that Stack Islands thing – because that's one of the places that Lepescu stashed your niece's crew.'

Vida noted Livadhi's turn of phrase. Run hot, run cold, that was Livadhi. 'And . . .?'

'And he turned up something interesting. Lepescu's juniors – the ones too far down to have been caught with their hands in the honey jar after he was killed – have been cycling through Stack Islands. Not as prisoners, but as guards. Not all the guards, of course, but some of them.'

'Oh . . . my.'

'If you wanted to recruit desperate and dangerous personnel – even those who serve their terms and aren't discharged are going to have that mark against them – you could hardly do better than to start there.'

'And you think they're up to something, of course. Any idea what?'

'Another mutiny – perhaps a breakaway –'

'In service to whom? What kind of financial backing do they have?'

'I haven't been able to find out anything. I've always rather wondered if Lepescu wasn't close to the Morrelines, given his involvement in Patchcock –'

'He made things worse – the whole thing rebounded –'

'Yes – but in the long run, it cemented Morreline control. Got the Familias as a whole bad publicity –'

'You didn't say anything about that at the time,' Vida said.

'No. I didn't realize it at the time. I was all the way over in One, chatting up those Lone Star Confederation diplomats. I hate staff rotations.' Vida didn't rise to that bait, and eventually Livadhi went on. 'It's only recently, after your – mmm – adventure there, that I began looking into it.'

'Well, there's nothing we can do now but go home like good little children,' Vida said. 'I hope they realize what an opportunity this is for foreign interests. Not to say anything against your family member, Gadar, but your new admiral minor almost turned up his toes when he realized he was about to be responsible for the sector most likely to be attacked by the NewTex Militia, with only thirty-six hours of OJT.'

'My heart bleeds,' Gadar said. 'I hope these are only temporary ranks, because the instant they check us out medically, I'm going to be back in my office.'

'I hope it's quick,' Vida said. 'But if someone wanted to get rid of us – or some of us – all they'd have to do is delay the medical.'

'You Serranos are so cheerful!' he said.

'You Livadhis are so lively,' she said, and cut the connection.

*

Vida could not remember a time in her adult life when she had had nothing specific to do for days on end. She'd taken leave, of course, but she'd always had plans. A trip to take, a course, a family crisis that needed her time and talents. She had money enough – she hadn't spent all her salary since she made lieutenant, and her investments had prospered. She could live quite well on half-pay. It was the idleness that bothered her, the sense of being cut off from her family.

Well . . . she'd go home, then, to the Serrano compound on Melander, that source of all – or at least many – of the Serrano family.

Making reservations on a civilian ship was annoying; she tried to laugh at herself for expecting people to jump when she said hop, but it wasn't easy. She'd so often thought of civilians as disorganized, but when you didn't have a staff . . . she grumbled at herself repeatedly, as she arranged to ship this and store that and decided what to carry on and what to stow in cargo.

She recognized other flag officers the first day on the ship; by mutual unspoken consent, they avoided each other. Though all wore uniforms at first – and of course they were entitled to do so, on leave – she and most of the others changed to civilian clothes early in the voyage.

Melander's orbital station had grown since she'd last seen it, but was still smaller than the huge combined Fleet/civilian stations she was used to. She saw plenty of people in uniform, but they ignored her – ignored *her*, just because she wasn't wearing hers, and they could not see the admiral inside the red civilian suit. She glowered at them anyway. Two of them, at least, were Serranos.

She caught a Northside shuttle, checked the arrival-station weather, and pulled out a warmer jacket. Early spring on Melander would be colder than the regulated temperature on ship or station.

The Serrano family compound lay along the shore of a
lake inaccurately named Serenity, since it seemed always
ruffled by the breeze channeled up from the sea between
the hills. A row of solid, respectable houses built of buff-
and-brown stone or brick, each with its neat green lawn
and floral border, rows of shade and fruit trees marking
the edges of yards, neat pebbled walks from the road up
to each house . . . it looked far less attractive than it had
the last time she'd seen it. That had been . . . nearly thirty
years ago, when the crabapple trees now in brilliant
bloom above her head had been tiny sticks, her aunt's
idea. They did look pretty, but she still didn't want to be
here.

All the Fleet families who built compounds tended to
the same organization . . . separate houses for the
guardians with young children, those with older children, for the transient younger officers, for the senior
officers on long leave, for those in retirement. Flag officers each had an apartment, which might be used for a
special guest when its owner was not in residence. Vida
had never seen hers, having qualified for it since her last
visit, but she knew it would be there, furnished with the
things she had sent home over the years.

It smelled of wax and wood and leather and the clean
sharp scent of top-grade electronics. It was just as she'd
imagined it, filled with souvenirs from all over the
Familias, arranged attractively . . . and she hated it. Why
had she bought that 'Design in Blues' which was now, no
doubt, worth four times what she paid for it? It reminded
her of her first cruiser tour, and now she didn't want to be
reminded. She turned on the music, Prescott's 'Andante
for Manamash Strings,' and spent the first half hour turning pictures to the wall. If she couldn't be on a ship, a *real*
ship, she wasn't going to have them staring at her from the
walls. Or the caricature of the young officer's promotion

dance. Or the view of Castle Rock from Rockhouse Major, with the old *Mordant*'s pods framing the continents.

Was it the rejuv going bad, or just frustration? Vida didn't know, and almost didn't care. The apartment was bigger than her quarters onstation, but it felt cramped, enclosed, in a way that ship compartments never did. She glared out the window at the lake. A walk, then, to work off this bad temper.

On the way downstairs, she saw Sabatino, the other Serrano flag officer, and her distant cousin. 'I hate planets,' he said by way of greeting.

'So do I,' Vida said. They had never been close friends, but they were both Serrano admirals, and thus had common interests.

'I'm going up in the mountains for a week or so,' Sabatino said. 'Leaving tomorrow.' She remembered that he had always liked wilderness camping.

'I'm going for a walk,' Vida said. 'Dinner?'

'Might as well.' He waved and went on into his apartment.

Out of doors felt entirely too exposed. The wind, no proper ventilation current, whipped the lake surface into choppy little waves and tried to push Vida sideways. Clouds rushed by overhead, and behind the clouds was that opaque lid which groundsiders insisted was beautiful, hiding the stars.

She had liked the planet well enough growing up on it. She hadn't minded the blues and grays and mauves and pinks of the sky then, or the many shades of cloud. Vida pushed herself to walk faster, down the pebbled walk, across the road, to the footpath by the lake. Far out, bright sails glinted in red and yellow against the water. One thing about planets, you could walk a long way without retracing your steps. She walked herself breathless heading east, well past the end of the Serrano estate. There had been a small cluster of shops down here at one time, where a public boat ramp gave access to the lake for those who didn't have waterfront property.

Recovering her breath while waiting in a line of noisy children for a drink and a snack – she chose tea and a cinnamon pastry, not the sweet drinks and cream buns the children were buying – she recovered her sense of humor as well. Planets were not that bad, all things considered. She settled on a bench, protected from the wind by one of the shops, and looked at the hills behind the estates across the road. She had wandered there, as a child, splashing in the creeks and exploring little hidden valleys. She had run down here, hot and thirsty, to buy the same sweet drinks. Not bad at all, planets, if you were there by choice.

She would have to find something useful to do. With that resolve, she started back to the family compound, and by the time she arrived, she was quite ready for dinner with Sabatino. They chatted about music and art – her collection of modern prints, and his of music recordings. He invited her to come hear Malachy vu Suba's new bassoon concerto in his apartment, and she spent a pleasanter evening than she'd expected, arguing about the merits of that controversial work. Vu Suba had chosen to write for the ancient instrument, not the modern one, which limited performance to those orchestras which possessed period instruments. Sabatino argued that the tonal qualities were different enough to make this worthwhile, but Vida contended that only a very few could hear the difference.

The next morning, however, he was gone and she still hadn't decided what to do. She turned her pictures faceout again, rearranged a few ornaments, checked for a third time that everything had been put away neatly.

Shrieks from outside brought her to the window of the second bedroom.

The smallest Serrano children played in the garden between the houses as she had done, screaming and laughing the way children always did. Vida looked down on their playscape with its ramps and towers and bridges, and found it hard to believe she had ever been that noisy. Now that she had noticed them, the noise seemed to pierce her head with little needles.

Maybe the archives would be quieter. She went downstairs, and down again, into the underground library that housed the oldest documents the Serrano family owned.

Rows of Serrano biographies . . . Vida reread Rogier Xavier Serrano, one of her favorites (he had every attribute of a hero, including having made love to and won the heart of a beautiful heroine as brave as himself), and Millicent Serrano, born blind but gifted with extraordinary spatial abilities. She'd always meant to read about her own great-uncle Alcandor, who had managed to get thrown out of the Fleet for smuggling a tricorn vermuge onto a ship as a prank . . . and had then been readmitted, because no one else could get it off. That story in the official biography wasn't nearly as good as she remembered from his tales on the front porch of Rest House when he was a retired commander with a gimpy leg and a strange green spot on his arm. The official biography didn't mention the vermuge's lust for coffee, for instance, or the creature's curious mating behavior.

Vida spent several days browsing the family biographies before she tired of that, and looked around for something else. Battle reports . . . she'd seen all she wanted of battle reports. Service records, leave records, slim volumes of verse by Serranos who thought themselves poets . . . she opened one of these and burst into laughter. Either Amory David Serrano wasn't a very good poet, or the language had changed a lot in the past two hundred years. Mercedes Esperanza, on the other hand, had written erotic verses that should, Vida thought, have ignited the whole archive . . . but Mercedes had died young, of a typical poetic fever. What kind of space commander would she have made?

Stories, even: a few Serranos had written fiction, most of it clearly intended for children, and most of it – to Vida's taste anyway – pretty bad. *Carlo and the Starship* was nothing more than a child's tour of a passenger ship, with a biddable child asking obvious questions and a friendly puppy answering them. She passed by *Carlo and the Power Plant*, and *Carlo Goes to the Mountains*, glanced briefly at the illustrations for *Helen Is a Good Girl* (little Helen shaking hands; little Helen sitting up straight at table; little Helen offering a toy spaceship to another child with an improbably sweet smile – Serranos, even in childhood, didn't hand over ships willingly), and almost missed *Long Ago on Altiplano*.

Altiplano. Her grandson's fiancee's homeworld. She pried it out of the tightly-squeezed group of skinny children's books. Its pages had turned brown and brittle; the illustrations were not drawn in, but pasted on, ancient faded flatpics.

'Long ago, on Altiplano, a great Family ruled.'

So they had, the family the Serranos had been bound to.

'A beautiful world, with magnificent snow-capped mountains, and great golden plains of grass. To this world, the Garcia-Macdonalds brought their people, who prospered there and spread across the fertile land. And their loyal guards and protectors, the brave Serranos, watched the sky above them, and kept their ships safe from piracy.' That, too, she knew. The Serranos had been their space militia; someone else had been their ground militia.

'But treachery surrounded them. They were betrayed by those they trusted to guard them.' Vida felt a chill. They hadn't been betrayed by Serranos . . .

'By their soldiers on the planet.' That was better. Not Serranos at all, someone else.

'And they were all killed, the mothers and fathers and all the little children, because of the wickedness of the rebels and traitors. And that is why when we say our prayers, we do not ask for blessing upon the people of Altiplano.'

What an odd book for a child! It was more like a diatribe, like a memoir. She looked on the other side of the gap in the row, but found only *Carlo Visits the Observatory* and *Helen Starts School*, followed by *Three Little Serranos Visit the Seashore*. Nothing else with the same faded brown binding.

Vida took her find over to the table, and paged back through it. Very, very odd. Hand-printed, of course, and the flatpics glued on with something that had bled through. They were all blurry and faded, but one appeared to show a house, and another a face. The rest might have been landscapes. The pasted-in pictures made the book fatter than its spine suggested – no wonder the whole row had been wedged tight.

Vida flipped every page, looking for any identifying mark. One of the flatpics fell off, and the paper folded behind it with it. She looked at it . . . thin, almost translucent, brown on the folds . . . it had been there for a very, very long time. Perhaps she should get the family librarian; she might damage it by unfolding it.

But she couldn't resist peeking.

CHAPTER TEN

CASTLE ROCK

Back at Castle Rock, Cecelia was surprised to find that
Miranda had left not just the Palace but the planet. She
checked the net and found that Brun was the only family
member onplanet. Brun had moved to Appledale, the
Thornbuckle family estates on Castle Rock. Cecelia had
always liked Appledale, with its pleasant view of rolling
fields and orchards. She called and, as she'd expected,
Brun invited her out to stay.

Brun met her at the front door, quickly directed the
staff to take her luggage upstairs, and then – even on the
way to the handsome downstairs morning room – frothed
over with indignation about Hobart Conselline, who had
gotten himself elected Speaker of the Table of Ministers.

'Hobart?' Cecelia blinked. 'He's not that bad, is he? He
was always polite to me. I never had that much to do
with him, but –'

'Hobart is a raging bully,' Brun said grimly. She waved
Cecelia to a comfortable chintz-covered chair and threw
herself into another. 'Just wait until you hear –' She took
off at a conversational gallop, surprising Cecelia with her

grasp of Family relationships. Had the girl been listening behind doors and actually paying attention when she seemed just a young fluffhead? It was always possible – this was, after all, the same Brun who had engineered her escape from the nursing home.

'I wouldn't have believed it,' Cecelia said at last. 'Are you sure . . . I mean, he's always been a bit pigheaded, but most of us are, from time to time.' A maid had brought in trays of pastries and sliced fruits, and pots of coffee and tea. Cecelia filled a little plate with apple slices and munched. They were just as crisp and flavorful as she remembered.

'He slapped down Great-Uncle Viktor in the meeting. Viktor! And Stefan didn't say a word. He's found excuses to get rid of most of the Ministers, replacing them with his own people – and now that he has the votes, it doesn't really matter if a few of Dad's are left.' Brun was ignoring the food so far, but Cecelia took one of the ginger curls as well.

'What about Harlis?'

'He's bought Harlis, I suspect with the help of his new Minister of Judicial Affairs, Norm Radsin. You know how helpful or unhelpful the courts can be in estate cases –'

'Indeed I do.' The old anger washed over her.

'Well, it's amazing how many rulings have changed in Harlis's favor since Norm took over that ministry. Without Kevil Mahoney, or access to his private files – and nobody, not even George, knows the access codes to Kevil's files –'

She did. Cecelia thought back to their last conversation, when they had discussed her own tangled legal problems in the wake of being declared incompetent. Kevil had trusted her with the voice codes for just this sort of situation.

'Has anyone tried to have Kevil declared incompetent?' she asked.

'Not that I know of. George certainly hasn't. Why?'

Why not, she thought, if Kevil was still incapacitated and unable to access his own files? Had no one in his offices tried to get access?

'I mean,' Brun went on, 'we could use the information, but we're not going to press for that – not after what happened to you.'

'Is he conscious?'

'Yes, but he can't seem to remember much, or concentrate. His doctors don't advise rejuvenation because of the extent of the neurological damage, and the recent discoveries of what went wrong with Fleet rejuvenations.' Brun finally poured herself a cup of tea, and took a pastry.

'I hadn't heard about that.'

'No, it came out after you left. Some of the senior NCOs, the chiefs, started going senile – I actually saw one like that, back on Copper Mountain, before I . . . before I left and all the rest happened. Memory loss, irrational thought processes. I mentioned it to Esmay, in fact, but then we had that fight. Anyway, there were more of them, a lot more, and when they did some research they found flaws in the process. They've put about half the flag officers on indefinite leave, because they were rejuved, just in case. None of them had shown symptoms yet, unless you count Lepescu.'

Cecelia frowned. 'Flaws in the process, or in the drugs themselves? Remember what happened on Patchcock . . .'

'That's what I thought of first, just a bad batch of drugs. I raised a formal Question in Council – the second meeting, that is, not the first – but Hobart claimed I was just trying to embarrass him, use it as an excuse for family rivalry, and one of his bootlickers got up and spouted a whole involved line about genetic susceptibility and the inbred genome of Fleet families.'

'What did Venezia Morreline say?'

'She wasn't there. And I can't get hold of Heris or Vida Serrano, either. Both Serrano admirals were taken off active duty; Fleet personnel offices claim not to know where they are. Heris has a ship, but it's out on patrol or something, inaccessible to civilians. Which doesn't make sense, because I've been able to contact Esmay, and she's on an SAR, way off at the remote end of Familias Space.'

'How is Esmay?' Cecelia asked, to give herself time to think about the rest of this.

'Pining for Barin, worried about his NewTex wives – apparently Fleet accounting has garnished Barin's entire salary to help support them – and getting a little bored with the SAR, I gather. Also she's found out that Fleet doesn't think Landbrides should marry Fleet officers.'

'But she *is* a Landbride. What do they think of that?'

'Yes – it's funny, really. She says they've got it all wrong, and she didn't want to be one anyway. But it's tied up the paperwork for her to marry Barin, even if he weren't going broke trying to support all those NewTex women. Poor Esmay.' Brun gave a wry chuckle. 'It's her first time in love; I remember how I pined for Tommy Rakeseller, the first time I had it bad, and thought the universe was dreadfully unfair because his parents sent him off to camp. I know this is more serious, but it's really hard on her.'

'And Barin?'

'Barin's at the other end of our universe, escorting a Lone Star Confederation Ranger back here.'

'What?'

'Yes. They warned me – or rather, Waltraude did, that crazy professor who's hanging around the NewTex women. It never occurred to anyone *official* that introducing me to a Ranger might upset me. Apparently, Hobart's new Minister of Foreign Affairs – he fired Cabby DeLancre for daring to contradict him – decided to shut the wrong barn door long after the horse had returned, and froze all the assets of Lone Star Confederation citizens, and closed the border.'

'But Lone Star had nothing to do with it.'

'You know that, my father knew that, even I know that. But all Hobart had to hear was the word "Texas," and the fact that they were Ageists, as he calls it. The Lone Star Confederation has been a reasonable trading partner for centuries; they were understandably annoyed, and insisted on sending someone to educate us.'

Cecelia leaned back in her chair. 'You know, Brun, I find it hard to believe that you, of all people, are being this politically minded.'

For an instant, the old grin flashed out. 'Me, too. I keep thinking, "This is not me; this is my evil twin." But one thing I did learn, in that hell, is what happens if you don't pay attention. So Mother's gone back to Sirialis, to dig out all of Dad's files that she can – some of them were never transferred here – and try to stave off Uncle Harlis's grab for the family properties. And here I am.'

'Yes . . . I see.'

'And . . . you did find a good home for the twins?' That in a tone almost wistful, and certainly pleading.

'Yes,' Cecelia said firmly. 'A very good home. They will be loved and cared for.'

'Good. I thought, after you left, that I should have suggested Raffaele, but then she's been cleaning up my messes for far too long. I'm glad you found someone else.'

Cecelia's brain tripped over that one and came up with a fresh topic. 'You said a new Minister of Foreign Affairs – who would that be?'

'Minor family, major pain. Pedar Orregiemos. You probably never heard of him.'

'As a matter of fact, I have. He –' She shut down that line quickly and shifted to another. 'He has event horses. I beat his entry in the Wherrin this year.'

'Good. I wish you'd managed to trample him at the same time. You should see him fawning on Hobart, and Hobart lapping it up. The man has *no* background in the diplomatic service, no experience in dealing with foreign entities. He thinks any political system which doesn't embrace rejuvenation is corrupt and probably about to attack us. He's already managed to insult the Crescent Worlds, and they're *ours*. Worse than that, he thinks he's the right person to comfort widows – he keeps hinting to me that he would make me a fine stepfather.' Brun mimed gagging.

Cecelia grabbed for yet another topic, anything but Pedar. She had never been in a conversation with quite so many landmines. 'Who's in Colonial Affairs, now?'

'Another Conselline lackey, Davor Vraimont,' Brun said. 'It's dawned on them – well, on everyone, I guess – that repeatable rejuvenation could cause the biggest population explosion ever, as well as locking up wealth in the very, very old. That'd mean a lot of ambitious, frustrated young people. So colonization has been speeding up for some time – I didn't know that; Buttons told me he'd talked to Dad about it. But I found out that Conselline Sept has major investments in development companies, and their projections for the rate at which excess population can be absorbed by development make no sense – unless there's a much higher failure rate than before. That bit of information I got from a clerk in Colonial who'd been fired for insubordination. Makes me suspicious.'

'Ummm. You remember that Ronnie is my nephew,'

Cecelia said, carefully erecting bombproof partitions in her mind against a loose tongue.

'Yes, of course.'

'His parents are concerned about the situation on the world he's moved to. I hear that some supplies in the contract weren't actually delivered, that there's the possibility of interference with communications. What if the Consellines are counting on a certain percentage of colonies to fail, because they get their profit from selling colony shares?'

'I could believe that. But how can we prove it?'

'I don't know. We need Kevil,' Cecelia said. 'I'd better go visit him.'

'It's – pretty bad. You know he lost an arm, too.'

'No, I didn't. When I saw him in the hospital, before I took off with the babies, he was just a shape in the bed. And I didn't have much time.'

'They're trying to grow a replacement, but so far it hasn't worked – they've lost three buds. And George says his memory's still damaged, and he can't concentrate.'

'Is he still in the hospital?'

'No; they moved him to a rehab center, and then George took him home. Our wonderful new Speaker decided he was a security risk at the rehab center.'

'Well, then. I'll go over tomorrow. Maybe I can be of some help.'

'You know,' Brun said more slowly, 'Uncle Harlis runs the planetary development corporations for the Barraclough Sept.' She took a long swallow of tea.

'What colony are Ronnie and Raffa in?'

'Excet-24.'

'Rats. I was hoping it was one of ours – that way I could pump them. Excet Environmental Group is a Conselline corporation. I wonder why they chose that one, instead of family? Not that it matters.'

'I don't know,' Cecelia said. 'Possibly the shares cost less?'

'Could be. Anyway, I'd bet something's going on in all these new colonies . . . I wish I had Kevil's background files, because I rather suspect the data in the main computers has been fiddled as well.' Brun stretched. 'And now that I've talked your ears off, both of them, how about a visit to the stable? We don't have much here, as you probably remember, but there are a couple of niceish mares we can take a ride through the orchards on, if you'd like.'

Cecelia shook her head. 'No, thank you, my dear. Everyone thinks of me as a thoroughly horse-besotted old woman, but one prerogative of old women is to surprise young ones occasionally. I shall go stroll in your gardens, if I may.'

'Well, then, I'm for the pool. See you at dinner.'

At the Mahoney house, a uniformed nurse met Cecelia at the door. 'Ser Mahoney is in the study, madam, but he is . . . not really himself.'

Cecelia thought of asking who he was instead – she had a lingering distaste for medical euphemisms – but resisted the temptation. She followed the nurse down the familiar wide passage to the double doors that led into Kevil's home office, steeling herself for what she would see. At the same time, she wondered where the security was. If Kevil was a security risk, shouldn't there be more protection around him? She had seen no guards at all.

'Ser George Mahoney is at the university,' the nurse said, over his shoulder. 'He won't be back until this evening.'

Cecelia frowned. No security, one nurse all day . . . something wrong here.

In the study, Kevil lay awkwardly in one of the big

leather chairs. His face looked strange, twisted; she realized that regen had not been able to repair all the physical damage, that part of his jaw was missing, and the skin over it rumpled oddly. In his eyes, Cecelia saw no recognition, just anxiety. Then, slowly, a spark . . . as if he were walking through a dark corridor with a candle, closer and closer.

'Cecelia . . .'

'Yes.'

'You look . . . younger. Dye your hair?'

Cecelia's heart sank. Of course she looked younger; she had rejuved several years before, to a nominal forty. He had known that. They had slept together after that. 'Rejuv, Kevil,' she said briskly. It was hard to look at him, but she knew she must. 'I'm sorry I wasn't here when you were hurt,' she said.

'Me . . . too. I can't . . . remember . . . all.'

Was the slurred voice from the injury, or from drugs? Cecelia glanced around, but saw no litter of pillboxes

'I've been to visit Ronnie and Raffaele,' she said. To her delight, the spark in his eyes brightened.

'How are . . . they?'

'They're fine, except that the developer's done something foul with the colony they're on.' She told him about it, gauging his attention span by his expression. For a few minutes at a time, he seemed the old Kevil – his eyes bright, his face intent. Then he would blink, and the expression slacken. She stopped, and waited, and when he seemed focussed again she went on.

'You're . . . really . . . talking to me.' He smiled, a genuine smile this time.

'Yes, of course.'

'You . . . understand . . .'

'Not completely, Kevil. But I know you need something to chew on.'

'Yes. They keep asking me . . . questions . . . tests . . . can't remember. . . .'

'I hated those,' Cecelia said, remembering her own convalescence, the idiocy of the questions in the standard tests.

'Name three vegetables, name five fruits . . .'

'Name the CEO of Excet Environmental Group,' Cecelia said, as if it were another on the list.

'Silvester Conselline,' Kevil said instantly, then looked blank. 'What was that?'

'A reasonable question,' Cecelia said. 'And one I wanted the answer to. Ronnie and Raffa are, as I said, practically marooned on Excet-24, and Brun says that's an Excet Group colony planet. I want to know who's responsible for shorting the colony of its startup supplies and staff.'

'Probably not Silvester,' Kevil said, sounding even more awake now. 'He's been spending most of his time trying to convince the universe he's a great composer. But he does tend to sign anything anyone puts in front of him.'

A tap at the door. The nurse looked in, his expression exactly the one Cecelia least liked to see. 'Ser Mahoney needs his rest, madam. Perhaps another time?'

'Go on – take a break,' Cecelia said to the nurse. 'I'm experienced with this – I've been a convalescent myself.'

'But his lunch . . . his diet –'

'And I can cook. Go on now.'

Finally he left, protesting and warning and muttering. Cecelia watched through the scan pickup until she had seen him go all the way down the street and board a tram.

'Officious,' she said to Kevil, when she came back to him.

'You think . . . he's up to something,' Kevil said.

'Nurses are always up to something,' Cecelia said. 'But

in addition to that, yes. Now.' She pulled the scrambler she carried out of her bag and turned it on. Kevil gave her a puzzled look. 'Remnant of my times with Heris Serrano and those Fleet refugees she foisted on me as crew. Oblo whatever-his-name-was. Good advice, I realized after awhile. Always carry a means of tapping someone else's data, and always protect your own conversations.'

Kevil grinned. 'You always were smarter . . . than people thought.'

'Yes, and so were you. Kevil – what's happened? Why only one nurse? Why haven't you had a proper limb replacement?'

'No money.'

Cecelia stared at him, shocked. 'But Kevil – you've always had money, pots of it.'

'No more. It . . . isn't there.'

'But – what happened?'

'I don't know. One day there, then – it wasn't. George tried – couldn't find out –'

'Someone fiddled the databases? But – people would notice –'

'Not unless it was their account. The people who normally handled my accounts would notice, unless they'd been transferred.'

'And that's not hard at all . . .' Cecelia mused. 'And there are new Ministers in the relevant Ministries, and a huge muddle all over . . .'

'Yes. I think . . . it happened . . . when Bunny died.'

If that were true, it would mean – no, *could* mean – that it was related. That the same person or persons planned the attack on Bunny's life, and Kevil's fortunes.

'I know . . . something . . . I know it's because I know something . . . but Cece, I can't remember what it is I'm supposed to know. I can't remember. I can't think –' A muscle in his face twitched; his hand shook.

'Kevil . . . relax. Please. Let me fix you lunch – yes, you come with me into the kitchen – and we'll talk some more. I know I can help.'

It took a struggle to get Kevil up, and Cecelia fought down her fury when she saw his unbalanced, lurching gait. But in the kitchen, he seemed more comfortable in the chair, his good arm propped on the wide wooden table, than he had in the study.

'I'm assuming you don't have a cook because of the money –'

'Yes.'

She fixed him fruit, bread, cheese. There were custards in the refrigerator, but she didn't trust them – custards could conceal drugs. He ate, clumsily, with his left hand.

'Kevil, do you remember giving me your access codes?'

A blank look. 'Access codes?'

'The second night. After we decided it wouldn't work. You said, "If I'm ever in the state you were in, I want to know you're on my side." And you gave them to me. You've forgotten, but I haven't.'

'Cecelia –'

'When George gets home, we'll get to work. Tonight. There's no time to waste.'

'I can't . . . help much.'

'You did that, years ago. We'll take care of it.' Somehow. Cecelia scolded herself internally – she was turning into everyone's helpful old aunt again. Well, if she was going to take her turn being civic-minded, helpful, and useful, she might as well make a thorough job of it. She'd had another brilliant idea.

Waltraude Meyerson, tenured professor of antique studies on loan to the Regular Space Service as a consultant on Texan history and culture, sat quietly in the corner of the room with her recorder on, watching the NewTex women argue about religion and education without getting involved. She hoped. This was the first conflict she'd seen among the women who had fled Our Texas, and she was fascinated.

It had been months, and only now was the rigid rank structure breaking down. The first wives of the Rangers had each run her own household without interference from the other first wives – Primas, they were all called. Prima Bowie, the one Waltraude felt she knew best, actually ranked second in the hierarchy; the Ranger Captain's first wife outranked her. That was Prima Travis, but she was older and had less vitality than Prima Bowie. Usually she let Prima Bowie make decisions, but not today.

They were arguing about schools again. Under Familias law, the children – all of them – were supposed to be in school. Parents could choose from a wide variety of schools, or school their children at home, and the requirements were – to an academic like Waltraude – minimal. All children must become literate in at least two languages, study some very basic science and mathematics, and the Code of Citizens. But these women had steadfastly resisted sending the children to school from the beginning. No one had been able to figure out why, because the women would not explain what they considered self-explanatory. Now, in the argument, Waltraude began to grasp the problem.

'Boys and girls together! I think not!' Prima Travis was holding firm on that. 'They'd become Abominations!'

'There are single-sex schools,' Prima Bowie said. 'Most are religious –'

'Not *our* religion!' Prima Travis sniffed again. 'They're heathens, or worse.'

'But –'

'We should never have come,' Prima Travis said. 'I – I

was wrong to come. We should go back.' Behind her,
Waltraude saw several of the junior Travis wives nodding, but one pinched her mouth up and looked
stubborn. Waltraude counted – third back, that was
Tertia.

'The men lied to us,' Prima Bowie said. 'They killed
mothers –'

'*You* said,' replied Prima Travis. 'I never saw that picture you said you saw.'

'You heard Patience – Hazel,' Prima Bowie said. 'She's
a good girl . . .'

'She is *not* a good girl; she is one of them. Prima
Bowie, has your brains run out your ears, or what? She is
one of them, an Abomination. She runs around wearing
men's pants, messing about with machines –'

'I'll bet she has an implant,' sneered Secunda Travis.
Prima Travis whirled and slapped her on the mouth.

'Don't you be saying those bad words, girl!'

'I just –'

'And don't you be arguin' with me! You see what it
comes to, Prima Bowie? We left our rightful place, and
now we have this – this arguin' and usin' bad language.'

'We can't go back,' Prima Bowie said. 'They'd kill us –'

'And so they should,' Prima Travis said. 'Our children
to grow up no proper way –'

'So you think we should just go back, die, let our children be orphans?'

'No, but we got to find a right way to live. Not hived up
like bees with nowhere to gather honey.' Having delivered this, Prima Travis led her family out of the common
room, back to their own little hive. More stingers than
honey, the way Waltraude saw it.

Waltraude shut off the recorder and waited until the
remaining women were seated, back at their endless
handwork.

'Prima –'

'Call me Ruth Ann,' Prima said. 'I'm not a first wife anymore. Mitch is dead, and that boy won't actually marry me – I see that now.'

'Ruth Ann, fine. Listen – where do you think you would be happy?'

'I won't be.' The woman's broad, rounded face contracted in a scowl. 'Not in this kind of world.'

'There are many worlds in the Familias,' Waltraude said. 'What sort of place, can you tell me? A city? A smaller town?'

'Hazel said there was, but how can we go there? We can't just up and ask some spaceship to take us, even if I knew. If I can't be home . . . I guess I'd like a quiet place. There's always noise here, machine noise. I'd like it where it's quiet. Open. Maybe where I could see the fields. I always missed that, after Mitch moved us to the city, not having the fields outside. The garden just wasn't the same, big as it was. Someplace where people didn't laugh at me for not being schooled, someplace where what I can do is worth something. But I doubt you got anyplace like that in your fancy confederation or whatever it is.'

Waltraude grinned. "Oh, but we do, Ruth Ann. What you need first of all is to be on a planet, not on a station in space. And then you need the kind of world where the basic skills you have are desperately needed. Your gardening, weaving, sewing, cooking . . . and tell me, do your boys know anything of tools?'

'The older ones do. Boys make most of the furniture in a house – they're so rough on it, they have to learn to fix it and make it.'

'Your world had trees, didn't it? Wood for manufacture?'

'Yes, of course.' Ruth Ann paused, brow wrinkled. 'Are there worlds without trees?'

'Nearly without, yes. Ruth Ann . . . the Familias has hundreds of populated worlds, and is opening new ones to colonization all the time. And the colony worlds need pioneers. As you pointed out so succinctly today, most of us can't boil water without a computer. You know how to build fires. You know how to make bread from wheat – and I'll bet some of your older boys know how to make a mill.'

'Of course they do,' Ruth Ann said. Waltraude could almost feel the slow smile working its way out of her confused heart, and just as she expected, it finally smoothed out the ridged brow. 'You really believe we could get to such a place? How? We have no money. . . .'

'I know someone who does,' Waltraude said. 'And they owe you a lot. The only problem is making the connection. But that's what scholars do.'

'Make connections?'

'Yes. It's our job, though most people don't think it is. They think of us in terms of collecting information – silly, anyone can do that. What we do is notice which bits make new connections.'

'You will help us? Why? You think we're ignorant . . .'

'Of history, yes. Of life, no. And of course I'll help you. Any decent person helps others; it's one of the things people are for.'

'What . . . religion are you?'

'You wouldn't recognize it, and it would only bother you.' Waltraude picked up her bag. 'Prima – Ruth Ann, I'm going to be gone for several weeks; I've been asked to escort a diplomat from the Lone Star Confederation back to Castle Rock. But let me just show you –' She took out some hardcopy ads for colony worlds. 'See this? You might like something –'

'But what would our protector say? He'd have to say it was all right –'

Waltraude thought of the scuttlebutt she'd heard about

young Barin Serrano and his problems with the women. 'I think he'd be delighted if you found a place you could be happy.'

'And living the right way,' the woman said, the scowl returning for a moment. 'Happiness isn't everything. Just because our men did wrong things doesn't mean they was wrong about everything. I want my children to grow up to be good, Godfearin' men and women.'

'I'm sure there's a place, Ruth Ann,' Waltraude said. 'When I get back, I'll help.'

Rockhouse Major had everything that two young officers in love could want, Esmay knew . . . if she could only get there. It should have been simple to get from the R.S.S. *Shrike*, over in Sector Seven, to Sector Seven HQ, and from there to the Castle Rock system. She had finally heard from Barin; Castle Rock was the one place they could reasonably meet, since *Gyrfalcon* would be there several days. Castle Rock lay on her route to her new duty station, and was admirably provided with shipping and passenger lines. But one thing after another had delayed her. She imagined Barin, on *Gyrfalcon*, making an effortless smooth transit . . . only to wait around wondering if she was even going to show up. He might even leave before she arrived, if this miserable tub of a ship didn't get a move on.

Barin saw Esmay just a moment before she saw him: saw her face with that harder edge, that warier expression. Then their eyes met, and she grinned.

'How long do you have?' she asked, as they settled at an empty table in the concourse.

'Four hours,' Barin said, angry all over again. 'It was supposed to be forty-eight hours on station, minimum, but all of a sudden –'

'Same with us,' Esmay said. 'I should have been here three days ago, but the blasted ship had a pressure-lock problem; we hung around for hours and hours at SecSev HQ, then they transferred us to old *Bowfin*, without time to send any messages, and then she couldn't generate more than seventy-two percent of her normal power, and we just came limping in . . . I was afraid you'd have left already.'

'So was I. I left a message for you at the mail drop already, just in case.' Barin put his head to one side and grinned. 'Surely, all this scramble can't be just to keep us apart,' he said. 'That's an expensive abuse of Fleet resources.'

'Whatever it is, it's a nuisance. Is your family still against us?'

'Yes. They think we should wait until the NewTex women are all taken care of. How am I supposed to do that? It could be years. What about you?'

Esmay handed over the message that had finally arrived, tied and stamped formally. 'The Landholders are upset. Can you read Kurlik script? Basically it says that it is unacceptable for a Landbride to marry offworld at all, and particularly to marry a foreign military officer.'

'But we're not *foreign*,' Barin said.

'I know that. You know that. But Altiplano –'

'I don't want to take away anything you have,' Barin said. 'You've explained about being Landbride – it's a wonderful thing –'

'It's a nuisance,' Esmay said. She straightened. 'I never expected to be Landbride, and I thought I'd lost you . . . and . . . anyway, I accepted it in a time of crisis, but that's past. My father realized very early that I might resign in favor of a legitimate heir. It's not done often –' It had never been done except in cases of insanity or other permanent disability or extreme old age. She didn't like to think of marriage as equivalent to insanity or permanent disability. 'But there is a ritual procedure. The hard part is going to be getting leave to go there. I can appoint a stand-in, but that's not the same thing as the next Landbride. My father says if I marry you, even though I've appointed someone, the Landmen's Guild could challenge, and intervene in our family affairs. And that would be bad.'

'I can see that.' Barin shook his head. 'And we still haven't figured a way around the Fleet regulations; even if you do resign as Landbride, you can't quit being a sector commander's daughter. Does it seem to you that this is a lot harder than we thought it would be?'

'Yes. If it were this hard for everyone, nobody would get married.'

They stared gloomily at each other for several minutes. Then Esmay sat up. 'Let's not waste it. We have four hours – or rather, three hours and forty-two minutes.'

'I don't suppose we could get married in three hours and forty-two minutes?' Barin said wistfully. 'Maybe an hour to get married, and two hours to enjoy it?'

Esmay laughed. 'It takes a lot longer; we couldn't possibly. But we can do something cheerier than sit here eating bad food in a noisy place.'

'Right. But you'll have to pay. I'm flat broke.' For some reason, this struck both of them as funny rather than annoying, and they thoroughly enjoyed their dinner.

CHAPTER ELEVEN

J.C. Chandler, President of the Lone Star Confederation, watched the newscube with his lower lip tucked under. This was trouble with a big T, and he didn't know how he was going to deal with it. They had had problems enough with the Familias Regnant, over the years, without *this* kind of nonsense.

'Looks bad, J.C.,' Millicent said.

'There's always crazies in the world,' Ramie said, leaning back with his hands folded over his belly. 'It's not our fault they call themselves Texans.'

The two obvious responses, J.C. thought, and neither of them useful right now. He said nothing while the newscube ran through the whole summary, then turned off the reader and put his hands on the table. Time to talk seriously.

'That new administration has closed the border to Lone Star citizens,' he said without more preamble. 'They say they can't guarantee our safety, and they did send this to explain why. And they haven't withdrawn their embassy staff.'

'But it wasn't us,' Millicent said. 'Those idiots are all the way across Familias space –'

'More like the length of it,' Ramie said, not moving. 'If you look at the actual geometry –'

'What matters,' J.C. said, 'is that they've done it – closed the border. Frozen our assets in their banks, too –'

'They can't *do* that –' Ramie said, sitting up so suddenly that his chair rolled back. 'The Treaty of Poldek clearly states –'

'They've done it.' J.C. tried not to enjoy interrupting Ramie again, but it was hard – the older man was so annoyingly difficult to get a rise out of, and here he'd actually made Ramie sit up.

'But I moved most of the family's liquid capital into Goodrich & Scanlon only a year ago; it's not reasonable –'

'They claim we might be financing our "countrymen" as they call them, even if we aren't personally involved. They want to be sure what our money's doing.'

'Making more money, just like theirs.' Ramie huffed his reddening cheeks out. 'What do they take us for, ignorant rubes?'

Probably they did, J.C. thought, but that wasn't at issue right now. 'What I want to do,' J.C. said, 'is tell the Cabinet and Congress that we're sending some investigators to help 'em out.'

'Help them? Help them what? Steal us blind?'

'No – help them with specifically Texan issues. They seem to be blundering around not knowing the difference between those idiots and the rest of us. We could help.'

'They've got a scholar, they said. That Meyerson woman.'

'Milly, why do you call her "that Meyerson woman"? That won't help our image.'

'I liked Professor Lemon,' Millicent said frankly. 'He

used to send me the nicest notes . . . all right, it's not fair. You're right. We should help them — even Meyerson — if they'll let us.'

From sheer force of habit and a fondness for tradition when it didn't get in the way, the Lone Star Confederation had retained the term 'Rangers' for its internal security forces. This hadn't bothered anyone — not even the Familias Regnant with their hoity-toity attitudes — in centuries, but obviously, the Familias Regnant had a reason to react badly to the title now. The abuse of the same word by the New Texas Godfearing Militia nuts made *real* Rangers wish they'd trademarked the name somewhere back down in history.

Still, it wasn't the fault of the Lone Star Confederation. Rangers had the right training to pursue an investigation — and they weren't about to change their names just to satisfy a twitchy Familias Regnant. They'd send a Ranger.

Which Ranger then became the issue . . . but not for long, because Katherine Anne Briarly was the obvious best choice. A woman like Katie Anne, and they'd know that Lone Star's Rangers weren't like those others in any way, shape or form. Especially shape.

And besides, it would get Katie Anne out of everyone's hair for a few months. She had been getting a mite big for her britches, though not in a physical way, ever since her uncle Beau got appointed to the Supreme Court. She'd taken to being even more Texan than the Texans could stand.

Ranger Katherine Anne Briarly arrived at the Familias Regnant embassy wearing a red two-piece suit that emphasized every asset she had except brains, which — in

Kate's view — couldn't be put on view anyway without making someone puke. A tumble of ash-blonde hair swirled over her shoulders; her bright blue eyes twinkled at the R.S.S. marine guards by the gate. Neither twinkled back.

'Hi,' she said, holding out her ID case. 'I'm Kate Briarly, and y'all are expecting me.'

The gate opened behind the motionless guards, and she was facing a squad of them. The leader or whatever came out and took her ID case, then looked from the image inside to her.

'You're Ranger Katherine Anne Briarly?'

'Yup. But that's an official picture, in uniform, and I didn't see any reason to get gussied up in uniform for just a friendly visit. I figured y'all'd have an ID scan unit anyway.'

'Quite so. If you'd come this way.' She followed the young man toward a portable booth set up in the courtyard, ignoring the scrape of feet as the squad fell in behind her. This was going to be fun.

She was who she said she was — retinals, fingerprints, voiceprints, the whole shebang — and in another ten minutes she was upstairs waiting to meet the ambassador.

'Sera — Ranger — Briarly —'

'Oh, just call me Kate,' Kate said, widening her smile. He blinked.

'It's irregular,' he murmured.

'I know,' Kate said. 'But who's to tell on you? Not me.'

'I have received permission for two Rangers to enter Familias space and help with inquiries —'

'You don't need two,' Kate said. 'I'll just go by myself, thanks.'

'But —'

'It'll be simpler,' Kate said. 'Less cost to you, too, keeping track of just one. Besides, it's traditional.'

She had seen the ambassador before, while running security at the Cattlemen's Association Ball three years before, but she'd been in uniform then, her hair slicked back into a neat French braid. He didn't remember her, she could tell that. All the better.

'Now I realize y'all are concerned that we might have some connection to those NewTex nuts –'

'Concern was expressed,' the ambassador said. 'Not by me; I've tried to reassure the Grand Council that you all . . . er . . . you . . . here, the Lone Star Confederation . . . are not part of that group.'

'Heavens, no,' Kate said. 'I'd like to see anyone making *us* wear clothes like that! And bare feet – shoot, I was as tomboy as they come, but you don't see me shuffling around in bare feet.' She pointed a long, elegant foot clad in a feminine version of the Texas style: high-heeled, but not a boot.

'It's the new government,' the ambassador said. 'We have a new Speaker and a new Minister of Foreign Affairs and Minister of Defense; one doesn't like to say it's inexperience, but they're just not listening to me. You've travelled in Familias space before, Sera . . . er . . . Ranger . . .?'

'Kate,' she said again. 'No, not me. I've been to Bluebonnet and West and Panhandle, but not to Familias. It'll be fun.'

At the border, Kate found she had an escort at the end of the docking tube.

A trim young man with a face like carved bronze. 'Lieutenant Junior Grade Serrano,' he said. 'Ranger Briarly, your luggage will be transferred –'

'Oh, call me Kate,' she said, smiling. He didn't smile back.

'You're to come aboard *Gyrfalcon*,' he said. 'It's the

fastest route to Rockhouse Major, where the task force has reassembled –'

'Are you arresting me?' Kate asked. She glanced around the docking lobby, decorated in what struck her as bland and chilly colors, muted blues and greens, and noted two men and one woman in R.S.S. uniform lurking by the entrance.

'No, ma'am,' the young man said. 'Just transporting you, ma'am.'

Kate cocked her head and considered him. In her experience, young men his age melted with only one smile, and he hadn't. Well, his preferences might lie elsewhere, but still . . . 'Fine,' she said. 'Let's go.' He turned as quickly as she moved, and walked beside her through the entrance, where the others lined up after them, and then guided her across the wide passage to what the sign said was a dropchute. Kate stopped short.

'I'm not going in there,' she said. 'I've heard about those.'

'You don't have them?'

'No – we like floors in our elevators. No one's looking up my skirt –'

'Fine – then we'll take the cross-station tram.' He led her to the station, plugged some kind of datawand into a port, and the next tram stopped, doors opening exactly opposite them. Kate was impressed, and said so. He still wasn't melting. She looked him over again. He couldn't be a mango; she had known lots of mangos and they had a certain . . . feel. So either he really hated Texans, or . . . he was resisting her because he had a girl.

Her first meal in the officers' mess gave her a chance to do more than mutter polite greetings.

'Have you ever visited Familias space before, Ranger Briarly?' asked the executive officer, on one side of her.

She was not sure what an executive officer did, but she had memorized the insignia, and knew he was a lieutenant commander.

'No – and I hope I'm going to see more of it than the inside of a transfer station and this ship.'

'What would you like to see?'

'Oh – all those sights the tourist brochures have. Langsdon's ice falls. Chuzillera's cloud forests. The Grand Council Chamber on Castle Rock. I'd like to have seen your king while you still had one.'

'Why?'

'It's so romantic,' Kate said. 'All those dramacubes, set in misty Vaalonia or – what's that place where they go running around on horses chasing after a fox? We just have ordinary people doing ordinary things –' She didn't really believe that, but wanted to see their reaction.

'The storycubes you people export are extraordinary enough. Those lawnhorns . . .'

'Longhorns,' Kate said. 'And the stories are old – last century's revival of Wild West –'

'Annie – that woman in fringes with all those guns –?'

'Stories,' Kate said firmly. 'Not real history. And that's what I'm here for, to talk about real history.'

'But you're a . . . Ranger . . .' No doubt about it, they were twitchy about that word. With reason, though the reason was a lie.

'I'm a Ranger,' Kate said firmly. 'They weren't. They were a bunch of maniacs with no legitimate connection whatsoever to real Rangers.'

'So you say,' said one voice down the table. Kate leaned forward.

'So I say. Are you calling me a liar?'

The air seemed to congeal around her. She smiled; the silence lengthened. The officer at the far end of the table cleared his throat.

'Mr. Chesub, that was rude; apologize.'

'I'm sorry, Ranger Briarly,' a young man said. 'I'm not accusing you of lying.' But by his tone he still wasn't convinced.

Kate let her smile soften. 'We have had just as many freaks and nutcases as any other culture,' she said. 'But the people who stole your Chair's daughter are not ours. The Lone Star Confederation wouldn't tolerate that kind of behavior. We Lone Star *women* wouldn't tolerate that kind of behavior.' Nervous chuckles. 'Not that we're . . . however you say it . . . hostile to men or anything . . .'

'Well, you don't look like the pictures of their women – but you're all from Texas originally, right?'

'Not really.' Kate settled into lecture mode. 'The Lone Star Confederation was organized for space exploration back on Earth, and most of its members then were North Americans – many of them from the exact region then known as Texas. But most of the people in Texas came from somewhere else, all over North America. Sure, there were some hard-shell Texans among them – people whose families had been in Texas just about forever – but a lot of them weren't. And Lone Star has always welcomed immigrants who share our philosophy –'

'Which is?'

'Fear God and nobody else, ride tall, shoot straight, never tell a lie, dance with who brung you, and never renege on a handshake.'

Another silence, this one slightly shocked, but responsive.

'"Dance with who brung you?"'

'Another way of saying honor your earlier obligations – don't just look at current profit.'

'Interesting.'

'And your philosophy?' Kate asked.

For a long moment no one answered, then young Lt. Serrano spoke up. 'If I understand yours, it's much the same. Tell the truth, keep promises, stand by friends, don't turn your back on an enemy.'

'I notice you didn't mention God,' Kate said. 'Is that because those NewTex nutcases have you scared, or what? Any of you folks got religion?'

This time the captain spoke up. 'The Familias legal codes – and those of the Regular Space Service – allow freedom of belief, and freedom of religious practices which are not directly harmful to others. Because of the wide variety of beliefs, many held strongly, we do not generally discuss religion with those we do not know.'

Kate cocked her head and gave him her best mischievous kid grin. 'In other words, it's bad manners to talk about God?'

'Something like that,' he said.

'You people must have been descended from Anglicans,' Kate said. 'Well, I'm not here to make you nervous, though I don't see why a good argument about God should do anything but keep your digestion going. It's one of our favorite forms of entertainment.'

'You . . . uh . . . are religious yourself?'

Kate looked him in the eye. 'You bet. So far as I know, every member of my family back to Old Earth has been, and I'm not about to break tradition.'

'And what, since you don't mind our asking, is your religion?'

'Baptist,' Kate said. 'But my mother's family was about half Anglican, and my dad's grandmother was Methodist. There's even the odd Presbyterian in there somewhere.'

Glances passed back and forth.

'Y'all don't have a clue what I'm talking about, do you?'

'Not . . . exactly.' That was a female officer.

'You do have Christians, right?'

'Certainly . . . many kinds, though I don't know all the names.'

'Then just call me a Christian, and don't worry about it. God'll sort it out.'

'Do you have any . . . uh . . . dietary or special needs we should know about?'

'No, that's somebody else. I'll eat anything I like the flavor of, any day of the week. We don't drink alcohol on the Baptist side of our family, 'cept when we're being young and sowing wild oats. Every once in awhile I sow an oat myself.'

She sensed the mood warming even more.

'What do your kind of rangers do?'

'Anything that needs doin'. We're a lot like a police force, but we tend to work alone. Keep order, track down the bad guys, help the people who need it.'

'How do you know who the bad guys are?' came a call from down the table.

'Same way you do, I expect,' Kate said. 'Liars, cheats, killers, the kind of people who'd pour gasoline on a dog –' She felt the total noncomprehension of that one, and stopped. 'You have dogs, don't you?'

'Oh . . . like . . . dogs? Hounds or something?'

'Dogs, like hounds, sheepdogs, cowdogs, even those awful nippy-yippy poodley things. And do you have mean people who hurt animals?'

'Yeah . . .' That more cautiously, as if the speaker weren't entirely sure.

'Well, we don't much like people who mistreat animals, kids, or old ladies. Or old men, for that matter. They're on my list of bad guys.'

By the end of that meal she sensed that most of the officers were at least neutral, if not actually friendly.

*

The next day, Kate met the antique historian, Professor Meyerson, and sighed to herself. So predictable, that type. The lady academic, tweedy and warty . . . not that Meyerson actually had warts, but she looked as if they should be there to complete the official look. Even on Bluebonnet, known for its beautiful women, a certain kind of academic woman looked like this, only with better tweeds.

At least Meyerson knew more about the Lone Star Confederation than the rest of the people she met. And she was finally able to clear up a question that bedeviled Kate for days.

'That young fellow, Barin Serrano?'

'Yes . . .' Meyerson, head down in a scanner as usual, didn't seem to be paying close attention.

'What do you know about him?'

'He's giving you trouble?' Meyerson's head came up, and her expression was mingled mischief and surprise.

'No, just the opposite. He's ignoring me as if I had bark like a mesquite tree, but I just can't believe he's a mango.'

Meyerson laughed, a surprisingly full-throated laugh for a frowsty old professor. 'He's not. He's engaged to another officer, in the first place, and in the second place he's burdened with all those NewTex women and children.'

'Why him in particular?'

'They consider him their protector, and for them this means he's the only one who can make decisions about them. The Regular Space Service has taken his pay to help support them, so he can't marry until he figures out what to do with them.'

'I suppose shipping them back isn't an option?'

'No, they'd kill them, at least mute them. He's stuck with them.'

'That's too bad.' Kate thought about it. 'He's a nice boy, and if he's minded to marry, he should have the chance. You suppose those women would listen to me?'

Meyerson looked her up and down. 'As a messenger of the devil, maybe. They're very serious about their religion.'

'And I'm very serious about mine, Wally.' They had come to first names several days before, and Kate refused to struggle with Waltraude after the first few tries. 'You don't have to go barefoot and wear rags to be a believer.' She cocked her head. 'You ought to send those women to us – we'll make real Texans out of 'em. They had to have some gumption to get up and leave in the first place.'

Day by day, the officers relaxed around her, and if she hadn't had the appetite of a healthy horse, she'd have starved, for all the talking at the table.

She talked more than she asked questions, and the information flowed her way without her having to ask. By the time they reached Rockhouse Major, she had most of them eating out of her hand, men and women, and had invited most of them to come visit sometime. She thought a few of them actually would.

All but the young lieutenant junior grade who had remained coolly distant no matter what. Well, if he wanted to sulk, let him. She had many, many other fish to fry, and others had told their own tales of Barin Serrano and Esmay Suiza. So he was in love with a hero – if the stories were true, Suiza would have made a good Ranger – and perhaps worried about whether she'd stick it out.

Security concerns kept her from touring Rockhouse Major, though she could tell it was much bigger than any of the orbital stations in the Lone Star Confederation. A

Fleet shuttle took her downside, and she got her first look at Castle Rock.

Boring, she thought, but did not of course say. The government buildings, mostly gray stone, looked substantial and dull. Insides matched the outsides; the Foreign Office was all dark paneling and dark tiles and thick dark green or blue carpeting in the offices she was led to. Everyone wore dark suits — men and women both — and had a dark, muffled, hurried way of speaking.

'Sera Briarly — so pleased —' That was the Minister of Foreign Affairs, the first person she'd seen in this dismal building who looked completely awake. He wore a different style of shirt, with a tiny ruffle at the collar, and he had several blue-and-silver rings in his ear. She knew what that would mean in San Antone, but not here. 'You are so . . . so *decorative*, my dear.'

This she had met before, twinkling of the eyes and all. 'Mister Minister,' she said, putting out her hand. 'I'm Ranger Briarly, but you can call me Kate.'

'But I thought your . . . er . . . Rangers . . . were sort of . . . er . . . policemen?'

'That's right,' Kate said cheerfully; she saw some of the man's staff wincing, and grinned at them, too. The way they acted, you'd think this solid stone building would fall over if anyone spoke louder than a murmur.

'But surely you — you're not — I mean, you're more of a . . . er . . . honorary title . . .'

That was going too far. 'Mister Minister, I am a Ranger, same as any other Ranger; I qualified on the same course, and I can and will demonstrate my skills any time you or anyone else questions them.' She had no weapon, of course, but she could break this fellow's neck — or any other bone — without one.

'Oh . . . certainly, certainly. Now, uh . . . we are having

a reception in your honor this afternoon, in the Palace. I
hope you aren't too tired . . .'

'Not at all.' She was never too tired to party.

The Palace was another pile of gray stone, with outcrops
on one side of a curious buff color. Inside, the formal
rooms had the same sort of dull, dark look as those in the
Minister's offices.

Kate was on her best behavior, smiling like a car
dealer. She had been through her share of fancy events,
and knew that her role, as honored guest, was to smile
and tell everyone how beautiful things were. She told the
new Speaker what an honor it was to meet him, and
thought what piggy eyes he had. She told his wife what a
lovely dress she had on, even though she longed to tell
the woman that she should never in this world wear that
shade of green, it made her look sick. She told the Foreign
Minister, whose name was Pedar Orregiemos, that she
liked his ruffled shirt, though she contemplated mentioning that a ruffled shirt plus those pretty rings in the
ears would have branded him an obvious mango in the
Lone Star Confederation. Then she overheard part of a
conversation and learned that the local slang for the same
thing was 'pet.'

It was all intensely boring, since she didn't know
enough yet to make sense of most that she heard. Her feet
hurt, and her head was beginning to throb. Then Pedar
bustled up to her leading a tall blonde woman whose
face Kate recognized from her briefings.

'And this is Ranger Briarly,' Pedar said. 'Brun Meager
Thornbuckle . . .'

Kate looked at the blonde woman who had been a
prisoner so long, whose father was dead, whose predica-
ment had led directly to her own presence here – and saw
a familiar shadow in those blue eyes. Automatically, she

softened her approach. 'Hi there – I hope you can forgive my havin' that kind of a title.'

'Well –' The woman's voice was slightly husky. 'You don't look much like *their* Rangers.'

'Hon, they aren't Rangers; they're trash. Lower'n a groundhog's burrow. A brick can call itself a diamond – doesn't make it one.'

The woman grinned, her face suddenly relaxing. 'And you're the genuine diamond?'

'Pure carbon crystal, that's me,' Kate said. 'Cubic, but not zirconium.'

'Excuse me?'

'Sorry – slang's hard to translate. Listen, my feet hurt – can we go sit down somewhere?' If she could make friends with this woman – and she liked her already – maybe she could get the embargo lifted faster than anyone had thought. Even Kate at her most optimistic hadn't thought she'd get to meet the cause of it all, or that the woman would want to meet her. But that was obvious from the satisfaction on her face: she'd come here with a purpose, and Kate was part of it.

'The reception's nearly over, Sera – Ranger –' Pedar said. 'The car will soon be here to take you back to your hotel.'

'Why don't you come with me?' Kate asked Brun, as much to annoy Pedar as anything else. 'We could have dinner –'

Brun smiled. 'Thanks – I'd like that.' Pedar scowled, and Kate grinned to herself. Had he thought he was going to move in on her himself? Fat chance.

They ate in Kate's suite, which was as dull as everything else she'd seen so far. What was the good of silk on the walls if it was gray? And muted green and blue upholstery . . . cold, unwelcoming, dull.

'You people don't like bright colors much, do you?'

Kate asked, halfway through a main course of some non-descript meat with a lot of fancy vegetables heaped over it. They hadn't even had steak on the menu.

Brun looked around. 'This isn't very bright, is it? I'm used to it, I guess. Castle Rock is pretty conservative.'

'That's what you call it? That Foreign Office is like a funeral home; the only color in it is your Minister, and he's –'

'Awful,' Brun said, wrinkling her nose. 'Such a little climber –'

'Climber?'

'Oh, yes. Minor family, so he pushes and climbs, trying to make himself bigger. Well, he got a Ministry, though who knows what he did for Hobart to get it.'

'Hobart's your Speaker?'

'Right. But Pedar wants more . . . you wouldn't believe, he's after my mother.'

'Your mother?' Kate reminded herself that this was Lord Thornbuckle's widow.

'Yes. He had the nerve to tell me, when Mother'd left for Sirialis, that he could now offer so much to a lonely widow – I nearly threw him out the window.'

Kate shook her head. 'I wondered if maybe he was a . . . what is it, *pet*? . . . with those rings and that shirt.'

'No – the rings are Rejuvenant rings. They're actually the medical codes: they can be implanted or worn, but a lot of people like to wear them.'

'How many times has he been pickled?'

'I don't know. I didn't count. Several. Why do you call it pickled?'

'Preserved, you know.' Kate held up one of the wrinkled green things she hoped was a pickled cucumber. 'Lasts nearly forever.'

'Mmm.' Brun ate silently a few minutes, then asked, 'What do you make of our Speaker?'

Kate looked at her, mind on full alert. 'You're asking a visitor to criticize your government?'

Brun flushed a little. 'He's a Conselline, and we're in the Barraclough Sept —'

'Is that families or religions?' Kate asked.

Brun made a face. 'Maybe both. Let's just say that the Consellines and the Barracloughs have been rivals for a long time, in a genteel sort of way. I don't like Hobart, but I wondered if maybe an outsider would see him more clearly.'

'He's nobody I'd buy a ranch from,' Kate said. 'Not without walkin' over every inch of it, and checkin' the title since God made it. He's got a mean mouth, and his wife's scared of him.'

'You saw that?'

'Oh, yes. Just like I saw that you didn't like Pedar with the rings and ruffles holding your hand when he led you over. But you wanted to talk to me.'

'You don't miss much, do you?'

'Rangers don't. Now why don't you get down to what you really wanted to talk about, so we can enjoy dessert later and not have to tippytoe?' Kate pushed her plate away and leaned back, fixing Brun with the look that had brought confessions out of the Harkness boys.

'I hate it when everyone is smarter than I am.' Brun pushed her own plate back.

'They aren't, when you leave your brain on,' Kate said. 'It didn't take a lot of intelligence to recognize that you wanted to meet me as much as I was glad to meet you.'

'You haven't met Esmay,' Brun said. 'She's smarter —'

'Spare me.' Kate ran her hands through her hair, fluffing it out. 'I heard plenty about Miss Genius on the trip over here. Everyone says she's so wonderful, and I'll bet she is. But — she isn't you.'

'No, she's —'

Kate wasn't about to let her take off down that trail, whatever it was. 'Lord, girl, you sound like you haven't got a friend in the world. Didn't you ever have a best friend?'

'Yes, but she got married.'

'Oh, brother. You and me both. Sally and I were closer than twins, and then she went all goopy over Carl, and that was the end of it. Two babies. She says she's still my friend, but all she wants to do is tell me about those two rugrats . . . which one put jam in the processor, and how the other one is smarter than any ten college professors. My mother told me she'll come out of it in a few years, but in the meantime I have to pretend to care what some grubby little kid is doing.'

'And you don't?'

'No. If there's supposed to be some instinctive maternal drive, I missed out at the feed trough. What about you?'

'Me, neither. I don't want to hurt them, but –'

'You didn't want to care for 'em either. Makes sense to me. Where are your boys?'

'A friend of my mother's took them, and found a home for them. But I worry –'

'Don't. I mean, don't worry more than you have to. And you're evading the subject. You didn't just accept a dinner invitation because you thought a stranger might be lonesome. You just about committed the impossibility of telepathic communication, wantin' me to figure a way we could talk.'

'Or to get away from Pedar; he's been wanting Mother's ansible call number. All right, all right, I'll tell you.' She scratched at a spot on the tablecloth. 'I want to find out who killed my father, and what kind of hold Hobart Conselline has on my Uncle Harlis, who's after my father's estate.'

'Now that's smart. That's a goal we can work on.'

'We?'

'Of course, we. Hell's bells, sweetheart, I'm not going to leave you to hunt this hog alone. And I need you, anyway, to help me find my way through this maze of protocol y'all live with. Besides, if you come out convinced that I'm not a monster, maybe you'll help me get your government to let up on Lone Star Confederation funds. You did know our citizens can't access their money in your banks, didn't you?'

'No!' Brun looked startled. 'When did that happen?'

'Right after the assassination. And all our citizens expelled, and the borders closed. Even your father realized we had nothing to do with that bunch of idiots who captured you. This embargo thing has put a real crimp in our economy; the Familias is our biggest external trading partner.'

'I didn't know,' Brun said. 'It didn't come up in the Council meeting.' She scowled. 'A lot of things seem to be happening without coming up before the Council . . .'

Kate glanced around the room. She had made it as secure as possible, but she didn't trust any public space.

'Maybe we ought to talk about this another time,' she said. 'Tell you the truth, I'm feeling the journey –' She noticed that Brun's gaze slid around the room too, as if she were also aware of the surveillance possibilities.

'Of course,' Brun said. 'Listen – I know some of you Lone Star people ride –'

'Ride!' Kate grinned. 'Hon, I started riding afore I could sit up, in fact afore I was born. Don't tell me they have horses in this city!'

'They do, but what I had in mind was our place out in the country. It's only a small stable, but we have some lovely views.'

'That's right nice of you. I don't know how busy I'll be

here – I'm supposed to spend my time convincing your government that we're harmless.'

'I'll introduce you to people,' Brun said. 'And it won't all be boring afternoon receptions like today's.'

'It wasn't that bad,' Kate said. 'Under the circumstances.' She winked at Brun.

CHAPTER TWELVE

Within a week, Kate had moved to Appledale. Brun took her to dinner with Viktor Barraclough, and hosted a garden party where she met a group of less senior Barraclough relatives. The Lone Star woman seemed unfailingly cheerful, brisk, and friendly. She persisted in wearing screamingly bright colors, and spent a long time every morning arranging her hair into its vast pouf, but aside from that, she might have been an old friend. Brun found herself explaining, over breakfast or in the intervals of their social commitments, everything she knew about the family business and her uncle's machinations.

The next time Harlis visited, Brun saw the Ranger in action for the first time. She had been coming downstairs when the bell rang; Kate waved off the maid and went to the door herself. Brun paused to see what would happen, stepping back so that she couldn't be seen from the door.

'Hi, I'm Kate Briarly,' she heard Kate say to Harlis, without moving aside for him.

'I want to see Brun,' Harlis snapped.

'That may be, but I don't know who you are,' Kate said. Brun was fairly sure that wasn't true – she'd shown Kate ID pictures.

'Harlis Thornbuckle – now go call Brun for me.'

A grunt followed, then: 'Now, Mister Thornbuckle –' in Kate's coolest voice.

'That's *Lord* Thornbuckle –'

'Back where I come from it is not considered polite at all for a gentleman to push his way past a lady –'

'You're no lady! And you hurt me!'

'Be that as it may, you pushed at me, and that just won't do. Now you be nice, and just wait there a minute, and I'll see if Brun has time to see you –'

'She'd better, or I'll –'

'Ah-ah-ah! No threats. Y'all know Brun's still under formal guard for any threat to her safety; you'd hate to be hauled off kickin' and hollerin' to spend the night in jail.' The door thudded shut softly, and Brun came down another few steps to see Kate standing with her back to it, shaking with silent laughter.

'You shut the door on Uncle Harlis,' Brun said, grinning.

'I truly hope your father was a better man than that, Brun, because that man is all hat and no cattle, where brains are concerned.'

'A lot better,' Brun said. 'But I'd better talk to him.' She reached for the door, and Kate stopped her.

'No – go into the drawing room and sit down in something comfortable.' Brun complied, realizing halfway there what Kate was about. She heard the door open again, and Kate's voice – all sugar now – inviting him in. Harlis stormed into the drawing room.

'Where is your mother?' he demanded.

'I'm not sure,' Brun said, carefully thinking of the possibilities – her mother might be in bed, or eating, or out riding – rather than the certainty that her mother was somewhere on Sirialis.

'Dammit – she has no right to take family property while the will's in question!'

'What property, Uncle Harlis?'

'Sirialis! I'll wager that's where she is!'

'It's a large universe, Mister Thornbuckle,' Kate said, before Brun could answer. 'Why do you think she's there? And what difference would it make if she was? She can't take off with a whole planet.'

Harlis glared at her, his face reddening. Brun tried to keep from laughing; he looked ridiculous.

'She had better not remove anything from the property,' he said finally. 'I have an injunction.'

Brun felt cold to the marrow, but Kate spoke up again.

'An injunction – not to dispose of property? In other words, not a dismissal of the original will?'

'Not that it's any of *your* business, no. She's enjoined from disposing of any of the property under dispute, until the case has been decided.'

'Suppose you just let me see that, Mister Thornbuckle –' Kate reached out an imperious hand; to Brun's surprise, her uncle put a hardcopy into it. Kate looked it over, one pencilled eyebrow elevated.

'It may be legal here, but it sure wouldn't be legal back home,' she said finally. 'Y'all have a really strange legal system, what with no proper constitution. But I guess you'll have to send Lady Thornbuckle a message about it.'

'You don't scare me,' Harlis said, and lurched out of the chair, grabbing the hardcopy from Kate on his way to the door, which he slammed.

'I don't think much of your security,' Kate said after a moment. 'Lettin' that man up to the door without warnin' us.'

'He's my uncle,' Brun said.

'And you never have family murders here? No, never mind. It's time I went to work.'

Kate looked and sounded a lot less Texan when she was detecting, Brun decided. She had acquired copies of all the relevant surveillance materials, on the grounds that she needed to prove that the Lone Star Confederation had not been involved in any way. Now her room was festooned with charts and lists and flatpic blowups.

'This here is a list of every person registered in the Monos Hotel; I don't think much of your investigators for only getting the list of those on the fifth floor and above. Sure, the shot came from that high, but people can go up as well as down. They know at least one shooter was here, in room 517 –'

'They didn't tell us that.'

'Well, they wouldn't. I wouldn't, if you were back home and I was investigatin' there . . . I'd have rules to follow, same as they do. Now, the couple in room 517 weren't there at the time. They were attending the annual convention of the plumbing contractors, and we have good surveillance pictures of them in their booth for two hours, and another two if you don't count the one trip each made to the john. Moreover, there's witness statements, and an order book with an automatic time stamp, to show they took orders.'

'They could have let someone else use their room –'

'Yup. First thing I thought of. But as it happens, the room door was forced, not unlocked. A string of DJ-8, and someone took the trouble to overpulse the mag relays so that no alarm would sound when the lock blew. They wouldn't bother with all that if they had a key. The Stringhalts might still be involved, but I doubt it. Right now I'm lookin' at eight possibles.' Kate pointed them out on her list. "Two hotel employees –

the assistant day manager, and the housekeeping supervisor –'

'Why them?'

'Access to files on which rooms were occupied, and
which rooms were occupied at what times. I don't want
to drag you through the gory parts, Brun, but look at this
here –' Kate put up another screen with the plan of the
hotel and street overlaid in colors. 'Your security personnel did a pretty good job, even though it wasn't good
enough. They'd moved all known foreigners out of rooms
overlooking the route from the court to the Palace; they'd
put spotters on the roofs, and the usual sort of net below.
They had roving patrols, including in this hotel. My
people might have made some changes, but nothing good
enough to keep your dad alive, if his route was known.
And his route was posted – everyone knew it.

'I can tell you this much . . . I'm convinced it wasn't
even an outside job. I think it was someone in the
Familias, who tried to make it look like the NewTex
Militia.'

'Well, I want to know who.'

'D'you have any ideas? Your population's a lot bigger
than ours, and we usually start with *some* idea of who's
trying to kill someone.'

Brun ticked them off. 'There's always my uncle Harlis,
though I don't think he would – he wanted my dad's
property, and he's doing his best to get it away from
Mother, as you saw. His son Kell, who's meaner than a –
what's your term?'

'Rattlesnake. And?'

'One of the Consellines, though I can't see Hobart
Conselline doing anything that stupid on his own.'

'Hmm. If it was stupid – he did end up Speaker. Well,
let's go after this another way. Leaving aside the murder,
for the moment, what else have we dug up?' Kate shoved

one mess of papers aside, and brought up a printout that looked to Brun like rows of figures.

'Are those numbers supposed to mean something?' Brun asked.

'Quite a bit,' Kate said. 'If you can follow the money, you can just about always find the criminal. I got these figures off the public newsfeeds, by the way, so I can't vouch for their accuracy. But here's some things to look at . . . see this? It's your uncle's shares in companies you told me were your family holdings.'

Brun recognized most of the names. Her mother had mentioned them, but had given no details.

'Brun, I need to talk to you.' Lady Cecelia, sounding very upset. Brun hadn't heard from her in days, and had been so caught up in Kate's research that she'd almost forgotten about her.

'Lady Cecelia, how –'

'Now,' the voice said.

'I have that Lone Star woman visiting . . .'

'I know; I heard the rumors. But can I come out for a few days?'

'Of course.'

A few hours later, Cecelia erupted into the house in what Brun recognized as a fine white fury. She didn't even glance at Kate.

'Did you know that Kevil Mahoney's been robbed while he was in hospital?'

'No! George didn't say –'

'George has been trying to cope without getting them in deeper trouble. Someone swiped their accounts, the day of the assassination, though George was too busy to find out about it for a couple of weeks. And he had no way to trace it by then.'

'But how? I thought the safeguards –'

'Were safe. Yes. So did I. But George is trying to take care of Kevil, and finish law school – they can't even afford a cook, and they're going to have to sell the house! The thing is, Brun, George didn't have the access codes and Kevil couldn't remember them. I have them, but I don't know how to interpret what's in the files.'

'You have Kevil's access codes?'

Cecelia reddened. 'Yes. And he has – had – mine.'

'So what they were saying about you and Kevil –'

'Was idle gossip. Brun, I'm ashamed of you! The man's hurt, his memory's damaged, he's been robbed, and all you can think about is that?'

'Sorry,' Brun said. 'It did come to mind.'

Cecelia looked at the papers and films spread all over the library tables, and then at Kate. 'What were you looking up?'

'Goin' through the public financial records, trying to find out how Harlis was gettin' so far with a ridiculous claim, and tryin' to cross the trail of the killer. Brun's mama's over at Sirialis, doin' the same thing.'

Brun looked at Cecelia.

'Kate, we need to join forces here. With the codes Cecelia has, and your ability to interpret the files, this might go a lot faster.'

'If you'll keep intruders out,' Kate said. 'Remember what I said about your inept security –'

'I worry more about Kevil,' Brun said. 'Why don't I go bring him out here?'

'Excellent idea,' Kate said.

'But that's all wrong, that's –'

'Somebody'd do all that, wouldn't stop at a little shootin'.'

By the time Brun got back with Kevil Mahoney, Kate and Cecelia were hard at work. Brun helped Kevil into the library, and moved a pile of printouts off a chair for him.

'Looks . . . like fun . . .' he said. 'You . . . must be the . . . Texan.'

'Ranger Briarly,' Kate said. 'Just call me Kate. Somebody sure knocked a hole in your stock tank . . . but I'll get 'em.'

'Kate has a healthy disrespect for thieves,' Cecelia said.

'I don't like people hurtin' people, and takin' advantage, 'specially of people that's just been shot.' Kate gave Kevil one of her wide smiles. 'I will bet my best show saddle that there's not but one or two villains in this drama, and I aim to catch every one of 'em.'

'You'd be interested in what I found at Kevil's, then,' Brun said. She held up a sack and shook it. 'Interesting meds to give someone with a brain injury . . .'

'I thought so,' Cecelia said. 'Was that nurse there? He's been harder to shake with every visit.'

'Oh, yes. Very eager to give Ser Mahoney a little something to make the trip out here easier. Then very eager to clear the shelves of the meds.'

'I don't suppose you have *his* access codes,' Kate said, looking up.

Brun grinned. 'When I got back home, and wasn't going out much, I spent my time building some of the gadgets Koutsoudas has . . . so yes, an illegal datasuck gave me every bit of data on him. Here.' She put it down on the table. 'Interfaces to the cube reader or the computer, whichever you want.'

Three nights later, Brun was dozing on one of the long leather couches in the library, an arm shielding her eyes from the light, when the breakthrough came.

'Gotcha!' Kate muttered. She no longer looked like the sexy blonde in red fringe; back-to-back all-night work sessions had flattened the hair, and put circles under her eyes. Instead of the tight red suit, she wore loose knit pants and shirt. But nothing could dim the grin she turned on the others. 'This is it, partners – we've got what we need.'

'Ummm . . .' Brun heard only the first of that, but managed to open a bleary eye for the last phrase. 'Got whom?'

'Your uncle Harlis, for starters. He's been acquiring stock in ways that are illegal even here – and I have to say, Brun, that your government needs to overhaul its legal system in a big way. There's holes you could drive a herd of longhorns through, with this bylaws arrangement. All you have to have is one generation of idiots, cowards, and a few bad guys, and it'd be all over for you.'

Cecelia's rumpled red head rose from the other couch. 'That s all very well, but what did he *do*?'

'He extorted stock by roughing up some of your weaker relatives . . . you remember tellin' me how surprised you were that your dad's aunt Trema left her stock to Harlis? That was no accident. I've got the paper trail where Harlis got some local toughs to come in and stomp on some of her favorite china, and tell her they'd break her bones just as easy. And he had the police around there in his pocket, told 'em she was a crazy old lady who dropped things and had hallucinations.'

'And they believed it?'

'Money makes a strong argument. Anyway, that's not all I've got, and the evidence ought to stand up even in a crooked court. Which is what you've got, I gather – Harlis contributed quite a bit to the education of certain judges' children. If you've got any kind of an opposition journal, this'll be meat and gravy for 'em.'

'I can . . . help write . . . the appeal . . .' Kevil Mahoney said. He was standing, leaning crookedly against the doorframe.

'You're up,' Cecelia said. 'You're supposed to be resting.'

'I've done nothing . . . but rest for . . . weeks. Enough. My memory's still as spotty as a Dalmatian dog, but if you feed me the facts, I can write. I think.' His speech had already improved, but now it smoothed even more the longer he talked.

'Good,' Kate said, with another of those blinding grins. 'Then I think it's time for this Texas gal to go have a rest and a shower. I must look like something the barn cat dragged in.'

Kevil Mahoney's name on the bottom of the petition for summary judgement upholding the late Lord Thornbuckle's will might have had little effect, but the thick stack of supporting evidence did. One of the court clerks called Brun that very afternoon.

'The judge hasn't heard of any of this before –' The clerk's voice was sharp with disapproval.

'Of course not,' Brun said. 'Ser Mahoney was critically injured, as you know; some of the family files were under his personal lock.' She said nothing about Kevil's other problems; a clerk wouldn't have reason to know anything about them.

'Is this all the data you have, or can we expect more?' That was sarcasm, but the clerk sounded uneasy.

'No, this isn't all; this is merely the preliminary filing. My mother, Lady Thornbuckle, is on Sirialis, getting additional data from the main family archives there.'

'I see. Well . . . you'll hear from us.'

Two hours later, Harlis came storming up the drive, only to be stopped by Brun's new security force. After they disarmed him, and checked with Brun, they escorted him to the door. Brun met him there, backed by Kate, Cecelia, and an upright Kevil, who was leaning on

George. Kate had reappeared in full Texan persona, but this time she wore her Ranger badge.

'Before you say anything,' Brun said, 'let me make it clear: we have all the evidence we need that you engaged in criminal activity to get control of family companies, and we are gathering more.'

Her uncle glared. 'I don't believe it! You can't do this to me! I didn't do anything . . . it was all perfectly legal. Hobart will take care of you –' Then he blenched.

'How very interesting,' Cecelia said. 'Hobart . . . Could you possibly mean Hobart *Conselline* . . . now why would someone in our sept be working with a Conselline . . .'

'I didn't say Conselline,' Harlis said. But he had changed color, and his voice shook. 'But it's my *right* –'

'You had no right to terrify poor old Aunt Trema,' Brun said. She was startled to realize that she sounded very much like her father, and wondered if the others noticed. 'And yes, we will press charges.'

'I'll – I'll see you in hell!' Harlis wheeled and strode down the front walk, shadowed by the guards.

'It's not over,' Brun said, as much to herself as to the others. Harlis wasn't ready to give up, and she didn't know what he might do next.

'No, but it's a good beginning,' Kate said. 'C'mon, hon, wait until you hear Cecelia's next good idea.'

'What?'

'She's found a place for all those inconvenient women and children that Lieutenant Serrano is stuck with. She's going to take them off to a pioneer planet she knows about, where they'll be happier and their skills are needed.'

'That's nice for Barin and Esmay,' Brun said. 'But I wanted her to go tell my mother what we've accomplished. She needs to know that we have evidence against Harlis. We can't trust that to ordinary communications –'

'You're right, but now that Harlis is on the run there's no hurry, is there? Your mother's not going to do anything rash.'

EXCET-24

Ruth Ann took a long look out the windows. It looked cool and green, and she didn't know if this was spring, summer or winter. Puddles reflected the sky, patches of blue and rolls of gray cloud like unspun wool.

No towering cities, no noisy crowds. When the hatch opened, the air that swept in was cool, moist. She could smell green growing things on that air. The red-haired woman led the way; Ruth Ann followed close behind. The ground felt good to her feet, even through shoes. It held still; it didn't vibrate.

The red-haired woman with the fancy name – Cecelia whatsis, a Rejuvenant – led the way into a little square building, where they each had to show their ID. Ruth Ann felt the oddness of it, that each person handled their own cards. And hers had her own name on it, Ruth Ann Pardue.

Once they were all finished with 'Customs,' whatever that was, and had new purple stamps on the cards, the red-haired woman led them down the street. This was scary. The little town looked like the backwater village where she'd grown up where she'd have been whipped till her legs bled for walking around wearing shoes and looking at people . . . but here were men and women, dressed almost decently, except that they all wore shoes, and the women didn't keep their eyes down. People looked at her, but with hope, not distaste. She recognized the admiring glances at the children.

They turned into the open doorway of a two-story building, and the red-headed woman yelled, 'Ronnie! Raffaele!' Immediately, a woman yelled back. 'Lady Cecelia! Just a second – I'm coming!' Then a clatter on the stairs, and a slender young woman with dark hair and eyes came running down, and gave the red-headed woman a hug. Then she looked at Ruth Ann. 'I've got dinner on – we're so glad you came; I hope you'll like it here. Ronnie's out trying to see why a machine won't work or something . . . he'll be back soon.'

Ruth Ann recognized, in the woman who introduced herself as Raffaele, the same signs of abomination she had seen in Brun. This woman had never lowered her eyes in respect; she had never stood back keeping silence; she had never been denied access to anything she wanted to learn.

But – from the smells coming from the kitchen – she had also never learned to do more than push buttons when she wanted something to eat.

'And we hope –' Raffaele was still talking, when Ruth Ann interrupted.

'What were you trying to cook?'

'Just some . . . some meat . . .'

'Let me take a look.' Ruth Ann sailed into the kitchen on a wave of unexpected delight. Sure enough, the place was a mess, sticky implements cluttering the counter – and not a big enough counter, either, that would have to change – and a stove leaking smoke from a badly-hung oven door.

'Secunda – Shelley Marie, you get that counter cleared. Tertia – Terry, get this floor clean. Benji –' Her oldest son stared at her, wide eyed. 'Benji, we need that stove fixed.'

'Pri – Mama?'

'Now, Benji.' She could feel her confidence coming

back. 'Simplicity, honey, you take the littles out into the garden – you do have a garden, don't you?' she asked Raffaele.

'Y-yes, but it's not – it's kind of a mess.'

'Not for long.' Messes she understood, and what to do about them. 'Simplicity, just you start the littles weeding, and make sure nothing bothers them.'

The dark-haired young woman was fluttering now, like a gaudy butterfly in a net. 'But – but Sera – Ruth Ann – I didn't mean for you to go to work – I was making dinner for you –'

'Never you mind – why don't you go set the table or something?'

'Come on, Raffa; I'll explain about Ruth Ann.' The tall lanky redhead led the younger woman away.

In a kitchen again at last, a real kitchen. Too small by far for all of them, but bigger than any of the cubbyholes called kitchens in the spaceships and space stations. Shelley had found a kettle and had water heating on the stovetop; Benji had already taken off the oven door. Inside was a lump of meat, charring on one side.

Shelley handed Ruth Ann a couple of folded towels, and she pulled out the cooking pan, wrinkling her nose at the smell. Raw inside, burnt outside; the girl had built up the fire too much too fast, trying to compensate for the ill-hung door. Probably she'd never cooked without the electric, and the electric was off.

Ruth Ann looked around for a worktable – none. It would have to be the counter, where Shelley swept aside the clutter to make room for her, then began rummaging in drawers for the knife she knew Ruth Ann would want. 'We're going to need a worktable,' she told Benji. 'They said they had plenty of wood, so that's something to start planning.'

*

'Cecelia, I feel terrible – but the twins kept me up last
night –'

'You haven't found anyone to take them –?'

'No.' Raffa blushed, a becoming color, Cecelia noted.
'I – we – we sort of – decided to keep them ourselves.
And one of the nursemaids ran off with a farmer, and the
one with children wanted to start a school, and besides
she has her own children to care for . . .'

'You?' This was an unexpected complication. 'Er . . .
do you think that's wise?'

'You mean, will Brun mind when she finds out?' Raffa
had always been too sharp. 'I don't think she will, but if
she does, too bad. I quite understand her not wanting to
keep them. It must have been horrible, and I wish it had
never happened But I like – no, I *love* the boys, and I
even love it that they're part of her. The way things are,
Ronnie and I may never get off this planet again – and
that's all right, but I do miss some things –'

'My dear – you don't have to stay here –'

'Yes, we do, and don't argue. We wanted a life of our
own, and we're getting it. It's not anything I imagined,
but – whether you believe it or not – we're happy. But the
thing is, children . . . it'll be years, because . . . well . . . I
don't fancy having babies without modern medical support. This way, we're helping Brun. And ourselves.'

Clearly it would do no good to argue. 'What did you
name them?' Cecelia asked.

'The redhead's Peter, for Ronnie's great-uncle, and the
brown-haired one's Salomar, for my mother's brother.'

Cecelia felt her eyes stinging unexpectedly. Family
names – and names she must know were in Brun's family
line as well. 'So – when do I see the little demons?'

'They're napping. They've had some illness – I know
it's only a childhood thing, and all children do this . . .
out here, I mean.'

'Well, we'd better set the table then. One thing I've found out about Ruth Ann, when she makes up her mind, things get done.'

'Was she one of the – one of the ones who hurt Brun?'

'No. Her husband was, but she knew nothing about it until long afterwards. Where's your table linen?'

'Used it for crib sheets,' Raffa said. 'All we can do is dust this off.' *This* had been an elegant dining table when Raffa and Ronnie brought it downside, but it had spent several years as a work surface, and looked it. Cecelia forbore to comment on the state of the floor – with no glass in the windows, let alone any household machinery, how could Raffa keep dust off the floor? – and helped wipe down the scarred tabletop.

'I still have most of the china,' Raffa said. She unlocked the big cupboard in the corner, and took down stacks of plates. 'Even if they look a bit silly on this bare wood.'

Incongruous was the right word, but Cecelia said nothing, laying out Pierce & Samuelson's famous 'Coronation' pattern, with the gold wavy rim. Partway through, she noticed that the smell from the kitchen had changed from singed meat and something sour to a delicious blend of roast and something that almost smelled like bread.

Suddenly Ruth Ann appeared in the doorway. 'Oh – you don't use tablecloths?'

'We don't have any left,' Raffa said. 'We had to use them for the beds –'

'Deary me! And us with all more than enough in the luggage. Cecelia, where are the boxes, do you know?'

'No, but I'll find out. Which box?'

'The one with the table and chair on the side.'

Cecelia headed for the shuttle and, from the piles of boxes being unloaded, located the one with the table and chair on the side. One of the crew carried it back for her;

she set it on the table and opened it carefully. Inside, it was stacked full of folded linens, brilliant with hand embroidery.

Cecelia lifted out the folded cloth. 'However did you have time to weave this?'

'Oh, that's not our weave,' Terry said. 'We had no space for looms. But Prima – Ruth – says we mustn't be idle. She got that Miss Waltraude to get us some cloth, and we embroidered it. Do you think it's good enough?'

Cecelia shook out the folds. On plain white cloth, the women had embroidered a broad band of flowers, trees, birds, stars, and what she supposed were religious symbols. 'It's . . . more than good enough.' It was splendid, and the Coronation pattern looked even better than it had before.

By this time the kitchen smells had attracted the twins from upstairs. The twins were much more mobile than before, and although they might have been sick the day before, they were full of life now. They made straight for the table, and Raffaele tried to intercept them. Terry grabbed Salomar just as Raffa caught Peter.

'What big boys!' Terry cooed. 'Yours, ma'am?'

'Yes,' Raffa said. 'But I'm not ma'am – just call me Raffa. If you could help keep them out of the dinner table –'

'I'll take them out in the garden, and help Simplicity keep an eye on them.'

When she'd gone, Cecelia cocked an eye at Raffa. 'They'll never believe you bore those children, you know. They'll realize they're adopted.'

'Yes, but not from whom,' Raffa said firmly.

Cecelia dared a peek into the kitchen. The floor could not gleam, being what it was, but it had the look of a floor that would gleam if only it were smooth enough. Ruth Ann worked a great lump of dough on the counter, which did gleam except where she worked. One of the

women was washing dishes; another was chopping something that smelled good. Older children were moving in
and out, bringing bits of fresh greenery from the garden,
carrying out trash, and – as soon as Raffa agreed – mop-
ping the dining room floor.

The lights came back on just before Ronnie came home.

'My God,' Ronnie said as he came through the door.
The women bowed their heads and waited. 'I mean – er –
it's a surprise.'

Ruth Ann looked up. 'We don't take the name of the
Lord in vain,' she said. 'I thought you were going to pray.'

'I know – I just . . . what did you do? Where did all this
come from?'

'It's just food,' Ruth Ann said.

'It's not just food,' Ronnie said. 'It's a feast.'

'Then you can say thanks to God for it,' Ruth Ann said.
She looked hard at Ronnie, who reddened and stumbled
through a child's grace Cecelia was sure he had not
uttered in over a decade. The NewTex women added a
hearty 'Amen.'

The roast fell into even slices, perfectly cooked. Puffy
rolls as light as clouds. Potatoes, crisp outside and mealy
inside. Fresh greens that weren't bitter or too sour.

'Truly a feast,' Raffa said. 'I can't imagine how you got
that horrid old stove to work. Ever since the electric went
bad, we've all been stuck. The bread machines don't
work –'

'You don't need machines to make bread,' Ruth Ann
said.

'I do,' Raffa said, with a smile that took the sting out of
the contradiction. 'I don't know how to make it otherwise. I tried to put the ingredients in a bowl that the
directions say to put in a bread machine, but it came out
the most horrible sour lump –'

'Did you knead it enough?'

'Knead? What's that? I mixed it up, isn't that what the machine does?'

Terry snorted, and Ruth Ann shot her a look. 'I don't mean to make fun,' she began.

'You can make all the fun you want, if you'll teach me how to cook the way you do,' Raffaele said. 'If I could make an edible loaf of bread, just once –'

'You don't make good bread by making it once,' Ruth Ann said, feeling more secure every moment. Cecelia had been right. Clearly this household needed her, needed the knowledge she had. 'You make good bread by making a lot of bread.'

'Well, here I am,' Raffa said. 'Ready to learn.'

Ruth Ann remembered Hazel, and had her doubts. This woman was much older than Hazel, and unless she had a natural knack, she might never be very good. Still . . . she could certainly learn not to stuff too much fuel in a leaky oven, and burn a roast on one side.

After dinner, the junior wives organized cleanup without even being told, and Ruth Ann discussed with Raffaele why they'd come, and what they wanted to do.

'We can use all the instruction you give us,' Raffa said. 'I told Lady Cecelia last time she was here . . . we have good, hard-working people, but none of us have ever done without electricity, or running water, or all the other things that we have on developed worlds. It's not just me – it's all of us, just about. We can't learn all this out of books or teaching cubes.'

'Let's start with you, then. There's room in this house; we can experiment –' She was proud of using that new word, of being able to think of it. 'When we know what you need, we'll know what the others need.'

The next day, work began in earnest. Ruth Ann had a clear picture in her mind of what the kitchen needed to be, so she and the others could work there without falling all over each other. She couldn't believe it . . . she was directing men. 'Make the counter this long,' she'd said, and they were making it that long. They didn't seem to mind, and she was enjoying it. So were the others. All those months of being told how backward they were, all those months of being confused by the humming machines, feeling awkward and uncertain. And now –

'If you arrange your beds so the tall plants don't shade the low ones, you'll get more yield,' Becky was telling Raffaele. 'See, you've got them crossways . . . if the plant rows went the other direction –'

'Oh . . . well . . . look, Becky, why don't you tell me how it should be, and I'll draw a plot of it for next season's planting.'

'Fine –'

Terry had gone upstairs to work on the bedrooms – although they'd slept last night, Ruth Ann had been very aware of the clutter and dust. The boys were at work in the front courtyard on simple furniture: rope-strung bunks to get them all up off the floor. When Ruth Ann looked out the tall dining room windows, she saw a crowd of men standing watching. It was backwards, men learning from boys, but it was right that the boys and men were together. She carefully ignored the two women wearing pants in the same group.

By dinnertime that day, the shuttle had brought the rest of their things down from the spaceship, including the popup cots Lady Cecelia had bought. The whole house smelled different, and Ronnie had the expression Ruth Ann liked to see on the head of a household. Of course, he wasn't her husband – she kept reminding herself of that – but she did enjoy watching a man eat with relish.

Cecelia left a few days later. Ruth Ann hardly noticed;

she had her worktable in the expanded kitchen, and had also set up a summer stove outside, for preserving.

'What we need is a school,' Raffa said, watching the crowd around the stove as Shelley demonstrated jelly testing. 'A really big kitchen, where everybody could come to learn cooking, and maybe a sewing room where they could learn sewing.'

'A weaving shed,' Ruth Ann said. 'That fabricator cloth is too harsh. And a really big bread oven.'

Raffa looked around. 'This would almost work, if Ronnie and I moved into one of the smaller houses.'

'No,' Ruth Ann said firmly. 'Your husband's the governor; you need this house. We'll build one.'

More quickly than even she had hoped, the school went up. The engineering cubes Cecelia had brought, and the bundles of reinforcing whiskers, made it possible to pour solid walls quickly. One of the other colonists, who had been a hobby potter on her home world, found a lens of good clay in the riverbank, and knew how to make tiles.

'Not really good ones yet,' she admitted. 'We don't have a kiln hot enough. But for starters, better than plain concrete or dirt.' The school was the first building to have locally made tile floors.

A proper school for proper women, with a kitchen in which they could all learn the way she had learned – from watching and doing and being knocked on the knuckles with a wooden spoon when they needed it. A big outdoor oven to handle dozens of loaves of bread at once. A weaving shed – she regretted the loss of the captive women, who had been such talented weavers, but Tertia Crockett – she used Anna now – was almost as good. Sunrooms for embroidery. Gardens for the children.

The gardens for the children produced another benefit –

everyone in the colony wanted their youngest children there, under Simplicity's gentle guidance, for part of the day. Raffaele brought her twins when she came to learn cooking, and the other women copied her. As Ruth Ann had suspected, Raffaele would never be more than a middling baker. Her hand was too heavy for pastry, and not firm enough for yeast dough, though both her pie crusts and bread were now at least edible. But the other women followed her lead, and the gardens were full of busy little children.

Raffaele's twins, though – the twins gave Ruth Ann a funny feeling in the chest. Salomar, in particular, was all too familiar . . . she had seen that quirk of mouth, that shape of eyebrow and set of eye, before. She looked again and again at Raffaele and Ronnie, trying to trace in their faces the source of those details of Salomar's. What kept nagging at her had to be impossible. She had to be imagining it. Didn't she?

She put her mind firmly back on the school. A few of the other former wives were being courted by men whose wives had died, but enough of the women wanted no part of remarriage that she was sure of enough teachers for years to come. Her daughters had suitors, too, the older ones.

And her sons, about whose acceptance she had been so worried, were every one of them more expert at tool use than these city folks, for all that those men had taken courses and been passed as expert enough. They may've been, Ruth Ann thought, with the fancy electric tools they'd trained on, but few of them knew anything of unpowered tools.

Everything from beds and tables to bowls poured out of the boys' workshop. Nobody minded that it was plain stuff, though one of the other colonists began making stains out of local plants to give the wood different tones of soft red and yellow. And nobody here minded if a few girls took up woodcrafting. All through the rest of that spring, and into this new world's long summer, Ruth Ann blessed the long series of chances that had brought them here.

'I never thought nineteen women and a bunch of children could make this much difference,' Ronnie said one hot afternoon. He'd taken to coming by to fetch the twins, and he often stopped to chat, leaning on one of the planters. 'You've galvanized the colony, is what you've done. The extra supplies helped, but it's you, Ruth Ann, you and the rest of them, who've waked us up and gotten us moving.'

She glanced sideways at him, thinking that he hadn't learned it all yet, even so. Greatly daring, but also confident, she reached to the basket of hand tools. 'While you're resting,' she said, handing him a weeder and nodding to the planter he leaned on.

He grinned at her. 'You never do stop working, do you?'

'You don't have to rush if you don't get behind,' she pointed out. 'Those stickery ones are the weeds.'

'Yes, ma'am.' He grinned at her. 'I'll learn in the end.'

'By the way,' she said, finding it easier to bring this up when he was bending over the tangled growth, weeding. 'Those twins of yours . . . I can't believe your Raffaele bore them – she's so tiny.'

Ronnie's ears turned redder. 'She didn't,' he said shortly. 'They're adopted.'

'It doesn't matter to God,' Ruth Ann said. 'What it is, though – and I know I'm being presumptuous, but – that Salomar. He reminds me of someone.'

The back of Ronnie's neck went three shades darker, not counting the sunburn. 'Who?' he asked, more coolly than Ruth Ann expected.

'I'm thinking,' Ruth Ann said, folding her needle away,

because her hand had started shaking. 'I'm thinking he minds me of my – of Mitch. And I'm thinking, if there's any reason he should mind me of Mitch, that you might be worrying that I'd notice. You've been awful good to us, and I don't want to worry you. So if – if it is that, what I'm thinking of, then – then I want you to know that I don't mind, and I'm glad to have the boy around. Both of them.'

Ronnie said nothing; his shoulders bunched, and the dirt flew.

'I won't say any more,' Ruth Ann said.

'It's . . . all right.' He turned around; his eyes were bright with unshed tears. 'I – we didn't know you were coming, or – but – Oh, I'm making a mess of this, Raffa will kill me. But if you've guessed, you've guessed –'

'I bore nine of that man's children; I know their stamp,' Ruth Ann said. She said nothing of Peter's father, though she knew exactly who that red hair reminded her of.

'Brun wanted a good home for them; she was afraid they might be stolen away and used against her.'

'You don't have to defend her to me,' Ruth Ann said. She still could not understand a woman not clinging to her own flesh and blood, but she wasn't going to argue that now. If their mother had been a natural mother, she herself wouldn't have this chance. 'You don't know what a blessing it is, to have those children here,' she said. 'I've worried and worried – that's the last bit of Mitch I'll ever see; I wanted to know the children were safe. Will Raffaele mind? I'm not going to interfere, I promise you.'

'She'll skin me, but she'll hug you,' Ronnie said. 'Ruth Ann – you are a very, very unusual lady.'

'I try to be a good woman,' Ruth Ann said, but a bubble of delight rose and would not be denied. She stood up, and let her head fall back. 'Praise God, you aren't angry with me for seeing what I saw, and you won't keep me from him. I never thought to be happy again, and here I am happier than I've ever been.'

CHAPTER THIRTEEN

**BENIGNITY OF THE COMPASSIONATE HAND
NUOVO VENITZA, SANTA LUZIA**

Confession, for a member of the Order of Swords who had been on a mission, must always be to a priest of the Order. Even so, there were things no one confessed, not if he wanted to live; the priests had the right – ecclesiastical and legal – to mete out punishment, including death.

Hostite Fieddi knelt in silence, awaiting the priest's arrival, and thought about what he had to confess, and what he had to conceal. As a young man, he had found distinguishing between debriefing and confession very difficult, but now it was second nature.

The soft chime rang; Hostite began the old, familiar ritual, 'Forgive me . . .' Even as his voice continued the opening phrases, his mind was dividing, as sheep from goats, the truths he must repent from the other truths of which he must not repent, as long as he was a Swordmaster.

'It has been a long time,' the priest said.

'I was on a mission,' Hostite said. 'To distant worlds.'

'Beyond the Church's dominion?' asked the priest.

'Nothing is beyond the Church's dominion,' Hostite said. 'But this was far from any priest of the Order of Swords.'

'Ah. Go on then.'

Category by category, he laid his soul's burden out, the temptations acted upon and those merely dwelt upon in the mind, the orders followed which ought not to have been followed, the orders not followed which ought to have been followed. He was heartily sorry for them all, for the necessities which his duty placed upon his conscience, when he would – were he other than he was – have been happy to live in peace all his days, with no more to confess than a lustful glance at someone's daughter.

'And have you any other sins . . . lust perhaps?'

They always asked about lust, though by now they should know that his conditioning had destroyed that possibility. He answered as always, and as always received his penance in true submission of spirit. When he was too old to be of service, when the Master of the Order of Swords commanded, he would confess the last of his sins, and go to his death clean-hearted, no longer the Shadow of the dancers, but filled with light. So it had been promised him, and so he believed.

There was no other life but this possible, and no other future to which he belonged.

'Hostite –!' The Master's call brought him out of the reverie which a long penance produced.

'Milord.' Hostite rose smoothly from his knees and turned.

'The Chairman would like an expansion of your report on the situation in the Familias.'

'Milord.'

'We will be granted an audience this afternoon. I will

accompany you, as will Iagin Persius.' Persius, another who had recently completed a mission in the Familias. Hostite was elder by three years, but he knew Persius as a competent agent. 'You will report to the Order's Clothier for a fitting now.'

'Yes, milord.' Hostite bowed; the Master withdrew from the chapel, and Hostite made his way to the store-rooms in which the Order kept all the costumes its members might need. He did not dwell upon the after-noon's meeting. Rumor had many things to say about audiences with the Chairman, but Hostite had been there before, and in any case feared nothing, including death.

The costume appropriate for a Swordmaster in this instance was simple enough. The bodysuit of black stretch-knit fit like skin and incidentally left no space for hidden weapons. The scarlet velvet cap matched scarlet velvet slippers, and denoted his Swordmaster rank. Looped through the shoulder epaulets were cords of gold, green, and red silk – the level of experience, the number of assassinations domestic and foreign, the whole story of his career, if one knew how to read it – and the Chairman certainly did. As he was checking the fit of the slippers, Iagin Persius came in. He nodded but did not speak. Hostite nodded in return. They could not discuss their missions until after the report to the Chairman, lest they be suspected of colluding in some error.

From then until lunch, Hostite reviewed his debriefing cube, correcting minor errors in transcription with a coded datawand; four seats down, Persius was doing the same thing. At lunch, they ate at different tables in the Order mess; Hostite restricted himself, as his penance required, to clear soup and water with a lump of 'sin-ners' bread' – a hard, sour, unleavened lump that offered just enough nourishment to ensure that the penitent could perform any necessary duty.

Outside the Chairman's office, the Master of the Order of Swords handed his red cut-velvet cloak to the gray-uniformed guards, and unbuckled his sword belt. Hostite wondered why the Master was required to wear full dress, and then relinquish the cloak and swords, but he pushed the question aside. Tradition required it, that was all. He and Persius doffed their velvet caps for inspection, then put them back on.

The Chairman sat behind his great black marble desk, his face reflected dimly in its gleaming surface. On either side, his personal guards.

'Fieddi, you were sent to see the Barracloughs . . . what, then, did you find?'

Hostite bowed, then began his recital, carefully gazing at the bronze plaque on the wall behind the Chairman's head. 'This was my third visit to the Barraclough senior branch, in the persona of a sabre-dance troupe's visiting instructor. On my fourth day there, the assassination of Lord Thornbuckle was reported. The dance troupe is comprised of locals, though they have been trained by Swordmasters; their reactions indicated that they were aware of friction between Lord Thornbuckle and his younger brother, and between Thornbuckle and certain Families: the Conselline-Morreline Sept in particular.'

'Did you have speech with family members?'

'I gave private lessons to six family members while there, including Stefan, the present head of Family; Mieran his wife; Rudolf and James, his sons; Katarin his daughter; and Viola, his niece. Stefan spoke only of the art of fence; he is proficient in three weapons, but wishes to become expert. He asked advice on hiring a permanent master; this request had been anticipated by the Master, and I recommended Alain Detours, as instructed. Mieran expressed the opinion that Lord Thornbuckle's death was a dreadful nuisance, but that he had brought it on himself, and she hoped that the New Texan assassins would be satisfied with one death.'

'How does she fence?' asked the Chairman.

'With that same wit,' Hostite answered. 'She answers a threat well enough, but always directly. She cannot see beyond the next thrust. Most women of the Seated Families are more astute.'

'And the others?'

'Rudolf prefers parpaun; he fences only because it is done in his set, and is content with mediocrity.'

'His mother's son . . .' the Chairman said. 'Go on.'

'James competes in school tourneys; he seeks praise from me when I visit. He may mature into a good fencer someday.'

'Weapon?'

'Epee, I think, though perhaps saber later.'

'Continue.'

'Katarin and Viola both fence well, for women.'

'You have no more to say about them?'

'No . . . they fence because it is done, as they play at nets or ball or swim.'

'Are they pretty, Fieddi?'

Hostite cast his mind back; he could see the faces clearly but he had no grasp of what the Chairman's standard of beauty was. 'They are young, and rich,' he said. 'They are not Dancers.'

The Chairman laughed. 'Your standards are strict, I see. Well, then . . . Iagin Persius. You were sent to the Consellines. What did you find?'

'Hobart Conselline continues in his belief that he is ill-treated. Although he is now the acknowledged head of that family and sept, he still hungers after the approval he feels was given his brother. He is ambitious for himself and his friends; he wants to ensure his secure hold on power for the rest of his life.'

'And he is a Rejuvenant?'

'Yes, a multiple. He despises the short-lived who cannot afford rejuvenation.'

'And does he know where the Compassionate Hand stands on rejuvenation?'

'He does, sir, and he says it is the one weakness of the Compassionate Hand.'

'His religion?'

'He has no belief in any higher power than wealth and influence, sir.'

'Ah. Such men are ripe for superstition. Hostite, how about the Barracloughs?'

'Some in the family are believers, but not in our faith. Theirs is debased, decadent, a descendant of those rebellious faiths of Old Earth, which broke away from Holy Church so long ago.'

'Hostite! I did not know you could be eloquent.' That arch surprise was dangerous; Hostite tried to empty his mind of all but his duty. 'So you are passionate about the Church?'

'Sir, I am a member of the Order of Swords; I have given my life to the Order since childhood.'

'I know that, Hostite. But I sense in you some deeper emotion. Have you ever had a vision or revelation of Our Lord?'

'No, sir, none that could not be explained as a child's wishful fantasy. But the contact with those unbelievers in the Familias has made me realize what a treasure the True Faith is. They play with their faith as a child with jacks and balls, putting it away in a mental box when it is not convenient. That is not real faith.'

'No, of course not. But let us go back to the matters at hand. How stand the Barracloughs on rejuvenation?'

'Most of them over forty have been rejuvenated, sir, but several of the seniors have refused. The Barraclough family has an elective power structure: Stefan, the current head of family, is not actually the eldest son of eldest sons. His older brother Viktor specialized in legal theory, and he refused rejuvenation. His objection was legal – the turmoil that would be caused by multiple rejuvenations. Viktor is now in his seventies. Viktor's daughter Viviane was rejuvenated with the new process at forty; she is now forty-five, but my sources say that she is determined not to repeat the process. Stefan is fifty-seven, and has received two rejuvenations, giving him an apparent age of thirty. However, he disapproves of what he calls "frivolous" rejuvenations.'

'Ummm . . . for either of you: to what extent do the non-Family citizens of the Familias regard rejuvenation as a legal or social or religious matter?'

Hostite paused, thinking, but Iagin spoke up quickly. 'Because Hobart Conselline is so willing to talk – more willing to talk than almost anything else – I have data on these points. He is very concerned about opposition to serial rejuvenation. This is fuelled both by concerns about the profit margin – Conselline Sept's family investments in rejuv pharmaceuticals are large, and until the Patchcock scandal, these had formed twenty percent or more of the profits – and by concern about the social constraints that might be put on serial rejuvenants. The Consellines introduced and strongly supported the repeal of the law against repeat rejuvenations. He feels that serial rejuvenation, conferring unlimited lifespan, is the earned right of those who have shown their fitness by accumulating the wealth to afford it.'

'Ah – and would he apply this same philosophy to foreign affairs?'

'In all likelihood. He follows up advantages in fencing – and, from what I've been able to gather, in other domains as well – with great vigor and intensity. I have observed him at table, and with his family, and would say that nothing is ever enough for him. If he had no access to rejuvenation and advanced medical care, he would eat and drink himself into the grave.'

'Truly, the discipline of the Faith saves more than souls,' the Chairman said, flashing a smile at Hostite. The Chairman, as lean and fit at sixty as he had been thirty years earlier, had not been rejuvenated and would not be: the Church forbade it. But neither would he inflict damage on his own body for selfish purposes. 'So . . . Hobart Conselline, who has become the new head of government, is a man of grudges and jealousies, scheming and ruthless, a man who will not feel safe until he controls everything. What, Hostite, will the Barracloughs do when he tries to control them?'

'Viktor will fight, with all the legal knowledge he has – but the Familias Regnant has no formal Constitution. Stefan will start by hoping for the best, but if Hobart angers him sufficiently he will lead his Family in opposition. He is not a man of great vision, however. He counters the obvious attack, but does not see the oblique one that covers.'

'Why, I wonder, did they elect him head of the Family?'

Hostite cleared his throat. 'Of the posssibilities, he seemed least likely to interfere with the others' lives. Lord Thornbuckle was already Speaker, in any case – he did not want the Family leadership as well. His younger brother Harlis was not well-liked. Viktor didn't want it. And although the Familias is far from strict on the gender issue, few of the great Families have women at the head. None of the Barraclough women were dissatisfied enough to make a run for it.'

'They have no renegade women?'

'They do, but their tastes run to inconsequentials. Lady Cecelia de Marktos, for instance, breeds horses.'

'She was on Xavier,' the Chairman said, with a cold contempt that almost loosened Hostite's bowels. He should have known that; he had been listening to what her family said about her. 'She might be just a horse breeder, but she has been inconveniently near several disturbances in our plans. She was on Sirialis when Lepescu was destroyed –'

'Lepescu was ours?' Iagin asked. The Chairman gave him a look Hostite would not have liked to receive.

'No. I would not use that filth. It is one thing to kill – even to maim, as a lesson – but quite another to treat an enemy as less than human. No, what I'm remembering is that Cecelia de Marktos was the one who took the Crown Prince back to his father, and meddled. I did not authorize our agent's attack on her – women are simply not reliable, and I suspect personal jealousy of some sort – but she showed up again interfering with the Patchcock situation. It passes chance that she – a woman never previously far from a horse – should be right at the scene of problems so many times.'

'Heris Serrano,' Hostite murmured. 'The commander was there also.'

'Yes. And the Serranos have always had the reputation for neutrality in the Familias. Here they are linked to a Barraclough repeatedly . . .'

'Heris Serrano had resigned her commission; she began her association with Lady Cecelia as a hireling.' That was Iagin.

'Easy enough to contrive that, if one wanted to form a duetto.' A bonded pair hunting together, that meant.

'Thank you both,' the Chairman said then, nodding. 'Master, if you will wait a moment . . .'

Hostite backed away from the Chairman's desk until

he felt the ridge in the carpet that signalled the correct distance, then turned to go.

Somewhat to his surprise, he lived to cross the threshold. He and Iagin strolled back to the vesting room, and Hostite felt the languid ease that always followed a moment of mortal danger survived.

The Chairman eyed the Master of Swords. 'Hostite is our oldest Swordmaster, is he not?'

'Yes, sir.'

'Unusual for a Swordmaster to live this long. And yet — extraordinary, would you say?'

'In his way, yes.'

'He has a clean stroke,' the Chairman said. 'He never misses his mark, and I hear from all sources that he is sober and submissive.'

'That is true, Chairman.'

'Yet —?'

'Yet I cannot warm to him, Chairman.'

'No. And that is why I insist he has not reached his end; I must have one Swordmaster whom the Master of Swords does not like.'

The Master bowed. They both knew this; they had said it before.

'I find the news of Hobart Conselline disturbing, however. Such a man might do anything, if he felt endangered. We thought the discovery that their rejuvenation drugs were so easily contaminated would slow down the rate of rejuvenation . . . why would someone risk insanity, senility, just for the chance of unending life?'

'They fear death?'

'It is not just that. They do it when they are years from death, just for pleasure. I told myself it was their decadent class structure, that rejuvenation would spread to the professionals and workers only rarely and later. But no. They do not want eternal life . . . they want eternal youth. That is not the same.'

'No, Chairman.'

'We did not realize that at first; we had no comprehension of their desires. And without the comprehension of desires, there can be no shaping of policy. It is beyond the understanding even of Holy Father, except as another example of their sinful nature. It poses a great problem for us. The strategy which we prepared for use in one situation may be useless in another . . .' His voice trailed away, and he turned to look out the window. Children. They were aging children, who did not want to earn anything or learn anything, who abhorred the discipline of faith. How could he influence aging children? He had a terrible vision of Hobart Conselline as he appeared in the data cubes, still spoiled and smug a hundred years hence, when he himself was dead and in his grave. His successor's successor might be dealing with that one, and all the rest – and how many there would be by that time.

It would not do. He must find a solution, and soon. His family, his vast extended family, the entire Benignity of the Compassionate Hand, relied on him to keep them safe and prosperous and orderly. It was his duty, and he was Chairman precisely because he had never yet failed in his duty.

'I may need to speak to Hostite Fieddi again,' he said. 'Please inform him to remain in the compound. I also need your analysis – is there anyone in the Seated Families who has refused serial rejuvenation, and if so . . . why? Are there any sane members of their Council?'

'Yes, Chairman.'

When the Master of Swords had gone, the Chairman turned to look out the window again. Aging children . . . senile children, if a merciful God limited the number of rejuvenations with even the best drugs. A terrible prospect, that great empire full of aging senile children. And in the interim, all that energy and expertise . . . their great space navy with admirals wiser than his, replenished constantly by commanders wise as admirals. But not enlisted personnel. At least they had taken care of that. Still . . . a grave, a very grave situation.

He would have to pray for Hobart Conselline. He would have to pray a very special prayer for the soul of Hobart Conselline . . . and for the soul of Hostite Fieddi, it might be.

In the Boardroom, the Chairman faced his Board, and explained what he had learned.

'So the Familias will be in even more turmoil?'

'And even more acquisitive. I have the Master of Swords looking into the possibilities of a coup d'etat, but we will need a suitable successor.'

'With due respect, Chairman, I thought our policy was to promote addiction –'

'You misunderstood.' A breathless silence, while everyone waited for the Chairman's next comment. 'We promote no vices; we do profit from them where faulty human nature allows them to flourish. But in this case, it was my most earnest hope that they would withdraw the drugs, either voluntarily, from shame, or involuntarily, as the evidence of the danger spread. We did not object to the damage done to their military, of course, but that damage was intended to shift their policy away from that process to a safer, more limited drug which merely prolonged life a decade or so.'

'Our resources –'

'Are unequal to full-scale war with the Familias. Yes. We lost an entire assault group at Xavier, and another such loss would be unprofitable. We need a way to protect ourselves, without risking ourselves.'

'To eliminate Hobart Conselline?'

'That's one possibility, certainly. Especially if the right man can be found to take his place, someone who understands that unlimited expansion brings explosive decompression in the end.'

His Board looked back at him. He knew what they were thinking, and knew that they knew he knew. A hundred, a thousand stalks of wheat fall before the reapers, and no one knows one from another but the Almighty . . . but the fall of a great tree brings down those around it and shakes the very ground. Perhaps God cared as much for a blade of grass as for a tall cypress . . . but mere humans noticed one more than another. It was his decision, but on them would fall the consequences.

SIRIALIS

Miranda walked down the hill to the stables in a chill evening drizzle that did nothing to cool her anger at the dapper little man who had been so sure of his welcome.

She had tried to be fair. She had tried to be reasonable. She had told herself that Cecelia often got things wrong, in her hot-headed enthusiasms.

But Pedar Orregiemos seemed determined to push her past her limits. He had written, expressing his delight in his Ministry. He had written again, complaining of her daughter's 'interference' in foreign affairs, when Brun had invited that Texas woman to be her guest at Appledale. He had called by ansible to insist that she be 'fair' to Harlis. Because, he explained, she didn't really need all that property. He could provide for her, and advance her interests himself, as Minister of Foreign Affairs.

And today, he had arrived at Sirialis, smugly certain that he was telling her what she did not already know, when he brought the results of the judgement for Bunny's will and against Harlis. Smugly certain of his welcome. Smugly certain that he could comfort a widow he was sure needed comforting.

If only he had let her alone. She glanced around, and saw only the grooms busy with the last evening chores. They nodded to her, and she to them, as she ducked into the passage between the stable offices and the vet supply storage. No one would be surprised to see her here; she often came down for evening rounds, or after, with a few sugar cubes for Bunny's favorite mounts.

If only he had left her alone, she would have done nothing. If only he had not flaunted his power, his connections, and hinted so broadly at his involvement that she could not ignore it. What did he think? That she had always loved him secretly, that she had been hoping to slough off an unwanted husband and take a lover?

Was he really such a fool?

She opened the door of the old smithy where bits and stirrups and buckles waited for repair. Above the long counter with its burners and torch tips, bottles of chemicals in neat racks. A small forge filled the end of the room, which had been built around it when the new smithy – much larger, and suited to a stable with more horses – had been built in the other courtyard.

Brun's information had been more complete than Cecelia's. Pedar was linked to the Rejuvenants and to Hobart Conselline . . . but while Hobart had refused to intervene to protect Harlis's interests, he would not cooperate in his own downfall. Neither Brun nor that Texan Ranger thought that the evidence they had would stand up, since the Speaker could dismiss and appoint Ministers and higher-court justices at will.

'I'm sure Pedar planned it,' Brun had written. 'I'm sure he hired the killers, though Cecelia says he could not have done it himself; he was in Zenebra. Kate thinks she's found a money trail – a tenuous one – but in a hostile court it probably would not hold. But whether he did it on his own, as a way of currying favor with Conselline, or on Hobart's orders, we can't determine. The reward seems to indicate a payment for services rendered – why else would anyone appoint Pedar to Foreign Affairs? – but we can't prove it. Unless you've uncovered something in the archives, we're at a standstill.'

The archives had thoroughly implicated Harlis Thornbuckle and his son Kell in financial chicanery, extortion, and intra-Family power plays – but not in the death of his brother, and not in connection with the Rejuvenants. At least, not that she'd found yet.

She moved about the room, then picked up a broken snaffle and sat down at the workbench. Was she sure, in her own mind, that Pedar had had Bunny killed?

Yes.

Was she sure, in her own mind, that he could not be brought to justice?

As long as Hobart Conselline was Speaker, and Pedar his Minister of Foreign Affairs, yes. Who would believe the hysterical accusations of a grieving widow?

Was she really willing to put herself at such risk, when nothing she did could bring Bunny back to life?

She thought about that, turning the bit over and over. If he would go away and leave her alone . . . no. No. He would not; it was not in his nature. He would wheedle and whine, year after year; he would act against her one way and another, to force her into his bed, as he had maneuvered when she was a young girl in love with someone else. But then she had had Bunny. Now she was alone, with no protection but her own wits.

She could do nothing about Hobart Conselline, the ultimate enemy, the one who, she was sure, had inspired Pedar to his actions, whether or not he had ordered them. But here, in her own house, she could deal with his minion.

She turned on the smaller torch, and played it over the bit in the clamps. She had first learned to work metal as a hobby, when she'd wanted a particular style of guard on her foil. Over the years, she'd learned how to make metal stronger, or weaken it; how to make it look old, how to make it look like something else entirely.

You may not approve, my love, but you will understand.

She hoped her children would.

Finally, she turned the torch off, and left the bit to cool. She had not mended it properly, but she had made a start. That was sometimes the best a person could do.

Neil waited by the outer gate.

'Goodnight, Neil,' she said. 'I made rather a mess in the old forge – that broken Simms bit. You were quite right; the little torch isn't hot enough.'

'It'll come right in the end,' he said.

She hoped it would. She would do her best to see that it did.

CHAPTER FOURTEEN

BASKAR STATION, BASKAR SYSTEM

Beatta Sorin, head teacher for the Little Lambs class of Shepherd's Glen Primary School of Baskar Station, led the way to the transit station. Every few steps, a quick glance behind showed her the neat crocodile of uniformed students, assistant teachers, and volunteer parent helpers. The adults wore an official tabard with 'Shepherd's Glen Primary School' on the left and a picture of a gamboling lamb on the right; in the pockets were their official IDs, their locator chips, their emergency kits. Around each adult neck, a lanyard and whistle to supplement the earpiece and mic, and the assistant teachers wore — as she did — an adult version of the school uniform, white shirt and plaid slacks. She herself held the braided end of the organizing ribbon, to which each child was supposed to cling. So far, they all had their little hands on it . . . but they were still almost in sight of the school. They could still be sent back, to spend a boring day in the nursery class.

At the station, she handed in the school's credit cube, and the file of seventeen children and ten adults moved into the loading area. This early in the trip, the children were still behaving well, though her experienced eye recognized that Poro Orinios already needed to use the toilet, and Mercy Lavenham had something sticky in her pocket and on the fingers of her left hand. She detailed her first assistant, Uri, to deal with Poro's needs, and herself excavated the pocket, wiping Mercy's fingers carefully as she did so. Mercy's mother, it seemed, could never resist sending her youngest out without a personal treat, even when it was strictly forbidden.

Uri came back just in time, and the crocodile edged its way on board the transgrav tram that would take them on a tour all around the station. Beatta, always organized and efficient, had made prior arrangements with station transit authorities, and this tram had enough slack in its schedule to allow extra time here. They had a reserved car, and each child was properly buckled into the seat, a motion-sickness patch in place, before the tram slid away from the station, one car entirely full of Little Lambs and their keepers.

Beatta had run this same field trip eleven times before. She knew from experience how to plan the route to provide the most in thrills, education, and efficiency. First, the slow part, through the densely populated shopping and residential district. Shrill voices piped up, pointing out home blocks, or the store where Mam bought bread. The tram stopped frequently. Then, as it swung away on the first of the transgrav segments, Beatta tapped her classroom bell for quiet.

'We're going to go oopsie,' she said. 'Everyone remember to breathe and hold on.' Safety bars swung down in front of each seat; Beatta took this opportunity to insert her earplugs. No amount of discipline would keep the children from squealing when the tram made gravity transitions, and the ear-piercing quality of Little Lambs would have rendered her deaf years ago if she hadn't taken precautions.

The tram gathered speed, rumbling a bit, and the lights blinked three times, a final warning of transition. Then the tram plunged into the dark, and Beatta's body tried to insist it had just fallen off a cliff. Even through her earplugs, the children's shrieks of mingled fright and excitement were painfully loud.

Gravity returned gradually, but not to normal. Heavy Cargo, their first stop, maintained only 0.25 G. Beatta, who had watched closely, noticed that none of her class had thrown up; this year, at least, the mothers had believed her about the need for a light breakfast. The tram emerged from a dark tunnel into a vast lighted cavern. Beatta flicked out her earplugs with a practiced twitch, and picked up her microphone.

'Attention, children! This is the cargo servicing area for most incoming shipments. Bri, your father works in Heavy Cargo, doesn't he?'

Bri, halfway down the car on the right, nodded.

'Well, this is where he works.'

'I been here before – he tooked me!'

'Yes, Bri, but the others haven't. Please pay attention. When we come to the station, you'll be able to see – out Bri's side – the exit hatches of the container transport system, and the tracks of the transport system itself. If we're very lucky, you'll get to see a line of cargo containers coming through.' She knew they would be lucky; she had scheduled the field trip for a time when one of the big container haulers was in, and she had checked on the transport schedule with its cargo chief. She also knew the color-coding and shape-coding for different types of containers, and was prepared to explain which carried food products and which industrial raw materials, or manufactured merchandise.

Bix and Xia were bouncing in their seats, testing the light gravity and their restraints ... Beatta looked at them with that immemorial teacher expression, and they settled back, a little sulkily. Twins were always a problem, in her opinion, and the current fashion for twins annoyed her. Thanks to Lord Thornbuckle's daughter Brun's well-publicized pair, hundreds of thousands of parents were opting for twins on their next pregnancy, and Beatta foresaw a great deal of work for teachers in a few years.

The tram slowed for the cargo handlers' station, and Beatta reminded the children to look out the righthand windows to see the cargo containers. Sure enough, huge colored bins butted through the heavy curtains at the hatches, and bumped and rumbled along their assigned tracks. Some shunted off this way, and others that, and Beatta answered the predictable questions without really thinking about it.

'The optical sensors read the coding on the labels, and there's a cross-check by color-coding from another set of sensors ... this allows the AI system to route each individual bin where it should go.'

'Where's my daddy?' asked Bri, now looking as if he were going to cry.

'Working somewhere,' Beatta said. 'I really don't know for sure.' She should have known; she should have made sure that Bri's father was in sight for this brief stop.

'There he is!' Bri said excitedly, patting the window in his glee. Beatta wasn't at all sure the orange-suited figure running a scanner along the markings on a cargo bin was Bri's father, but if it made him happy — her breath caught as someone in a tan shipsuit stepped out and hit the orange-suited one over the head. The top of the bin lifted, and four ... eight ... twelve ... more tan-suited men crawled out. The orange-suited one lay motionless on the floor.

'Somebody hit him,' Bri said. His voice rose even higher. 'He's hurt, my daddy's hurt!'

'I'm sure he's not, dear,' Beatta said. Experience kept her voice even, and experience made her look quickly out the other side of the car for something to distract the children. 'Look!' she said, before her brain had finished processing what she saw. 'Look at all the funny little cars they run around on!'

It was too late to wish she hadn't done that, because all the children except Bri had turned obediently, and had clear view of the firefight as the passengers on the funny little cars attacked first the workers on the floor, and then drove right up to the tram.

The tram gave a convulsive jerk, as if the driver had started to pull away, then stopped again. Three of the children started to cry; the other adults stared at Beatta with white faces.

'Now, children,' she said, in her best teacher's voice. 'There's nothing to cry about, just a little bump. Stay seated, please. Mag, would you help Bri calm down, and Sivi, you see to Crowder —' The adults responded, and by the time the man with the obvious weapon opened the car door, the children were all sitting quietly, listening to Beatta tell the story of the Brown Bunny and the Spotted Snake.

'Oh, shit!' the man said. 'There's *chillen* on this tram!' He had a strong accent made all too familiar by newscasts of the previous two years.

'We don't use that sort of language,' Beatta said firmly. The muzzle opening on his weapon looked big enough to swallow the tram, but she made herself look at his face. 'Please do not upset the children.'

'Just stay there,' the man said, backing out. Beatta had no intention of doing anything else.

*

On the transportation board, a light blinked twice and then went red.

'Babytrain's got a problem,' Kyle said. The yearly field trip had its own code name which the school knew nothing about.

'What?' His supervisor, Della Part, was trying to listen in to a conversation between an R.S.S. security advisor and her own supervisor.

'Don't know yet.' Kyle hit the com button. 'Transgrav 4, what's your problem?' No answer. Any problem that could pull a transgrav tram driver off his seat might really call for help. If one of the kids had been hurt –

'What compartment's Babytrain in?' Sash called across the control room.

'Heavy Cargo Two.'

'I've got a slight but significant rise in pCO_2, and ambient temp's up slightly.'

'Kids got loose? Running around?'

'Where's our video?'

'Blank – it's been blinky the last few days.'

'Ask station security.'

Kyle called down to the stationmaster. 'We've got a problem in Heavy Cargo Two. What've you got on scan?'

'Lemme see.' Pause. 'CO_2's up a bit, O_2 consumption's up, also ambient temp . . . visual . . . the transgrav's stopped at the station. Wasn't Babytrain on for today?'

'Yeah. They've popped a red and I can't raise 'em.'

'Looks normal. Cargo containers coming in from *Freedawn 24*. Cargo handlers – wait – what color's Heavy Cargo this year?'

'Orange. Changed from tan –'

'Would anyone be in the old – oh, hell!'

'What?'

'None of the Heavy Cargo crews would be carrying firearms. We have an intrusion.'

'In *there*? What about the kids?'

In the appalled silence that followed, Kyle could almost hear his heart thudding. He gulped, hit the supervisor's code, and said it. 'We have a Level Five emergency. Hostile intruders in Heavy Cargo Two, and a trainload of kids – that preschool field trip.'

The R.S.S. officer opened his mouth and shut it again, but looked sideways at the supervisor.

'Cut out the alarms to that sector, put us on Level Five Alert. Patch to the stationmaster and the emergency response teams. Call in the second shift as backup . . .'

Then to the R.S.S. advisor, 'What else?'

'How many certified emergency personnel do you have?'

'Counting security, medical, damage control – maybe five hundred.'

'Find out – you need to know exactly. And I recommend you inform the picket as well; we can presume this intrusion is of foreign origin.'

'Stationmaster'll have to approve –'

'I do.' Kyle was relieved to hear the stationmaster's voice over the com.

'Can they help?'

'Maybe. Then recall all R.S.S. personnel on station and collect them – check MSOs . . . specialties . . . for security, demolitions, and emergency medical.'

Sergeant Cavallo had chosen to finish out his present tour in mess, in part because the supply and mess personnel had more chance of a few hours on stations during otherwise boring picket duty. The weekly green run always meant 24 hours on station, and sometimes more. He liked the bustle of the markets, he had – thanks to his grandmother's gardening passion – an unusually good eye for quality produce. He knew that Purcell's Family Grocers sometimes imported fresh fruits from planetside groves, and hoped to find either cherries or cherrunes. The exec's tenth anniversary was coming up, and he liked cherries. The other part was his sense of the ridiculous: few if any neuroenhanced troops ever had the chance to indulge a harmless interest.

He was only five minutes from the station when a red light came up on the board. The shuttle pilot grimaced, and switched channels. Cavallo saw the telltale hardening of the jaw, then the pilot's hands moving to change settings on the board.

'What?' Cavallo asked.

'They've got an intrusion,' the pilot said. 'They don't know what, but armed hostiles in Heavy Cargo – and they've taken hostages, a whole tramload of preschool kids.'

Cavallo started to ask what a tramload of preschoolers had been doing in Heavy Cargo's 0.25 G, but that wasn't the most urgent question. 'Who've they got with anti-terrorist experience?'

'I don't know, but they've got a Major Reichart on station, and he's ordered all Fleet personnel to assemble – that's why we're shifting docking assignment. Sorry, Sarge, but it looks like we're all part of this for the duration.'

Cavallo said nothing; he was aware of the irony of his present position. He had chosen mess duty as a welcome break from the tedium of being a Special Response Team leader on a picket ship where nothing happened . . . and here he was, back in his own territory, but without any of his equipment or a trained team.

'Better let the major know I'm coming in,' he told the pilot, who shot him a quick glance.

'You, Sarge? But you're a cook –' The pilot had known Cavallo only in his present duty; perhaps he thought the extra bulk was a supply sergeant's overindulgence.

'Not entirely,' Cavallo said. 'My primary specialty is NEM Special Response.'

The pilot looked nervous, the usual reaction to someone discovering that he was sitting next to one of the few Fleet personnel trained to kill in hand-to-hand combat. 'You're a NEM?'

'Yup. So call me in.'

'Yessir.'

Although the supply shuttle had not been fitted out with a combat mission in mind, all Fleet shuttles carried some basic emergency equipment. There was no combat armor to fit Cavallo, but he grabbed the largest p-suit and the ready pack of demolitions supplies, intended to create a small hull breach if that should be necessary in an emergency. Three bricks of LUB explosive, five standard fusing options and the components for others, detonation signallers . . . he checked it all, and by the time the shuttle docked, he had repacked it and was ready to dive out the tube.

Sarknon Philios had been celebrating the successful auction of the *Mindy Cricket II* – the old tub had sold for more than he paid for her, though not more than he'd sunk into her – and the sale of his interest in the minerals they'd towed in. His crew, equally delighted with the outcome, and the promise of a new – or at least better-quality used – ship on the next run, had joined the celebration as well. While they hadn't quite drained the *Spacer's Delight* dry, they'd made its proprietor richer, and as the morning commuters rushed past, Sarknon was finally ready for bed. Bed was two stops away on the station tram; he gathered his crew and led them across to the tram stop.

There a man in Security green demanded their IDs –

even though they wore their shipsuits with patches prominent on the left shoulder, and even though it should have been clear who and what they were.

'What is, man?' asked Sarknon. 'We been at the *Delight*, you musta seen us crossin' oer. We's shipcrew, we bother nobody.'

'Your IDs, Ser.' Station Security normally went unarmed, but this one carried an acoustic weapon slung over his shoulder. Down the platform, Sarknon could see two more Security men, now looking this way. Annoyed though he was, Sarknon didn't intend to cause trouble.

'Foodlin' shame, I say, leapin' on folks as is just shipcrew come to spend money at station.' He fumbled in his shipsuit's pocket and brought out his ID folder. ''Tisn't enough to let yon pubkeeper charge twice too much for his wares, now you have to act as if you don't know who we are.'

Even when Security did ask to see ID, which happened rarely, they always just glanced at it. Not this time. Sarknon stood, swaying slightly as the man glanced from his papers to his face, again and again, and finally had had enough.

'What, you think I am not Sarknon Philios? You never heard of *Mindy Cricket*, of our strike? Or am I too ugly for you?'

'Take it easy,' the man said, closing the folder and handing it back. 'We've trouble – we're looking for rock-hoppers with demolitions experience. Looks like you're it.'

'A contract?' Sarknon blinked; he knew he was not a good negotiator when he was drunk; that's how he'd ended up paying too much for the *Mindy Cricket II*. 'Can't talk contract now, m'head's fuzzled. Next shift, maybe, when the drink's left me.'

'Now,' the man said. The other two had come nearer, without Sarknon noticing, and now he found himself facing drawn weapons.

'Trouble, Harv?' asked one of the others.

'No – found us a demo crew, but they're soused. Help me get'm to medical.'

Sarknon had paid good money for his drunk, and was not inclined to see it dispersed for nothing. 'I'm not goin' to med; they'll just waste my money . . . I earned that drunk; it's mine –'

He saw the hand coming towards his face, but was too uncoordinated to evade it. When he woke again, he was on a cot in the station medical clinic, and he woke entirely, in an instant, with the unnatural clarity of the detox patient. 'Dammit,' he said. 'An' I bought a whole jug of that Surnean ale!'

'Never you mind,' said the young woman who slid the needle out of his vein. 'You save those kids and I will personally buy you two jugs.'

'Well, then.' Sarknon sat up, not regretting the headache he didn't have, thanks to detox, and looked around for his crew. 'If it's that kind of job . . .'

'It's that kind of job.' He didn't recognize the man's uniform, but the tone of voice was unmistakable. Sarknon followed him along the corridor to a compartment full of people in EMS vests, and five minutes later he was explaining all he knew about demolition.

Instead of the organized, disciplined planning groups Cavallo was used to, a roomful of civilians were muttering, arguing, and even (in the case of one fat man in the corner) shouting. Cavallo spotted the major at once, and made his way over. 'Sgt. Cavallo, sir; NEM Special Response Team.'

'That's good news – how many of you?'

'Just me, sir. I was inbound on a supply run – I've been acting as supply sergeant for the picket boat.'

'A NEM supply sergeant? No, don't tell me – later, when we have time. We have a real bad situation here.' Quickly, the major laid it out – the intruders, the preschool field trip, the information he had so far on station resources. 'They don't have anything equivalent to your training,' he said. 'Good basic emergency services, but nothing to handle large-scale terrorist actions. They'd been warned, but they didn't really know where to get the information they needed. That's why I was here. And those kids are really our problem now. The med staff has told me that they're more susceptible to sudden pressure changes than adults – they get shock lung more easily, and it's harder to treat. Same is true of chemical riot-control agents, or the acoustics. We're going to end up hurting the kids no matter what we do, so we have to be very, very fast.'

'Negotiation, sir?'

The major shrugged, with an expression Cavallo couldn't quite read. 'They've got the usual complement of mental health professionals, and two of them have some experience in small-scale stuff. Man holding his ex-wife hostage and threatening the kids, that sort of thing. But nobody with this kind of experience, and I'm not sure they realize how different it is. I suspect that our bad guys wouldn't talk to a Fleet officer . . . and as you can tell I have an accent that won't quit.'

'These those New Texas guys?' Cavallo asked.

'Don't know yet. So far we have no contact. The stationmaster cut all com right away; I've been unable to convince him to reopen at least one line. He's afraid they'll override the security precautions to the main computers, I think.'

'We can fix that, sir,' Cavallo said. 'I brought the

demolitions and communications kits from the shuttle.'

'Good man. Let me get you to the stationmaster.'

'If they want to kill the children, to make a statement o something, the kids are as good as dead – if they aren' already. We can't prevent it. What we can do is talk t them. Our sources tell us they have very strong family connections, especially to their children. We can hop they are less likely to kill children, more likely to negoti ate where children are concerned.'

'But they think our children are heathens –'

'Yes, but they didn't hurt the children from the *Elia Madero*. They wanted to save them. They aren't likely t have planned this for the one day a year the preschoo has its field trip.'

Cavallo's Irenian accent had amused his Fleet associ ates at first. After twentysome years he could turn it on and off like a tap – his implants helped – but at the moment it might be useful.

'Anybody there?' he asked, drawling it out.

Silence followed. Then, in a thick accent made famil iar by the newsvids of Brun's captors, 'Who you?'

'I'm lookin' for that teacher – Sera Sorin. We're wor ried about those children.'

Silence again, but not so long. 'What children?'

'Those children in the tram. It's time they was home don't you think?'

'What you mean havin' chillen in a transgrav tram' Don't you care about 'em?'

'Of course we care; that's why I'm callin'. Can I talk t the teacher, please?'

'Puttin' chillen in the care of a woman like that. Boys too. Downright disgustin'. No, you cain't talk to her; she' doin' what she's tol', keeping them chillen quiet.'

'But they're all right? I mean, you know kids, they

need the bathroom, and they get hungry and thirsty –
you got enough snacks for 'em?'

Another voice, this one older and angrier. 'No, we
don't got food for kids. Your kid down here, mister?'

Cavallo had considered trying to impersonate a parent,
but kids that age couldn't be fooled easily. If he claimed
to be some boy's father and the boy said 'That's not my
dad!' they'd be worse off than they were now.

'No,' he said. 'Not mine – but it might's well be.
Children are everyone's responsibility, where I come
from.'

'And where's that?'

'Irene.' They might or might not know anything about
Irene, but if they did, that would fit – Irenians had a
Familias-wide reputation for idealistic child care.

'Oh.' A pause; Cavallo wished he'd been able to get a
vid tap in; facial expressions would tell him a lot. But the
vid pickup was still snaking its way through the utility
lines, a good seventy meters from Heavy Cargo Two.
'Well . . . it's too bad about the kids, but –'

'I can get you supplies for them,' Cavallo interrupted.
'Food and water. For you, too,' he added as if this were a
new thought rather than an orchestrated tactic.

'Listen, you, whoever you are –'

'Fred,' Cavallo said, choosing an uncle's name at
random. 'Fred Vallo.'

'Well, Fred, thing is, these chillen are dead if we want
'em to be.'

'I understand that,' Cavallo said.

'So you better give us what we want –'

'If the children die,' Cavallo said, letting the steel into
his voice, 'none of you will get off this station alive.'

'If you want 'em alive, you do what we tell you,' the
voice said. Behind it, another younger voice protested,
'But we can't kill *children*.'

Cavallo smiled to himself. Trouble in the enemy camp, and talking to a negotiator . . . they had already lost. If only small children hadn't been involved.

'I need to speak to someone who can assure me that the children are unharmed,' he said. 'If not the teacher, one of the other adults on the tram.'

'Wait,' said the older voice.

Cavallo muted his mike and turned to the major. 'You heard, sir? There's at least one who's going to cause their leader trouble if he hurts the children, and so far they're willing to talk.'

'Yeah . . . but how long will it last? Wonder if he'll really let you talk to one of the adults?'

'I –' The light blinked on his set, and he turned the mike back on.

'Go on –' said the voice he was used to. 'Tell them the chillen aren't hurt.'

'But they want to use the toilet –' came another voice, a man's.

'Tell 'em.'

'Uh . . . this is Parkop Kindisson . . . with the Little Lambs field trip? . . . you know about that?'

'Yes, Ser Kindisson,' Cavallo said. 'Are the children unharmed?'

'Well, they aren't *hurt*, but they're scared, especially Bri because he saw his father get hit, and they need to use the toilets, and they won't let us, and they're getting hungry, and they won't let us get them anything at the tram station snack bar, and –'

'Enough!' The angry voice was back; Cavallo could just hear the distant protest of the other man. 'You know this Kindisson fellow?'

'Not personally, no,' Cavallo said. He had skimmed a file on all the adults with the field trip, and knew that Kindisson was a single parent, taking a day off his job as a coater for the housing authority to help chaperone the children.

'Seems kinda excitable, not like a normal man –'

'He's worried about the children. So am I. How about if we arrange some snacks for 'em? Or carry-pots, so they can use the toilet right on the tram?'

'The tram has toilets?'

'No – that's why I said carry-pots. Families have them here, to take along with a small child, if there's not a toilet around.'

'There's toilets in the tram station, though, aren't there?'

'Sure, but if you don't want to let them off the train. Little children – I'm sure you know about them, and how they run around getting into things – it's smart of you to keep them safe, in one place.'

Flattery couldn't hurt, he was sure.

'We want to talk to our women,' the voice said.

Cavallo felt his eyebrows going up. 'Your women?' he asked cautiously.

'Don't pretend you don't know. Those Rangers' wives you stole, and their chillen – we want to tell 'em to get theirselves home.'

'Just a second –' Cavallo blanked the mike and called to the stationmaster. 'Are there any of those NewTex women at this station?'

'No, they left awhile back. Why?'

'Because these fellows came to take them home, that's why. Do you know where they went?'

'No. I can look on the passenger lists, but that'll only tell me which ship.'

'Which we don't want to tell these lads,' Cavallo said. He flipped the mike back on and spoke into it. 'I just asked the stationmaster, and he says they aren't here. They were, but they left awhile back.'

'Yer lying! You git us our chillen, or we'll take yours.'

'I can get you a list –' Cavallo waved, and the station-master came back over. 'We need a list or something, so these men know those women aren't here –'

'There's a directory accessible from the public data-ports in Heavy Cargo, but we cut the lines –'

'Well, put in a shielded line.'

'We're gonna blow up this whole place if you don't give us our women and chillen!' That was another voice, one that sounded entirely too excited. He heard a confused scuffle in the background, and a yelp. He hoped it was from an adult.

'Now just a minute,' Cavallo said. 'We don't none of us want children hurt. Let's see what we can figure out here –' Someone held a display screen in front of him, with the message DATA DISPLAY AT TRAM STATION ACTIVE FOR OUR USE. It's true your children aren't here anymore – and it's true I don't know where they are. You – what'd you say your name was?'

'Dan,' said the older voice. 'You kin call me Dan.'

'Dan, I reckon you think children should be with their parents –'

'Yeah, that's right. So if our chillen ain't here, we wanta know where they've gone.'

The vid scan was in, though distorted by the wide-angle lens. Scan specialists ran tests, converting the image to a corrected 3-D version. Cavallo made himself ignore that, until they were done, and someone moved a screen close to him so he could see it.

Now when Dan spoke, he could see the computer's best guess at the face – middle-aged, as he'd guessed, the face of someone who had taken difficult responsibility before.

'How'd you plan to get 'em away?'

'Steal a ship. We done it before.'

'Good plan,' Cavallo said, mentally crossing his fingers. He scribbled *Find a small, cheap, simple ship* on the pad and handed it to the major.

'We kin just take these chillen instead, if ours is really gone.'

'But it's not the same,' Cavallo said. 'And these children should be with their families.'

'You offerin' to let us go?'

'Would you?'

'Might.'

Cavallo watched the man put down the mike and turn away, talking to the others. He boosted the audio pickup.

'You said they was here!' he heard one man say; he couldn't pick out features from the fish-eye view.

'That's the best word we had.'

'I tell you, I'm gettin' sick of this. We come all the way from home, workin' like dogs on that damn ship, because you didn't want to spend the money for tickets, which would've been worth it if we'd killed the old buzzard, but we didn't, on account of somebody else beat us to the draw.'

'It wasn't supposed to take that long –'

'And who picked out that ship? Then you say let's go get those kids back – and they're not even our kids – and we have to work our passage again, comin' here, and when we get here they ain't. I don't know's I believe they ever have been.'

'Ever'body in that bar said they was!'

'Ever'body in that bar was drunk, Dan. They ain't here, and they ain't been here, and what in Sam Hill are we gonna do now?'

'I'll think of sumpin' – just give me a minute, will you?'

'We could take these kids –'

'Hell, Arnett, I don't want these kids. These ain't *our*

kids, or Ranger kids. And what'd we take 'em in, anyway?'

'Well, what d'you want to do, give up and let them kill
us like they did them Rangers?'

'We ain't done nothin' yet they'd kill us for.'

'I ain't surrenderin' nothin'.' That was Arnett, Cavallo
could tell by his voice.

'Well, I'm not killin' any chillen.' That was the one
who had protested in the beginning. 'Why don't we trade
'em for a ship out of here?'

'A whole ship? You think godless heathens would give
us a whole ship for just a bunch of chillen? They don't
care about chillen.'

'How's it going?' the major asked. Cavallo sat back,
still watching the vid.

'They're fighting over whose fault it is. If I understand them right, this bunch wanted to assassinate Lord
Thornbuckle, and when they found out someone else
had, they decided to hunt up the women and children
and capture them. I don't think they're NewTex Rangers;
I think they're a bunch of idealistic fools that went off by
themselves.' He tapped the mike, and heads turned in
the vid. Dan came over, almost reluctantly, to pick it
up.

'Dan! Dan . . . listen. Are the children still all right?'

'Yeah, yeah, they're fine for now.'

'Dan, the stationmaster tells me the women and children left eleven days ago on a passenger ship, the *Dolphin
Rider*.'

On the vid, two of the other men threw up their hands,
and one spat on the deck.

'Now I can't change that, Dan, but here's what I could
do.'

'What?'

'I don't know if you'd – but if you'd – I mean, if we

could get you a ship, Dan . . . and then the children wouldn't get hurt –'

'You mean trade the chillens for a ship? You'd do that?'

'Yeah, of course. It's children we're talkin' about.'

'A whole ship – a ship that actually works?'

'Of course.' Cavallo glanced up as someone leaned over and handed him a pad with *Mindy Cricket II* scrawled on it.

'I dunno. We'd need supplies.'

Cavallo dared a grin at the major, as he flicked the mike off. 'They're gonna take it,' he said. 'Now if they don't cross us – and there's some of them I'm pretty sure won't – where's that ship docked?'

It had taken another twelve hours of ticklish negotiation before the children were reunited with frantic parents, the NewTex terrorists were finally aboard the *Mindy Cricket II*, and the little ship lurched away from the station with her usual grace.

'You didn't really have to do anything,' Sarknon said. 'She's not goin' to get 'em anyplace real fast.'

'Especially not now,' Cavallo said. He had applied the bricks of LUB to best advantage. *Mindy Cricket II* wouldn't make it to jump distance in one piece. Two hours out, a safe distance from the station, and she'd blow. 'We don't need that kind of scum wandering around causing trouble.' He stretched, and grinned at the major. 'Guess I'll go finish the shopping now, if it's all the same to you.'

CHAPTER FIFTEEN

R.S.S. *GYRFALCON*

'Jig Serrano to the captain's office . . .' Barin tapped his code into the wall-hung unit to signal his receipt of the message, and turned to the sergeant of the compartment.

'I'll finish this inspection later,' he said. 'And I expect you'll have done something about those lockers.' The lockers had been unlocked, and Barin had already found three major discrepancies.

'Yes, sir!'

All the way upship, he wondered what he'd done. He couldn't think of anything, and Major Conway had actually complimented him the day before.

Captain Escobar's clerk gave him no warning glances, just smiled and waved him through. Barin came to attention and waited.

'Ah . . . I thought you'd like to know you have pay.' Escobar handed a data cube across to him.

'Sir?'

'Apparently your . . . dependents . . . have found honest work somewhere. They're off Fleet's hands.'

'Where are they?'

'Some colony world. Apparently Professor Meyerson and that Lone Star Confederation diplomat found them a place, and someone paid their colony shares. Also paid off at least part of what Fleet spent on them, and HQ has forgiven the rest. So you have pay again. I suppose this means you'll be marrying?'

Barin felt himself go hot. 'I – hope so, sir.'

'From one fire into another. Better give your family time to get used to it. Have your parents ever met Lieutenant Suiza?'

'No, sir. But now that I'm getting pay again, if I could get a little leave –'

'You'd get married.'

'No, sir, not right away. I'd get her together with my parents, though.'

Escobar considered. 'You have plenty of leave stacked up. Tell you what – figure out a time that will work for your parents and her, and I'll do my best.'

'Thank you, sir.'

R.S.S. *NAVARINO*

'You have mail, Lieutenant.' Esmay wondered what it was this time. Her last mail had been a stiff notice from Personnel advising her that she should have informed them before accepting appointment as a Landbride, and that any request for a variance would have to work its way through the chain of command in her sector, then at Headquarters.

A cube from Barin. That had to be better than something from Personnel.

Her heart soared as she read it. Out from under the responsibility for all those women and children. Getting paid again. He'd talked to his parents; they wanted to meet her. He could get leave – what about her? He was

sure he could enlist the senior Serranos to aid in bending
the restrictions about Landbrides. . . .

She, too, had accumulated leave time. Surely it would
be possible to meet for a few days, even a week.
Somewhere private – she didn't mind meeting his parents, but she wanted at least some hours alone with
Barin.

COPPER MOUNTAIN

Although Fleet's Copper Mountain Training Base, named
for the red-rock formation of the original landfall, had
become the generic term for the entire planet, Fleet had
other bases where neither mountains nor red dust were in
view. Most NCO training courses, though reached by
shuttle from Copper Mountain, were actually dispersed to
other facilities on the same continent: Drylands, in the
northern plains, Camp Engleton in the coastal swamp,
Big Trees far to the west. Permanently assigned school
staff had their own recreational areas which students
never saw: the long sand beaches far east of Copper
Mountain where the carnivorous hunters of the deep had
been carefully fenced away. Eight Peaks Mountain
District, which offered far more than eight peaks, though
the rest of them weren't quite eight thousand meters.

Among these lesser-known bases were the Stack
Islands facilities. Rising almost vertically from the cold
waters of what someone had unimaginatively called Big
Ocean, the old volcanic plugs of the Stacks had been engineered into even more forbidding shapes than time, wind,
and water had created. The Stack Islands group had three
Fleet bases altogether, two for research (biomedical and
weapons) and one to supervise the confinement of its
most dangerous criminals.

That proximity was no accident; although the Grand

Council knew nothing about it, research into neuro-biology used prisoner subjects, some of whom emerged from the program with new identities. But the proximity was on a planetary, not local, scale: though less than an hour by aircar to either of the other Stack Islands bases, the prison was distant enough to keep its prisoners secure. The research bases were only a few kilometers apart, on neighboring stacks, but the prison base lay at the east end of the group, out of sight from either and far beyond swimming distance, even if water temperature and sealife had not intervened.

The security personnel at Three Stack, as the prison base was colloquially called, made no attempt to prevent prisoners from committing suicide; it was the general feeling that suicides saved everyone a lot of trouble. So little attention was paid to preventing escape attempts that were certain to be fatal. Prisoners could jump off the cliffs into the cold water if they felt like it; if they survived the fall, and the numbing cold, they were easy prey for the native sealife, which in these latitudes was toothy and voracious. Although guards patrolled the corridors and exercise courts, and the base's aircars were carefully guarded, no regular watch was kept on the cliffs.

Commanding such a base did nothing to advance an officer's career, and most loathed brig duty. For a few, however, Stack Islands Base Three offered exactly the milieu in which they flourished.

Corporal Gelan Meharry, second-shift guard at Three Stack, wondered what it was about his new commander that bothered him. Prison COs were invariably bent in some way – Tolin had been soft, slovenly, entirely too fond of his own comfort, and easily handled by the senior NCOs – but this Bacarion person was clearly not bent that way. What had she done, to get sent here? A tour at a high-security brig was no disgrace to the enlisted security force, rather the contrary, if nothing went wrong, but . . . he had an uneasy feeling about her.

After the change-of-command ceremony, his immediate superior, Sergeant Copans, dismissed the second shift to eat and prepare for their shift. Gelan racked his ceremonial staff, and changed from his dress to his duty uniform. As always, he made sure that his gear was perfectly aligned in his locker before heading for the mess hall. Then he checked his bay in the barracks. Sure as vacuum, that new commander would pull an inspection, and he intended *his* unit to pass.

On the way to mess, he stopped by the base data center, and called up the Officers' List. At least he could find out about his new commander's official biography. Her image on the screen showed her with the insignia of a lieutenant commander – she hadn't had her image updated since her last promotion. He scanned the notes below. Top quartile in the Academy, so she wasn't stupid. Command Track with her junior duty on a series of front-line craft. As a major she'd done the usual rotation in staff, this time on a flagship, the *Dominion*. There she'd seen combat, though from the staff viewpoint.

What was it about *Dominion*? He should know that name . . . he scrolled to the flag's name. Lespescu. Bacarion had been on *Lepescu's* staff? In the engagement where Heris Serrano refused to follow Lespescu's orders, and by so doing won the battle but lost her command? Gelan clamped his jaw, hoping his expression had not changed. Thanks to Lepescu, Serrano's crew – including his oldest living sib Methlin – had been tried and imprisoned. Bacarion deserved a prison appointment, he thought sourly. She deserved to be a prisoner, really. He had not seen Methlin since her release, but he'd heard all about it. Lepescu was safely dead, but this Bacarion . . .

He switched off the unit, smiled a careful smile at the clerk in charge, and went to lunch with a gnawing pain in his belly. Partway through the meal, he stopped eating abruptly, with his fork halfway to his mouth. What if this wasn't punishment for Bacarion? What if she had wanted this assignment? What if she, like Lepescu, wanted to play games with prisoners?

He was going to have to be very careful indeed. When she noticed that she had a Meharry aboard, she was going to assume he knew . . . and knew she knew.

Gelan Meharry had not even been born when his oldest brother Gareth died in the wreck of *Forge*. He had been in school when his sister Methlin was sent to this very prison. His recruit training had been spent under the shadow of her disgrace, though his drill instructor had told him — after he passed — that he personally thought she'd been framed. He had acquired, from his family and their history, a keener awareness of social nuances than most young corporals, and the certainty that anyone keeping things from him had a bad reason for doing so.

When nothing happened during the first few weeks of Bacarion's command, Gelan did not relax his vigilance. He asked no questions; he said nothing he had not said many times before; he continued to be, to all outward signs, the same quietly competent young NCO he had been all along.

Inside, he felt himself caught in a storm. What Bacarion had done, so far, was call in each officer and NCO, in turn, from the most senior down. Each had returned from that interview looking thoughtful; a few had also looked puzzled or worried. None had had more comment than 'She's one tough lady.'

That in itself was slightly bothering. On such a small

post, gossip about each other was the main entertainment. From short encounters came small bits of information, painstakingly assembled into the common understanding of each individual. Gelan knew that their former commander, Iosep Tolin, had an aunt who bred flat-faced long-haired cats, a cousin in the wine business, and a daughter from whom he was estranged – Tolin blamed his former wife, who had left him for a historian.

But about Bacarion, nothing. 'A tough lady.' His sister Methlin was tough . . . he had not known, while she was in prison, just what prison was, or how difficult, but now he did. At least from the other side of the doors. His throat closed whenever he had duty on the women's side, thinking of Meth in there, and he wondered if any of the women were like her, unfairly condemned.

His turn with Bacarion would come soon. She had access to his service record, which included a list of all relatives formerly or presently in service. What would she say? What would she ask? What should he say, since the truth – *I want you dead, like Lepescu!* – would not do.

Tolin had not been a slob, but Bacarion's offices already looked shinier, neater. Everything gleamed, smudgeless. Every paper on the clerk's desk aligned perfectly with every other.

A martinet, like Lepescu. In the inner office, Bacarion waited, sitting motionless behind her desk like a carved figurine.

'Corporal Meharry reporting as ordered, sir.' It was hard not to react when her cold gaze met his.

'You don't look much like your sister,' was her first comment. Then she sighed, and gave a mock smile. 'Why is it the men in a family so often get the looks, I wonder?'

He felt his neck go hot, then the flush spreading up his face. Her smile warmed.

'Sorry, Corporal. Didn't mean to embarrass you.'

Didn't she, indeed! Gelan hoped that looking like a silly boy was the best strategy now.

'I met her only a few times, of course,' Bacarion went on smoothly, as if reading from a script. Perhaps she was. 'I was shocked and surprised when I heard she'd been sentenced to prison, and delighted when her name was cleared again.' A wrinkle appeared in her forehead; Gelan was sure it was intentional, intended as a sign of sincerity. 'It may be hard for you to believe, Corporal, but when I was serving on Admiral Lepescu's staff, I had no idea that he was capable of any dishonesty. He seemed so . . . so focussed on defeating the enemy.'

That was one way of putting it. If you ignored the way that Lepescu's allies paid the price of his focus, as well as the enemy, the fact that he liked seeing blood shed, in quantity, and didn't much care whose it was.

'I hope we can work together,' Bacarion was saying, now with a little frown, as if he'd failed to carry out some order.

'Yes, sir.' Gelan tried to inject some enthusiasm into the familiar phrase. Bacarion's face relaxed, but whether that was good or bad he could not tell.

'Did you request assignment here because your sister had been here?' she asked.

'No, sir.' He had anticipated this question. 'Personnel noticed I hadn't had a tour in my secondary specialty, and yanked me off *Flashpoint* right before deployment. I asked for Sector Three, so I'd at least be in the same sector as my – as the ship – but they sent me here.'

'Do you find it difficult?'

'No, sir.'

'What do you think of the general loyalty of the officers and men on this station?'

What kind of a question was that to ask a corporal?

'Loyalty? I'm not sure I know what the commander is asking about. '

'Don't play innocent, Meharry! Any time you have prisoners and guards, you have the possibility of collusion, even a breakout. I'm asking you if you know anything about such a situation here.'

'No, sir,' Gelan said. 'Nothing like that.'

Another searching look. 'Very well. Dismissed.'

The autumn evening was closing in, a fine cold mist blowing across the courtyard. Gelan shivered. It was a week yet until time to change to winter uniforms, but it wasn't the outward cold that chilled him. The ten kilometers to Stack Two and twelve to Stack One might as well have been the thousands of kilometers that stretched to the next continental mass, for all the good it did him. He could not pilot any of the aircars even if the aircars had not been kept under close guard. There were no surface watercraft; the Stacks had no beaches or harbors where such craft could land. Water met rock with brutal suddenness twenty meters below the lowest accessible path; in storms, the spray of that meeting shot upward thirty and forty meters. He could swim, but he could not swim ten kilometers in water that cold, even if the sea creatures didn't eat him.

No escape. He was trapped as surely as any of the prisoners. He had no doubt that Bacarion would try to have him killed, and in such a way that it required the least investigation. Which meant probably not shooting or stabbing or even a fatal blow to the head – any of which would require sending his body for forensic examination. She might or might not have a collaborator in the medical facility on Stack One. Though such a murder could be blamed on a prisoner, far more useful for her purposes would be a disappearance, something that would leave

the blame on him. If he went AWOL – as he had been
thinking of doing, he realized with a start – Bacarion
would be free to make up whatever story she liked about
him.

The most likely thing was a quick toss over the cliff,
alive or dead. Alive, probably, because then Bacarion's
agents could honestly claim not to have harmed him. She
would not order an attack until she was sure it would
succeed – until she was sure she had enough support. He
had a little time to make his preparations, minimal
though they could be.

Three Stack had fifty Personal Protective Units,
Planetary, in storage. In theory, a PPU would protect its
wearer from the rigors of a planetary climate, as well as a
variety of traumas. Abstracting a Personal Protective Unit
from stores would definitely attract attention, but they
were inventoried only once a month. Would the attack
come in that time? Probably, he thought.

But a PPU wouldn't be enough to keep him alive in the
ocean. He needed something else.

Aircraft carried survival gear; they did occasionally
come down in the ocean, and the crew did occasionally
survive to use the life rafts and other gear. There was a
manual – he had seen a copy once – on surviving such
wrecks, modified from one written by people who liked
to sail around in boats. But he had read the manual out of
boredom, while waiting for a shuttle flight, and with the
casual contempt of someone who would never be stupid
enough to get himself in a situation where the details
presented would be important.

Methlin had always said learn everything you can.
Meth had survived worse.

Why did big sisters have to be right so often?

Spare survival gear for the aircraft based at Three

Stack – the commander's personal aircar shuttle with a capacity of four besides the pilot, and the two mail/utility vehicles which would hold 20 in a pinch – was stored in a locked bay on the shore side of the hangar. In his first month onstation, when he was still learning where everything was, he had been part of the inventory team that preceded the annual IG inspection. He remembered clearly the fat bundles, like sausage lumps, that were stacked next to the outer wall. Heavy, awkward, and not something he could tuck under his arm.

So . . . where could he stash something like that? Before he took it, he had to have a place to hide it, and he spent the next few off shifts looking. Everywhere on the limited surface of the Stack, someone else had reason to be. The two main lava tubes were in regular use; one had a small lift tube fitted into it. Personnel were up and down several times a day, though most didn't venture beyond the stacks of reserve supplies piled at the foot, and the little nest of discarded clothing just around the corner, where those who wanted to keep their encounters private bedded down in the warmer months.

Still . . . it was the only place. The smaller of the tubes opened to the outside, above the high-tide level except in storms. Generations of guards had broken a connection between the two; he was not the only one who had stood in the sea opening watching the waves at closer range and even trying to catch one of the native sea creatures on a moly line. As long as no one saw him actually dragging a deflated life raft into the sea cave, his presence in the tubes would cause no notice. He hoped.

He felt clever about figuring out a way to get the folded raft through the buildings and into the lift tube without detection. He didn't have to take it himself; he'd stenciled it with a supply code, and simply told a pivot to take it down with other supplies when the next load came in.

Supply drops were chaotic enough that no one noticed – or seemed to, he cautioned himself – when an extra container went down. Later, he found it, and – having borrowed an AG dolly – floated it down the tube, through the gap, and to his chosen hiding place.

He felt better after that, even though his chances were still, he felt sure, closer to zero than a hundred. At least he had a chance, if a small one.

Once that was done, his mind turned to Bacarion's plans, not his own. What was she up to? He was as sure as if he'd crawled into her head that she had sought this assignment. But why? She would not have come here because of him – surely revenge on Methlin's little brother wasn't profit enough for three years on Stack Three – but what was her purpose? What could she do with a prisonful of convicts and guards, isolated in the midst of the ocean?

When he put it that way, he had to wonder what she could have done with a prisonful of guards and convicts on the mainland, or in space . . . and the answer chilled him. Lepescu's protegees, he was sure, had not become exemplars of sweetness and light since Lepescu's death. Indeed, Methlin had warned the family against having anything to do with any of them. Next thing to traitors, she'd said. So involved with their own game that nothing else mattered.

What he should do was find out what Bacarion was doing, and report it. But how? He was not in Bacarion's confidence and he had no access to the administrative offices anyway. That would just get him killed faster.

As the days passed, Gelan found that acting normal stretched his nerves almost past bearing. Inspections, chores, guard duty . . . wondering which of the guards and which of the prisoners were in on the plan, and yet again what the plan was. It had to be more than just killing him. Bacarion might take pleasure in killing Methlin Meharry's little brother, but she would not have finagled an assignment here just for that. If only he knew what was going on . . . but although it became increasingly obvious that something was – that he was being left out of meetings and plans – he could not find anything out.

He had not considered himself a trusting soul, but now, trying to trust no one, he realized that he had the normal human desire to be part of a group, not a complete outsider.

Margiu Pardalt had accepted a position as junior instructor in the Schools, and discovered that she enjoyed teaching. As the weather eased, bringing the occasional cool breath from the far north, her spirits lifted. Xavier had never been quite as hot as Copper Mountain in summer, and she looked forward to winter here. Unlike some of the others, who never took to planetside life, she enjoyed learning more about the world she was on. The Regular Space Service had facilities scattered around the planet, from the frigid polar caps to the balmiest of tropical islands. Most were used for training of some kind, or testing equipment; it did not occur to Margiu to wonder why a space force would do so much training and testing on a planet. Instead, she hoped she would have a chance to see the steppes near Drylands, so much like her homeworld, and maybe climb a mountain when she had some leave coming.

Her first chance to travel came in the break between class sessions, and she didn't even have to use leave time. Priority directives of very high classification had to be hand-carried from base to base. Ensign Pardalt was the obvious choice.

So on a morning that was not quite crisp, but at least not stifling, she accepted a case full of the directives, locked it to her belt, and climbed aboard one of the regular supply aircars headed for Camp Engleton. She sat on a sack of something lumpy and uncomfortable for two hours – the supply aircars had no passenger slings – and watched the red-sand brush country give way to dirty-green coastal grasslands and then dark-green trees standing in brown water.

She had only fifteen minutes to deliver the directives to the base commander, but fifteen minutes of the sticky heat and sulfur stench of the swamp forest was more than enough to quench her curiosity. She was glad to climb back into the aircar, now headed for Drylands. The lumpy sack she'd been sitting on had been unloaded, along with others, and the crew chief now had room to rig a seat of sorts.

That flight took several hours; she fell asleep in the noisy cargo compartment, waking when the aircar came down through the late afternoon sun. This far north, a chill wind rattled the few fading leaves left on the trees planted around the base's central drill field, and the short prairie grass had turned various shades of russet and maroon. She handed the base commander his copy of the directives, and signed into the TOQ for the night. When she walked around outside, she could almost believe she was on Xavier – until dark, when the night sky looked very different. Were they really that close to the Scarf?

Next day, she was scheduled for a long-distance flight to the west coast bases, Big Trees and Dark Harbor (she wondered again who had been allowed to name these places), and then she would embark on the more dangerous journey to the Stack Islands bases.

The long distance flight was not by aircar, but in a pressurized aircraft flying much higher than the 'cars;

beneath her the land faded into a dim patchwork of dun and wrinkled brown, with white tips on the tall mountains she hoped to see in person some day. Also on the flight were replacement officers and enlisted; she was crammed into her seat with only a brief glimpse through the window whenever the neuro-enhanced marine beside her leaned back for some reason.

Still, it was travel. She had come to learn, and this was learning. She memorized everything she could about the inside of the aircraft.

They landed at Big Trees, the runway a long gash in the forest. She had grown up among trees, clumps and woodlots and scattered groves on the meadows, but those trees had been rounder, softer. She had seen more, and taller, trees during her years at the Academy. But the trees had always had space around and between them. Despite the pictures, she had not really imagined what this forest would be like – great spires many times the height of the buildings on base. After delivering her package to the base commandant, she found she could not get transport to Dark Harbor until the next day.

'You should see our trees,' she was told. 'There's nothing like them anywhere else.'

So she wandered out into the afternoon light, and up to the margin of the forest. Behind her mowers buzzed, trimming the emerald grass in the quadrangle; she could hear the closer click of feet on the walkways. Looking away from all that, she faced a massive dark bole like a slightly curved wall. Ferns the height of her head grew near it, trimmed back in a straight line on the base side. Between the chinks of its bark – she thought it must be bark – other plants grew, mosses and ferns and something with bright yellow flowers like tiny fireworks.

She edged around the tree, following a vague path. Under her feet, the ground felt spongy, and when she

had cleared the curve of the great tree's bole, she realized
she could not hear the base . . . the great tree lay between,
soaking up the sound. Uneasy in the thick growth, she
went back the way she'd come, and then back across the
quadrangle to base housing.

Her flight up the coast the next morning, again in an
aircar, revealed how little of the land had been touched
by humans – the great forest lay green and unbroken from
the base to the foothills of the mountains, and almost all
the way to Dark Harbor, where it eased gradually into
smaller trees, and then into broken shrubland.

In Dark Harbor, she had to wait several days for a
trans-ocean flight to the Stack Islands bases. A storm
system had moved in, and no one was going to risk a
flight during it, not for a mere courier. In the meantime
she was supposed to familiarize herself with cold water
ocean survival techniques. It was already early winter in
the northern Big Ocean. Margiu learned to wriggle into
the PPU and fasten the hood with one hand; she went
over lifeboat drill and abandon-craft drill at least four
separate times.

Corporal Asele Martin-Jehore stood satellite watch at the
remote Blue Islands facility. Unlike Stack Islands, the
archipelago known as Blue Islands lay in warm equatorial waters. Assignment to Blue was as coveted as Stack
Islands was feared: the big sea predators which lay in
wait for escapees from Stack were force-netted away from
the beautiful white beaches and turquoise lagoons of
Blue. All the permanent personnel onplanet tried to
wangle at least a week's leave time on Blue.

Martin-Jehore had worked years to earn this assignment, but help from a friend in Personnel didn't hurt. He
had proven himself time and again – he had recalibrated
the number four signal array after a seastorm, when his

senior supervisor was out with gut flu. And – because he showed talent with recalcitrant electronics – he had been permanently assigned to MetSatIV, the weather and surveillance satellite responsible for covering the northern third of Big Ocean.

MetSatIV had been a problem since it was installed. The contractor had replaced it twice, and each time found nothing wrong. The second time, the contractor's project engineer had made the unwelcome suggestion that someone in Fleet was screwing up the software. That had been Jurowski, who held the position before Martin-Jehore. It hadn't, in fact, been anything Jurowski did which bollixed the bird, but in the interest of satisfying the contractor that all steps had been taken, Jurowski had been taken off the roster for MetSatIV.

MetSatIV was still buggy. Martin-Jehore was sure it was an AI glitch – so was Jurowski, but Martin-Jehore had one vital piece of information Jurowski lacked: the command set for MetSatIV's AI.

In theory, every transmission from Blue Islands was logged. In practice, a very good communications tech could tightbeam a satellite without detection. Not often, but occasionally. Martin-Jehore had chosen his moments carefully, gradually gaining control of MetSatIV's AI at a level no mere communications tech was expected to reach.

Now he needed only the cover of a routine test transmission to cause the desired failure.

MetSatIV's AI compared the instruction set to those previously received, and agreed that they matched in syntax and content. Then it turned off its IR scan, and tipped itself 30° around its z-axis.

In the observatory below, one of the dozen screens in satellite surveillance went from a clear visual of a seastorm in progress, a vast swirl of white, to an eye-wrenching jiggling blaze of hash.

'Blast. There goes Watchbird again.' Martin-Jehore glared at the screen. 'I'll bet it's a clock problem.'

'Nah – it's too random.' Jurowski wasn't going to agree with anything Martin-Jehore said. Eighteen months, and he was still sore about losing his place as Watchbird's senior tech.

'Well, let's see if C-28 will get it back.' Sometimes command C-28 would bring Watchbird back online, and sometimes it wouldn't. This time it wouldn't, but Martin-Jehore punched in that command sequence, anyway. The hash on his screens remained. 'Not this time.' When C-28 didn't work, the problem usually took longer to fix, but so far he had always been able to do so.

'Try the 43-120 set,' Jurowski suggested. While he could not resist the initial jibe, he was a generous-hearted man, and always willing to help. Martin-Jehore nodded, and entered it. It wouldn't work either, but it would eat up several minutes while not working. The screen hash changed to a finer grain, but nothing else happened.

'Somebody rejuved its AI,' Jurowski said. The whole room chuckled appreciatively. Headquarters might not know about any connection between rejuv and mental problems, but the lower ranks had figured it out long since.

As required by regulation, Martin-Jehore reported to his superior that MetSatIV was ineffective within the hour, when the first three standard interventions didn't bring it back online. CPO Gurnach sighed, and told him to keep trying. Martin-Jehore could tell she wasn't really worried. Big Ocean was mostly empty, and the storm MetSatIV had shown was already in the model. Stack Islands already knew about it – in fact, it was just clearing them now – and it wouldn't reach the mainland for days.

MetSatIV's other capability, that of detecting small craft atmospheric penetration, didn't concern CPO Gurnach either. At last report, the only ships insystem were, as always, Regular Space Service vessels. A hostile landing would have to come from a hostile deepspace ship, and there weren't any. Why worry about a hostile landing? Besides, Polar 1, now at the south end of its orbit, carried sensor arrays designed to spot any intrusive traffic; MetSatIV was really redundant.

Martin-Jehore knew it was crucial to keep MetSatIV offline for five hours or more. He did not know why, nor did he care. He had convinced himself that it was probably a matter of smuggling something really profitable (given the size of his payoff), and he didn't think smuggling actually hurt anybody. So what if some porn cubes got past customs without paying duty?

CHAPTER SIXTEEN

STACK ISLANDS BASE THREE

The attack came on a dank gray afternoon, with thin rain spitting out of a low sky and visibility just reaching from the parapet of the exercise courtyard to the administrative offices. Gelan Meharry had outside duty, and had checked the first three posts when he found that number four was missing. Even as he thumbed the control on his comunit, he felt the prickles rising on his arms. Not at night after all, but with enough daylight to see if his body caught on any of the rocks.

'Spiers here,' came the answer to his call. Spiers, whom he had not seriously suspected.

'Number four outside post's empty,' Gelan said. 'Should be Mahdal – has he called in?'

'No, Corporal. Want me to check sickbay?'

'Request backup at this post,' Gelan said. 'And run a com check on the others, would you? Then check sickbay.'

'Sure thing.' Spiers's voice sounded normal, with only the slight concern appropriate to a missing sentry.

Gelan looked around. Number four post gave its

occupant a view of the prisoners' exercise court, the entrance block beyond, the upper part of the administrative block overlooking the forecourt, which was itself out of sight, and the peak of the stack itself rising beyond that. To his left he could see the helmet of number three post; to his right and down, on the outside of the entrance block, he should have seen the bright dot that was number five.

He didn't. He leaned out over the parapet of number four, to check the path below. There, far below, a bright yellow splotch, and a white dot near it.

He used his com again. 'Spiers, this is Corporal Meharry again. There's a man down on the westside path. Have you raised number five yet?'

'No, Corporal.' Now Spiers did sound worried. 'Sergeant says he's on the way. Want me to call Medical?'

'Better do it. I'll go on down and see . . .'

As the blow fell, he lunged forward, so that his skull took less than the intended blow. The unexpectedness of that lunge loosened his captors' grip, and he got in another good shove as he went over the edge.

For an instant, hanging in the air with the sea spread out below him, he was euphoric. They hadn't knocked him out; he'd fooled them. He was going to make it; his plan would work.

Then he was close enough to see the height of the waves — mere wrinkles from above, here taller than he was, and smashing into the sharp rocks. *And no helmet*, he thought, just as he plunged into water so cold it took his breath, with force enough to nearly knock him out.

He fought his way to the surface by blind instinct, helped by the surge of the rising tide. When he shook the water from his eyes, he saw a black wall rushing toward him, covered with sharp shells. He threw out his arms; the water slammed him into the rock with crushing force, but the PPU gloves protected his hands, and then his body, from the sharp edges of the shells, and the wrist grapples locked onto the surface. When the water dragged back, he was able to stay on the rock. In that brief second, he curled up, jamming his boots into a crack, and deployed the PPU's lower grapples.

Cold water roared over him again, smashing him into the rock, then sucking his body away . . . the grapples held; his arms and legs strained. In the next trough, he released the wrist grapples, flung himself upward, and locked the wrists again just as the next wave hit.

Minute by minute he fought his way upward, racing the tide and the limits of his own strength. Distant clamor battered his hearing, even over the roar and suck of the waves. He looked upward, only to get a faceful of cold water.

Just above high tide, well within the splash zone, he clung to the rock. Despite the PPU, he was chilled; without it, he would have been dead. He could feel his arms and legs stiffening from both cold and bruising, and out there somewhere . . . the killers were looking for him.

Gelan stripped off the last of his duty uniform, ripping it free with the grapple claws of the PPU. He hoped it would look like the damage of sea creatures if the killers spotted it. Underneath, the PPU's programmable outer surface took on the mottled dark color of the rock . . . now if they looked down, they would see only rock, not a splash of yellow. He unhooked and unrolled the hood, and pulled it over his head. At once he felt better; the hood cut the windchill. He sealed it close around his face, then pulled up the facemask. The last bite of the wind disappeared. He wasn't comfortable, but he was no longer in danger of hypothermia. Not soon, anyway.

He touched the controls on his chest, and the PPU's circuitry delivered a boosted audio signal. Another control released a fine antenna to pick up transmissions.

'– Went over right there, sir. No chance to grab him – and he went right down – may've hit his head on a rock –'

Darkness closed in early. Gelan could see lights above; he waited until they were gone, then longer: they would be scanning in infrared as well. Though his suit reflected almost all his body heat inward, to protect him from the cold, a sensitive scan could pick up a human shape in movement. But well after local midnight, he moved – stiffly at first, then more smoothly – toward the lava tube where – he hoped – his survival kit was still concealed.

Once in the mouth of the tube, he risked a brief flash of his torch. There it was.

And there was Commander Bacarion, a weapon levelled at his chest.

'I thought they might have underestimated you,' she said. 'I didn't.'

He said nothing.

'I will be glad to take your ears,' she said. 'I might even send one to your family.'

The thought of Methlin's reaction if she got one of her little brother's ears in the mail made him grin in spite of his fear. 'Do that,' he said.

Then tossed his torch aside and dove toward her dominant hand, and used the suit grapples to catch and fling himself in a tumbling arc toward her. Her weapon fired, but the needle went wide. Gelan pivoted on one suit grapple, and slammed both booted feet into her side; he felt the crunch of bone and heard her grunt, but it was dark now, and she wasn't dead. She would have more than one weapon.

He scrambled towards her, raking with the suit grapples. A thin red beam appeared, the rangefinder of her next weapon, and the sharp crack of a hunting rifle turned to the clatter of falling rock where it hit. Gelan felt something with one glove, and yanked hard; she cried out, then something slammed into his shoulder. He swung elbows, knees, feet, and took hard blows himself, barely softened by the suit. Then the blows weakened; he hit again and again. And again.

Silence, but for the sound of his own breathing, and the pounding of waves outside the tube. Was she dead, or feigning? Had she been alone? He fumbled around, trying to find the torch, but finally gave up and used the suit's headlamp.

Bile filled his mouth. His suit grapples glistened, brilliant red in the light; he had torn her face off, in that last struggle. An ear dangled from one grapple tip. He shook it free.

She took ears.

He was a Meharry.

He was a Meharry who had killed an officer, an officer who was, as far as anyone knew, his legitimate superior merely doing her duty. He couldn't just go tell the sergeant about it. Not this time.

Methlin had said there would be days like this, he'd told himself often enough. She had never told him he might have to murder his commander and then figure out how to explain it.

He needed to search Bacarion's body. Surely if she intended some serious wrongdoing – beyond having him killed – she would have some evidence on her. She would not trust everything to an office safe. But not here, not where her confederates might be on their way, alerted by some signal he knew nothing about, or simply by her failure to show up at a meeting. If she had evidence on

her, he would have to take her corpse along, or they
would destroy it.

A gust of icy wind curled into the tube and it res-
onated like a giant organ pipe. Was it a storm coming? He
couldn't wait. Grunting with the effort, Gelan dragged
his purloined life raft down the tube to the lip, and then
considered what to do with Bacarion's body. Finally, he
decided to bring it along. It was heavier than he expected,
awkward to heave and tip into the raft, but he secured it
carefully before shifting the raft — and himself — to the
very edge of the rock.

A more violent gust of wind caught it and whirled it
through the air to land hard on the water; Gelan almost
lost his hold. Even through the PPU, he could feel the
water's chill, and its power. He yanked the vent control,
and the raft ballooned around him. Bacarion's body
lurched into him as the raft whirled, tilted, whirled again,
on the wild waves.

Daylight came late, and weakly; the raft was driven
ahead of sleet-laden wind over tossing waves that had
long since relieved Gelan of everything in his stomach.
He didn't want to use his headlamp to find the medkit; it
might be seen from the base. So in the dingy gray light,
with Bacarion's grisly stiff corpse rolling into him with
every lurch of the waves, he finally spotted the medkit on
the raft's bulwark and edged over to it. He peeled back the
glove of his PPU, opened the medkit, and found the
antinausea patches. In a few minutes, he felt slightly
better, and very hungry. First, though — he used the raft's
suction pump to clear bloodstained water from the raft's
interior, and dared a peek out the canopy.

Nothing but tossing waves, dimpled by sleet, receding
into murky dimness. At least they were out of sight of
Three Stack. He resealed the canopy and explored the
rest of the raft interior.

It had been designed to hold eight crash survivors. Tucked into one compartment was a manual – the same one, he realized, which he had read so carelessly that other time. On the first page, he saw a diagram of the raft, clearly marking the location of the water purifier, the direction finder, the food stores, the repair kit . . .

Lieutenant Commander Vinet waited none too patiently for the signal he expected. Today or tomorrow, Bacarion had said, depending on weather. It had to be cloudy, so that nothing would show on a satellite scan if the scan hadn't been disabled; it had to be daylight enough that her men could be sure Meharry was safely drowned. With the storm moving in, surely it had been cloudy on Three Stack – it had been cloudy here since before dawn, and as evening closed in an icy mix of sleet and snow pelted windows.

He ate dinner as quickly as possible. If only he could contact her – but she had forbidden it, and he knew her to be a ruthless critic of those who disobeyed. Something had caused a delay – certainly the next day would be the one, then. He fell asleep at last.

Morning brought the height of the gale, the waves below beaten down by wind, scraped by sleet into patterns that looked as dangerous as they were. Through triple insulated windows he felt the power of that gale, the chill of the wind. By noon he was unbearably restless again, pacing from desk to window and back, then down the passage to the little enclosed overlook that gave him a clear view of the entire west end of the stack, and across to several others. No more sleet and snow, now, nothing but the cold wind; the two trees in the courtyard below flailed bare limbs against the wall that protected them.

Towards evening, the storms slid off to the south, and

cold green light speared under the trailing edge. Still nothing. Something had gone very wrong indeed. What should he do now? He couldn't contact any of the others; Bacarion controlled the recognition codes. He couldn't do anything with the research teams or the weapons without additional forces. Bacarion knew he had only a few reliable men. She knew that, and still . . . he made himself sit down again, but nothing could quiet his mind.

Gelan had lashed the commander's corpse to the far side of the raft, repaired the slashes he'd accidentally put in the inner hull, eaten, and slept again. The storm had eased, but he had no idea where he was in relation to the Stacks. Fear of being blown back to them warred with fear of drifting on the vast ocean until he died. Death either way – which was worse?

Surely the commander's conspiracy, whatever it was, didn't include everyone on the planet. He ought to be able to count on the people at Search and Rescue, if no one else.

He looked at Bacarion's corpse, and shuddered. He could not bring himself to look for papers or whatever else she might have had. Well, then he could write his account of what happened: the survival manual had a thick pad of water-resistant sheets and a waterproof marker. Gelan hadn't written anything by hand in years, but he decided to put down what had happened before he unlocked the beacon. That way, even if he died, there'd be some record of events from his point of view.

If someone didn't just destroy them.

No use thinking like that. He set the pad on his knee, and tried to form legible writing as the waves lifted and dropped. It was harder than he'd expected, and after three sheets, he gave up.

*

'Commander Bacarion's not in her offices, sir.' Sergeant Copans looked worried. 'The commander's not answering any call, and the locator's not lit.'

'If it's not one thing it's another.' CPO Slyke didn't need this. Corporal Meharry's carefully staged suicide had gone exactly as planned, along with the murder of Major Dumlin, the senior unaligned officer. But Bacarion should have been there, unless she was playing some game of her own . . . and even then, she should have been back by now. Her games were usually short ones.

CPO Slyke had been a member of the Loyal Order of Game Hunters for sixteen years, the first enlisted recruit. He had served with then-Major Lepescu, and admired the officer's grasp of the real nature of war – a test of survival, of ultimate fitness. Born and raised on Calydon by Priorists who believed that fitness in this life was determined by effort in the life previous, Slyke knew he had *earned* his superior skills and toughness.

Now, facing the implications of Bacarion's disappearance, he knew his moment had come. Although he had not been briefed on the whole mission, his part had required him to know more than any other NCO and most officers. He could – he *would* – take over.

They had been lucky. Severe weather cut off communication immediately after the commander's disappearance, giving him time to do what he could to obscure the evidence, and search the buildings. The underground storage and lava tubes were an obvious target. He insisted on leading the search party himself, with his most trusted companions, all full members.

The commander had left tagtales. Very sensible of her. What had she known about that he didn't, and why hadn't she told him? He pushed that thought aside, grunting as he squeezed into the second tube.

There. The search lights picked up the glint off the

hunting rifle's barrel first, then he saw the little red dot on the far wall. The laser sight was still on, the power pack unexpended. His breath came short. Was it a trap? Her trap, to test her followers? The sea boomed outside, and filled the tube with a wash of cold wet air; the walls glistened with it.

Closer . . . and he realized that some of the glistening surface was blood, not seawater. Smears and pools of blood, a few shreds of flesh . . . and something had been dragged, something heavy, from *here* to the edge of the tube, to the sea, where a crumpled wet tarp lay, its edge flapping with every gust of wind.

That damnable, conniving, fornicating Corporal Meharry must have survived the fall . . . climbed here, hoping for refuge — no, to retrieve a life raft he'd stowed here. And the commander had figured it out, had been waiting for him, only in the struggle one of them had killed the other (such a lot of blood, and he was a man who could estimate spilled blood accurately) and escaped in the raft.

But which? Logic said Meharry; Bacarion would have come back.

Unless that was part of her plot. Unless she had planned to betray them all, and escape herself. She had, after all, come down here without telling anyone. Perhaps she had counted on Meharry's death, and the life raft was for her own use.

He chewed his lip, trying to figure it out, and finally decided it didn't matter. They were in it up to their necks, and a witness — which witness didn't matter — had escaped.

He would have to go on with it. Too many clues might remain, even though he had used a firehose to flush the lava tube of evidence. If they could get offplanet before the person in the life raft made contact with anyone, the plan could go on as originally formed.

He ran his thumb under his belt, along the strips of ears that he had taken. They were, he was sure, only the beginning.

Within the prison population, tension had risen in the past few days. Prisoners studied jailers in both their roles, as the predators they had been (and were in spirit) watch prey, and as the prey watch predators around them. Slyke knew exactly which prisoners were supposed to be released, but his own assessment suggested a few additions. First he had to find a way to contact the conspirators in orbit, and convince them of his identity.

Establishing the contact was easier than he'd feared.

'We heard.' The voice contact, generated from random snips of synthetic speech, would defeat voice recognition software.

'Ready to initiate Bubblebath,' Slyke said.

A long hissing silence. Then – 'You?'

'Better go ahead,' Slyke said, leaving out 'sir' with an effort. 'Investigation of the major's disappearance –'

'Affirmative. ETA stage one?'

Slyke had calculated this carefully. 'Two-seven minutes plus original.'

'Good.'

Now he had to signal his fellows. Sergeant Copans and Sergeant Vinus looked worried, but heard him out.

'But sir – with the commander's disappearance, Fleet Security will be all over us like crushers on a broken spacer.'

'Yes, and if we wait around here, chances are they'll find something the commander left that will incriminate us. Either we do it *now*, or there's a very good chance we'll be in there' – he jerked his thumb at the cell block's outer doors – 'with them. Is that what you want?'

'No, but –'

'Did you earn your *ears*, Sergeant?'

'Yessir.'

'Then hop to it.'

R.S.S. *Bonar Tighe* requested permission from Traffic Control to practice LAC drops into the Big Ocean. Many of the warships which visited Copper Mountain took advantage of the opportunity to test their drop crews. Traffic Control approved the drop zone – 200 klicks south of Stack Islands – and also advised them that the only traffic was a prop jet doing SAR to the northwest.

Bonar Tighe's crew had coalesced around the charismatic Solomon Drizh, hero of Cavinatto, and just too junior, like Bacarion, to be closely investigated as a Lepescu protégé after the admiral's demise. The conspirators had learned from the mutiny aboard *Despite*, and the proportion of those supporting Drizh and his allies was much higher in every ship, the chain of command much tighter. This time they were not acting for the Benignity, but for themselves . . . the Loyal Order of Game Hunters.

Fleet had gone soft, Drizh had declared; the whole Familias Regnant had gone soft as a rotting peach. With anyone of real vision in charge, there would have been no piracy, no incursion by the New Texas Godfearing Militia – and certainly no attempt to preserve the lives of those scum once they'd taken the Speaker's daughter. All the NewTex worlds would be taken, their vicious militia subdued . . . though Drizh had to admit that he rather admired the men who would attack big ships with little ones.

The Loyal Order of Game Hunters had survived Lepescu's death and, in the years since, had even grown. Its leaders used one political event after another to demonstrate the need for more toughness, a more realistic attitude towards war, more loyalty between brothers in arms. Weakness in high places – from the king's abdication to Lord Thornbuckle's inability to keep his daughter in line – proved the need for a stronger, more warlike, military arm.

Like Lepescu, they saw themselves as more loyal, more dedicated, than other Fleet members, and the others as wishy-washy, irresolute, and ultimately ineffective. They recruited widely, more often in the NCO levels than Lepescu had – as Drizh said, if their founder had a fault, it was his misplaced belief in high birth.

The removal of senior NCOs and flag ranking officers because of problems with rejuvenation gave them an obvious window of opportunity. The following burst of temporary promotions gave the group a flag rank member again. He might be only an admiral minor, and only for the duration of the emergency – but that emergency would last long enough for his purposes.

Bonar Tighe's three LACs dropped into atmosphere under control of the orbital Traffic Control. Atmospheric Traffic Control on Copper Mountain was minimal except near the main training centers – and the Big Ocean had none. Once below 8000 meters, they were automatically untagged on orbital screens.

Still they stayed on course until under 2000 meters, when they angled northward, towards the Stack Islands.

CPO Slyke did not know exactly how Commander Bacarion had intended to deal with the prisoners and guards who were not part of the conspiracy. For his part, he had no intention of leaving witnesses behind, even on that isolated base. When the storm passed, and the radios once more punched through with the usual demands for daily reports, he'd had to say something to divert suspicion, and had reported Meharry and Bacarion both as 'missing, presumed swept away by waves.' Incredulity had followed; he knew that someone would send an investigative team as soon as possible, along with a new CO. No one must be left to talk about it. Even if the mutineers gained support of the orbital station, they wouldn't have the whole planet by the time someone could get here and write a damning report.

His confederates first took care of those members of the staff who were not part of the conspiracy. Those bodies he left in place . . . he hoped later investigators would think it a prisoner breakout. Killing the uninvolved prisoners was another matter. He had them brought out into the courtyard and then turned the riot weapons on them. They had time to scream . . . and when the prisoners he'd recruited came out, they were more respectful, just as he'd hoped.

By the time the LACs were in atmosphere, he had the prisoners lined up and waiting. The most reliable had the weapons and PPUs out of the guardroom. When the first LAC screamed out of the sky, and settled on the cold stone of Three Stack's landing pad, Slyke didn't wait for the hatches to open – the men were in motion, running. The first LAC lifted, and the next settled in place. Sixty more men raced aboard, just ahead of another rain squall. Then another sixty, and another. Slyke rode the last one up.

Behind him, a driving rain battered the corpses sprawled in the courtyard, washing the blood into gutters, and finally through drains down into the sea. When the squalls moved on, the seabirds came, and for a time made a column of flickering wings above the towering stack.

Bonar Tighe's LACs screamed south, and rose from their designated drop zones back to orbit an ample twelve minutes before Martin-Lehore finally fixed MetSatIV's glitch.

MetSatIV picked them up at near-orbital level, but they were outbound, carrying Fleet beacons; the satellite's AI tagged them as friendlies.

The first LAC eased into *Bonar Tighe*'s drop bay and settled onto its marks. Pivot Anseli Markham, who always read manuals and followed them to the letter, aimed the hand-held bioscan at its fuselage.

'Put that down,' growled her boss, Sergeant minor Prinkin.

'But sir, the manual said –' Anseli goggled at the readout. The LACs had gone out empty, with flight crew only, and her instrument was showing dozens and dozens of little green blips.

'Put it down, Pivot; it's out of order.'

'Oh.' Anseli racked the instrument. So that's why it was showing troops aboard an empty LAC. 'Should I take it to the repair bay, Sergeant Prinkin?'

He gave her a sour look. 'Do that, Pivot. You're no damn use in here anyway.'

Anseli unracked the bioscan and headed toward the repair bay. She was tempted to turn it on and see if it worked when it didn't have to read through hull material, but she could feel Sergeant Prinkin watching her. He'd never liked her; he was always sniping at her, and she tried so hard . . . she let her mind drift into her favorite reverie, of how much better she would treat pivots when she made sergeant minor.

The repair bay for small scan equipment was out of sight of the LAC service bay. Once around the corner, Anseli experimented with the bioscan. When she pointed it at her foot, a green blurry foot-shaped image appeared. When she aimed at the squad coming down the passage, it showed all eight of them. When she aimed it at a bulk-head, there were two squatting shapes . . . and then a rush through the water pipes that made her blush. She hadn't *meant* to do anything like that.

Chief Stockard, in the repair bay, took the bioscan and gave her forms to fill out.

'But I think it's working now,' Anseli said, trying to fit the entire thirteen-digit part number into a space only two centimeters long. Print clearly, the directions said, but how could she print clearly that small? And why did she have to fill out forms at all, when the computerized ID system would read the part number right off the bioscan itself? She did know better than to ask that one; it wasn't her first trip to the repair bay. 'I tried it on people coming along here, and it always registered them.'

'If your sergeant said it wasn't working, then it wasn't working,' Stockard said, folding his lips under. 'It may be working now, but it wasn't working then. What was he trying to do when he said it malfunctioned?'

'He wasn't using it, Chief. I was. I was taking a bioscan reading of the incoming LAC, just like it says to do in the manual, and he said put it down, it's not working right. And I guess it wasn't, because it said the LAC was full of troops.'

'LACs usually are,' Stockard said, the corner of his mouth twitching. 'I don't see what's wrong with that.'

'But they dropped empty,' Anseli said. 'I was there; I scanned them going out, just like the manual says, and they carried only flight crew. It was just a practice flight.'

Stockard froze, his hands flat on the counter between them. 'Are you saying the LACs went down empty and came up full?'

'Well . . . no, sir, not really. They couldn't have. It's just this bioscan unit, but since it's malfunctioning –'

'You just wait there a minute.' Stockard turned away, and Anseli could see him talking into a comunit, though she couldn't hear him. He turned back, shaking his head, still muttering into the comunit. Then he gave her a rueful look. 'I guess it malfunctioned . . . I just asked Chief Burdine if the LACs carried troops, and he said no. Oh – he says for you to take a detour up to Admin and pick up the liberty passes for the section. We'll be docking in a few hours.'

'Yes, sir.' No chance that her name would be on the list, given Sergeant Prinkin's animosity, but maybe he'd go, and she'd have a few hours of peace.

Chief Burdine, on the LAC service bay deck, strolled over to Sergeant Prinkin as if making his usual round of stations. 'Just had a call from Stockard in repair – that idiot pivot of yours told him all about the malfunctioning bioscan showing the LAC full of troops. I think Stockard bought my assurance that they're empty, but how much chance that pivot will blab to someone else about the bioscan reading?'

'Near a hundred percent,' Sergeant Prinkin said. 'The girl's got no sense.'

'Is she popular?'

'She's got friends. Hard worker, shows initiative, always willing to help out.'

'A milk biscuit.' That with contempt.

'Oh yes, all the way through.'

'I wish we didn't have any of that sort aboard,' Chief Burdine said. 'They could have a happy life milking cows somewhere; what'd they have to join Fleet for?'

'For our sport,' Sergeant Prinkin said.

'That's true.' Burdine grinned at him. 'Though it's little sport someone like her will give us.'

Running up to Admin from the repair bay meant running up a lot of ladders, which other people seemed busy

running down. Again and again Anseli had to stand aside
while one or more officers or squads of NEMs clattered
down. She wasn't really in a hurry, because the longer
she was away from Sergeant Prinkin the better, but standing at the foot of ladders wasn't her idea of fun. Her mind
wandered to the LACs and the bioscan. If LACs could
drop and pick up troops . . . or drop troops off . . . why
couldn't they pick troops up? Go down empty, come back
full? And if you didn't bioscan the LACs, how could you
tell?

'Stand clear!'

She flattened herself to the bulkhead yet again, not
really seeing the uniforms flashing past her. What if there
were people on the ship who weren't crew? People from
down on the planet?

Of course, everyone on this planet was Fleet, so it
didn't matter. Did it?

Anseli knew that pivots weren't supposed to think —
well, not beyond memorizing instruction sets in manuals.
But she'd always had a sort of itchy feeling in her head if
she didn't get things straight. Machines either worked or
they didn't, in her very clear interior universe. A bioscan
which reported on real, verifiable human-sized beings
behind one wall didn't turn liar and report that there
were people where there weren't any. That very same
bioscan unit had reported nothing in the LAC holds when
the LAC left . . . when it was known to be empty. So *how*
did the sergeant know the LAC was empty when the
bioscan said it was loaded with troops? Sergeants knew
everything, but . . . her mind itched.

A non-itchy part of her mind began its own commen-
tary on the crew members who kept coming down the
ladders. There had been no general alarm, so why were
the ship's security details on their way to the LAC bays?

By the time she reached Admin, her mind was worse

than a case of hives, and the only way she knew to scratch it was ask questions. The chief in Admin growled and handed her another job to do. How was she supposed to learn if no one answered her questions?

Bonar Tighe reported its LACs recovered, and requested and received permission to dock at the orbital station. This, like the request to practice LAC drops, was standard procedure, and the Traffic Control gave *Bonar Tighe* a docking priority assignment based on her ETA. The stationmaster approved station liberty at the captain's discretion, and forwarded the station newsletter. Ships of *Bonar Tighe*'s mass could not microjump so close to a planet, so the cruiser had to crawl patiently in a spiral to catch up with the station, a process which took several hours.

CHAPTER SEVENTEEN

Margiu Pardalt boarded the odd-looking aircraft before dawn. If not for the briefings, she'd have had no idea that such craft existed. On Xavier, she had seen only surface-to-station shuttles and low-flying aircars or flitters. Her years at the Academy had introduced her to high-altitude passenger aircraft like the one she'd been in from Drylands to the coast. But this uneasy compromise between aircraft and boat looked like something a mad scientist would come up with: four fat engines on the high-set wings, with whirligig propellers set into adjustable ducts; a peculiar blob hanging from the end of each wing, suspended on a thin pole. The bottom of the fuselage had the conchoidal shape, scooped and ridged, that she associated with shattered glass. She found it hard to believe it would actually fly.

This time the craft carried only three passengers besides its crew. One was a gray-haired major, with a pinched mouth and a narrow line of decorations which she recognized as efficiency awards. Admin, most likely. He went to the head of the little line waiting on the dock as by rights, boarded first, and installed himself in a seat midway down the port side, where he immediately flicked on his seat lamp and opened a handcomp.

The other passenger had waved Margiu ahead, with a flamboyant gesture that matched his flamboyant appearance. In the harsh lights of the harborage, his leather jacket blazed a garish yellow, and the metallic decorations glittered. Margiu climbed over the entrance coaming, and followed the major, almost stumbling once when the gentle motion of the seaplane on the water surprised her.

She picked out a window seat, on the starboard side. As she buckled in, she looked up to see the third passenger watching. One of those? He had pulled off his cap, revealing fine gray hair fluffed around a bald pate, and in this light she could see that his yellow jacket might be some theatrical troupe's idea of a uniform. Its shoulders were decorated with loops of green braid, and there was a line of stars on the upstanding collar, now open to reveal a green shirt; his dark pants were actually green.

'May I?' the man said, in a surprisingly sweet voice. 'I'm really quite harmless.'

She had hoped for a quiet ride, perhaps even a nap. But courtesy demanded that she say yes, so she nodded.

A crew chief checked to be sure they were all wearing the PPU, and a life vest, and that all the survival gear aboard was actually in place. Predictably, the man in yellow wasn't wearing his PPU. Unpredictably, he was quite cheerful about having to change, and quicker than she would have expected. Margiu had flown between the stars, but never over large bodies of water; she began to realize that this was serious.

Then the pilot swung the stumpy plane around, revved the engines, and Margiu felt acceleration shoving her back. The plane slammed its way across the low ripples of the harbor, spray blurring the lights outside. A few moments later they were airborne.

The headlands of Dark Harbor, edged with lights, fell away behind and below them, and then it was nothing but darkness below. Down there somewhere was water, invisible to the eye but cold and wet. Margiu shivered. To her relief, her seat companion turned a little away and started snoring almost immediately. By dawn, they were flying under high clouds, and the water below looked like a vast sheet of wrinkled silk patched with shades of blue and green and silver that she could not identify.

The man beside her woke up, and gave her a sweet smile. 'I hope my snoring didn't keep you awake,' he said.

'No, sir.'

'I'm no sir, milady. I'm Professor Gustaf Aidersson, if you want my dull, boring, everyday name, which goes with my dull, boring, everyday profession, about which I cannot talk, or we will both be in serious trouble. Or you could call me Don Alfonso Dundee, most noble knight of the Order of Old Terra, and we could have a pleasant conversation about anything you wish.'

'I'm sorry?' She had no idea what he was talking about.

'No, I'm sorry.' He hit himself dramatically on the forehead. 'Never accost young ladies before breakfast with strange tales out of distant mythology. You've heard of SPAL?'.

'No, sir.'

'Ah. Well, it's the biggest collection of galoots and misfits in the universe, and the letters stand for the Society for the Preservation of Antique Lore. Antique lunacy is more like it – I have no faith whatever in the actuality of our tomfoolery, but it is fun. We got the idea back when the rich folks in the Families first took up antique studies and arts – long before your time, milady – and we put our own interpretation on it. Let them flit about with fencing masters from the Company of Sabers, create titles for themselves, and imagine that they're re-creating scenes from Old Earth history. They're so serious about it, it takes all the fun out.'

Margiu listened to the rolling flow of words and wondered if the man were entirely sane. His bright sidelong look seemed to catch her thought in midair, as if it were a ball being tossed.

'You wonder if I'm crazy. Of course you do. I'm not sure myself, and my wife tells me regularly that my pot is a little cracked. But the fact of the matter is, craziness is not necessarily a bar to genius, and my kind of craziness consists only in boring total strangers to distraction in airplanes. Or spacecraft. Or anywhere else I can trap them.' He grinned at her with such obvious good humor that Margiu felt herelf relaxing.

'What is that yellow jacket?' she found herself asking.

'Good question,' he said promptly, in a tone that she could well believe went with a professor of something. 'There was a colony world – second-order colony out of Old Earth by way of Congreve – which had successive waves of settlers. They didn't get along, so of course they started fighting. Back then fabricators were pretty basic machines – couldn't turn out any useful sort of protective garments. So the colonists started using leather from their herds of cattle. The color told what side they were on. Mine is a semiaccurate reproduction of a Missen-Asaya officer's uniform of the Third Missen-Asaya/Tangrat War. Except the insignia. I should have a little wooden bird, but I couldn't find it before I left. My wife swears I must have left it at the last awards banquet . . . so I just took the stars off a model spaceship. Not a very good model, either; Rose-class ships never had double batteries of beam weapons. I told Zachery that when he showed me the model, but he got huffy about it and threw it in the corner, the one where Kata drops her dirty boots. That's why I knew where to find stars when I wanted them. And I thought stars might be more impressive when I had to travel with Fleet officers, but of course they see that yellow canary-jacket and try not to laugh.'

It was like drowning in treacle.

'But I'm talking too much about myself. Just whap me on the head when I do that, that's what my wife does. Or ignore me and look out the window if you want. I can see you're an ensign, with red hair exactly the color of my niece's, but – who are you?'

'Margiu Pardalt,' Margiu said. 'From Xavier.'

'Xavier!' His face lit up, and her heart sank. 'You know, the tactical analysis of the most recent engagement is fascinating. I was most impressed with the fire control of the Benignity ships –'

'The Benignity ships –' She couldn't help that, or the tone it popped out in.

'Yes. No disrespect to Commander . . . er . . . whoever it was –'

'Serrano,' murmured Margiu.

'But the Benignity performance was markedly better than expected. And there's new data – from this very facility – well, not where we're going but where I assume you've been, the Copper Mountain base – to indicate that they upgraded one of our ships they captured. For instance, the time to recharge – no. I mustn't get onto this.' Margiu could see the effort it cost him to rein that enthusiasm back. 'Tell you what, let's talk about wet navies. Here we are, flying over a superb large ocean, and I'll bet you've never studied wet-navy history, have you?'

'Only a little,' Margiu said. Her mind scrabbled frantically in search of some crumb of data to prove that she had studied it at all, but only the word *Trafalgar* rose up.

She couldn't remember if it had been an admiral, a ship, or a battle. 'Trafalgar,' she said.

'Of course!' He beamed at her. 'A mighty battle indeed, that was, but perhaps a little remote for our purposes. Are you familiar with the application of Nelson's sail tactics to colonial naval battles?'

'Uh . . . no, sir.'

'Consider, if you will, the archipelagos of Skinner III.' He spread his hands, as if touching a particular geographic area, and Margiu wondered if she ought to admit she didn't know what an archipelago was. She didn't have time. 'Forty thousand islands, at least. Colonized with intent to exploit its obvious advantages for aquaculture, but, as always, underfunded and subject to piracy. Abundant timber, so –'

Margiu's com beeped; she pressed the button. Her companion watched, bright-eyed. The pilot spoke: 'Ensign, Major –' She glanced back and saw the other officer sit up; he met her eyes across the plane. 'There's some kind of trouble at Stack Islands. Apparently personnel are missing, believed lost at sea –'

'What personnel?' the major asked.

'Base Three commander and a guard corporal. There's also a life raft missing from the Three Base aircar hangar, and evidence of a struggle . . . they're saying the corporal may have gone crazy and kidnapped the commander. But anyway – we're to join the search; they don't have any long-range craft, and they suspect the life raft was blown west by the storm into the North Current.'

Margiu started to say that her orders were to get those directives to the base commanders without delay, but decided not to. The pilot knew she was a courier, and if someone were down there in a raft, surely that had to come first. She hoped.

They were still at least an hour east of the Stacks, but

Margiu could not help scanning below for the life raft. She had no idea how big it would look from whatever altitude they were flying.

Dark dots appeared on the sea. 'Those are the Stacks,' the pilot said. Margiu stared at them . . . a scatter of tall black rocks, whose height above the water was hard to judge in this flat light. The plane lost altitude again in a sudden lurch. 'We'll be over Stack Island Three in an hour.'

The Stacks looked impossibly forbidding – too tall, too narrow on top, too bleak. Why had Fleet put bases out here at all? She'd read the cubes, but it still seemed ridiculous. The plane droned on, and the Stacks rose up and sank, appearing and disappearing . . . a total of 98 visible at high tide, 117 at low, according to the cube. Some so small that not even an aircar could land vertically on top.

They left the Stacks behind, and Margiu stared at the sea from her side of the craft with more intensity.

'Signal!' the pilot said suddenly. 'I've got a beacon! And confirmation from upstairs.' The plane heeled on one wing, and Margiu gulped her stomach back into place. When she laid her forehead on the window, the glass felt colder than before.

The major spotted it first; Margiu heard him call out, and the pilot swung the plane around again. Now she saw the little yellow chip on the gray-green sea. Was anyone in it? Alive? She could not imagine what it must be like.

'We're going down,' the pilot said. Margiu clamped her jaws shut. Going down? Was something wrong with the plane?

'It's all right, Ensign,' the major said, catching her eye. 'This is a seaplane, remember. It can land on the water.'

Margiu drew a shaky breath. Water, yes: in a protected

lagoon, shallow and calm. She hadn't known any aircraft could land on open ocean without sinking. She wasn't sure she believed it.

'Hoods on,' the pilot ordered. Margiu plucked the hood of her PPU from its curl around her neck and put it on. If it was so safe, why this precaution? She put her hands into the gloves, too, and made sure the wrist and boot grapples were locked back. She peered out. They were much lower now, and she could see that the surface of the ocean heaved slowly in broad swells, reflecting the bright yellow canopy of the life raft. Through that clear, quiet water, she saw something swimming – some long, narrow shapes.

'Isn't this exciting?' asked her seatmate. 'A most excellent adventure, my first water landing in an aircraft.' He didn't look frightened at all. Margiu was scared, though she wasn't going to admit. it. 'Of course, if we come in too fast, or too steeply, we'll be killed, which would be a shame. Let me see . . . this planet's gravitational attraction is 1.012 that of Earth, and that means . . .'

Margiu closed her ears; she wanted to close her eyes, but she could not look away from the water's surface . . . the smooth water looked less smooth the closer they came. Then spray fountained past the window; the safety harness dug in as the plane lurched and swayed. The plane slowed, settling in the water; she could feel the movement of the ocean take over from the movement of the air, lifting and dropping the plane in a leisurely oscillation. The inboard engine on her side stopped, and her window cleared. She remembered the briefing, that in event of an emergency landing, the craft would keep two engines going, with the ducts adjusted to minimize blast on the escape rafts. Presumably the same technique would keep the prop blast from blowing this life raft away.

As they rose on the swell, she could see the yellow

canopy of the life raft in the distance. The pilot's voice came over the roar of the engine. 'We don't have current weather data – MetSatIV's down again – and although it looks dead calm now, I don't trust it. We're not going to be down one second longer than we have to be. You will all do exactly what my crew chief tells you.'

The crew chief beckoned to them. The professor climbed out and let Margiu into the aisle after the major had gone past.

'Major, you and the ensign will need to hang onto this line . . . steady . . .'

Margiu wrapped her gloved hands around the rope. Line. Whatever they wanted to call it, it was rope to her, familiar from the family farm. The major, ahead of her, blocked half her view of the outside, but she could see water not that far below, and nothing but water to the horizon. She shivered in spite of her PPU.

'Why not just tie the rope to the plane?' the major asked.

'Sir, we never secure the aircraft to something like the raft. Should it capsize –'

'It's a life raft,' the major said. 'It's made to not capsize. I shouldn't have to stand here holding a stupid rope.'

'Right, sir – just let me take that a moment.' The crew chief took the rope from the major, passed the slack to Margiu, and then back to the professor, who had come along without being asked.

The canopy flap opened; a head poked out, shrouded in a PPU hood.

'Who are you?' croaked a voice.

'Chief Stivers,' the chief said. 'And you are . . . the missing Corporal Meharry?'

'They've reported me missing?' The voice sounded odd; Margiu could see the strain on that face. 'I was supposed to be dead.'

'Where's Commander Bacarion?'

'She's – her – she's here.' Meharry pushed the canopy flap farther to the side. Margiu couldn't see what that revealed, but the major stiffened.

'That's – she's hurt, she's –'

'She's dead, sir,' Meharry said.

'There'll have to be an investigation,' the major said.

'Yes, sir. But first, sir –'

'No buts, Corporal. Chief . . . er . . . Stivers . . . you will place this man under arrest –'

'Sir, he's been on a lifeboat for days . . . he needs care . . .'

'He's a material witness, if not a murderer. Under arrest, Chief, at once –'

'We have to get him aboard first.'

'And the deceased. And the raft.'

'Sir, I'll have to ask Pilot Officer Galvan. It's not going to be easy to get the raft aboard safely.'

'We can't leave valuable evidence at the scene –'

The pilot had other priorities. 'First, we get that man aboard. He's been adrift for days, in freezing weather; it's a wonder he's alive. Major, you take that line; Professor, get back to your seat for now.'

As the pilot ordered, Margiu and the major each took a line, and wrapped it around a projecting knob inside the aircraft. The pilot had a name for the knob, but Margiu ignored that and concentrated instead on the need to keep the line taut and the raft snugged up to the aircraft. The copilot and the crew chief helped Corporal Meharry clamber over the raft's inflated rim and into the plane.

He was haggard and pale; when he tried to stand, he staggered against the bulkhead. The copilot and crew chief half-carried him back to the seats, and draped him over two of them. Professor Aidersson bustled over;

Margiu heard his sweet voice over the others. The major spoke to her.

'Ensign – get in that raft, and prepare the commander's body for removal.'

Margiu stared at him, but swallowed the 'Me, sir?' that almost came out. She glanced at the copilot, hoping he would say something, but he was doing something to the corporal's PPU.

She had never envisioned herself clambering into a blood-smeared life raft in the middle of a vast ocean to retrieve the dead body of a murder victim. Gingerly, she eased over the inflated rim and into the raft. The fabric dipped and shifted under her; she felt very insecure. She had seen dead bodies before; she had seen dead bodies days old, for that matter. But that had been on dry land, in the warm, dry climate of her homeland. She had never seen so much water in her life, and to be bobbing up and down in a raft in the middle of the ocean, with a cold stiff body, terrified her. When she looked back at the plane, it looked much smaller, entirely too small to be reassuring when everything else was water.

The next thing she noticed was the smell; cold had retarded decay, but there was a sickening odor of human filth and death both, held in by the canopy. When the raft rocked to the swell, Margiu struggled not to gag. As quickly as she could, she unfastened the canopy tabs and rolled it back. Even the aircraft fumes were better than this.

Bacarion's body . . . she tried not to look at it, especially not the ruin of the face. But it was heavy – the woman had been both taller and heavier than Margiu – and she could not get the right leverage to move it.

'Hurry *up*, Ensign,' the major said.

'Sorry, sir,' Margiu said, breathless, as she struggled to unlash the webbing that held Bacarion's body still. She got the last one loose, and the next swell rolled the body toward her. When she tried to lift, the additional weight pressed her knees into the raft floor, which sank, and the body rolled into the depression. It would have been hard enough on a solid support, but she had none.

'Tie a line around her and we'll haul from here,' suggested the professor, who had reappeared in the aircraft's hatch.

'Don't be ridiculous!' snapped the major. 'All she has to do is lift and slide the body across –'

'No – she'll need the basket. Hang on, Ensign. Be right back.' The crew chief, who had come forward, now disappeared back into the plane.

'I don't think much of your initiative,' the major said to Margiu; behind him, the professor winked at her. The crew chief reappeared, with a bright-orange object that looked like a long skinny basket. 'Here you go, Ensign –' He slid it over the rim of the life raft to her. 'Ever used one of these? No? Well, just roll the body into it, then hook those lashings over.' He turned his head to look back into the plane and yelled, 'Just a second, sir –'

Margiu positioned one edge of the basket thing next to the corpse.

'Now go to the other side and give it a push,' said the major.

'Stay where you are,' the professor said. 'Your weight will make it roll toward you.'

'Keep out of this,' the major said, turning to glare at the professor.

'It's simple physics,' the professor said. 'A child could see –' He gestured. 'Her weight depresses the life raft floor, and the corpse rolls –'

A gentle swell lifted her up, then dropped her, and the corpse rolled into the basket. Margiu hooked the lashings quickly, then glanced back at the plane. A line of cold green water widened between her and the plane; the two men argued in the doorway, hands waving, and the rope ran smoothly out beside them. She felt an instant of panic so strong that she couldn't even yell.

'Idiots!' The crew chief lunged past them and grabbed the trailing line. 'Don't pull!' he yelled to Margiu. 'We won't lose you.' Even as he said it, an end of rope slipped out and splashed into the water. Panic gripped her again, until she remembered the line attached to the Berry.

Another voice yelled from forward in the plane. 'What's going on, Ker? We need to get back in the air sometime this century. Swell's picking up, if you hadn't noticed.'

'Loose line, sir.' The crew chief did not turn his head this time, Margiu noticed. 'Now, major, if you'll take hold behind me, and then you, professor. Let's bring her in . . .'

Margiu made herself look away from the plane, and recheck the lashings on the basket. Then she began hauling in the rope attached to the basket. Something yanked on it, hard, and she fetched up against the life raft's inflated rim.

'Hurry up, Ensign,' the major said. 'The pilot wants us to leave.'

'Yes, sir . . .' Whatever it was yanked again, putting a sharp crease in the inflated rim. Then it let go, and she fell back into the smelly slime of the lifeboat floor. She reeled the line in, hand over hand, and was able to toss the dripping end into the hatch when the raft bumped the plane again.

'All right, Major – if you'll let go this line, sir, and take hold of that one –'

Margiu did her best to lift the ends of the Berry unit over the inflated rim as the major pulled, and after some minutes of breathless struggle, the corpse was aboard the plane. Margiu crawled out after it, her knees shaking. The plane might be tiny compared to the sea, but it was more solid than that life raft. She pulled herself upright, and hoped no one had noticed her fear, as the copilot came forward and slid into his seat.

The pilot peered back over his shoulder.

'Hurry it up, back there. I don't like the look of the horizon, and I'm still not getting current feed from MetSat.'

'We simply must take the raft aboard,' the major said.

'We're going to take off before that squall line gets here,' the pilot said. 'And the chief says it would take at least an hour to deflate and pack the raft, which will put us marginal on weight, since it'll be wet. Forget the raft.'

'Dammit, it's *evidence*.' The major visibly fumed for a few moments, then said, 'Fine, then. We'll leave Ensign Pardalt in the raft to secure the evidence; another flight can pick her up later. Ensign, get back in the raft.'

Margiu's heart sank. Leave her alone on the ocean with a storm coming?

'I don't think –' the professor began; the major rounded on him.

'You have no place in this discussion; you are only a civilian. You have caused enough trouble already. Go sit down and be quiet!'

The professor's eyebrows went up, and his head tipped back. 'I see, sir, that you are a bigot.'

'Ensign, get into that raft and prepare to cast off,' the major said without looking at the professor. 'We will inform Search and Rescue where you are, and they will come find you.'

The pilot burst out of the cockpit. 'Ensign, take your seat. You too, Prof.' Margiu followed the professor quickly into the cabin. 'Major, if you do not shut up, I will put you in the raft. I'm in command of this craft –'

'What's your date of rank?' the major asked. Cold anger rolled off him in waves.

'You're a paper-pushing remf,' the pilot said. 'Not a line officer, and not my CO. You have a choice – you can either go sit down and be quiet, or you go out the hatch, right this instant, and I don't much care if you land in the raft or the water.'

Margiu watched the little group by the hatch – did the major know that behind his back the crew chief's broad hand was poised to push him out? She doubted it; he was too angry with the pilot.

'I'll complain to your commander,' the major said, turning away; Margiu could see how red he'd turned, and looked down. This was not something she wanted to witness.

'So will I,' the pilot said. Already the crew chief was coiling the wet line that had held the raft to the plane. He pulled the hatch shut, dogged the latch, and secured the dripping coil of rope to the cleat on the forward bulkhead. Margiu could not see the raft from her side, but she saw the propeller of the inboard engine begin to turn, and the duct flanges move. Gouts of blue smoke, then spray, as the propeller blast whipped the surface of the sea. The plane swung in a tight circle; now she could see, through the wavering streams of water on the window, the bright yellow of the life raft rocking on the swell. The engines roared, and the plane moved jerkily at first through the water; then, with a series of shuddering slams, reached takeoff velocity and lifted away from the water. As the window cleared, Margiu looked back. A tiny yellow dot, already hard to see, and behind it, a darkening line of the oncoming storm.

She could have been down there. She could have been huddling in that miserable foul-smelling life raft, struggling to learn how to survive in a storm.

'I don't think I quite like that major,' the professor said. Margiu glanced at him. His amiable face had set into an expression of cold distaste. 'Not someone with the right grasp of priorities.'

Safer to say nothing, especially since her stomach was leaping around with the turbulence.

'Are you all right?' he asked, then answered his own question. 'No, I see that you are not. Here –' He put something chilly and wet on her cheek, the only exposed skin. 'Antinausea patch. I put one on while they were still arguing. Close your eyes, and lean back – takes about thirty seconds.'

Margiu counted to herself, and by twenty-seven felt that her stomach had settled. She opened her eyes. Behind, over the noise of the engines, she heard the major retching, but even the sour smell of vomit didn't make her stomach lurch. The professor leaned away from her. 'Here, Major – an antinausea patch –'

The man said nothing, but the professor's hand came back empty, and he turned to wink at her. Margiu smiled uncertainly.

'Always come prepared,' the professor said. 'Nausea adds to no one's ability to think and act effectively. You're better now?'

'Yes,' Margiu said.

Once the plane was in level flight, the pilot spoke over the intercom.

'I realize all of you have urgent orders to the various Stack Islands bases, but we have some problems to deal with. MetSatIV is offline, and has been for several hours. We do not know what our weather will be, and there's an additional concern about security at Stack Three. They can say what they like, but with the commander dead – we're heading back to Dark Harbor.'

'I'm going to see what I can do for that poor lad,' the professor said, unstrapping himself.

'But the major –'

'Has no authority over me – as he so rudely pointed out, I'm a civilian. And he's not any of the military officers to whom I report – he can bluster, but that's all. Besides –' He pointed, and Margiu craned her head to look. The major was sleeping, ungracefully slumped in the seat with one hand dangling to the deck. The professor winked at her again.

'There are antinausea patches and antinausea patches,' he said. 'He'll be out for several hours.'

The rescued corporal, though swathed in blankets at the rear of the cabin, looked miserable enough. He had not thrown up, but his face had a greenish cast. Across from him, the corpse had been wrapped in another and lashed to the deck.

'How about giving him a patch?' the professor asked the crew chief.

'Fine with me – I notice our major is sleeping peacefully –'

'Nausea is so exhausting,' the professor said. 'Here, now –' He put a patch on the corporal's cheek. 'That should help.'

'He really needs fluids and calories,' the crew chief said. 'If he can hold 'em down.'

'In a minute or two,' the professor said. 'What do you make of this?'

'A mess, sir. This lad's a Meharry – may not mean much to you, but it's a family with a proud history in Fleet. Meharrys are known to be a tough bunch to tangle with, but they've always been loyal.'

'So – what do you think happened?'

'I don't know, sir. The major, he said no one was to talk to him –'

'And the major's authority –'

The crew chief sucked his cheeks in. 'Well, sir – he outranks me. The pilot's in command here, but he's busy

with the craft and I don't like to bother him. It's always a
pain when one of the MetSats is out.'

'How often does that happen?'

'MetSatIV's been buggy for the past two years or more.
There's a new youngster at Blue Islands who's been keeping it up more often, but even he slips sometimes.'

'Mmm . . . and how long has he been there?'

'Oh – eighteen months, perhaps.'

'Is MetSatIV our communications link?'

'No, it's a general surveillance satellite. Outplanet, it's
part of the passive sensor array for the whole planet;
inplanet, it's a broad-band visual and EM scanner. If it
had been up, for instance, we'd have found that life raft
with less trouble.'

'But the life raft's beacon –'

'Oh, it has a direct signal to GPS satellites. But they're
not set up for visual scans. And the beacon has to be
turned on by the occupant, after which it puts up a signal
every two hours minimum. You can drift a long way in
two hours.'

'Tell me, Chief: if there hadn't been a life raft or a flight
out here, and MetSatIV was down, would anyone have
spotted a landing out here?'

'Landing, sir?'

'Landing . . . like . . . oh . . . drop shuttles from a warship?'

'On Copper Mountain? Well, Big Ocean is a training
area for wet drops, but a ship couldn't get that close without the other units spotting it, even if MetSat IV were
offline.'

'What about the drop shuttles?'

'Once they were down below the horizon – I suppose –
there aren't any ground scanners out here, of course.
But – what made you think of that? And what difference
would it make?'

'With all due respect for the honor of the Fleet, Chief, I've never known a society of saints. If there is a way to smuggle contraband and make a profit off it, people will do it. I can't think of a better way to smuggle than to be able to turn off the lights when you wish.'

The chief flushed, but finally grinned. 'Well, sir, you're right about that. I've never been on a ship that didn't have at least one unauthorized animal, person, or substance, be it what you will.'

'So my question is, what might be smuggled that would involve the commander of the prison?'

'I don't know, sir.'

'Nor I. But since I was headed for Stack Islands myself, I am naturally interested. Smuggling goes both ways – persons or materials can be introduced, or removed. The Weapons Research Facility naturally comes to mind –'

'Sir –' That was the corporal, his face now pale but no longer waxy greenish. His voice was weak, but clear enough.

'You need water and food,' said the crew chief. 'And I'll need to tell the pilot you're able to talk.'

'I can give him something,' Margiu said. The crew chief handed her one of the self-heating soup packets, already squeezed and warming, and went forward. When its heat stripe matched the dot at the end, Margiu put the tube to the corporal's mouth.

The professor waited until he'd finished, then said, 'You had something to tell us?'

'Yes, sir. Commander Bacarion was one of Lepescu's followers,' the corporal said. Margiu felt a sudden chill.

'Means nothing to me,' the professor said. 'You?' The crew chief shook his head. Margiu nodded.

'Admiral Lepescu was using prisoners as prey . . . . he was part of a secret society that held manhunts. They used human ears as recognition symbols.'

'How'd you know that?'

'I was reading up on Commander Heris Serrano –
because of Xavier, it's my home planet, and she saved
us – and found that after she resigned her commission,
her crew had been condemned and used as prey. So I
read what I could find on Lepescu. But – you're sure
Bacarion's one of his followers? They were all arrested, I
thought.'

'Yes. She admitted it to me, when she tried to kill me
the second time.'

'The second time?'

'Yes. The first time she had someone push me off the
cliff.' Corporal Meharry coughed, then went on. 'You
mentioned Commander Serrano, sir – my sister Methlin
Meharry was one of Serrano's crew. She was imprisoned
here, and then hunted later. She survived; she's back in
Fleet now. So when I found out Bacarion had been on
Lepescu's staff, I knew she'd do something. That's why I
made preparations, and even so she almost got me. But
that's not all – not just private vengeance, I mean. I'm
sure she was up to something, but I couldn't figure out
what.'

'But now that we've thought of something – vague
enough, still.'

'The prisoners!' Meharry said. 'Lepescu used prisoners
before, as prey. What if she were using them a different
way – as troops?'

'To do what?' the chief asked.

'Nothing good,' the professor said. 'Maybe she was
going to sell them off to someone who wanted to hunt
them, or maybe she was going to use them to hunt something . . . but whatever it was, it's bound to be bad.'

'We must tell someone –' The same thought must have
occurred to them all at once, from the startled glances.

'Yes, but who?' The chief shook his head. 'Now our

pilot, I'd trust – but you don't know him. For that matter, you don't know me.'

'A bit late to worry about that now,' the professor said. 'And the pilot must know, you're right. And must inform as many others as possible. You do not run a major conspiracy from such a small base as Stack Three. You run a small one which you hope will become big. There must be plenty of people not involved within radio range.'

'Big enough if they're behind turning off MetSatIV,' the chief said. 'And if it involves bringing a ship in. Using LACs means conspirators on that ship, a lot of them. The LAC flight crews, for instance, as well as a majority of bridge officers.'

'What if they did embark convicts? Just the ones they'd picked? Then attacked the orbital station? They'd control access to the whole planet . . .'

'And the system defenses,' the professor said. 'And the weapons research labs. A fine start to a mutiny, if anyone wanted to start a mutiny.'

CHAPTER EIGHTEEN

By the time Margiu and the others landed at Dark Harbor, their worst guesses had been confirmed.

'They've got the orbital station,' an angry major told them, the cold wind whipping his uniform around his legs as he stood on the end of the quay. 'We bounced your call up, but it was already happening. *Bonar Tighe* picked up convicts from Stack Three with its LACs, and armed them – used them as shock troops. We think – we hope – that somebody on the station got a tightbeam out and tripped the ansible alarm, but we aren't sure. The mutineers have cut off all communications from topside, and they can control the system defenses from there too. We know of six other ships insystem – anyone care to lay odds on how many of them are mutineers?'

No one did.

'So what can we do?' asked the pilot.

'Damn little. Polacek over at Main has declared a state of emergency, of course, but there aren't any jump-capable ships onplanet, not even little ones. We don't have any missiles capable of taking out the station or any of the ships in space — why would we? We're stuck down a gravity well. I hate planets!'

Margiu had heard this before, from many a Fleet officer, but she was just as glad to be on something solid.

'Think they'll try to invade?' asked the professor.

'I don't know.' The pilot shrugged. 'Who knows what they're going to do? They're not telling us anything. Let's get all of you under cover, and see what else you might know. Does that corporal you rescued need a medical assist?'

'No, sir; I can walk.' Corporal Meharry still looked pale to Margiu, but he was reasonably steady on his feet.

'Good. Chief, get this craft secured; I've arranged transport for the corpse. We'll need statements from all of you . . . where's that major?'

'Still pretty groggy, I imagine,' the professor said. 'I'm afraid I may have administered a stronger antinausea patch than necessary. I'd like to talk to your base commander, if I might.'

Margiu looked at him. He had been calm and even cheerful until he'd thought of the mutiny, but now his face had stiffened into a grim mask. He caught her eye and managed a smile, but with none of his earlier warmth.

The little base headquarters seethed with tension and activity both. The major who had met them ushered them to the base commander's office. Lieutenant Commander Ardsan glowered at them for a long moment.

'It's not your fault, but I could wish you'd figured it out an hour earlier,' he said. 'Even an hour might've given those people a chance.'

Margiu felt guilty, but the professor clearly didn't. 'Nonsense, sir,' he said. 'An hour before, we were dealing with a corpse, a survivor, an oncoming squall . . . and I doubt very much that hour would have done more than prolong the carnage. The mutineers will have had accomplices on that station, as they had on Stack Three.'

'You're probably right,' Ardsan said. 'But it's so frustrating – we don't have land lines everywhere, and with the mutineers in control topside, we can't get anything through the relay satellites.' He pushed a data cube from side to side on his desk. 'We have short-range ground radio, but they can interdict that from topside if they choose. They've cut off the weather information, too, which is going to make it hard to fly from one base to another. Polacek wants everyone to gather at Main, but that just makes us a handy target, the way I look at it.'

'Are we sure of his loyalty?' the professor asked.

'I'm not sure of anyone right now. I never thought anything like this would happen, but then the whole Xavier mess shocked me. I don't understand it –'

'I think the point is how to handle it now,' the professor said. 'I have a very specific problem in mind. I'm a weapons specialist; I was on my way to Stack Two to consult on the progress of some of their research.' He handed Ardsan a flake. 'You'll want to check my clearance, of course.'

'Of course,' Ardsan murmured. He swung around and slid the flake into a slot in the cube reader. Margiu caught a glimpse of the screen before Ardsan flicked it off. 'Well, that's clear enough.' He looked pale. 'I don't think I ever saw a –' he glanced at Margiu and away '– anyone with that level clearance before.'

'Probably not,' the professor said. 'But we put our pants on one leg at a time, the same as you. Now. I happen to know that there are weapons under development there which you do not want the mutineers to have. And the fact of the matter is, if someone on that base is not part of this, I'll be very surprised.'

'Why do you say that?'

'Why else would they start a mutiny here, in this system? Why not meet in some quiet out-of-the-way location, safe from discovery? I would wager that if Commander Bacarion had not been killed – if all had gone according to plan – one of those LACs would have picked up personnel and weapons from Stack Two. I suggest you check the records of the personnel stationed there very carefully.'

Ardsan frowned. 'We don't really have the facilities for that, Professor. I can look up who's in command, but that's about all. I'm not even sure I can get a list of personnel. With the mutineers in control of our communications, we can't access the personnel records back at Main, and we don't keep copies here at Dark Harbor.'

'I see.' The professor drummed his fingers on his knee for a long moment. 'Well, Commander, if I were you I'd figure out a way to send some troops out there to secure the base.'

'But – how?'

'We flew out there before. Can't we do it again?'

'But we have no weather data – they've cut off our feed from the weathersats.'

The professor leaned forward. 'Commander, I'm telling you – if you don't secure that base, and keep the mutiny from getting hold of those weapons, you'll wish you had to the end of your life, which will probably not be a long one. Now several things can happen. We can try to go back and not make it and crash in the sea. We can try to go back and – if enough of the personnel are involved – they might shoot us out of the sky, if they happen to notice us. We can get there and fail to secure the base, although I believe if you send along enough troops that won't happen. We can get there and secure the base, and the mutineers topside can land a force and drive us off . . .

but if we have enough time, we'll have destroyed at least the worst of the weapons. Or we can sit here and do nothing, and be dead with no chance of helping out.' He sat back. 'I personally think that is the worst option.'

'I – I should contact Commander Polacek.'

'No, Commander, you should not. You've already said you aren't sure of his loyalty You know communications are compromised. You know what my authority is.'

'He's right,' Margiu said, surprising herself by speaking up. 'If we're going back out there, we have to do it before they send shuttles down.'

Ardsan looked from one to the other, frowning. Finally he sighed. 'All right. All right . . . let me think. We need transport that can land at Stack Two and carry troops –' He touched his desk comunit. 'Chief – look up what we have on the personnel at Stack Two. And give me an estimate of our security forces here.'

The professor interrupted. 'Are there any heavy cargo craft based here?'

'We have the heavy-duty aircars we use along the coast, but we don't like to take them out over the open ocean. They sink like rocks if the power plant fails. That's why we use the amphibs.'

'How long would it be before the mutineers could send shuttles down?'

'Depends on whether the station had any short-field shuttles ready to go. The usual shuttles require longer landing fields; there are only four long fields on the whole planet, and two of them are only used for emergencies. The LACs from *Bonar Tighe* can do it, of course, but they'll require refueling and service – at least a couple of hours of turnaround. Those other ships . . . I don't know which had LACs, and if those LACs were ready for drop. Then unless a ship did a low pass, the LACs would need several hours – I don't really know how many – to fly in.

If they launched additional LACs immediately after taking the station, the mutineers could be on that island now. Or, if they're delayed, it could be tomorrow or the next day.'

'And the flight times of your available craft?'

'Depends on the windspeed and direction – and we have no weathersats now. Five hours, six – I can't say exactly.'

One of the enlisted men poked his head in the door. 'Sir, Stack Two has thirteen civilian scientist personnel, five officers, and twenty-nine enlisted. Commander's a Lieutenant Commander Vinet. We've got fifteen NEM assault troops, and thirty ordinaries, plus the base police.'

'Thank you. Carry on.' Ardsan grimaced. 'Enough to tempt us into trouble, and not enough to get us out – and if I strip Dark Harbor, there's no one to protect the people here –' Then he shook his head as if to clear it. 'All right. It's something definite, at least. Professor, I assume you're going –'

'Absolutely,' he said. 'You need me to disable those weapons, and the scientists and engineers know me.'

'Ensign, I'm assigning you to the professor, since he seems to have confided in you before. You are weapons-qualified, right?'

'Yes, sir.' She had gone hunting as a girl; she knew she was good with firearms, and her qualifying scores had always maxed out.

'Good. I'll have the armsmaster issue you weapons; I want you to stick to the professor like glue, and watch his back. Just in case any of the people we send along aren't as loyal as we think they are.'

'Yes, sir.'

'Professor, it'll take some time to fuel the aircraft, brief the aircrew, and assemble the troops. You'd better eat and rest while you can. Ensign, you too – but you stick with him, you hear?'

'Yes, sir.' She realized suddenly that she was very hungry, and also tired, and that she would have to go back out over that cold, wet, vast ocean . . . in the dark.

In the mess, where she and the professor ate, she overheard another conversation.

'It's that damned rejuvenation stuff,' the crew chief said. 'It doesn't take a grand admiral strategist to see what enormously prolonged youth will do to the career curve of anyone below rejuv age. Promotions started slowing down ten or fifteen years ago, right about when they were doing those senior NCO rejuvs . . . you don't spend all that money on rejuvenating someone and then retire 'em, now do you? And the people who might expect to step into that job see they won't have a chance. Expansion helped some, but how big a space force do we need?'

'But . . . mutiny, Chief. Can you see mutiny?'

'Not right away, no. And not for me, personally, ever. But there's been a rumor that something was wrong with the NCO rejuvenations, and some people – not me – said they were bollixed on purpose. It was one thing to have too many young-old admirals, but they didn't want the enlisted getting ideas.'

'Now that makes no sense,' the professor broke in. 'Senior enlisted are the backbone of every successful military organization – always have been. Admirals are fine, and if you have a strategic genius you certainly want to keep him, but day to day, you need senior NCOs.'

'Militaries have made that mistake before. Rank-heavy, officer-dominated . . .'

'Well, I used to work in Personnel Procurement,' another chief said. 'Back when I was a young sergeant. I saw projections of need by rank and grade, and back then, at least, the planners knew they needed more master chiefs than admirals. So I don't think they'd deliberately sabotage a rejuvenation program for chiefs.'

'Somebody sure did. Remember Chief Wang last year? We had to watch him every second, or he'd put a six-star fastener in a four-point hole, and tell everybody to do the same. I never saw anything like it, and it wasn't pretty.'

'I thought they said it was some brain virus or something, from his fishing trips to the mountains.'

'That's what they said then, but when we got that directive on removing rejuved chiefs from active duty until they'd been checked, that's who I thought of. 'Course, he was medically retired by then, but I asked Pauli in sickbay, and he said he thought it probably had been a bad rejuv.'

'Bad rejuvs would let the people below move up . . .' a sergeant said softly. 'Not that anyone would do something like that . . . I saw Chief Wang right at the end.'

'Maybe they didn't know what it would do. I remember giving my mom's pet sarri a cookie once, just sharing, y'know, and it went into convulsions and died. I had no idea they couldn't eat our kind of food. But it was just as dead as if I'd poisoned it on purpose.'

'That's true. Never attribute to malice what could be stupidity. It's just as likely to be a cost-containment effort by procurement or even the manufacturer.'

Margiu had not even realized that some Fleet personnel had been rejuvenated; she couldn't remember anyone mentioning it in the Academy. She wondered if any of the people in that room had been rejuved. How could she tell?

When the professor finished eating, he touched her sleeve. 'Ensign – we'd better get some rest while we can. Do you remember where Commander Ardsan said we could bunk?'

Margiu showed him to the assigned room – clearly an officer's quarters, now theirs for a few hours. They took turns in the shower, and changed into clean clothes. But before either of them dozed off, the commander told them that transport was ready.

This time the professor donned his PPU over street clothes, and then put his yellow leather jacket on top. 'My friends out there will recognize this,' he pointed out.

'You're a fine target that way.' The major who had met them at the quay was in charge of the mission; Margiu now knew his name – Antony Garson. A Lieutenant Lightfoot commanded the troops.

'True, but if we have to make a hostile landing, at least our side will know who I am.'

Margiu, who had on a clean PPU set to midnight blue – the default night-camouflage color, caught the major's eye. He shrugged, and went to check on the rest of the group. Though it was only afternoon, the heavy cloud cover and spitting rain made it seem much later.

By the time they neared the Stack Islands again, daylight had faded into murky night. They'd had clouds all the way, which was supposed to be protective, though Margiu found it dreary as the plane seemed to crawl between two layers of darkening gray. As the light failed, no lights came on in the plane – for security reasons, she was told – but she could feel, all around her, the bulky shapes of the NEMs. The professor had fallen asleep, snoring as musically as the first time, and Margiu leaned cautiously against his shoulder, letting herself doze. She couldn't lean the other way; the unfamiliar sidearm poked her. She woke when the plane slanted downward, and peered out the window into darkness.

'Umph!' That was the professor, almost choking on a final snore. 'See anything?'

'No – it's all dark.' How were they going to land? What if they ran into Stack Two, instead of landing on it? She could feel the plane sinking under her, and her ears popped repeatedly.

Then a sparkle of light appeared, somewhere in the gloom . . . a tiny bright line, then another line.

'Lights,' she said to the professor.

As they drew closer, she could see that the lights outlined an ordinary runway, and other lights showed in buildings nearby. It looked so normal. . . .

The plane landed hard, bounced, came down firmly, and she rocked forward as the brakes caught. Instead of rolling up to one of the lighted buildings, the plane swung aside near the end of the landing strip. The NEMs were on their feet as soon as it landed. Margiu, lacking orders, stayed where she was; she and the professor had earbugs set to the same communications channel. Another plane, then another, came to a stop near them. In the dark, with only faint light from the runway lights, Margiu could just make out dark figures leaving one of the other planes.

Then someone forward opened the hatch of their plane, and a cold breath of sea air swirled into the plane, past the dark forms. Someone else muttered an order, and the troops began to move out into the night. Major Garson's voice in her earbug sounded calm: 'Professor – you and the ensign come on, now.' The professor heaved himself up, and Margiu scrambled out of her seat to follow him.

Outside, it was colder, but slightly less dark; Margiu could tell the professor from the others as a slightly lighter blur. She pulled up the hood of her PPU against the chill and stayed close to his side. A delicate red line pointed the way; someone had their laser guide on. She could feel the rasp of the runway surface under her boots. Was it safe? No one had fired a shot yet, and the troops seemed to know where they were going. She wasn't sure

where the first troops had gone; she couldn't see them
anymore.

'Looks secure for now, Professor.' The major's voice
spoke again in her earbug. 'Come on inside.'

Margiu felt more than saw the troops closing in around
them, a protective cordon, guiding them to one of the
buildings near the landing strip. Ahead, a door opened,
spilling out yellow light. She blinked, tried not to stare at
the welcome light, but watched for any threat. She
couldn't see anything but the troops who had come with
them, and the dark night beyond.

Inside, Major Garson was talking to a lieutenant commander; both of them looked tense and unhappy. Armed
guards stood at each exit. Margiu looked past them to the
civilians – the other scientists, she supposed – in the
large room.

'Oh, Lord, it *is* Gussie,' one of the civilians said to the
others. 'Complete with that ugly yellow jacket and a cute
redhead in tow . . .'

'She's not a cute redhead in tow, she's Ensign Pardalt.'
The professor nodded at her. 'Show some respect; she's a
very intelligent young woman –'

'Meaning he talked your ear off and you didn't object,'
the other man said, flashing a smile at Margiu. 'I'm
Helmut Swearingen, by the way.' He turned back to the
professor.

'When you didn't show up this morning, Gussie, and
then those people took the station, we were afraid you'd
been captured –'

'How far have you gotten?' the professor asked.

The other man grimaced and nodded toward the officers near the door. 'Nowhere. As soon as we heard – and
Ty was on the radio, trying to find out where you were, so
we heard right away – I went to our base commander and
told him we should start dismantling the work in

progress, destroying notes. He wouldn't have it – insisted he had to wait for orders, that we were under Fleet discipline. Even said we might be mutineers ourselves. He's had us under guard, in this room –'

'What's he like?' the professor asked, in a lower voice.

'A worrier. The only good thing about him is that he's technically trained, so at least he's understood some of what we're doing. He's actually got an advanced degree, studied with Bruno at the Gradus Institute. But he's got a serious addiction to regulations, and he claims regulations won't let him make any independent decisions about what we have here.'

'We don't have time to waste. What's his name?'

'Alcandor Vinet.'

The two officers were glowering at each other now. Margiu looked from one to the other.

'Excuse me,' the professor said. 'Commander Vinet? I'm Professor Aldersson; you were expecting me this morning –'

'You're late, Professor,' Vinet said. 'But I suppose, under the circumstances, this is understandable.'

'Yes,' the professor said. 'Now that I'm here, I'm taking charge of the research unit. We'll need to start clearing away files before the mutineers can capture –'

'You can't do that,' Vinet said. 'It's out of the question. I've had no orders from Headquarters –'

'Under the circumstances –' the professor began.

'He's got the highest level clearance and authorization,' Garson said. 'And I've got orders cut at Dark Harbor, directing you to give your complete cooperation.'

'Dark Harbor's not in my chain of command,' Vinet said. 'And you don't have the rank, Major. How do I know you're not all mutineers, anyway?'

'All of us?' the professor's eyebrows rose steeply. 'That's an interesting hypothesis, but do you have any data to support it? Why would mutineers want to deny other mutineers highly effective weaponry? I'm more inclined to suspect someone who tries to preserve it intact for capture.'

Vinet turned red. 'Are you accusing me of being a mutineer?'

'Not at all,' the professor said. 'I'm merely pointing out that your refusal to carry through on the very reasonable suggestions of my colleagues, or the orders I'm giving you, could be misunderstood in case of later investigation.'

'That's ridiculous! This installation is extremely valuable; the equipment alone is worth –'

'Worthless to the Familias if it gets into the wrong hands. Worse than worthless. Don't you understand that?'

'Well . . . of course, but there's no proof the mutineers are after it. They may not even know about it.'

'You're assuming they're stupid? That's not a good position to take. Commander, I'm afraid I must insist on your cooperation.'

Margiu noticed Garson's signal to his troops. So, she saw, did Vinet. He sagged a little.

'Very well. But it's over my protest, and I will log this. If you had not barged in here with overwhelming force, you'd find yourself in the brig for such nonsense.'

'Thank you,' the professor said, with perfect courtesy. 'I appreciate your position, and your assistance.'

He led Margiu back to the cluster of civilians.

'Gussie, we had an idea –' one of them said. 'Maybe we could mount the –' He lowered his voice, and Margiu heard only a mumble. 'And then attack the mutineers.'

'Mount it on a planet?' The professor pursed his lips. 'That's interesting – that might actually work, if we have time. Do we have the supplies for adequate shielding?'

'Yes, if we dismantle a couple of other things. Oh, and

Ty was working on breaking into their communications before Vinet snatched him out of the communications shack and stuck him in here with us.'

The professor glanced at Margiu. 'Ensign, you're going to be hearing many things you should not hear, and which I advise you to forget as quickly as possible. Do you have any specialty background in technical fields?'

'Aside from growing up making what we needed from scrap, no. Basic electronics and carpentry.'

'Well, that may be useful. Come along; we're going to the labs . . .'

They began with a short meeting in what looked like a snack lounge, with a row of programmable food processors on one wall and battered chairs and couches around the others. A half-finished child's model of a space station cluttered the low table. Margiu had not suspected scientists of playing with such toys, and someone quickly moved it to a far corner.

'What have we got for communications?' the professor asked. 'Ty?'

A skinny man with a bush of black hair came forward. 'They've got the sats, but we can reach mainland with something I cobbled together. I want to send the specs for it over there, so they can build their own quickly. Getting into the mutineers' lines is going to be harder; they've got tight-link capability up there. But they've transmitted some outside that – I suspect to downside confederates – and that I can grab, if I have access to the equipment. I can tight-link if you give me an hour or so – it only takes reconfiguring some modules from one of the labs – but we don't have anyone to send to.'

'What about scan? Can we detect anything beyond atmosphere?'

'Well – only for whatever's in our horizon. The

problem's going to be tracking, not to mention what's below horizon. Knurri had a telescope with a motorized equatorial mount we could've used, but he took it with him when he went on leave. We can point something up, but we won't have an accurate fix if we do find a ship.'

'Do you need anyone else to help you?'

'No, not really. There's a pretty decent enlisted tech I could use, but I'm a little worried that the mutineers had one or more agents on this base – and he'd be the logical one.'

'Fine – Ensign, get Ty an escort from our group to the communications shack, would you?'

She was supposed to guard his back, but this required only going to the door. Lieutenant Lightfoot was outside, waiting; he called over two NEMs who went off with Ty.

'Now – Cole, you said you had an idea?'

'Yeah – Jen and I think it might be possible to rig the big guy for planet-to-space work. We've been trying to come up with the best way to acquire and track the target –'

'Which target?'

'Well . . . we're pretty sure we can take out the orbital station, and any ships docked there. Distant stuff, without the use of satellite-based scans, is going to be harder –'

'But I think we could do it,' a woman said. 'If we take out the station, then get the satellites linked to us –'

'How many hours?' the professor asked.

'Six or seven to mount the weapon, and it'll take a lot of personnel.'

'We may not have six or seven hours,' the professor said. 'We need to know if they're coming, and how soon. Jen, what about scan within atmosphere? Is there any way to get access to the satellite data?'

'Not right now. What we have here is basically old-style radar, for spotting and guiding air traffic, and a little local-weather scanner. The range is so short that we couldn't spot incoming LACs in time to do anything useful. We haven't needed more than that; we had the satellite data for longscan. We really need those satellites, and for that we'll need to break their lock. It's not going to be easy, and it's going to take time.'

'Which, again, we may not have. Bob, what about Project Zed?'

'Operational. And we really don't want them to have it.'

'It actually works?'

'Oh yeah. If this were a ship, and not an island, I could flip the switch and they'd never find us. A big improvement over the earlier models. Unfortunately, as it is an island, it's easily located no matter what cloud we wrap around ourselves.'

Margiu realized with a start that they were talking about new stealth gear.

'Could it be used to cover a retreat in the aircraft? If we took the data and ran for the mainland?'

'I suppose.' The other man looked thoughtful. 'We haven't tried it on aircraft . . . how much can those planes lift?'

'I'll ask,' the professor said. He glanced at Margiu, who headed for the door again. She passed the question off to Lightfoot, and went back to the professor. In that brief interval, the discussion had already turned too technical for her understanding, but it came to an abrupt end when someone pounded on the door.

'Come in,' the professor called.

Ty came in. 'I've found two things – one's a datalog showing transmissions to this station from Stack Three five days ago. From Bacarion. I think someone here's on their payroll.'

'Most likely,' the professor said. 'And?'

'And a transmission from orbit to this station, just now. Personal for Lieutenant Commander Vinet.'

'For Vinet! I'd never have guessed he was part of it,' Swearingen said. 'He's such a fusspot. Did you answer it?'

'No, just acknowledged receipt, using the same sig code that was logged for reply to the others. But I did take a look –'

'Wasn't it encrypted?' someone asked.

'Yah, but a simple one. Not hard to break. Thing is, he's not only part of it, they were telling him they'd be coming down in a day or so, and not to worry – that they'd prevented anyone from sending word from the station. So here we are, nobody else knows what's going on.'

Margiu spoke up. 'We have to get word out somehow!'

The professor looked at her. 'You're quite right, Ensign. And we have to keep them upstairs from finding out that we're here, if possible, to give ourselves time to work – to get word out somehow, to destroy what we can't protect.'

Margiu noticed that he didn't say 'to get away safely.'

'We'll need the troops that came with you, Gussie, to keep the baddies out of our hair.'

'Right. Ty, did your guard come back with you?'

'No, I left him there to guard the equipment.'

'Ensign, we'll need Major Garson.' Margiu told Lightfoot, who hurried off, and in a minute or two Garson appeared.

He listened to Ty's report, scowling. 'I'll put Vinet under arrest, then. I wonder how many baddies were with him.'

'And I wonder how many are with you, sir,' the professor said.

'None, I hope,' Garson said. 'Can you people take care of the rest of it?'

'Building a tightbeam with the power to a ship in-system, yes. Building a scan to locate such a ship, yes. Destroy the more delicate research, and the records, yes. But it will take time, Major. There are only fourteen of us, and some of the work is specialized enough that only one person can do it. So we'd best get at it.' He nodded to Garson, and the major withdrew. The professor turned to the group. 'One thing worries me.'

'Only one?' Swearingen asked, grinning.

'If they don't know we're here, they won't be in as big a hurry to get down here . . . but when the cloud cover goes, they'll be bound to take a look. And they'll see our transports sitting there like a sign in capital letters: TROUBLE HERE.'

'We could send them back,' Swearingen said. 'But then we'd be stuck here. Besides, the latent heat would still show on a fine-grain IR scan.'

'If you just want to hide the planes from scan,' Bob said, 'we can do that with Zed. Set it for just those parameters. It'd be a good test –'

'And if it fails, they'd not only know we were here, but they'd also know about Zed.'

'It's a lot quicker to dismantle and destroy than the big guy,' Bob said.

'How many more hours of darkness? And does anyone have a clue about the weather?' The professor looked around the group.

'Local sunrise is at 8:13 tomorrow; it'll be light before that, of course, if it's clear.'

'And we have no weathersats . . . but we can always go outside and look.'

When they opened the door, a squad waited to accompany them. The professor told Ty to get back to the communications shack; half the squad went with him. With the others he went outside to look at the weather.

Outside, a cold wet wind scoured the ground. Margiu stayed close to the professor, looking up only once to see that no stars showed.

'I can't tell,' the professor said finally. 'Bob, go on and rig Zed to cover the planes. We'll start dismantling the other stuff –'

'Professor –' That was Major Garson. 'We can't find Vinet, or several others. I want all of you back inside, until we find him.'

'That could take days,' Swearingen said. 'Some of the labs are underground, connected by tunnels.'

'Ty's at the communications shack,' the professor said. 'He has guards, but –'

A flare of light, followed in moments by a *whoomp*. Down the runway, one of the planes was blazing, the flames shooting up to glow on the underside of the clouds.

'Great,' Garsón said. 'They can spot *that* right through the cloud cover. Go on now – get inside, get under cover.'

'Where's Lieutenant Lightfoot?' Margiu asked.

'I don't know – he's not answering the com.' Another, brighter flare of light painted one side of the major's face, and another explosion rolled through the night. The second plane. 'Ensign, switch your PPU mask to enhanced, and get these civilians back under cover. That yellow jacket makes a fine target.'

Margiu fumbled for the mask controls, and hit suit reflectivity by mistake. Her suit turned silver, then back to dark blue as she turned it off. Then she found the right set of buttons, and instead of dark clouds and a distant fire, she was looking at a scene painted by someone with a passion for shades of amber and orange. She could see little orange figures moving around, some with green triangles for heads; the blazing fire looked black. As her eyes adjusted, she noticed that the professor had a green triangle, and so did the NEMs around them.

Then a turquoise line stabbed across her vision, to crawl up the professor's sleeve toward his head. Margiu threw herself at him, hooked a leg behind his, and they fell together as a shot whined past and smacked into the armor of the NEM on the other side. He staggered, then all of the NEMs dropped as one.

'Target acquired,' the one beside Margiu said. 'Mark hostile –' Margiu turned her head and saw that one orange figure now had a red square on top. Another of the NEMs fired, and the distant figure went down. She lifted her head, and the NEM shoved it back down. 'Not yet, Ensign. May not be dead, and may be others.'

'Casualties?' That was Garson, on the com.

'No, sir. Small arms fire only; didn't penetrate armor. Civilians all unharmed.'

'Who's on high guard?'

'Turak and Benits – report!'

'No activity on the roof – nothing, sir.'

'Let's get them inside.'

The NEMs formed a double row of armor, and the civilians crawled carefully between them into the building, but no more shots were fired. Margiu took a last look through her enhanced mask, and the orange figure still lay where it had fallen. Then a network of turquoise lines appeared, coming from several angles to converge on the antenna cover of the communications building. She leaned out to see, and a NEM yanked her back.

'Are you trying to get killed?' a woman's voice asked.

'No, I just –'

'Get inside, stay inside, take care of your professor!'

Margiu followed the others into the windowless break room; the professor was looking at her in a way that made her uncomfortable.

'What are they doing?' Swearingen asked.

'I think they're trying to destroy the antenna array,'

Margiu said. 'It's under that dome on the communications building, isn't it?'

'Yes. And if they succeed, we're not going to be able to use a tightbeam, even if we construct one.'

'Why a tightbeam?' Margiu asked.

'Goes farther, carries more data. We might even be able to reach the system ansible, if we can get a fix on it. That would get word out.'

'But – wouldn't a regular broadcast disperse more widely, giving you more chance to warn any incoming ship that wasn't part of the mutiny?'

The professor looked thoughtful. 'You mean – like old-fashioned broadcasting?'

'Yes. If you have enough power –'

'And the antenna is much easier to make. You may have saved more than my life, Ensign.'

The R.S.S. *Vigor* came through the jump point in textbook fashion. Just because they knew they were coming into a secure system, just because nothing could possibly be wrong, was no reason to be careless. Captain Satir would not have paid attention if anyone had complained, and no one did: Satir was a good captain, and his fussy adherence to every little jot and tittle of the rules had saved lives before.

Now *Vigor* slowed to scan the system defenses and monitor system message traffic before proceeding in-system, even as her beacon automatically informed the system who she was. As she dumped velocity, the communications officer stripped one message after another, hardly glancing at them as they came off the printer – Captain Satir demanded hardcopy, even if that did mean plenty of recycling. He handed them to the captain's runner, who took them to Satir. Satir was already alert, peering at the system scan.

'I've been to Copper Mountain eight times, and the outer loop's never been *all* red,' his scan officer was saying.

'I've been here ten times and never seen this many big ships insystem. What's going on, I wonder?'

'We're ten minutes out – twenty delay on queries.'

'I don't think I want to talk to the station. Put us at battle stations, Tony, but don't light up the weapons.' The alarms rang through the ship; colored lights danced across the various control boards reporting systems in operation. Satir glanced at the sheets of paper in his lap. Trouble. Major trouble.

'Sir, there's an odd signal coming in – you need to see it now.'

'Odd how?'

'Not the usual frequencies, for one thing. It's surface propagated, but not a coherent signal – it's like they didn't care who picked it up. It'd dissipate to noise within this system, though.'

'And it says?'

'It's in clear, and it says there's a mutiny at Copper Mountain, that the mutineers have the orbital station and control of system defenses. It's begging somebody to get the word out.'

Captain Satir looked at his bridge officers. If this was a hoax, reacting as if it were real could end his career. If it was not a hoax, he had only one chance to get away.

Even as he hesitated, a bank of lights on the scan desks came alight.

'They're aiming at us,' his scan officer said. 'Tracking us –'

'Full ahead, find us a slot and take us to jump,' Satir said. 'We're getting out of here while we can.' *Vigor* had the speed and the angle; none of the ships insystem could catch them in straight flight, and he was prepared to jump blind if necessary to put more distance between them. The system defenses were preset to defend certain arcs which he could easily avoid. 'Make extra copies of all scan data, and try a squirt at the system ansible as we go by – they may have reprogrammed it, but it's worth a try.'

Four days later, *Vigor* came in range of an ansible in another system, and transmitted an emergency override command set, followed by the entire load of scan data she'd collected.

CHAPTER NINETEEN

SIRIALIS

The long room with its high ceiling would have held twenty pairs of fencers, and had before. The walls were pale green above the mirrors, and the gilt beaded molding around the ceiling was echoed by the molding around the mirrors. The east wall, a bank of French windows, let in the natural daylight and overlooked a rose garden. This morning, bars of yellow sunlight lay across the polished wood floor. Only a few roses had opened, the early white single ones like showers of stars, but their perfume entered on the slightest movement of air. Down the middle of the polished parquet floor ran the strip, deep green.

Miranda finished her stretches, and picked up her practice foil. Facing the mirrors, she could see that Pedar, though still stretching, was watching her. She moved through the parries, smoothly but not fast, feeling for the rhythm that would best suit her needs. He finished his stretches, but made no move to pick up his own blade. He stood watching her instead. She met his eyes in the mirror, then turned.

'What? Am I doing something wrong?'

'No, my dear. I was thinking how lovely you are – and how incongruous it always is to see a beautiful woman holding a deadly weapon.'

'This?' Miranda laughed, touching the button, and bending the blade with only a little pressure. 'Even if it weren't so whippy, it could hardly kill anyone.'

'It's the principle of the thing,' Pedar said. 'And I've seen you with stiffer blades.'

Miranda grimaced. 'I was younger, then.'

'You were Ladies' Champion in epee . . . I have never forgotten your grace, that day.'

'I was lucky. Berenice ran out of breath – I've always suspected she had a cold. Usually she beat me.'

'But still – if you had live steel in hand, in the old days I don't doubt you'd have been a formidable opponent.'

'I'll take that as a compliment,' Miranda said. 'Shall we?'

Still he didn't move. 'I was going to ask a favor.'

'A favor? What?'

'I see you have Bunny's old collection here – in the hall. I know he never let anyone actually use it, but – do you suppose we could?'

Bait and hook, taken faster than she'd expected. She frowned a little. 'The old weapons? But Pedar – they're *old*. I don't even know how old, some of them.'

'If I could just hold them – just feel them.'

'I don't even know if they're really mine to lend,' Miranda said. 'I mean, they're here because Bunny brought them along, but they are his family's heirlooms. You're the one who said I should be fair to Harlis –'

'Harlis need never know,' Pedar said. 'It's just – the oldest steel I've ever held was that antique Georgy has – you know.'

'Oh, that old thing.' Miranda allowed herself a sniff.

'It's not a day over two hundred, whatever he says. These are much older –'

'I know, that's why I asked. Please?' He cocked his head and put his hands together like a polite child.

'I suppose it couldn't hurt,' Miranda said. 'If we're careful . . .' She could feel her heart speed up, safely hidden under her white jacket, as she led the way back to the hall.

She unlocked the case, and stood back. Pedar reached past her, and took out, as she'd expected, the big saber with the heavy, ornamented hilt. He ran his thumb down the blade, and nodded. 'Still –'

'Bunny said they were still usable,' Miranda said. 'But he didn't want to take a chance on breakage. They're not replaceable.'

'No . . .' Pedar breathed on the blade, then buffed it with his sleeve. 'Derrigay work, look at that pattern! And the ring –' He rapped it with his nail, and the blade chimed softly. Miranda shivered, involuntarily. Pedar set the blade back, and took down another. 'You have no idea of their age?'

'Bunny always said that one – the epee – was the oldest, and the rapier the next oldest. He said it was just possible those two were from Old Earth from an era when they might have been used.' Used to kill, intentionally. Used as she would use a blade today.

'Amazing.' Pedar put the rapier back, and took the broad, curved blade for which she had no name. 'And this?'

'I don't know. It looks more like a chopper to me – for very large potatoes.'

He chuckled. 'Not a blade for artistry, no. An executioner's weapon, perhaps, from a very bloody period.' His hand reached again, this time for a foil. 'So – this is your weight now?' His hand stroked the blade, bent it. 'Not so

whippy as the one you were using, but – light enough, I'll
warrant.'

'Oh, probably. I still practice with heavier blades now
and then.' She had to be fair. She had to be scrupulously
fair, and let his own folly put him in danger.

'Let's fence with these, not the modern ones.'

'I don't think it's a good idea . . . I don't know what
they would think –'

'They? What "they"? Who could possibly dispute with
you, now that the judgement has gone your way? What
harm could it cause?'

'I don't know,' Miranda said again. 'What if a blade
breaks? What if Harlis appeals, and then finds out I've
destroyed a valuable asset?'

'He needn't know. He isn't a fencer; he's probably
never paid attention to them. Besides . . . I'll explain it
was all my idea.' Pedar nodded at the helms. 'Look – let's
do it right. Use all the old gear, masks as well. It would be
like fancy dress.' He had always liked fancy dress; he
had worn it to balls where other men wore conventional
clothes.

'But –'

'Just this once. There's no one to see. Please?' Again
that tip of the head, the pleading expression, then an
impish grin. 'I'll bet you've always wanted to. Haven't
you?'

Miranda smiled. 'As a matter of fact . . . I did sneak that
one out once –' She nodded at the blade in his hand.
'There's something about it – knowing it's old, knowing it
was used by people long dead –'

'Yesss.' He drew out the syllable, nodding. 'I thought
so. Just as you enjoy old porcelain, or jewelry. Those who
appreciate such things should not be forbidden the use of
them. So you will humor me this once, Miranda?'

She glanced around, as if nervous of watchers. 'I

suppose – and after all, if we do break one, and Harlis finds out – as you said, he's no fencer. He can hardly skewer me.'

'Well, my lady – choose your weapon.' Pedar set the blade he'd been holding back in the rack and waved her forward with an extravagant gesture.

Miranda reached, pulled back as if unsure, and finally took the blade he had just replaced, the longest of the foils, with a weighted hilt to balance it. He took its partner.

'Let's complete the mischief,' Pedar said. 'As I said, with such blades as these, our helms too should match. I've long fancied myself in one of these – had my armorer make a replica, but it's not the same.' He tried on one, then another, until he found one that fit . . . the others had, as she knew well, inconvenient and uncomfortable lumps beneath the linings.

Miranda raised her brows at him. 'It can't be safe, Pedar – blades last, but old metal screening –'

'Pah! It will stand up to a blunted stroke, and if I cannot defend my face at least I'm not much of a fighter. Come, my dear . . . if you are nervous, you must wear your usual mask, but permit me my conceit. The only way you will strike my eye is with your beauty.'

It needed only that to erode the last grain of sympathy Miranda felt. She could have shot him where he stood, but she was not going to trial for the murder of a murderer.

Back in the salle, after they had clipped the buttons to the tip of the blades, Pedar moved out of the shadow to stand in one of the bars of sun, a glowing white figure with a shining golden-bronze head; the old helm gleamed in the light. She could not see his face through the pierced metal. From within her own mask, the world narrowed to the strip itself, and the opponent across from her. Could he see her face? She let herself smile now, with no guarding tension.

She brought her blade up in salute, as did he. Then he advanced.

They began with the formal introduction, the 'Fingertips' as advocated by the fencing master Eduardo Callin, two centuries before. This allowed the fencer who wished a match to carry more meanings to suggest them by the quality of his touch, and this first contact, feeble to feeble, set up that possibility. Miranda's blade tapped crisply, to signal no particular intent, but Pedar's drew along hers, or tried to – the signal that for him, this match's metaphor was Courtship.

Miranda could feel her lip curling, within her mask, and fought down the rush of anger. Here, at the ritualized beginning, she must maintain her ruse. At the fourth touch, her tip wavered a little – someone who had recognized his offering, and was not yet rejecting it. Thinking about it perhaps. His fifth touch, the last of the right-hand touches, attempted a spiral along her blade, which she did not allow, but did not bat away. That signified Shyness, not Rejection.

They switched hands for the next five Fingertips. His tip continued its swirl, a stronger plea of Courtship; Miranda allowed hers to droop, on the ninth and next to last. Uncertainty – the last thing she felt, but an emotion she hoped he would have for one last instant. Then the tenth – a clean tap by both to signal the end of that segment. She stepped back, as did he, and switched her blade to her right hand again. Another bow and salute, and they were into the next phase.

Miranda presented a quite ordinary opening in Fourth, and Pedar accepted. In a friendly bout such as this, there was no hurry, so they crossed blades in easy parry-riposte combinations for some fifteen exchanges.

'You're so graceful,' Pedar said, his voice muffled slightly by the mask.

'You're so quick,' Miranda said, out of her throat so that she would sound a little breathless.

'For you, I would gladly slow,' he said. His next stroke was slightly slower, and she met it just an instant late. If she could convince him to slow, if she could set a pace that lulled him into the wrong rhythm . . .

'I used to be faster,' she said. 'I know I did –'

'It's that blade, my dear. It's heavy for you.'

'I need something –' She blocked his stroke, threw one intentionally slow which he blocked easily. 'Against you, I need the extra length, and the stiffness –'

'Bah. I'm not going to press you harder than you can handle. You should know that, Miranda. When was I ever importunate?'

'You weren't. It's just –'

He stepped back and grounded his blade. 'Come – let's exchange blades. That was made for a man; you can tell by the weight of the hilt.'

'Besides, you want to try it,' she said, chuckling.

'True. Indulge me, my dear?'

'Very well. But I'm going to do more conditioning, I swear I am. I didn't realize how out of shape I was. All those days of the funeral, and arrangements –'

'Of course.' He handed her the foil hiltfirst over his arm, with a bow. If only his courtesy meant something. She handed him her weapon with equal grace, and they exchanged places on the strip, as always after an exchange of weapons.

Miranda was sure she knew which of the old weapons had actually drawn blood. She knew nothing would show on analysis; she knew her belief was irrational and indefensible, but . . . the foil conveyed to her an eagerness for blood that matched her own

It had from the moment she first handled the old weapons.

They were just poised to begin again when her com-unit chimed. 'Milady – Lady Cecelia de Marktos called; she has docked and taken one of the personal shuttles.'

Cecelia coming? Bright anger washed over her. She had been so close; she might never have another chance. Why couldn't Cecelia mind her own business? And where was she coming from? How many minutes did she have, now, to finish Pedar?

With an effort, she regained her concentration. She would figure out something . . . as long as it was over before Cecelia walked in . . .

She found it hard, at first, to conceal the speed the foil lent her. Beat, parry, parry, beat, beat. Her heart ham-mered, more excitement than effort; she dared not use her own pulse for a timer. She dared not wait too long, either.

She backed a pace, then another, then, with a quick disengage, lunged and made the touch. With contact, she twisted her wrist and pushed, taking Pedar's tip on her left shoulder. Through her hand, she felt the faintest give to the tip.

'We're both dead,' she said with a smile. The mask across from her gave no hint of Pedar's expression; he stepped back as she did to salute and begin again.

Was the tip gone? The foil felt no different; she parried his next stroke, and his next, and then she heard it. The tip gave way, flipped by her blade's elastic recoil into a para-bolic arc; she had to drag her eyes away from it to check the break. Pedar froze an instant, then started to withdraw.

'I'm afraid a blade broke –' he said. She saw the tilt of his helm, as he looked to check his own, saw it move back.

She waited, until she knew he had time to see her blade, the sharp tip exposed by the spiral fracture.

'Miranda –?' For the first time, his voice was uncertain.

He was good; he almost parried the lightning thrust she sent at his mask – but he had dropped his arm, lost his rhythm, and responded that fractional second late. The tip of her blade – stiffer now and sharp – slammed into her target, a particular perforation in the metal of his mask. Around it, the weakened metal gave way, and she thrust on, the broken tip grating over the orbit's rim into the eye she could not see, into the brain behind it, with a wrist motion that ensured more than a single damage track. Her blade snapped again, on the back of his skull, and quickly as she withdrew it, he was already falling.

'Ohhh . . .' She sank with him, still watchful until his hand loosened and dropped his weapon. Then she dropped her own sword, grabbed at his shoulders. 'Noooo. . . .! Pedar! NO!!'

Cecelia heard the cry as she came through the door, and saw Miranda, recognizable by both form and the golden hair that spilled out the back of her helm, facing away from her, clutching at the shoulders of her opponent, who was collapsing. She moved forward quickly. Was it Pedar, or someone else?

Miranda was scrabbling at the other person's mask trying to get it off.

'Miranda – let me help. Call medical –'

'It won't come off – it won't come off!' Miranda seemed frantic, her gloved fingers clumsily yanking at some kind of latch. Now Cecelia could see the blood trickling out where the mask had given way, and the blood on the broken short length of blade. 'I told him! I told him it was dangerous! Bunny always said no one should use the old blades, or trust the old armor, but he wanted to – he insisted –'

Cecelia discovered that her mind was already working again, when she recognized all this as elements of alibi. She worked at the other side of the man's helm, wondering why the ancients had made everything so complicated. Surely this hadn't been made before the advent of pressure locks.

'What happened?'

'The blade broke – I was lunging – and it just shattered –'

Cecelia looked, but could see only the shadowed shape of Miranda's face behind her mask.

'I thought you said fencing was safe.' Pedar had said that too, at the Trials. *As long as it is only steel*, he had said.

'It is. It's – he wanted to use the old blades, the ones Bunny would never use. He knew Harlis wouldn't allow it, but . . . then he said, why not the old helms. He was in one of his moods – you know how Pedar is. He'd brought me a lace scarf. He began with the Courtship, in the Ten Fingers.'

Cecelia had one side of the helm loose now, and began working on the other.

'You didn't call for medical help.'

'Cece – when a blade goes in the eye, there *is* no help.'

'In the eye?'

'This old helm – the face mask failed. My blade went straight through, into his eye. You know how it is – well, you don't, but when you thrust, if your blade snaps, you're already moving, you can't stop. I tried – but all I did was make it worse.'

'How?'

'The blade had already pierced his eye and the orbit – of course I yanked it back, but it was already in his brain. I didn't realize – it was so awful –'

She had the other side of the helm open, and lifted it

away. There was Pedar's face, one eye open but dulled already with anoxia, and the other a bloody hole.

'Miranda.' Cecelia looked at her, trying to see through that mask. But sunlight blazed on the metal, and behind it was only shadow. She looked down at the gloved hands, one streaked with blood . . . at Miranda's neck, where the high collar of her fencing habit hid her pulse.

The door slammed open now, and a crowd of servants rushed in. Where had they been all this time? Was it a plot?

'Milady! What happened –'

'We were fencing, and the blade broke . . .'

Miranda took her own mask off slowly, her hands trembling. Tears had streaked her cheeks; she looked paler than usual, with red-rimmed eyes.

'You cried –' Cecelia said.

'Of course I cried!' Miranda glared at her.

'I've never seen you cry before, except for Bunny –'

'You didn't see me when I heard about Brun's capture. Or when the babies were born.' She turned to the man in the gray suit; Cecelia did not recognize him. 'Sammins, we'll need a doctor, though I know it's too late, and the militia. This man is – was – Minister of Foreign Affairs; we'll have to have an investigation.'

All though the questions that followed, Cecelia sat quietly to one side, watching Miranda, listening to the timbre of her voice. Pedar had been coming to fence twice weekly since arriving on Sirialis. Pedar had initiated the practices; he had also come to talk business, and – she hesitated, and a faint color came into her cheeks – to propose a Familial alliance. On that day, they had begun as usual, but Pedar had asked – as he had before – about the antique weapons in the hall. Where were they going, and who would inherit them? He had wanted to handle them, fence with them. Bunny had never allowed it, but Pedar had begged –

And she had given in, agreed to fence with the old weapons, though they had not been inspected.

She must have scan data, Cecelia realized. She would not dare go into such detail if scan would not support what she said. And therefore – it could be an accident, just as Miranda said. Or she was even cleverer at arranging matters.

Slow anger churned her stomach. These had been her friends – or at least people she had known, people of her class. Wealthy, urbane, sophisticated . . . she had known them all her life. They collected fine art; they supported composers and artists and musicians; they had beautiful houses and landscaped grounds. They dabbled in this or that – china painting, horse breeding, designing exotic space stations – in between power plays in Family politics and acquiring more money and more power and more possessions. They wore beautiful clothes, and indulged in elaborate games of social intercourse.

And now they were killing each other off. Lorenza, trying to poison her. Kemtre, agreeing to poison his own son. Someone – Pedar, by his bragging – arranging to kill Bunny. Miranda killing Pedar.

Were they all crazy?

And if they were . . . why? And who benefitted?

She could not find her way through that maze, except in terms of the familiar, beloved world of equestrian sports and horse breeding. If she'd had a stable full of highbred horses, all carefully brought up, schooled . . . and if they had suddenly begun to act strange, to attack grooms and each other . . . what would she think?

Somebody got at the grooms.

Fine, but rich people didn't *have* grooms.

Her mind stopped short, like a horse overfaced by a huge, unfamiliar obstacle on the cross-country.

Yes, they did have grooms, and veterinarians. They

called them maids and valets and doctors and nurses. They all depended on pharmaceuticals for rejuv. They had all been rejuved multiple times. Lorenza, Kemtre, Pedar, Miranda, even her own sister Berenice. Some had access to other illicit drugs, like the neurotoxins Lorenza had poisoned her with.

Once she'd known Lorenza was dead, she'd given no serious thought to the source of that drug. Lorenza was a mean, vicious, sadistic woman . . . that was the threat, not the drug. It's not the weapon, it's the person who misuses it.

But . . . she knew. She knew about Patchcock, though she'd put it out of her mind when Ronnie and Raffa were safely married. Bad drugs. Bad rejuvenation drugs, and who knows what else, and the fallout might be worse than anyone had thought.

Was Miranda sane? Were *any* of them sane? The Grand Council of the Familias . . . without Bunny at its head, or Kevil Mahoney to advise, with Pedar – evil as she now believed he was – dead and stiffening on the floor in the fencing salon . . . what were they going to do? Was there *anyone* she could trust?

Those who had never been rejuved. Those who had been rejuved only . . . somewhere the drugs were reliable. Marta Saenz? But just because Marta was a biochemist herself, with her own labs, did that mean her drugs were good?

No. But she could not distrust everyone. She wasn't made like that; she had to have sides, someone on hers and someone against her.

Finally the initial interviews were over, and Cecelia went up with Miranda to her suite. A white-faced maid brought them a tray of food and hot tea. Miranda stripped off her fencing whites, and took a shower while Cecelia stared out the tall windows to the hummocky country of the Blue Hunt. By the time Miranda came back in, wrapped in a thick quilted robe, Cecelia had her own questions in order.

'Miranda . . . remember when I told you what Pedar told me, shortly after Bunny died?'

'Of course,' Miranda said. 'You told me that you thought Pedar knew who had killed him, that it was not the NewTex Militia.'

'Is . . . that . . .?'

'Cecelia, Pedar has always been a bit of a boor, you know that.'

'Yes, but –'

'He thought himself a man of power; he wanted to improve his status within the Conselline Sept. So naturally he claimed to have knowledge you didn't have.'

'You didn't take him seriously.'

'Not at first, no. He came courting, you see.'

'Courting!'

'Yes. Hinting that if I had his protection, I need not fear Harlis's challenge to the will. That I would get to keep Sirialis – he meant *he* would get Sirialis.'

'He honestly thought you would marry him?'

'Apparently. He asked if he could come here; I put him off several times, but finally consented.'

'But why?'

Miranda shrugged. 'I wanted to know what he knew – how he was so sure he could do what he claimed. It's not the kind of thing you can ask over a com line: "Do you really have the power you say you have?" I thought, if he visited, I could assess his abilities and intentions better.'

'But you weren't going to marry him –'

'Heavens, Cecelia, you do stick like a burr! No, I was not going to marry him. I'm not going to marry anyone. I'm going to fight Harlis, on Buttons' behalf, and save the inheritance, but I'm not going to marry. I had the best for most of my life; why would I settle for crumbs now?'

'I don't know – I just worry –'

'No need.' Miranda stretched, then strolled over to the pool. Fat orange goldfish rose to the surface and swam nearer. 'I'm not crazy; I didn't get my rejuv drugs from the Morrelines, and I'm not going to rejuv again. Once I get my children settled –'

'I thought I'd never get rejuved,' Cecelia said. 'Wouldn't have, if not for the poison. But I rather like it now.'

'I understand that,' Miranda said. 'You have more things you want to do. But, I'm nominal forty now, actual – well, you know the actuality – and have another sixty years of health without rejuv. Sixty years without Bunny is plenty.'

'You might find someone else.'

'And gold might drop from the sky in showers. If I do, I can rejuv then, if I want. But it's not something to plan on. End of discussion, Cece. Tell me, have you been down to the stables yet?'

'No –'

'Then you should. Just in case something happens, and Harlis ends up with Sirialis after all, you should know if there's anything here you'd like to put a bid on.'

'I can't believe he'd be stupid enough to shut down the stables,' Cecelia said.

'A horse broke his foot when he was a boy, and then he cracked some ribs falling off into rocks trying to keep up with Bunny. He thinks horses are large smelly abominations, a drain on the income – which they are, actually. We've never made money off the horses.'

'Miranda – you're distracting me with horses, and I'm not that foolish. Did you kill Pedar on purpose?'

Miranda gave her a long, silent look. 'Do you think I would do something like that?'

'I don't know anymore what people will and won't do.

I didn't think Lorenza would poison me and gloat over me while I lay helpless. I didn't think Kemtre would drug his own sons, or connive at cloning. I didn't think Bunny's brother would terrorize an old lady into giving up her shares. Or that Pedar would have Bunny assassinated to get a Ministry.'

'We're not answering each other's questions,' Miranda said. 'And I think that's probably wise. But I will remind you of that old, old rule.'

'Which one?'

'A lady is never rude . . . by accident.' Miranda put a dollop of honey in her cup, then sipped the tea. 'I needed that.'

'Sticking a blade into someone's brain and stirring goes beyond mere rudeness.' Cecelia felt grumpy. She was sure she knew what had happened – or part of it – and yet Miranda wasn't reacting as she should.

'That's true,' Miranda said. 'But the rule applies in other situations as well. Cecelia, if you're going to make a fuss, please do so.'

'You're not even asking me not to . . .'

'No. Your decisions are yours, as mine are mine.'

'What are you going to tell your children?'

'That Pedar died in a fencing accident. They have brains, Cecelia, and imagination; they will put on it what construction they please.'

Cecelia ate another jam-filled tart, and stared out the window again. After a long silence, she said, 'I suppose it sends a message to Hobart . . .'

'I hope so,' Miranda said.

CHAPTER TWENTY

Esmay scowled at the message strip the clerk handed her. They'd had it all arranged, she thought. Why meet in a private room, and not in the restaurant? She scanned the lift tubes, looking for the right range. Thirty-seven to forty . . . odd. Most tubes served at least ten floors. She tapped the access button.

'Room and name, please?'

What was this? If Barin had been there, she'd have whacked him in the head, but he wasn't. '3814,' she said instead. 'Lieutenant Suiza.'

The lift tube access slid open, with the supporting grid glowing green for up. Esmay stepped in, and found herself in a mirrored cylinder that rose smoothly, with none of the exuberance of most lift tubes. Her ears popped once, then again. It was only thirty-eight floors – what was happening here?

She stepped out into a green-carpeted foyer, the walls striped in subtle shades of beige and cream. The pictures on the wall . . . she caught her breath at the bold geometric. Surely that was a reproduction – she stepped closer. No . . .

the thick wedge of purple, that cast a shadow in every reproduction, cast a different shadow here, lit as it was by a pin spot on the opposite wall. Genuine Oskar Cramin. Then that might be a real Dessaline as well, its delicate traceries refusing to be overborne by the Cramin's almost brutal vigor. Quietly, with the confidence of greatness, the little gray and gold and black Dessaline held its place.

She shook her head and looked around. Beyond the foyer, a short hall had but four doors opening off it, and one was labelled SERVICE. Barin must have spent a fortune . . . 3814 was the middle door. She moved into its recognition cone, and waited.

The door opened, and she was face to face with . . . a middle-aged woman she'd never seen. Before she could begin to stammer an apology, the woman spoke.

'Lieutenant Suiza! How good to meet you – I'm Podjar Serrano, Barin's mother.'

Barin's mother. Panic seized her. She had been prepared for Barin, for a few stolen moments of privacy . . . a chance to talk before she met his mother.

'Come on in,' Podjar was saying. 'We're all dying to meet you.'

We? What *we*? We *all*? She could hear a low hum of voices, and wanted nothing more than to run away. Where was Barin? How could he lead her into this?

Podjar had her by the arm – Barin's mother; she couldn't just pull away – and led her inside, to a room that seemed as big as a planet right then.

'Here she is at last,' Podjar said to someone else, a short thickset man who had Barin's grin but nothing of his grace. Brother? Father? Uncle? 'This is Kerin, my husband,' Podjar said. Esmay hoped that meant he was Barin's father, because otherwise she hadn't a clue.

Farther into the room, her stunned wits began to register additional details. Not only was the room big, and arranged for entertaining, but it was comfortably full of people who all seemed to know each other. Barin's family?

'Esmay!' Her heart leapt. That was Barin, and he would get her out of this, whatever it was. He came toward her, clearly gleeful and full of himself. She could have killed him, and hoped he understood steel behind her fixed smile.

'I'm sorry I wasn't at the lift to meet you,' he said. 'I had an urgent call –'

Esmay couldn't bring herself to be polite and say it didn't matter. 'What is this?' she said instead.

Barin grimaced. 'It got out of hand,' he said. 'I wanted you to meet my parents, and they were coming through here on the way home. Then Grandmother –' He waved; Esmay followed the gesture to see Admiral Vida Serrano at the far end of the room, surrounded by an earnest cluster of older people. '– Grandmother wanted to talk to you about something, and thought this would be a good opportunity. And then . . . they started precipitating, falling out of the sky . . .'

'Mmm.' Esmay could not say any of what she was thinking, not with his parents standing there smiling at her a little nervously. 'Are we . . . going to have a chance to talk?' By ourselves she meant.

'I don't know,' Barin said. 'I hope so. But –' His gaze slid to his mother, who quirked an eyebrow.

'Barin, you know it's important family business. We must confer.'

Great. The only leave she'd been able to wangle, in the current crises, and it looked as if she'd be spending it conferring with his family instead of hers.

'How was your trip, Esmay?' asked Barin's father. He had lieutenant commander's insignia, with a technical flash.

'Fine, though we lost a day at Karpat for unscheduled maintenance procedures.' She couldn't keep the edge out of her voice.

'Mmm. That's typical.' Barin's father nodded across the room. 'Let me show you to your room.'

'My –'

'Of course you have your own room here. We may have descended in force, but we're not entirely uncivilized. You have to stay somewhere.' Across the room, through another door, into another corridor . . . Esmay was by this time beyond astonishment when he showed her to a small suite, its sitting room wall showing a view of the station's exterior. 'This is yours – and I'm sure the staff are sending up your things.'

'I have only the carryon,' Esmay said.

'Well, then. Come out when you're ready.' With a smile, he turned away and closed the door behind him. Esmay sank down onto one of the rose-and-cream-striped chairs. What she wanted to do was put her head in her hands and scream. That wouldn't be productive, she was sure. But what was going on?

A tap on the door interrupted her uneasy thoughts. Her carryon? 'Come in,' she said. The door opened, and Barin stood there looking sheepish.

'May I?' he asked. Esmay nodded; he entered, shutting the door behind him, and pulled her up from the chair. She stiffened for a moment, then relaxed against him.

'Your family –' she began.

'I'm sorry. It wasn't my idea, but it is my family. They're . . . headstrong.'

'And you aren't?' She wasn't ready to think it was funny; she wanted to indulge her annoyance – such justified annoyance – a little longer, but suddenly her sense of humor kicked in. She could just imagine Barin, having planned this quiet little retreat, being maneuvered by his powerful and numerous family. She stifled the giggle that tried to come out.

'Not headstrong enough,' Barin said, with a rueful grin. 'I tried to tell them to let us alone, but you see how well I did.'

Esmay lost control of the giggle; she could feel it vibrating in her throat and then it was out.

'You aren't angry?' he asked hopefully.

'Not at you, anyway,' Esmay said. 'I suppose a quiet few days alone was too much to hope for.'

'I didn't think so,' Barin said. 'You would think the entire universe was playing tricks on us —'

'Ummm . . . I've read that lovers always put themselves in the center of everything.'

'I'd like to put us in the center of a bed, a long way from everywhere else,' Barin said, with a hint of a growl.

'We'll get there,' Esmay said. Her arms tightened around him; he felt as good as ever, and she wanted to melt right into him until their bones chimed together.

Someone knocked on the door. 'Barin, if you don't let her get dressed, we'll never get to dinner —' A female voice, one she hadn't met yet.

'Oh, shut up,' muttered Barin in Esmay's ear. 'Why wasn't I born an orphan?'

'It would have been too simple,' Esmay said. 'Let me go — I want to change. And are we eating up here, or in public?' Not that the entire Serrano family wasn't public enough.

'Here. It's coming up.' He let go, went to the door, and opened it. There stood a woman in her thirties, about Esmay's size, with the Serrano features.

'Esmay, I'm Dolcent. Barin — go away, I need to talk to her for a moment.'

'I hate you,' Barin said, but he left. Dolcent grinned.

'Listen – I gather you were expecting a quiet evening of entertainment and you have only one carryon. If I were in that situation, I'd have brought only the clothes I meant to wear, which weren't exactly family-meeting ones . . . so may I offer you something?'

Annoyance returned, a wave of it – who did they think they were? – but then she remembered the contents of her carryon. Clothes for a casual day or so with her fiance, one nice dress to meet the parents . . . blast the woman, she was right.

'Thank you,' Esmay said, as graciously as she could while swallowing another lump of resentment.

'I wouldn't like having to borrow clothes, but there are times – look –'

She had to admit that Dolcent's offerings were better than anything she'd brought, and Dolcent's blue tunic over her own casual slacks met both requirements. Esmay thanked her.

'Never mind. I'll raid your wardrobe someday. If you make my little brother happy, that is.'

'Otherwise you'll blow it up, eh?'

'Something like that,' Dolcent said. 'Or if you call me Dolly . . . just a warning.' She grinned.

Dinner was less formal than she'd feared; the hotel staff brought in a buffet and left it, and people served themselves from it, sitting wherever they fancied. Esmay had a corner of a big puffy sofa with a table at her elbow, and Dolcent beside her, offering explanations. A man's voice emerged from the general babble.

'And I told him that technology wasn't mature enough, but he's determined –'

'Iones – a distant uncle. In material research; you just missed him when you were on *Koskiusko*,' Dolcent said. 'He's a terrible bore, but what he knows he really knows.'

Then a woman, close enough to see. '– and if she *ever* takes that tone to me again, I'll rip the brass right off her –'

'And that's Bindi – never mind her; she's not as bad as she sounds.'

A shrimp came flying through the air with deadly accuracy, to bounce off Dolcent's head. 'Am I not, you miserable eavesdropper?'

Calmly, Dolcent picked up the shrimp and ate it. 'No, you're not. Nor am I an eavesdropper, when you're talking loud enough to be heard three rooms away.'

Bindi shrugged and turned away.

'Is it always like this?' Esmay asked.

'Usually worse. But I'll be accused of dire things if I try to explain Serrano family politics. You come from a large family yourself, right? You should know.'

'Ummm . . .' There was, after all, some of the same flavor in the interactions. The loud ones, staking out their space and their areas of power; the quiet ones in the corners, raising a sardonic eyebrow now and then. Bindi would be an Aunt Sanni; Barin's mother, like her stepmother, seemed to be a quiet peacemaker.

Heris Serrano pulled up a chair to the other side of the end table, and sat down, and put her plate beside Esmay's. Esmay had never thought of Commander Serrano wearing anything but a uniform, but . . . here she was in silvery-green patterned silk, a loose tunic over flowing slacks.

'Esmay – I don't know if you remember me –'

'Yes, si – Commander –'

'Heris, please. This room's so full of rank otherwise, we can hardly talk to each other. I don't think I've seen you face to face to thank you for saving our skins at Xavier – and not just ours –'

'Heris, not during dinner – I know you're going to talk

tactics to her sometime, but not now.' Dolcent pointed with a crab leg, a gesture that would have been a deadly insult on Altiplano. 'She's going to be married; you could at least choose a more suitable topic.'

'And you'd talk clothes to her, 'Centa? Or flowers, or which way to fold the napkins at the reception?'

'Better than old battles during dinner.' Dolcent didn't seem perturbed by Heris's intensity; Esmay watched with interest.

'Picked out a wedding outfit yet, Esmay?' Heris asked, with too much sugar in her voice.

'No, s – Heris. Brun says she's taking care of it.'

'Dear . . . me. How did that happen?'

'She just . . .' Esmay waved her hands helplessly. 'She found out I had no ideas, and then the next thing I knew she was sending me fabric samples and talking about designers.'

'She is something, isn't she?' Heris chuckled. 'You should have seen her years back, when she was really wild. If you're not careful, she'll organize the whole wedding.'

Esmay was feeling reasonably relaxed and almost full when she saw Admiral Vida Serrano coming toward her, with an expression far less friendly than those around her. Like almost all the others, she wore civilian clothes, but that failed to disguise her nature. Esmay tried to get up, but the admiral waved her back.

'There's something you must know,' Admiral Serrano said. 'I haven't told the others because it didn't seem fair to tell them behind your back. It's not widely known – in fact, it's been safely buried for centuries. But since those idiots in Medical sent most of the flag officers off on indefinite inactive status, several of us decided to clean up the Serrano archives, and transfer them onto more modern data storage media.'

'Yes, sir?' She would call Heris by her first name if she insisted, but she wasn't going to call the admiral anything but 'sir,' whether or not she was in uniform.

'You know the official history of the Regular Space Service – how it is an amalgam of the private spacegoing militias of the founding Families?'

'Yes . . .'

'What you may not know is that despite the effort made to eradicate the memory of which Fleet family once served which Family, these realities still influence Fleet policy. Perhaps more than they should. The Serrano legacy – to the extent that we have one – consists in the peculiar fact of our origin.'

A long pause, during which Esmay tried to guess which of the great families had once had the Serranos as no-doubt-difficult bodyguards.

'Our Family was destroyed,' the admiral said finally. 'We were the spacegoing militia; we were, at the time of the political cataclysm that wiped out our employers, far away guarding their ships. After that, we could not go back – for obvious reasons – and when the Regular Space Service was organized some thirty T-years later, most of our family petitioned to be enrolled. We were considered, by some, safer . . . because we were unaligned.'

Esmay could think of nothing to say.

'This much is well-known, at least to most of the senior members of Fleet, and it's been at the root of some resentment of the Serrano influence. Every generation or so, some smart aleck from another Fleet family tries to suggest that we were part of the rebellion against our Family, and then we have to respond. If we're lucky, it's handled at the senior level, but a couple of hundred years back, we and the Barringtons lost two jigs in a duel.'

Admiral Serrano cleared her throat. Esmay noticed

that the room had grown quieter; the others had come nearer, and were listening.

'The Family we served was based on a single planet – many Families were, in those days. And that planet . . .' She paused again; and Esmay felt a chill down her back. It could not be. 'That planet, Esmay, was Altiplano. Your world.'

She wanted to say *Are you sure?* but she knew that Admiral Serrano would not have said it if it hadn't been verifiable.

'That much the Serranos know – we all know – and there were some who argued against you on those grounds. I didn't; I felt that you'd make my grandson a fine partner, and I said so.'

There were murmurs from the others. Esmay looked at Barin, trying to read his face, but she couldn't.

Vida Serrano went on. 'There's more, and I think I may be the first person to see this for centuries. I was down in the family archives, bored enough to look at a row of children's books written by some very untalented ancestor, when I found it.' She held up a dingy brown book. 'I don't think it's a children's book; I think it's someone's private journal, or part of it. The conservators think it dates from the time of the events it describes, or closely after, and the pictures it had were pasted-in flat-pics. The conservators couldn't find anything in the vid archives corresponding, and with maximal image-boosting, this is the best we could get . . .'

She slipped a package of flatpics out of the book, and opened it. The images were still blurry, but Esmay caught her breath. Altiplano . . . she could not mistake that pair of mountain peaks. And the building – the old part of the Landsmen's Guildhall, as shown in the oldest pictures she had seen in her history classes.

'You recognize it?' Vida asked Esmay.

'Yes . . . the mountains are the Dragon's Teeth –' And below them, an ancient bunker . . . she didn't want to think about that now. 'And the building looks like the Landsmen's Guildhall the way it was before they added onto it in my great-grandfather's time.'

'I thought as much. Behind one of the flatpics, hidden by it, I found this.' She held up a piece of paper that didn't look old enough. 'This isn't the original, of course – that's back home, with the conservators humming over it. This is a copy. And, Esmay Suiza, it makes clear that your ancestors earned the enmity of mine, by rebelling against their patrons and slaughtering them all.'

'What?'

'Your ancestors led the rebellion, Esmay. They massacred the family we were sworn to protect.'

Esmay stared. 'How can you know that? If no one survived –'

'Listen: *Against these our oath is laid: the sons of Simon Escandon, and the sons of Barios Suiza and the sons of Mario Vicarios, for it is they who led the rebellions against our Patron. Against their sons, and their sons' sons, to the most distant generation. May their Landbrides be barren, and their priests burn in hell, for they murdered their lawful lord and all his family, man and wife, father and mother, brother and sister, to the youngest suckling child. There is blood between their children and our children, until the stars die and the heavens fall. Signed: Miguel Serrano, Erenzia Serrano, Domingues Serrano.*'

Silence held the room; Esmay could scarcely breathe, and cold pierced her. She glanced around; the faces that had been welcoming an hour before had closed against her, stone-hard, the dark eyes cold. All but Barin, who looked stunned, but not yet rejecting.

'I never heard this,' she said finally.

'I don't suppose they would brag about it,' Vida said. 'What story did you hear?'

Story. She was already sure that anything Esmay said would be a story, would be false. 'In our history . . . there was a war, but also a plague, and a third of the population died of that, including the Founders.'

'Is that what you call the Family?'

'Yes . . . I suppose, though I never knew there was one great family. I'd always thought of them as many families.'

'You never heard the name Garcia-Macdonald?'

'No. Neither name.'

'Ah. I've no doubt the rebels destroyed all evidence. There was nothing to show against them when Altiplano joined the Familias Regnant three hundred years later. All we could do was watch – and we did not then know which of the people on Altiplano had been involved. By then the Regular Space Service had formed around us.'

'Was that the family? Garcia-Macdonald?'

'Yes. A family Serranos had served beside as far back as the wet-navy days of Old Earth. Tell me about this war, as you heard it.'

'The Lifehearts and the Old Believers,' Esmay said, dredging up what she remembered of those childhood lessons. 'Um . . . the Founders wanted to bring in more colonists, free-birthers and Tamidians, to work the mines and develop the land. There had been a charter – a compact, they called it – promising to settle Altiplano only with those acceptable to those already in place. The Old Believers objected to the number of Tamidians the Founders wanted to import – they knew that they'd be outnumbered in two or three generations because of the freebirth policies. And the Lifehearts wanted development to proceed with due regard for the underlying ecosystem. But the Founders wanted a quick profit – they brought in shiploads of Tamidians, and the Tamidians brought diseases alien to the Altiplanans – diseases they were immune to, genetically.'

It came back to her now – the accusations and counter-accusations. Infant mortality soared among the Altiplanans, as the diseases spread into an unprotected population; they would be outnumbered in decades, not generations. The Tamidians had mocked their beliefs, throwing down shrines and trampling the icons into dust. The Founders had moved people off the open land, herding them into cities, where they sickened faster. Her great-grandmother had told her about the Death Year, when no Altiplanan baby had survived a week past birth, and about the Landbride who had called a curse on the unbelievers, at the cost of her own soul.

'For Landbrides do not curse: they bless. But she was taken from her land, and her children had died, and she escaped from the city to the mountains, and there with blood and spit and the hair of her head she made a *gieeim*, and offered her soul to the land if it would destroy the invaders.

'I don't know what she actually did,' Esmay said. 'My great-grandmother never told me, if she even knew. In her view, the hubris of the Founders angered God and brought a just punishment upon them. But a plague came out of the mountains and the plains, and up from the sea, and in the first year the Tamidians died as our children had died, spewing blood and rotting as they fell. It was said that they begged the Founders to let them leave, but the Founders brought in more, until the cities stank of death, and the Founders themselves sickened.'

'A bio-weapon?' someone said, behind the admiral.

Esmay shook her head. 'No – at least, nothing I know of, and Altiplanans do not use bio-weapons today. But when the Altiplanans wanted to leave the cities, and go back to the land, the Founders denied them, and then there was war . . . but not to massacre them all, only to get back to the land from which they had been driven.'

'That's not the report we have,' Admiral Serrano said. 'That's not what this says.' She fluttered the paper.

'It's all I know,' Esmay said. 'Are you sure your report is reliable?'

'Why wouldn't it be? A servant . . . someone . . . escapes –'

'How? To what?'

'Atmospheric shuttle, to the orbital station. Unfortunately, he carried the disease with him, and it infected the station crew. Only three of them lived, but they passed it on . . .'

'I don't believe it!' Barin reached for Esmay's hand. 'How can you believe a little scrap of paper stuck in a child's book –'

'Not a child's book –'

'Whatever kind of book. How can you believe that the real, secret truth was lost so long, and only comes to light just in time to keep me from marrying Esmay?'

Voices rose in an angry gabble, but Barin shouted over them. 'I don't care! I do not care that she's from Altiplano. I do not care that this – this scrap of paper says her family were murderers hundreds of years ago. Are all Serranos saints? I love her, and I admire her and I'm going to marry her, if I have to leave the family to do it!'

'Barin, no!' Esmay grabbed for his other hand. 'Wait – we have to find out –'

'I already know what I need to know,' he said, looking into her eyes. 'I love you, and you are faithful and true and brave – and you love me. That is what matters, not what happened then.'

'There was an oath sworn . . .' Vida said.

Barin rounded on her, and this time Esmay could see

the family likeness as if stamped in living bronze. 'And are all oaths worthy? That's not what you told me, Grandmother, when I swore to keep Misi's secrets. There are oaths and oaths, you said, and it's a wise soul that swears rightly, which is why we swear few.'

For an instant, Esmay thought Vida would scream her reply, but her voice, when she spoke, was soft.

'Then we must find the truth of this matter, Grandson — whether the story as we know it, or as the Suizas know it, is the truth. For if we know at last the names of those who killed our patrons, I see no possibility of peace between us.'

'We have an oath to the Familias,' Heris Serrano said. 'As you keep telling the other Fleet families, when they remember who were their patrons. Would you have Serranos unravel Fleet, and possibly the Familias as well, to seek vengeance for ancient wrongs?'

Silence, an uneasy silence in which Esmay could almost hear the unspoken arguments based on rank, active service, combat experience. Barin broke it.

'It doesn't matter. I'm sticking by Esmay no matter what you say.'

'The question is, will she stick by you, or will she turn traitor like her ancestors?' That was not Vida, but a male Serrano at the rear of the crush.

'Nonsense,' Heris said. 'The question is, does she love him?'

That set off another uproar, in which *Love is nothing but hormones!* clashed with *Love is more than just hormones!* and a dozen other comments Esmay had heard before. Through that, the shrill pipe of a communications alarm cut like a knife; the noise level dropped.

Someone across the suite picked up the com, and absolute silence spread from that focus toward the group still muttering softly about love and betrayal and honor.

Heads turned; people moved away, looking in that direction.

Finally Esmay could see. A Serrano she hadn't met yet stood, one hand up for silence, listening, his face more gray than brown with some shock. He put the comunit down, finally, with exaggerated care.

'Mutiny. There's been a mutiny, on Copper Mountain, and the mutineers have ten ships already.'

'What?'

'All leaves cancelled, all personnel return to their ships at once –' His eyes sought Vida Serrano's. 'They're calling the inactive flags back, sir; you're to take the fastest possible route to Headquarters.'

'Who?' Heris called. 'Did you get anything on who started it?'

'*Bonar Tighe* was the first ship, Heris, but they took the Copper Mountain orbital station with convicts from Stack Three, and the commander there was named Bacarion.'

'Bacarion.' Heris thought a long moment. 'Lepescu's staff – one of his staff officers. It's that bunch again, our own little Bloodhorde. And you know how Lepescu's crowd feels about Serranos.'

Barin pulled Esmay to her feet and wrapped his arms around her. 'It's always something,' he murmured. 'But I do love you, and I will marry you, and *nothing* – not Grandmother, or history, or mutinies, or anything – is going to stop me.'

She hugged him back, oblivious for a long, long delicious moment, vaguely aware of people moving in the room, of doors opening and closing. Finally someone coughed loudly.

'You've made your point, both of you,' Vida Serrano said. 'But right now, you'd better get in uniform and get going.'

Esmay lifted her head from Barin's shoulder and saw

nothing but uniforms now, Serranos with carisacks and rollerbags, one after another emerging from the side rooms and heading for the door to the lift tubes.

'I do love him,' she said, right into Vida's face. 'And I'm not a traitor, and I won't hurt him.'

Vida sighed. 'There's a lot more at stake than the happiness of you two,' she said. 'But for what it's worth, I hope it works out for you.'

Barin turned into his own room, and Esmay went back to hers, stripping quickly out of the borrowed clothes and putting on the creased uniform she'd been wearing – not even time to have it pressed. She looked at Dolcent's clothes, considered leaving them on the bed, and then remembered having seen her, in uniform, leaving with two others. She stuffed them into her own luggage – maybe she'd run into Dolcent on a ship out of here – smoothed her wayward hair, and went out to find Barin waiting for her. In the hall, the last eight of the Serrano family were clustered at the lift tubes, waiting.

'I will never again complain about having to come to a boring family reunion,' said one, a woman who looked to be in her forties. She gave Esmay a sidelong look. 'First we find out that what had seemed to be an ordinary inspection of a potential spouse is almost the lynching of an old enemy, and then there's a mutiny.' Nervous chuckles from half the others. 'Is it you, my dear, or the conjunction of Heris and Vida? Those two are certainly lightning rods.'

'Lightning *and* rod, I would say today.' That was a bookish-looking young man. 'Sparks were definitely flying.'

'She knows that.' Another speculative look at Esmay that made her face heat up. One of the tubes opened, and they crowded in, descending so fast that Esmay felt her stomach hovering near the back of her throat.

The hotel lobby swarmed with a crowded mass of men and women in R.S.S. uniforms, some struggling at the counters, trying to check out, and others crowding to the exits. 'Don't worry about registration,' the man who had spoken said. 'I'll take care of it – we were last out, and that's my job.'

'Cousin Andy,' Barin said, in Esmay's ear. 'Administration. Let's go.'

The crush continued on the slidewalks and trams to the Fleet gate of the station. Every newsvid display had the story, with serious-faced commentators talking, while scenes of Copper Mountain played in the background. Esmay didn't stop to listen, but there was a clump of people near every display.

More and more people in uniform got on at every stop. Not only Serranos had been here, and Esmay wondered how they were all going to get where they were going. At the Fleet gate, she found out.

As the long line snaked through the security gate, they were divided into crew and transients: crew members of docked ships went directly to their ships, and transients were divided by specialty and rank. Within a couple of hours, Esmay and Barin both had new orders cut, sending them out on a civilian liner to join a battle group forming for Copper Mountain. They walked back down the concourse, and found eighteen other Fleet personnel in the waiting lounge for the *Cecily Marie*. Thirteen more appeared before they boarded, and a knot of angry civilian passengers were by then complaining bitterly to the gate agent.

'Welcome aboard, please take your seats, you'll be shown your cabins later –' The steward looked tense, as well he might. Thirty-three last-minute military passengers, a mutiny in Fleet, who knew what else? Esmay and

Barin sat down together in the observation lounge, and she wondered if he felt as peculiar as she did. Probably not. She had come off this very ship not six hours before, and now she was back on it.

The senior Fleet officer aboard was Commander Deparre, who quickly organized the others as if the ship were Fleet and not civilian. Esmay had had a brief fantasy of spending the time with Barin – the time they had still not had, the time she had been longing for since before Brun's rescue. But Commander Deparre wanted to impress upon them the seriousness of the situation, and be sure they grasped the importance of upholding Fleet's reputation among the civilians of Familias Regnant.

The civilians aboard *Cecily Marie*, Esmay thought, were more alarmed than reassured by the way Commander Deparre controlled his little group. If they had been mutineers plotting to take over this very ship, they could not have been more ominous – always together as a group, always apart from the others. Commander Deparre, however, seemed to relish this opportunity for leadership: he was, it turned out, normally in charge of payroll processing at Sector Four HQ. He assigned Esmay responsibility for the female personnel – she was actually the senior female officer – and insisted that they should be protected from intrusion by posting a watch outside their quarters at night.

'But sir –'

'We cannot have the slightest whisper of irregularity, Lieutenant,' he said firmly. Behind him, Barin rolled his eyes expressively, but Esmay felt more ready to scream than laugh. The maidens whose virtue she was supposed to guard were, all but one bright-eyed young pivot major, older than she was, and two of the seven were senior NCOs who had been travelling with their husbands. This made no difference to Commander Deparre, who insisted that it would be 'unseemly' for them to share cabins with their husbands. Why, exactly, he would not explain, and Esmay could not understand.

At least these older women understood that the vagaries of officers like Deparre should not be blamed on their subordinates, and that argument was futile. More difficult were the sergeant and corporal who had spotted civilian men they fancied, and wheedled endlessly for a chance to chat with them.

She and Barin were separated even at meals, because the commander felt that the women should dine at a different table. They could chat – cautiously – in the half-hour twice daily that Commander Deparre felt necessary for the officers to sustain their professional associations and exclusivity from the enlisted, who had the same half-hours to chat without an officer present. Lucky enlisted, Esmay thought, because they at least didn't have to have Deparre around, while she did . . . and the commander felt it his duty to have a little chat with each of 'his' officers at least once a day.

'Nothing lasts forever,' Barin said. 'Even this voyage has to end sometime . . .' It hadn't been that many days, but it felt like years.

'With our luck, we'll end up on the same ship as Commander Deparre for the rest of our careers.'

'No . . . he'll go back to his accounting, I'm sure.'

'I hope so.'

CHAPTER TWENTY-ONE

OLD PALACE, CASTLE ROCK

'Mutiny!' Hobart Conselline glared at the face on the screen. 'What do you mean, mutiny?'

'Copper Mountain, milord. Mutineers have taken it over, the whole system –'

Copper Mountain was a long way away – Hobart had no idea how far, exactly, but far enough. A training base, wasn't it? Probably a bunch of disgruntled trainees, and nothing to worry about. 'Who's in charge?'

'Milord?'

He was surrounded by idiots. 'Who is in charge of Copper Mountain? The base there?' A blank look, followed by a confused gabble about Main Base and Camp This and Island Something. 'Never mind – just put a cordon around it.'

'A cordon, milord?'

Did he have to explain everything? And these were supposed to be military personnel. 'Cut them off,' he said firmly. 'Blockade or cordon or whatever you people call it. Just isolate them, and they'll run out of supplies soon enough.'

A different face appeared, this one somewhat older. 'Speaker, you do not understand. The mutiny began at Copper Mountain, but the mutineers now control the entire system – they have the orbital station, and the system defenses – we know at least ten warships are involved. That's enough to mount an attack on any other orbital station, or even one of the more lightly defended planets.'

'But why would they do that?'

'We don't know, Lord Conselline, and not knowing their plans we must take what precautions we can to protect the most vulnerable population centers –'

'Damn them! I want to know who they represent! I want to know now!'

'Milord, the first thing is to secure –'

'I'll wager it's the Barracloughs – or the Serranos –'

The face on the screen seemed to stiffen. 'We have no information –'

'Well, find out. I'll expect a report immediately.' He shut off his unit, and swung his chair around so fast he banged his knee on his desk and caught his breath. Blast them. Smug, condescending . . . all they wanted was to feather their own nests, anyway. He sensed, as he always did, the vast sticky web of someone else's conspiracy, someone else's malice and opposition. It was unfair . . . why couldn't they see that he was only trying to make things better for the *real* Familias Regnant, that mental image of hard-working beneficent lords and ladies, and hard-working appreciative lesser families and workers, for whom he was grinding himself to nothing between two stones? Why did they always have to argue, talk back, bicker, complain? If they would only do what he told them, at once and without argument, the government could move smoothly, quickly, responding to whatever crises came up.

But no. They let personal ambition, mere selfishness and silly pride, get in the way . . . They were sabotaging his effort to save the Familias Regnant. Tears stung his eyes, and he blinked them away. It was tempting to resign, and let them find out what a muddle – what a disastrous quicksand pit – they'd be in without him. He'd certainly done his part; he'd earned respite. But no – he would do his duty, as he had always done it. He would uproot the lazy, conniving schemers who laughed at him behind his back, and save the realm in spite of itself.

He placed his own call . . . he would not work through that lemon-faced Poisson . . . and demanded of the man's secretary a word with his Minister of Defense.

'A terrible thing,' he was saying even as his face slid into pickup range.

'Don't you start,' Hobart said. 'I'm getting no help out of the Grand Admiral's office –'

'They're upset – you know, Lord Conselline, the Grand Admiral was a mere one-star before the other flag officers were sent away –'

'Don't make excuses, Ed! Mutinies don't come out of nowhere. I want to know who's responsible for this outrage. Names, dates, the whole drill. Heads will roll, do you hear me, Ed?'

'Absolutely, Lord Conselline. As soon as I know anything, I'll report –'

'I have enemies, you know,' Hobart said. 'There are those who would like to embarrass me. I could name names . . .'

'In the Fleet, milord?'

'Not exactly, though I understand that the Serranos were quite close to Lord Thornbuckle and his daughter. Weren't they involved in her rescue, that flagrant misuse of government resources?'

'Yes, milord, but no Serranos have so far been identified as crew members of any of the vessels involved. In
fact, a large group of them were attending a social function –'

'A flagrant alibi,' Hobart said. 'Suspicious by its very
nature.'

'Uh . . . it was a betrothal party, I understand. Milord,
Fleet asked my permission to cancel the order removing
rejuvenated flag officers from active duty, and of course I
gave it –'

'Why?'

The man looked at him blankly. 'Because we need
them, milord. With part of the Fleet in mutiny, we need
loyal officers, and especially the command structure –'

'How do you know they're loyal? How do you know
they didn't engineer this mutiny just to be put back in the
cushy jobs they had before?'

'Lord Conselline, there is no evidence –'

'If you're going to *argue,* Ed –' Hobart began, feeling
himself growing hotter by the moment.

'Milord, I'm not arguing, I'm only telling you what the
facts are as we know them.'

'And you don't know anything worth knowing!'
Hobart cut the connection, started to whirl his chair, and
stopped just short of banging his leg again. He was surrounded by complete incompetents. He had *made* that
man. He had taught him, shaped him, and brought him
into the government, and this – *this* was his reward.
Insubordination, incompetence . . .

He could fire him, of course. But whom could he
appoint in his place? None of them had lived up to his
hopes for them. Instead of working with him, supporting
him, helping him, they all acted like spoiled prima
donnas. Could he find anyone better?

*

'Goonar – wake up, man!' Goonar rolled over and glared at his cousin.

'It is my off watch. The ship is now in pieces. Go away.'

'Goonar, listen – we just sucked a priority one report –'

'Is Laisa crazy? If we go sucking Fleet data, they'll –'

'There's a mutiny, Goonar.'

'Mutiny?'

'Ten ships they know of, all in the Copper Mountain system. Who knows how many elsewhere.'

'*Open* mutiny?' He was wide awake now, his stomach in a cold knot.

'That's what it said. A ship sent down LACs to a prison downside, brought up a bunch of dangerous criminals, used them to break the orbital station, got control of communications and systemwide defenses, and has declared that system to be part of the Society of Natural Men.'

'And who is that when it's at home?' It sounded like nothing he'd ever heard of. Natural men? What did they do, run around naked and eat raw fish?

'My guess is it's some of those bloodthirsty lot who hung around with Admiral Lepescu. Remember the bald man who got blind drunk and wanted to show us trophies that time, after the fight in the bar? And what Kaim told us?'

'Lepescu's dead,' Goonar said.

'Meanness isn't, just because one mean man dies.' Basil shifted his shoulders restlessly. 'I wonder if Kaim's all right, or if he's mixed up in this some way.'

'He'd have told us . . . family . . .'

'Can you see real conspirators confiding in Kaim? He's so sure he can't be fooled, he's like the man holding his wallet and showing pickpockets where it is. I'd hate to have a Terakian involved, even by accident.'

'I'm more concerned about the rest of the family.

Mutiny in Fleet's going to play hob with shipping schedules, ours included. Things were unsettled enough before.'

'Which is why I woke you up. We're playing skip-the-loop with the *Terakian Harvest*, and Laisa says we're almost in tightbeam range.'

'We don't have to tube over, do we?' Goonar asked. He hated ship-to-ship transfer tubes worse than being woken out of a sound sleep.

'No. Or rather, you don't; I do. But they want to talk to you.'

Goonar groaned, but rolled out of the bunk, and rubbed his head vigorously. He was not any good fresh out of sleep; he could have smacked Basil just for looking so brisk and awake.

On the bridge of *Flavor*, Laisa grinned at him. 'Exciting times, Goonar.'

'I never prayed for excitement,' he growled. He just wanted to live his life in peace, he thought, holding the memory of dinner around the table on Caskadar . . . the mellow lamplight, the smell of the food, the children's sweet piping voices. He sighed, and linked in to *Harvest*'s com officer.

'Your analysis, Goonar?'

How was he supposed to have an analysis when he was barely awake? Yet though he could barely speak, he could feel the little rolls moving in his brain, the numbers flickering past, faster and faster.

'What's your cargo?'

'Class D. Tungsten shell casings in the number four hold, conformable explosives in number three, the rest unremarkable.'

'All of it.' They never wanted to tell you all of it, but it was the little things which might turn a profit projection on its head.

'High-fashion software to eight destinations, plumb-ing supplies – plastic joints, mostly, but also some flapper valves, and a gross of solar-powered pumps – a cube of stuffed dates, and two bales of synthesilk, undyed.'

Goonar knew from experience that the dates and the synthesilk wouldn't be on the manifest. Crew's personal possessions, not for sale . . . except at a profit. 'Fine – and your destinations and route?'

That came in a long string, directly into his deskcomp.

He looked at it and let the little gears and rollers in his head have their way. Then, just as Basil – suited up – waved at him from the bridge entrance, he had it.

'Xavier.'

'What? That's not on our list at all!'

'I know . . . but I'll bet they need your Class D, and they're listed as a priority destination in the Fleet direc-tive of last week. Nobody wants to go out there.'

'Neither do I!'

'Yes, you do. It's a long way in the wrong direction from Copper Mountain. Nothing to attract mutineers: no ships to grab, no weapons factories to raid, no rich com-merce to prey on. There's a Fleet presence, but after what happened, it'll be the most loyal crews they have. It's an ag world, livestock breeders, minimal hard-goods manu-facturing. Also Xavier's still rebuilding – they'll take the plumbing supplies, too. They use a lot of synthesilk, and they have their own dyers. After that go to Rotterdam; they're also agricultural, and they have a little cross-trade with Xavier.'

'What about the high-fashion software? It's only sal-able in a skinny window.'

'Tube it to us, and I'll send it on by the next one we meet, when things are more settled.'

'If they ever are. Fine, then. Godspeed.'

DOUBLE-SUN LINES, *CECILY MARIE*

At Chinglin Station, the censorious commander found orders taking him in one direction, while his very relieved companions had orders directing them to other ships. Barin and Esmay took the opportunity to stop by a dessert stand in the concourse that led from civilian docking lounges to the Fleet gate where they were to join the R.S.S. *Rosa Gloria*. They had less than two hours of time alone, with 'alone' defined generously, but it was a great improvement on a suite full of Serranos or the watchful eye of the major.

'It's like Rondin and Gillian,' Esmay said, swinging her feet against the counter. She felt like a child, sitting on this tall stool and spooning up ice cream. 'Old family quarrels and all.'

'You mean Romeo and Juliet,' Barin said. 'Shakespeare, very old.'

'No, I don't,' Esmay said. 'I mean Rondin and Gillian. Who are Romeo and Juliet?'

'You must have heard of it; maybe the names changed in your version. Montagues and Capulets, traditional enemies. Duels and banishment and finally they died.'

'No, they didn't.'

'Yes, they did. She took a potion that made her look dead, and he thought she was dead, and killed himself, and then she found him and killed herself.' Barin took another spoonful of ice cream. 'Tragic but stupid. He could have asked a doctor, though my teacher said they didn't have doctors back when the story was first told.'

'Not Rondin,' Esmay said. 'I met him.'

Barin stared. 'You're talking about real people?'

'Of course. Rondin Escandera and Gillian Portobello. Their fathers had quarrelled years before, and forbade them to marry.'

'Why?'

'The quarrel? I don't know. I never heard, being a girl. I think my father knew, though. It was all very exciting . . . Rondin rode across our land to get to Gillian, because her father had sent her to my great-grandmother to wash Rondin out of her head, he said. That's where I met her; I was a child, and she was a young woman. Then one night Rondin came and she went out the window.'

'How did he know where she'd gone?'

'Everyone knew – her father made no secret of it.'

'Was she beautiful?'

'Oh, Barin, I was nine . . . ten, maybe. I knew nothing about beauty. She was a grownup who talked to me, that's all I knew.'

'So what happened?'

'Oh, her father came and yelled at my father, and wanted to yell at my great-grandmother; my grandfather and uncle yelled at him – there was a lot of yelling, and I hid out in my room most of the time, so no one would ask me any awkward questions.'

'Ask you – what did you know?'

Esmay grinned. 'I was the one who'd carried the messages back and forth. Nobody paid much attention to a scrawny nine-year-old who was already known to be fond of walking the hills alone. Gillian was nice to me; I'd have done more for her than carry a note a few miles. And I knew where they'd gone. My great-grandmother tried to talk Gillian out of it, said it would be a disgrace for them both, but finally gave them permission to live far in the south, on our land, as – there is no word, in this language, but they are under Suiza protection, but also under Suiza law. They do not own the land.'

'Are they happy?'

'I don't know. After the yelling died down, I heard no more about them. But my point was that we are like that, our families opposed to our marriage, and we also must choose to lose our familes or each other.'

'I don't want to lose you.'

'Nor I, you.'

'It's not fair to blame you for what some ancestor of yours did –'

'*If* they did,' they said in unison.

'For all they know,' Esmay said, 'I'm actually the last living heir of that family, whatever its name was. Maybe they should be cheering me on, instead of hating me.'

'They don't hate you. They're just confused. It's all Personnel's fault anyway.' He reached out and touched her hair, a touch so light she could hardly feel it. Even that was risky in public; she felt her face going hot.

'Personnel's fault?'

'Well, if they hadn't put the rejuved admirals out of work, Grandmother wouldn't have been bored in the family archives. Imagine what it must have taken to get her to look at a row of children's books.'

Esmay couldn't help giggling. 'After she'd sat on the porch – is there a porch?'

'Oh, yes. She sat on the porch and looked at the lake, I'll bet. Then she took a walk. Then she read the news-flashes, and then she thought she should do something useful and improving . . .'

'Like read children's books.' It was hard to imagine the redoubtable Admiral Serrano reading children's books. She must have been very bored indeed.

'I don't want to read children's books . . .' Barin gave her a long look.

'No . . .' She stared into the ice cream, trying not to blush again. She knew exactly what he wanted, and what she wanted.

'Esmay . . . everything's against us – both families, the mutiny, maybe a war, the whole universe doesn't want us to get married. They're so sure they know why we shouldn't, what we should do to be happy ten or twenty or fifty years from now. But I want to marry you. Do you still want to marry me?'

'Yes.'

'Then let's do it. In spite of them, in spite of the mutiny, in spite of good common sense . . . let's *do* it.'

A rush of warm glowing joy suffused her, banishing embarrassment. 'Yes. Oh, yes! But how?'

'If nothing else we'll hold hands over a candle, but we have an hour – maybe more – before the ship gets here. If we don't waste it –'

'Let's go.'

When they looked on the board, the *Rosa Gloria* was seventy-two minutes from undocking. Seventy-two minutes. Finding a magistrate with the authority to perform the ceremony took thirty-three of them. Persuading him to do it – both of them talking, proving their identification, showing all the paperwork – took another twenty-six. Thirteen minutes left . . . they stood hand in hand, and the magistrate rattled through the legal requirements as fast as possible, then added something Esmay presumed was a blessing in his religion, though not in hers. Signing and stamping and sealing the various documents took another eight minutes, and they were both racing back to the Fleet side of the station as fast as they could.

'We're crazy,' Barin said, after they'd signed through Fleet Gate. His hand felt as if it were welded to hers.

'I love you,' Esmay said. 'I – rats, it's gone yellow –'

'Come *on*.' Hand in hand, they ran for it, stride and stride, as faces turned toward them; people stared, someone yelled – she didn't care. They hit the far end of the access tube just as the light turned red, and a very disgusted petty major held her fist on the controls to let them in.

'Welcome aboard sir . . . sirs.' Her tone would have preserved fish for a century.

Behind her was a major; Esmay got her hand untangled from Barin's, and they both saluted.

'Jig Serrano and Lieutenant Suiza, I presume?'

'Yes, sir.' She hadn't had time to think about whether she wanted to change her name.

'You cut it rather close, didn't you? We almost had you down as possible mutineers.'

'Us?' Barin said. He sounded outraged.

'You,' the major said. 'We're treating no-shows that way – what did you expect?'

'Sir, we need to report a change of status.'

His brows went up. 'We?'

'We,' Barin said firmly.

'I assume you mean a change of status that could affect billeting,' the major said. He rolled his eyes. 'All right. For now, we're assigning transient officers half-shift duties. You'll be on second shift, second half for now. Let's see – Lieutenant Suiza, we'll be meeting *Navarino* when the battle group is formed, and you'll be rejoining her – she's in jump transit right now. Jig Serrano, you were about to leave *Gyrfalcon*, but the ship you were assigned to has gone over to the mutineers, so your assignment's still up in the air.'

'*Goshawk* went over?'

'So I hear.'

'But it wasn't anywhere near Copper Mountain –'

'Serrano, I don't know any more than I've said. For now, you can wait for your chance at Admin and the captain in the junior officers' mess.'

'Yes, sir.'

The junior officers' mess was a buzzing hive of ensigns, jigs and lieutenants, who were much more interested in the latest news than in personal matters. Once they found that Barin and Esmay had not spent the two hours onstation watching newsvids, they went back to rehashing Fleet gossip. Barin and Esmay were able to sit together in a corner of the room, shoulder just touching shoulder, as they watched the status board for their turn to report to the captain.

'You've *what*?' Captain Atherton said.

'Got married, sir,' Esmay said. As senior, she had made the announcement.

'But – but you didn't tell anyone.'

'No, sir.' Never mind that her CO, and Barin's, were perfectly aware of the engagement.

'Your paperwork's not even complete.'

'No, sir.' She didn't explain about that, either, or the unlikelihood that it would be complete any time in the foreseeable future.

'You know this could be voided by Personnel –'

'Yes, sir.' She heard the stubborn tone in her own voice. Personnel could void what it wanted, but in her heart she was married, and nothing could change that.

'Why – no, never mind why. Because you're both idiots with dung for brains, pulling a stunt at a time like this.'

'That's why, sir,' Esmay ventured. 'Things keep happening and we wanted –'

'This is not a romance storycube, Lieutenant. This is a warship in time of war. I don't care if you two are in love or if someone spiked your cocktail . . . we don't have time for this. You shouldn't even be on the same ship.'

Esmay stole a glance at Barin, who stole a glance back. They hadn't been on the same ship when they weren't married, since the *Koskiusko*.

'Why couldn't you just have had mad passionate sex and gotten over it? Why did you have to get married?

Atherton turned to Barin. 'Do you have any idea what your grandmother's going to do to me when she finds out?'

'It's not your fault, sir.' Barin looked a little grim, and Esmay knew what he was thinking. It wasn't the captain of this ship who would bear the brunt of Admiral Serrano's anger.

'No, it's not, but she'll blame me for not stopping it. You –' He stopped in mid-bellow. 'You're not laughing, are you?'

'No, sir,' they said.

'Good. Because while this entire situation is so bad that laughter is the only sane response, I don't like to be laughed at, and I'm not laughing, so you can't laugh with me.' He shook his head at them. 'This happens in every crisis we have. I don't know what it is about youngsters – and you, Lieutenant Suiza, are really too old for that category – but every time there's a military crisis, a bunch of you decide to leap into the sack, and a few of those leap into marriage. It must be some atavistic quirk from the childhood of humankind.'

'It's not like that. We didn't rush into it. We'd waited, and waited, and filled out paperwork, and argued with our families –' Esmay knew she was saying too much, but for once she couldn't stop.

'And then Grandmother came up with something really awful –' Barin added. Esmay shot him a warning look.

'And then the news of the mutiny came in, and everyone was rushing around –'

'Mmm-hmm. And you got married because your personal happiness was more important than anything else.'

'As important as,' Barin said. 'Sir, I don't see how being miserable makes us more efficient, and right then we were miserable not being married, and being apart.'

'So you'll function better if you're together?'

'I think so,' Barin said.

'Good. Prove it. I see you're on second shift, second. We're certainly crowded enough to make sharing a cabin during your sleep rotation reasonable. But the first time one of you is groggy on duty, I swear I'll space you both. Clear?'

'Yes, sir.'

'And you will both inform your families immediately, while we're still within range of the system ansible. We'll be in jump transit before a reply comes, no doubt, but at least you'll have told them. You have one hour.'

'Yes, sir.'

'You're letting them bunk together?' the exec asked. He had overheard enough.

'It saves time. They'd get together somehow if we put them on alternating shifts with shifting bunk assignments . . . this way they don't waste any time or energy hunting each other down. My guess is, from their records, that they'll be just as efficient as anyone else.'

'The Serrano family won't be happy.'

'Well . . . as they said, it's not my fault. I didn't arrange it, or sanction it; it was done when I got them. Besides, I'm not a Serrano.' His face relaxed for a moment into a reminiscent smile. 'Back when I was an ensign on *Claremont*, and she was commanding, Vida Serrano chewed me out for spending too much time with my girl-friend. Said I'd outgrow the silly chit. Well, I've been married twenty-eight years now to that "little chit," and the day I outgrow Sal, I'll be dead. It's only justice that her grandson falls in love with someone she thinks is unsuitable – though how she could object to Lieutenant Suiza is beyond me. Maybe these two will be under-standing of one of my kids someday.'

*

The compartment was predictably cramped, with a second narrow bunk rigged above the first, and they would share it with four other officers. It was their space only during their assigned sleep shift. But they were alone, with a locked door between them and the rest of the universe. For now, that made all the difference.

'Sorry about the hurry,' Barin said, into Esmay's ear.

'Hmmm?'

'The beautiful dress Brun was having designed for you. And the ring I'd ordered. And a ceremony you would recognize . . .'

'We can do that later, if we have the chance. I'd rather have this.' *This* engaged both of them more than adequately for some time.

'Still . . .' Barin said, coming up for air at last.

Esmay poked a finger in his ribs. 'Don't . . . distract me.'

CHAPTER TWENTY-TWO

THE CHAIRMAN'S OFFICE, BENIGNITY OF THE COMPASSIONATE HAND

Hostite Fieddi had always known this day would come. The Chairman sat behind his desk, and on the desk lay the knife, the ancient black-bladed knife, the hilt to the Chairman's left.

'Hostite, you have been a good and faithful servant.'

'Sir.'

'You have been long in our service.'

'Sir.'

'You are the blade I trust.' The intonation suggested a pause, not a completion, and Hostite waited. 'We have an enemy time will not wound for us.'

'Sir.'

'You are my Blade, Hostite . . .'

'To the heart, Chairman.'

'To the heart, Hostite, without prejudice.' A kill, a kill beyond the borders, but one only. For that he was glad that only one kill would burden his soul in eternity.

'Come near, and I will aim my Blade.'

He was already dead, though he walked; coming near

could not increase his mortality. Hostite waited, and the Chairman said nothing for long moments.

Then: 'It is a grave thing to order the death of one who has never been under your authority. I give this order reluctantly, Hostite, not only for what it means to you and to me, but for what it means to the peoples . . . the clients. But there is no other way; the man is swollen with ambition, and would force on us all his ungodly ways.'

'They are heathens, sir.'

'Not all like this. Hostite, I bid you kill Hobart Conselline. None other of his family; him only.'

Hostite bowed.

'The method, sir?'

'Your choice.'

His last assignment. His death at the end. And the death of the Chairman, who would no longer have his personal Swordmaster, the Shadow of the Master of Swords, to ward him from that danger.

He felt the honor, and it warmed him. Death had not been a stranger to him for years, and nothing waited for him in age but someone's blade when he faltered. This – this he could do for his people and his faith, and he almost smiled, thinking of it.

'Go now,' the Chairman said, and Hostite withdrew, already thinking how he would do it.

OLD PALACE, CASTLE ROCK

Hobart slung his clothes into the hamper angrily. Worse every day, those damned idiots.

He put on his fencing tights, and began his exercises. When the door opened, he glanced up, expecting Iagin Persius. But he had never seen this Swordmaster. An older man, a bit stockier, in sleek black stretch with a funny-looking red cap and red slippers. In his hands he carried a sword unlike those Hobart used.

'It is time,' he said, in a voice as soft as rainwater.

'All right.' Hobart straightened up, and pushed past him into the salle. 'Where's that other Swordmaster? I'm used to him.'

'He was indisposed, Lord Conselline, and asked me to take his place, that you might not be inconvenienced awaiting his recovery.'

Hobart stared at the man. 'You're certainly more formal than he was. What's that blade you've got? Do I have to work out with that? I suppose you want me to learn yet another stupid archaic weapon . . .'

'Not if you don't wish it. What weapon would you prefer?'

'Rapier.' Hobart looked around, and realized that his coach wasn't there either; he would have to get his own gear, since he didn't think this old man would oblige him. But to his surprise, the Swordmaster moved quickly to the racks, and brought him a rapier – his favorite, he realized – and a mask.

'You seem angry,' the man said.

'I am,' Hobart said. He didn't want to talk about it; he came to exercise to forget – or at least ignore – his problems for a time.

'Did someone illtreat you?' asked the Swordmaster.

'Yes – but I'm here to fence.'

'Of course. My pardon, Lord Conselline. Swordmaster Iagin told me of your dedication, your seriousness.'

'He did?' Hobart had never been sure the Swordmaster approved of him, though the man had always been courteous and respectful.

'Yes . . . he said you were unusual, a man who took everything seriously.'

'That's true enough.' Hobart adjusted the mask, and

bounced a little, loosening his knees. He had skimped on stretching, and if Iagin thought him serious, then he had better be serious. 'Not many are – you would not believe – no, never mind . . .'

'But if you need to stretch out, and ease your mind with talk as your sinews with the exercise, then you should, milord.'

'Oh – very well.' Hobart laid his blade down on the mat, carefully, and leaned over to grasp his ankle. 'I hope it doesn't bore you, and you must realize it's confidential –'

'Of course. You need to turn your wrist a little more, milord.'

'It's these idiots – these dung-for-brains weaklings that I sponsored to high office. I made them what they are, I led them and taught them and groomed them for office, and now that they're in power . . . they simply will not do what they're told.'

'Ah. And now, milord, another centimeter of pull . . . yes. And now the other leg . . . remembering to keep the wrist rotated in . . . yes.'

'I don't know what it is, Swordmaster, but no matter how smart they are, or how much initiative they show when I start working with them, no sooner do they get into a position of real responsibility than they turn on me. Insubordinate, arrogant, selfish –'

'If you can tilt the head now – yes, like that – and a little more –'

'And they're supposed to be my supporters, but do they support? No. They go off and do stupid things, like that idiot Orregiemos . . .'

'And to the other side, now, milord . . .'

'It's enough to make a saint spew rocks,' Hobart said. Amazing how easy the fellow was to talk to. The combiation of the warm, quiet room, and familiar scents of leather, steel, oil, sandalwood, cedar, and the quiet, patient, steady hands of the older man molding him into one shape after another that stretched out knots he hadn't even realized he had . . .

'It is difficult when subordinates are not obedient,' the Swordmaster said.

'Exactly. I've tried reasoning, scolding, even threats –'

'And they resist.'

'They certainly do. If they only realized, I'm trying to make things better.'

Hostite had studied the files; he knew Hobart Conselline as well as anyone could, who had only files to go on. But the man in reality had shocked him. He was so miserable, so full of anger and fear and envy that the whole room stank of it. His body had been stiffened and deformed by it; the very muscles of his face were saturated with his rage and fear.

He was a skin bag of poison.

He was immortal, being a Rejuvenant, as the silver and cobalt rings in his ear boasted to the world.

So old, and yet so full of folly. He had learned nothing, Hostite saw, in all those decades of renewed vigor that rejuvenation had given him.

Pride . . . was his own pitfall, Hostite reminded himself. Yes, this man was proud, and bitter, and angry, but why? He had never yet killed without understanding why those he killed were as they were.

He must offer the opportunity for understanding, for contrition, for repentance, though he could not offer – must not offer – any chance of escape. He must give the soul a chance, while giving the body none.

But how to do that with unbelievers, with those who were not aware of the soul, of anything beyond the body? Hostite had studied unbelievers of all kinds, over the years, and found them all to have beliefs of a sort, just wrong ones. They believed in wealth, or security, or the kindness of strangers, or something other than the True Faith. And so what they believed in failed them, eventually, and they were brought low . . .

All that Lord Conselline was saying could be considered a confession, but in a true confession the sinner knew that what he confessed was sinful. Hobart didn't seem to grasp that at all. Everything that went wrong was someone else's fault. Hostite felt a wave of sympathy for these stupid uncooperative men who so angered Lord Conselline. They, too, were heathens, and enemies, and the Chairman might find it necessary to have them killed, but they had certainly suffered from long association with Lord Conselline.

He listened to all of it, eliciting more and more by merely being there, a neutral and unwisely trusted ear. Hobart's envy of his brother, and everyone else whose personality drew others. Envy of everyone, in fact, for he could always find something in which another had received unearned benefit. Pride – a towering pride, certainty of his own rightness, and the moral weakness of others. Anger at everyone, avarice – for nothing was ever enough, even for a day; lust, and a wide streak of cruelty that enjoyed humiliating others. And all of it, every sordid detail, drenched in self-congratulation.

A Swordmaster must know when enough was enough, and Hostite had that moment of revelation: this man would not ever realize his errors, not even in the moment of death. Poor soul, so benighted, so hopeless of a better eternity, so ignorant. But God gave each soul enough time, if it chose to use it, and Lord Conselline's soul had had the same chance – years, in fact – to come to a better understanding.

'Come now, Lord Conselline,' he said finally, and stood

back. 'You are feeling better; it is time for your lesson.'

'Yes – I am feeling better.' He clambered up, rapier in hand, in body a little straighter than he had been, his mind a little clearer in the aftermath of confessing, even so inadequately, his current crop of sins.

'It is not your associates,' Hostite said. 'It is you.' He was sure Conselline would not understand, but he had to try.

'What?' Lord Conselline's eyes widened as he saw the movement of the great dark blade, the backswing which promised such power.

'Your failure.' The blade swung forward; Lord Conselline tried to parry with the rapier, and the blade sliced it short, sweeping on; Conselline jumped back, mouth open to yell, and Hostite pursued, choosing to dance the figure rather than step it. He could hear the music in his head, his favorite music, Lambert's 'All On a Spring Morning, the Bright Trumpets Sing.' His pursuit, and Conselline's fear, used up the man's breath, and what should have been a shout came out a series of breathless squeaks.

'No – what are . . . you doing? Help – stop – security!' Lord Conselline glanced from side to side, clearly frightened, and grabbed at another weapon off the rack.

'I am your Death, your life is over.' Another swipe that parted a practice foil as if it had been a blade of dry grass. 'Ask forgiveness from your God.' The man had none, but again, he must offer the chance.

'I didn't do anything,' Lord Conselline gasped. 'It wasn't me. Don't –'

Hostite had never been one to play with a victim, past giving him a chance to repent; the great blade took Lord Conselline's head off with one stroke, and the harsh stench of death overtook the sweet spicy scent of cedar and sandalwood.

*

The Chairman of the Board of the Benignity of the Compassionate Hand faced away from his desk, looking out the tall windows at the formal garden. A boisterous spring breeze whipped the tops of the cypresses, and even swirled stray petals from the early roses along the pebbled walks. From here he could not see the fountains, but he could imagine the spray blowing out behind, a long damp veil that would slick the marble rim of the cascade, the seats behind it where the old ladies sat in their black dresses on fine days, watching the sea and the children playing. He lifted his gaze to the horizon, to the blue sea, its glittering tessellations flinging the sun back in his eyes.

He had had, on the whole, a successful life, and since he had just made his final confession, he was conscious of it as a whole, a story nearly complete, the defining moments as clear as if they had been painted by a fine artist. This and this he had done well, and that and that he had done less well. On occasion, the grace of the Almighty had protected him from the consequences of his own errors, and on other occasions he had taken the blame for what was not his fault. Not in God's eyes, of course, but in the eyes of the Benignity. All this was to be expected, and he regretted none of it, for regrets were useless. It had been a life of human shape and human content, and he was glad of it.

If regret had been part of his mental furniture, he might have regretted – he almost regretted – this last necessity. It was not his fault that the Familias Regnant had fallen into the hands of Hobart Conselline, and that he had been forced – he had seen no alternative – to order the man's execution. It would have taken supernatural ability to foresee all that had happened to bring Conselline to power, and to shape him into someone who could be so dangerous, and offer so little maneuvering room to the

Benignity. And no one expected supernatural ability of a Chairman.

Only that if he failed, he must pay the price.

Those in the Benignity were in his power, absolutely: if the Chairman ordered that a potato farmer must die for the good of the whole, then the potato farmer would die, in the manner and time prescribed, and this was as it should be. He might pity the potato farmer, and the potato farmer's wife and squalling brats, but he would order that death without a qualm, and without a qualm it would occur. This was not even cruelty. Death ended every life; death healed the sick and the badly injured; death opened the gates to endless life.

But outside the Benignity . . . the rules changed. To compete, to convert, even to invade – that was allowable. To corrupt, and to have secret agents providing information and forwarding the interests of the Benignity – that was inevitable. But to call for the assassination of a foreign king – whatever the foreigners called their heads of state, and they called them many foolish things – that was proof that a Chairman had failed. Had not seen trouble coming, had not managed affairs in another way, had not done – by means of stealth or influence or intimidation – what needed to be done.

Still, no tool, no method, was forbidden. God in His wisdom knew that emergencies happened. If, to protect the Benignity, a foreign king must die, then the Chairman could so order, and so it would occur.

So also would occur the death of that Chairman, who had shown himself to lack the qualities of a Chairman. Whether he was stupid, or old and tired, or misled by advisors, did not matter: he had failed his people, and he must pay the price. Not unexpectedly, not cruelly, but surely and certainly and with all due ceremony.

Some Chairmen never had to make that decision, and

it was the accumulation of errors which brought them to their final confession. He had expected it would be so with him, as his years advanced, until he'd realized, too late, what Hobart Conselline's leadership of the Familias Regnant would lead to. In the instant he'd seen it, he'd also seen his own folly, his own blindness: he could have recognized it years before. Whether that would have changed events or not, he could not know, nor did it matter. He had blundered; he had done what he could to fix it, but it was not enough.

No guards were in the room today. He had made his last confession, and his heart was as light and sunny as the spring breeze.

When he heard the door, he turned. Some had chosen not to look, but he had never been afraid of the man who would kill him, only of the man who would let him fail his people.

The Master of Swords stood by his desk, formally dressed, and carrying the dark blade they did not use for fencing.

'You know my reasons,' the Chairman said, without meeting his eyes. It was impolite to look into the eyes; it could be intepreted as pleading.

'Yes.'

'I have made my confession,' the Chairman said.

'Yes.' The Master of Swords stepped to one side, and raised his blade

'Fiat –'

'Nox.' The Master of Swords swung, and the blade that had taken the life of sixteen Chairmen sliced through skin and sinew and bone as easily as a hot knife through butter. Blood spurted as the head thumped onto the desk and rolled, but blood was nothing new in this place, and the servants knew how to clean it up.

'In nomine Patrem,' the Master said, saluting *his*

Master. He wiped the blade with a square of scarlet silk, and laid that silk over the Chairman's head. 'Requiescat in pacem.'

Then, as he was, naked blade in hand, with flecks of Pietro Alberto Rossa-Votari's blood on his cloak, he strode out of the office, through the anteroom – where the secretary was now already calling for servants, and would soon be notifying the family – down the hall, and into the Boardroom, where the Board had been waiting for the Chairman to appear and open the meeting.

'The Chairman has made his last confession,' he said without preamble. Faces paled, but no one spoke. 'The Board will elect a new Chairman,' he said. Anxious looks back and forth, and at him. Some of these men had never been through the election of a Chairman; Rossa-Votari had held that office for eighteen years. The Swordmaster stood by the door, with nothing more to say, as the low murmurs started, as they looked at him and away and back and away . . . it was nothing to him what they did, and nothing they said would he ever repeat, but they would not leave this room alive until one of them had been elected Chairman by acclamation.

R.S.S. *ROSA GLORIA*

The ship had been in downtransit only a couple of hours when the captain called Barin and Esmay into his office.

'I have messages from your families,' the captain said. He didn't wait for their response. 'They say they have more important things to worry about than you two. They're not happy with you, and they don't approve, but in the present emergency, they're not doing anything except talking about it. To each other.'

'To each other?'

'Yes. Admiral Serrano and General Suiza both signed

this –' He handed over the hardcopy. 'Actually, all the Admirals Serrano and Generals Suiza – I don't know what you thought you'd accomplish by running off together, but you seem to have unified a substantial number of high-ranking officers in at least one thing – you're in trouble.'

'But we're married,' Barin said.

'It's worth it,' Esmay said.

'It better be,' the captain said. 'Because when everything settles down and there are no wars, mutinies, invasions, terrorist attacks, pirates, or other distractions, your families are going to come down on you like one planet hitting another.'

This was, Esmay thought, a fairly accurate description of the probable interaction of Serranos and Suizas anyway, with the exception of themselves.

'Now get out of here, and go back to being the frustratingly competent officers you both are.'

They did not scamper away in glee, because officers did not scamper.

'When everything settles down, eh?' Barin said, grinning. 'That'll be the day.'

'If they wait that long,' Esmay said, thinking of her father and uncle talking to Barin's grandmother and great-uncle. If they didn't kill each other right off – and the combined message suggested they hadn't – what a dangerous combination *that* was, to have running around the universe!

'They'll get used to it,' Barin said. 'We aren't half as bad as we could have been – suppose I'd married Casea?'

Esmay gave him a look, and almost burst into laughter. A trail of suppressed giggles followed them down the passage to their tiny – but adequate for the immediate purpose – cabin.

Orbit titles available by post:

☐ Hunting Party	Elizabeth Moon	£5.99
☐ Sporting Chance	Elizabeth Moon	£5.99
☐ Winning Colours	Elizabeth Moon	£5.99
☐ Once A Hero	Elizabeth Moon	£5.99
☐ Rules of Engagement	Elizabeth Moon	£5.99
☐ Sheepfarmer's Daughter	Elizabeth Moon	£5.99
☐ Divided Allegiance	Elizabeth Moon	£6.99
☐ Oath of Gold	Elizabeth Moon	£6.99

The prices shown above are correct at time of going to press. However, the publishers reserve the right to increase prices on covers from those previously advertised, without further notice.

ORBIT BOOKS
Cash Sales Department, P.O. Box 11, Falmouth, Cornwall, TR10 9EN
Tel: +44 (0) 1326 569777, Fax: +44 (0) 1326 569555
Email: books@barni.avel.co.uk

POST AND PACKING:
Payments can be made as follows: cheque, postal order (payable to Orbit Books) or by credit cards. Do not send cash or currency.

U.K. Orders under £10	£1.50
U.K. Orders over £10	**FREE OF CHARGE**
E.C. & Overseas	25% of order value

Name (Block letters) . . . .

Address . . . .

. . . .

Post/zip code: . . . .

☐ Please keep me in touch with future Orbit publications

☐ I enclose my remittance £ . . . .

☐ I wish to pay by Visa/Access/Mastercard/Eurocard

Card Expiry Date
